"WITH MIRIAM MINGER, YOU'RE ASSURED OF A GOOD READ!"
—*Heartland Critiques*

Her captivating tales of medieval passion have fired the imaginations of readers everywhere. Here's what the critics are saying about award-winning author Miriam Minger . . .

PRAISE FOR *THE PAGAN'S PRIZE*

"BRILLIANTLY IMAGINATIVE . . . *The Pagan's Prize* will totally engross the reader. This novel will be perused so often that the reader will regret not having purchased an extra copy!"
—*I'll Take Romance*

"FIVE STARS . . . It is filled with rich detail that takes the reader on a rare trip to Russia in the eleventh century and is told so skillfully that the reader feels as if they have been there . . . *The Pagan's Prize* should be at the top of your shopping list!"
—*Affaire de Coeur*

"OUTSTANDING . . . This is a well-written, moving story that shows the tremendous skill of the author . . . *Marvelous* barely describes my feelings."
—*Rendezvous*

WILD ANGEL

MIRIAM MINGER

JOVE BOOKS, NEW YORK

WILD ANGEL

A Jove Book / published by arrangement with
the author

PRINTING HISTORY
Jove edition / January 1994

ISBN: 0-515-11247-X

A JOVE BOOK®
Jove Books are published by The Berkley Publishing Group,
200 Madison Avenue, New York, New York 10016.
JOVE and the "J" design
are trademarks belonging to Jove Publications, Inc.

PRINTED IN THE UNITED STATES OF AMERICA

10 9 8 7 6 5 4 3 2 1

FOR
Bev, Randy, Tim and Gracia,

You've always been there for me.
This one's for you.

WILD ANGEL

Prologue

Ireland, 1190
Wicklow Mountains, Leinster

A BABE'S CRIES led him to the carnage.

Grim faced, Fineen O'Toole leaned his bow against the thick trunk of an oak and sank to his haunches.

The woman was dead. That much was plain. Fatally gored by the wild boar he had found collapsed beneath a rock outcropping only a few yards away. Its yellowed tusks red with blood, a jeweled dagger embedded deeply in its throat.

Fineen made note of the woman's ravaged gown—a foreign cut fashioned from the richest blue cloth he had ever seen— as he pushed aside a silky sheaf of blond hair that covered her face.

God grant her peace. She must have fought like a tigress to have felled such a beast. Her ashen cheeks were still wet with tears; her slim white arms, marred by cuts and deep slashes, were wound protectively around the wailing child. But Jesu, Mary and Joseph, what had she been doing in these woods? A fine Norman lady with the countenance of an angel straying unguarded into the Wicklow Mountains. It was unheard of.

Shaking his head, Fineen pried the howling babe from the woman's arms. A girl child with the strong lungs of a banshee, she was a pretty wee thing, her chubby face framed by bright coppery gold curls. He guessed that she was no more than six months old. And such fat tears from one so little! Hoping to soothe her, Fineen settled her into the crook of his arm.

"Sshh, sweeting . . . sshh," he crooned, his gruff voice lowered to a comforting whisper. To his amazement the baby abruptly fell silent, a small frown puckering her downy brows as she gazed up at him. Her eyes, fringed by long dark lashes, were not the typical blue of babes, but rather a green as brilliant as the fragrant moss beneath his feet.

"Aye, you don't know me, sweeting, but you've nothing to fear from—"

A low feral growl nearby made Fineen stiffen, the hair rising on the back of his neck. He looked up to see a lean-ribbed black wolf skulking among the trees.

Accursed demon dogs. It never took them long to track down the scent of fresh blood.

Fineen rose swiftly to his feet. Freeing the babe from her blood-soaked swaddling blanket, he flung the stained cloth at the animal. He was not surprised when a half dozen wolves emerged from the gathering mist and leapt upon the blanket, the snarling beasts ripping it to shreds.

"A whole pack of you, I see," muttered Fineen as he settled the naked babe inside his leather jerkin. Startled by the commotion, she was crying again but he had no time to calm her now. He grabbed his bow and expertly set an owl-fletched arrow to the string.

Normally he would consign any dead Norman's soul to burn in eternal hell's fire, but this wretched lady had stirred his pity. After he dealt with the wolves, he would give the woman a Christian burial, then decide what was to be done with the child.

Fineen took careful aim at the lead wolf whose gleaming gold eyes were fixed first upon him, then upon the woman's body.

"Aye, come on, you damned hellhound. Come on . . . What the devil?"

Fineen spun as the wolves faded like wraiths into the trees, the sudden pounding of hooves growing louder. He didn't wait to discover if the advancing riders were friend or foe. Sliding the bow and arrow into the leather case slung over his shoulder, he lunged behind a nearby tree and thrust a knuckle into the babe's mouth.

"Not a peep, sweeting," he whispered, grateful when the babe quieted and began to suckle contentedly.

"This way, my lord! The crying came from just beyond the rise!"

Startled, Fineen paid no heed to the prickly bark digging into his back and thighs as he pressed closer to the tree, nor to the sweat trickling down his spine.

By God, Normans. Yet it was strange that they had ventured so far from the safety of the plains. Usually the land-stealing, murdering spawn of Satan knew these mountains were the domain of the O'Byrnes and the O'Tooles. Too bad he had ordered his clansmen to track their quarry in the woods nearer the stockade so he could enjoy the solace of hunting alone. If they'd been hunting together, they could have bagged some fine prey indeed.

"There, my lord! Beneath that tree!"

Fineen skimmed his hand over the jeweled dagger he had pulled from the boar's throat to the smooth wooden hilt of his hunting knife. But the riders galloped past him, four, maybe five in all. Scarcely daring to breathe, he listened as the Normans drew to a sudden halt and dismounted no more than ten feet away.

"I fear the lady is dead, Baron. And her babe is gone."

"God's teeth, I thought my brother's whelp too young to crawl! Find her!"

Fineen tensed as the baron's minions went crashing through the undergrowth.

"Wolves have been here, my lord! Our horses must have frightened them away. There are tracks and look, shreds of cloth."

"The babe's swaddling blanket. Splendid. A plump little heiress should make the beasts a fine supper. And they've saved me the trouble of dispatching the dratted chit myself."

"Bastard," Fineen breathed fiercely, hugging his tiny charge closer to his chest. The Norman monster spoke so callously of murdering a child. The man's own niece from the sound of it!

"Wrap the lady in your cloak and hand her up," came the baron's next command, his voice harsh. "It grows dark and this forest is cursed by rebels and thieves. We've already tested our luck by riding this far."

Fineen started as the babe suddenly tugged upon his beard, her berry red lips pursed and pulling hard at his knuckle. He smiled at her, but he sobered when the riders once more moved past him, the baron's voice a low growl.

"Pity about Eva, especially after I went through such pains to make her a widow. She could have been my bride instead of a corpse. Foolish bitch."

Sickened, Fineen was tempted to hurl his hunting knife and silence the man forever. That one was a Norman doubly worth slaying! But the babe yanking upon his beard stilled him. He would only endanger her life, and she'd already faced enough threats for one so small and helpless.

Poor wee orphan. Now she had only Fineen O'Toole, chieftain of the Imaal O'Tooles, to protect her.

He didn't step from behind the tree until the mailed Norman troupe was almost out of sight, the baron at the lead with the lifeless woman slung over his saddle. In the fading summer light, Fineen spied a coat of arms emblazoned upon the baron's shield.

Bloodred on black, a fearsome three-headed dragon with wings outspread. He did not recognize the emblem but in time would learn this baron's name.

"Aye, you fiendish whoreson, your evil deeds must have won you much," Fineen spat as the Normans disappeared from view. "But you'll not have this little one here. I'll see to that."

He walked back to the place where the woman had fallen, the spongy emerald moss stained a dark reddish brown with her blood. Solemnly, he made the sign of the cross above it.

"Rest your soul, Eva. Norman or no, you needn't worry about your daughter. From this day, I adopt her as my own. She'll be safe with me. On my life, I swear it!"

He glanced down to find the babe had fallen asleep, one tiny pink fist tucked up beneath her chubby chin, the innocent sweetness of her expression tugging at his heart. He'd always wanted his son, Conor, to have a little sister.

Fineen suddenly frowned, remembering the two boys he'd left behind with his men.

If he didn't meet up with them soon, that hotheaded Ronan O'Byrne would convince Conor that they should set out to look for him. And right now, that was the last thing Fineen wanted.

At twelve his impetuous godson possessed a lust for vengeance that matched any ten Irishmen. Fineen could no longer count the times Ronan had sworn mightily to do his part to drive the French-tongued invaders from their green isle. Begorra, if Ronan knew that Normans had strayed into their mountains . . .

"He'd chase them down and challenge them all," Fineen said aloud with a fond grunt. Aye, he loved the boy. Admired his fierce courage, too, an amazing trait in one so young. But Fineen didn't like his penchant for recklessness.

"Godfather!"

Muttering an oath, Fineen hoped the Normans hadn't heard the boyish cry that echoed through the darkening woods. Bracing his arm beneath the sleeping babe, he didn't wait for Ronan to reach him but set off at a fast lope, meeting his black-haired godson halfway up the rise.

"Where's Conor?" he demanded between hard breaths as Ronan drew his snorting mount to a halt, a powerful red gelding that the strong-limbed boy handled with ease.

"Coming, Godfather. We decided to race to find you. . . ." Ronan's voice trailed off, his startled gaze moving to the plump bundle in Fineen's arms, at the small white arms now flailing the air. But before he could say a word, Fineen hastily concocted a story to silence him.

"The babe's parents are dead. Wolves. I found the poor thing tucked in the hollow of a tree, crying her lungs out. Take her now—while I climb up behind you."

His gray eyes widening, Ronan appeared at such a loss to have a squirming bare-bottomed babe thrust into his arms that Fineen almost laughed. His bold godson undone by a wee bit of a girl? That was worthy of some teasing tonight at supper.

"But . . . but what if—"

"Begorra, lad, it would do you no harm save to your pride," Fineen broke in, settling himself behind Ronan. "Hand me the child and let's be off."

Ronan seemed more than relieved to surrender his burden, especially when the babe's tightly curled fist caught him squarely on the jaw as he handed her over his shoulder to Fineen.

"I don't think she likes me, Godfather."

"Nonsense, boy. She'll like you well enough. Just give her a chance."

Ronan's eyes grew all the rounder. "You're going to keep her, then?"

"Aye, I'm going to keep her! Did you think I'd be throwing her back to the wolves? Now ride with you, Ronan O'Byrne. Save your hundred questions for when we're out of these woods."

Gently cradling the babe once more inside his jerkin, Fineen was glad when Ronan obeyed and kicked the eager gelding into a gallop. He was gladder still when he saw Conor appear at the top of the rise, his handsome, good-natured son unperturbed that Ronan had beat him. They were as close as brothers.

"Conor, look what your father's found!" cried Ronan, throwing a secretive grin behind him at Fineen. "Tucked in the hollow of a tree, no less!"

Although deciding he couldn't have invented a better story, Fineen knew he'd have to tell his wife of twenty years the truth. There was no use in attempting to keep anything from Alice; she could read him as if he were the clearest mountain stream. But all would be well.

Alice had a good heart. She would understand the need to protect the child, no one other than herself ever to know that the babe was Norman. Besides, like him, she had always wanted a daughter, having been barren since Conor's birth.

"Aye, Eva, your wee one will be safe with us," Fineen whispered fiercely to himself as Conor drew his sweaty horse alongside them. His son's blue eyes grew as round as Ronan's had earlier as Ronan grinned and gestured to the babe nestled in Fineen's arms.

After all, he had sworn.

Chapter 1

Ireland, 1210

"AH, YOU MUST make haste, make haste! He has little time left!"

Barely inside the stockade gates, Ronan O'Byrne dismounted heavily, obliging the wizened, stoop-shouldered healer who had rushed forward to greet him. His countenance grim, he had only to nod to his men for them to understand they should wait for him there. Then he strode with the healer toward the hall, the stockade yard eerily silent around them. O'Toole clansmen stood in somber knots while the women went about their work silently. Wide-eyed children, forbidden to play, forbidden to make a peep, clustered into doorways to watch curiously as Ronan passed by.

" 'Tis Black O'Byrne, the rebel! Chieftain of the Glenmalure O'Byrnes!" he overheard one disobedient young boy exclaim to a taller youth who answered with awe in his voice.

"Aye, would that I were old enough to join his daring band."

"Oh aye, me, too!" proclaimed the younger one just before both boys were silenced by a sharp cuff to the ear from their stern-faced mother.

"Have some respect, lads! The O'Toole is dying."

The woman's words cutting through him as cleanly as an ice-cold knife, Ronan missed nothing as he and the healer crossed the yard.

It was strange how everything appeared much the same. Even though Ronan had not entered this stockade for twelve years the memories were still fresh; the pain always with him. Twelve long years ago Fineen O'Toole had banished him forever from the glen of Imaal, cursing Ronan for Conor's death.

It had been a freakish accident, yet Fineen's terrible grief had left him blind to reason. Over the years, Ronan had made several attempts at reconciliation only to be rebuffed. Even when Fineen lost his beloved wife, Alice, five years past, Ronan's message of sympathy had been refused. Now his stubborn godfather had summoned Ronan to his deathbed and he had come, unsure what to expect.

"It is bad, Ronan, very bad," the withered little man warned him as they entered the tomblike hall. He followed the healer into the sleeping chamber on the left; someone gently closed the door behind them.

The stuffy candlelit room reeked sickeningly of death, making his eyes water. Fineen's wounds had putrefied and now nothing could save him, not even the cowled priest, stout as a barrel, who intoned prayers in the corner. Clenching his jaw so hard that it hurt, Ronan moved to the bed and looked down upon the man whom he had loved as a second father.

The robust Fineen O'Toole he had known was gone, his full russet beard now scraggly against sunken cheeks as yellowed as parchment, his once powerful physique wasted.

"Lord, he is here," announced the healer in a hushed, respectful voice. He gestured for Ronan to draw closer. "Your godson, Black O'Byrne, is here."

With apparent effort, the dying chieftain turned his head. Ronan ignored the stool offered to him by one of the veiled women in the room. Instead, he knelt on one knee beside the bed.

"Ronan?"

"Aye, Godfather." Again Ronan had to swallow against the choking tightness in his throat. If Fineen's body had changed, his piercing gaze had not. His blue eyes, so very much like Conor's, still burned brightly.

"I knew you would come." The familiar gruff voice, half whisper, half rasp, struggled on. "I was wrong . . . about Conor . . . blaming you. Forgive me."

Stunned, Ronan could not speak. He had waited a long time to hear those words. As Fineen offered his bony hand, Ronan took it, astounded by the fierceness of his godfather's grip.

"My adopted daughter . . . Triona," Fineen continued brokenly, his breathing labored, his pale cracked lips barely moving. "She will have no one when . . . when I am gone. Swear to me, Ronan. Swear you will protect her."

Triona. The copper-haired babe Fineen had found crying in the woods, her parents killed by wolves. The babe who'd grown into a sweet little girl who adored her older brother, and mayhap Ronan as well. She'd always seemed delighted with the small trinkets he brought her whenever he came to Imaal although other than that, he'd scarcely had time to pay her much heed.

She couldn't have been more than eight winters when last he had visited Imaal. At that time he had come from his home glen to fetch Conor to join him and his clansmen on a raid. Except Conor did not return alive.

Sighing heavily, Ronan thrust the painful images of that day from his mind.

"Your daughter has no husband to look after her?" he asked, realizing Triona would be twenty by now and long past the age when she should have wed.

Ronan was surprised by Fineen's response, a dry cough that sounded suspiciously like a chuckle.

"No . . . not married."

Must be ugly as a hound, Ronan thought, although he recalled the girl as being pretty enough. Perhaps the pox had scarred her face. Or perhaps she was overly pious.

His musing was interrupted as Fineen's cough became a long hacking spell that left the chieftain visibly weaker. As if he sensed that the end were drawing near, Fineen once more met Ronan's eyes.

"You must swear, Ronan. You were like a son to me . . . family. Swear you will take my daughter into your care!"

Puzzled by the urgency of Fineen's request, Ronan nonetheless nodded. In truth, he wanted no such obligation, his raids upon the hated Normans and the pressing cares of his clan already consuming him. But he could not refuse a dying man.

"Say it, Ronan!"

"Aye, I swear. She has my protection."

His words were greeted by a rattling sigh as Fineen closed his eyes, his head lolling upon the stained pillow. Ronan heard one of the veiled women burst into tears. Triona? he wondered.

"It cannot be long now," said the healer, running his palm across the chieftain's sallow forehead.

At this pronouncement more women joined in the weeping, and the priest began to pray louder when Fineen still did not open his eyes. As if he were praying in unison the chieftain began to mumble, but Ronan could not understand what he was saying until he leaned closer.

"Must not . . . must not know the truth about Triona . . . Must not know . . ."

Glancing at the healer, who shrugged and shook his head, Ronan whispered in Fineen's ear, "What do you mean, God-father? I don't understand. . . ."

Ronan's query was answered by a low gurgling sound, Fineen's shriveled hand once more gripping his as tightly as a claw. Then it abruptly went limp.

For a long moment, Ronan stared at Fineen's face, oblivious to the wild keening crescendoing behind him. But at last he sighed and rose to his feet.

Except for the glowing candles at the head of the bed, the room was dark, the grief stricken women swathed in shadows. He wondered again which one might be Triona. As a dutiful daughter, he imagined she had kept a close vigil in this room, but was too modest to come forward. That pleased him. Such maidenly virtues would make his task as her guardian all the easier.

Ronan looked up at the sudden commotion beyond the door.

"What do you mean my father summoned that bastard Black O'Byrne to his bedside? Get out of my way! I will enter, I tell you!"

At the sound of a scuffle outside the chamber, the women's wailing became shocked gasps. Ronan frowned as the door burst open, five strapping clansmen spilling into the room.

At their center, he saw a flash of copper hair and two slender arms thrashing wildly.

"I said let me pass! Murchertach O'Toole, you may be my father's Tanist but you've no right to hold me back like this! I want to see my father!"

"Begorra, man, look out for her fists!" warned one of the clansmen.

"Aagh, Triona, why'd you have to stomp on my foot? I think you've broken my toes!" another cried out.

"You deserve worse than that for blocking my way, you . . . you—"

"By God, let her pass!" Ronan's stern command was answered by stunned silence as all faces turned toward him. "Is this riot the honor owing to a dead chieftain?"

"Dead?"

The hoarse exclamation had come from the petite, disheveled figure who shoved her way free of the clansmen before Ronan could reply. Dressed in a leather jerkin, shirt and trousers, her lush curls flying, she rushed past him and sank to her knees beside the bed.

"When?"

Ronan's gaze lifted from the young woman's curious clothing to her exquisite profile which was limned by candlelight. A smooth forehead, graceful nose and cheekbones, delicately curved lips. Triona O'Toole was no poxed hound, that much was clear.

"A few moments ago."

Expecting an immediate womanly flood of tears, Ronan couldn't have been more surprised when she rose, her small hands clenched at her sides.

"I will avenge you, Father. I swear it! I'll not rest until the Normans who attacked you feel the sting of my arrows!"

And you will not cry, Triona told herself fiercely despite the heartrending grief twisting inside her. Not now. Not until she was alone . . . and not until *he* had left Imaal.

She spun, her contemptuous gaze sweeping from head to foot the grimly silent man who towered above her. Considering she had last seen him as a child, it was amazing to her that he could look even taller than she remembered, his shoulders broader, his chest wider, an air of command emanating from him even as he was standing still, damn him. Boldly she met his eyes.

"Black hair, black clothes, black cloak. You look like Satan himself come to call! How dare you darken my father's last moments, O'Byrne!"

Ronan saw unshed tears glistening in her eyes, the trembling of her chin, and told himself to be patient. She had just lost her father after all. Yet it was apparent from her hostility toward him that Fineen had spoken of Ronan none too kindly over the years, Triona adopting her father's view. No doubt she, too, blamed him for Conor's death.

"So you remember me," Ronan said evenly, appraising again her unmaidenlike garb. His gaze lingered upon the snug fit of her trousers to shapely hips and thighs . . . until he realized he was staring. A damned dangerous combination, was men's clothing on a female form, and one he intended to remedy, Ronan decided, looking up to find Triona scowling at him. "You've changed altogether. You were just a little girl—"

"Spare me your recollections, Ronan O'Byrne. You will leave Imaal at once. You're not welcome here. Go back to Glenmalure where you belong!"

His eyes widening at her insolent command, Ronan felt his anger pricked and his patience vanished. No one gave him orders. No one.

"*I* will decide when to leave this glen, Triona O'Toole, and when I do, you will accompany me. Your father summoned me for a reconciliation and made me swear an oath. You're now under my protection. It was his last wish and I intend to fulfill it." Seeing her bristle with disbelief, he added, "The priest is my witness. If you'd been by your father's side like any devoted and respectful daughter, you would know I speak the truth."

"Like any devoted . . . ? Why you . . . you presumptuous . . ." sputtered Triona, so outraged that she was tempted to strike this overbearing rebel whose eyes glittered silver in the candlelight. "Do you dare to think because I wasn't his blood daughter that I've been any less devoted to him? It was only because he yearned for a taste of venison that I left his side. I just now returned from the hunt to discover I was barred from the hall, my cousin Murchertach informing me that Father had a visitor. You!"

Triona did strike him then but not upon the face. He was too damned tall. She balled up her fist and hit him squarely in the stomach, but her blow might have been a feather light tap for all she hurt him. Her hand was throbbing, however, his muscled abdomen as hard as rock.

"Did that ease your temper?" he asked tightly, his silvery eyes gleaming. "Now I understand what your father was mumbling just before he died. Why he enlisted his five men to keep you out until I had sworn. You're hardly the sweet-natured girl I remember—"

"Aye, so I'm not, and you'll get more of the same if you're fool enough to stay in Imaal a moment longer!" Triona shot back, although she doubted her poor hand would survive such abuse.

"Watch out for your shins, O'Byrne!" came a warning from one of the men near the door. "And your toes! She's a kick on her that can splinter wood!"

"Please, please, this unseemly strife must cease!" cried the flush-faced priest who pushed his girth between them as if anticipating Triona's next move. "Have some respect for the dead and take this matter outside!"

"Aye, so we will," Triona agreed, eager to be done with this intrusion so she could return to her father. Brushing past Ronan, she glared at the clansmen who had blocked her way and especially at Murchertach who, as her father's Tanist, was now the new chieftain of the Imaal O'Tooles.

"I could have been with him if not for you," she said to him with bitterness, fresh tears smarting her eyes.

"Do not blame me," replied the big-boned Irishman, his deep voice holding no apology. "It was your father's command that he speak with Ronan alone."

Feeling betrayed by her own clan, Triona said no more. She dashed out of the hall and ran to her tethered horse, seizing her bowcase from the leather sheath strapped to the animal's broad back. By the time Ronan appeared in the doorway, Triona had already strung her bow and set an arrow to the string.

"Aye, Laeg, I see him," she muttered to the tall bay stallion who tossed its great head as Ronan stepped outside, his black cloak swirling. "Bright June sunshine and the man still looks like the very devil."

An admittedly handsome devil no matter the stern look on his face, she thought as Ronan stopped dead in his tracks when she took aim. Even more so than she remembered as a young girl when it had made her heart pound just to look at him. When she'd believed the moon, the sun and the twinkling stars in the night sky spun around Ronan O'Byrne. But that had been before he'd murdered her brother.

"Might I ask what you're doing pointing that arrow at me?" came his query, his voice tinged with just enough authority, just enough condescension to infuriate her. "I thought we came out here to talk."

"I've little more to say to you than this, Black O'Byrne. If you think I'm going anywhere with you, think again!" She released the deadly missile with an ominous zing, skewering the hem of Ronan's long cloak to the wall.

Chapter 2

STUNNED, RONAN LOOKED from the owl-fletched arrow that had narrowly missed his calf to Triona's satisfied smile. That wily old Fineen! His new charge was no more a modest and dutiful female than Ronan was a lover of Normans. The disobedient chit seemed intent upon defying him.

"You see that I don't need your protection," she declared, deftly fitting another arrow to the string. "I've taken care of myself for years and intend to continue! Now mount your horse and leave me in peace!"

· "And if I don't?" Swallowing his surprise at her skill with the bow, Ronan yanked his mantle from the wall and strode toward her. He didn't flinch as a second arrow winged right past his ear, piercing the earth harmlessly behind him. "An oath is an oath, Triona, and I intend to honor it . . . with or without your consent."

The third arrow sliced into the ground at his feet and Ronan stopped, incensed.

"Go on, test my aim! Take another step!" she dared him, tossing a lustrous mass of coppery gold ringlets over her shoulder. "But I warn you, my father taught me how to shoot and he claimed that my skill equaled his own. Try to touch me, O'Byrne, and I swear the next arrow will fly straight to your heart. A fitting end to match the one you gave my brother!"

Wisely, Ronan didn't move.

Cursing under his breath, he found it strange that at such a moment he would notice the brilliant color of her eyes, now trained so intently upon him. The hall had been so dim that he had not noticed earlier, and he'd forgotten such a detail from her childhood.

Vivid emerald green . . . like a forest glade in morning sunlight. Beautiful. And deadly. He did not doubt that she would make good upon her threat.

He decided not to lunge for her. The thought of trussing her up and carrying her by force to his stronghold was very tempting and no less than she deserved for such willfulness, but he would reason with her instead.

But only this once. And he doubted she would listen to him unless he offered something that might appeal to this misguided hoyden.

"It would be a pity if you killed me," he said bluntly, his eyes holding hers.

"For your widow perhaps."

"I've no wife. No children." Ronan took a step forward, but froze when she began to pull back the string.

"Move again, O'Byrne, and I promise you'll be greeting your grave."

Bridling his anger, Ronan kept his voice calm. "I've an offer to make, Triona. One I believe will intrigue you."

He was answered by a most unmaidenly snort of derision. "Offer? What could you possibly offer me other than your agreement to leave Imaal and never show your face here again?"

"That's not exactly what I intended. I heard your oath to your father. I, too, am determined to seek out his attackers. If you come with me now, we could avenge him together. You could ride with my men and I—"

"Ride with you?" Triona cut in sarcastically, although she was surprised at this offer. Her father had rarely spoken a good word about Ronan, had rarely spoken of him at all for that matter, but he had never faulted Ronan's crusade against the Normans. The bold raids of Black O'Byrne and his clansmen were legendary among those Leinster Irish who still refused to accept the invaders' presence in Eire. In fact these Leinster Irish were branded as rebels by other clans who'd submitted to the Normans like stupid sheep. Aye, Ronan's was a brave cause, but it had been during one of these raids that she had lost her brother. "And risk falling to one of your arrows like Conor?" she added. "Not likely."

She saw Ronan stiffen, a muscle flashing along his jaw.

"I no longer use a bow, so you've nothing to fear." His eyes swept over her—not silver now but a stormy slate gray—as if taking her measure. "Then again, mayhap you're not as brave as you appear. Mayhap your oath of vengeance was only a fine show for your clansmen. From the way you hesitate, I would even venture to guess that you're afraid to join us on our raids—"

"Afraid?" Indignant, Triona lowered her bow. "I'll have you know that I'm a better shot than most men and I've the practice targets full of holes to prove it! If you don't believe me, ask my clansmen. Ask them, too, if I've ever flinched at the hunt. You'll find that Triona O'Toole's never once fled from a charging boar. Never!"

Given what he'd seen of her thus far, Ronan found it wasn't difficult to imagine her facing down an enraged beast—which didn't please him. Hunting was hardly a fitting pastime for a young woman. Yet, for now, he would humor her and tolerate her boasts.

"I would expect nothing less from you," he conceded, "seeing as your teacher was the finest bowman in Wicklow. But hunting is one thing, raiding against Normans entirely another. Who knows? In the heat of an attack, you might decide you'd rather be safe at home than faced with enemies who'd love nothing more than to slit your throat."

Now Triona was really angry. She must be red faced, her cheeks were so flame hot. How dare this arrogant man even hint that she might shrink in the face of danger!

"My father taught me to fend for myself, O'Byrne, and I've already survived enough scrapes to know that I could stand up to some fool Normans!"

"Then prove it. Accept my offer."

Triona almost shouted that she would, damn him, but cold reason doused her response just in time.

"I don't have to prove anything to you," she said surlily, once more taking aim. "I'd rather win vengeance on my own than ride with a man who could murder his best friend—"

"Enough, Triona! You disgrace your father's passing with such talk!"

Startled, Triona lowered her bow as Murchertach left the hall and stood beside Ronan.

"The good priest has told me everything, and 'tis true that your father and the O'Byrne reconciled before his death," continued the strapping young chieftain, his ruddy face stern. "The past has been forgiven. All blame set aside. Bridle your sharp tongue, woman, or you'll only shame Fineen's memory with your spite."

"I would never shame my father," Triona said stiffly, affronted that Murchertach would rebuke her so harshly and in full view of her clansmen. Glancing around her, she saw that her heated exchange with Ronan had drawn many onlookers, including her longtime maid, Aud, who was nervously wringing her hands.

But then again, Triona fumed as the new chieftain turned to confer in conspiratorial tones with Ronan. Murchertach had held a grudge against her since she had refused his offer of marriage. Mayhap he was repaying her for the slight. But she'd only rejected him as she had done all the rest; she'd marry no man who wanted to take away her freedom.

And Murchertach had threatened as much! No more hunting or late moonlit rides or the choice to go where she pleased when she pleased as a man might, but managing a home and servants and bowing to a husband's every whim, as wives were expected to do.

Mayhap if Fineen had reared her differently, she would have been contented with such a lot. But after Conor's death, she'd practically become the son that he had lost. No needlework and staying indoors for her—well, other than for occasional lessons in learning from a visiting priest—but training in archery and the ways of the woods and its creatures. Aye, she'd marry if she found a man who'd respect her skills as her father had, a man who wouldn't make her give up the things she loved. But until then, she'd be taking no husband. Not if she had breath in her body to say anything about it.

"I'd rather drown in a bog than settle for the life you offered me, Murchertach O'Toole," she muttered to herself, glaring resentfully at her former suitor.

"What was that?" he demanded, facing her. He crossed his brawny arms over his chest, clearly reveling in his role as her father's successor, the clan's new chieftain.

"I said I'd die before I'd disgrace my father's memory," Triona answered.

"Wisely spoken. Then I'll hear no more dissent when I say that you will honor Fineen's last wish and accept Ronan O'Byrne, chieftain of the Glenmalure O'Byrnes, as your guardian and protector."

So the two men had been conspiring against her, she seethed, certain now that Murchertach had been waiting for the chance to wield his newfound power over her and had finally found it in Ronan. Well, she wouldn't give him the satisfaction.

"Your fine speech wasn't needed, cousin," she said icily. "I've already decided to accept the O'Byrne's offer to ride with him and his men on their raids. A far more enticing prospect than embroidering shirts or warming some loutish chieftain's bed, wouldn't you say?" She ignored Murchertach's vehement oath and shot a glance at Ronan. "That is, if your offer still stands."

Ronan wondered if Murchertach's face could possibly turn any redder, and for a brief moment admired her for so easily quelling the man's smugness. "Aye, the offer stands."

"Then the matter's settled. Now if the two of you don't mind, I'll return to my father. Alone."

Ronan heard the telling catch in her voice, but it didn't match the look of pure disdain she threw at him as she shouldered her bowcase and stalked back into the hall. Or had it been directed at Murchertach? He couldn't be sure.

All he was sure of was that she was accompanying him of her own free will. At least that would buy him a temporary reprieve from her hotheaded temper until they reached Glenmalure.

Or so he hoped . . .

Chapter 3

"JUST BECAUSE I'VE agreed to join you on your raids doesn't mean that I have to like you, O'Byrne. I don't."

Taking his eyes from the rugged line of mountains to the south, Ronan glanced at the young woman riding bareback beside him.

So Triona had deigned to speak to him at last. She hadn't uttered a word to him since she'd accepted his offer two days ago. With Fineen's burial behind them, Ronan's stronghold only another hour's ride away, he had begun to think she would remain stubbornly silent for the entire journey. He might have preferred that she had.

"And just because my father forgave you doesn't mean that I'll ever forget what you did to Conor," Triona continued.

"That makes two of us," Ronan muttered to himself, frowning now as Triona's gangly gray wolfhound went crashing into the underbrush after a snowy-tailed rabbit. "You'd do well to keep that unruly beast of yours under control. He could startle the horses."

His terse advice was greeted by an indignant glare. "Conn isn't unruly! I'll have you know I trained him from a pup. He's obedient and loyal and would come back with a single command if I wanted him to. But I'd rather let him run. If you O'Byrnes raid as often as I've heard, Conn and I will have little time for hunting once we reach your stronghold."

More aptly put, Triona, you'll have *no* time for hunting, Ronan vowed silently, his gaze falling to the sleek white cat stretched across her lap.

He hadn't expected Triona to meet him at the stockade gate

20

with a menagerie in tow. But then he hadn't expected her to possess a majestically powerful bay stallion any man would be proud to own either. Another surprise. It amazed him now that the copper-eyed feline held no interest in the hooded falcon perched on Triona's shoulder, but it did hiss and spit when Conn came bounding from the trees, his red tongue lolling.

"Aye, that's my Conn! Conn the Hundred Fighter!"

As Triona leaned over to pat the huge wiry-haired animal, Ronan realized he was staring at her again, a creamy glimpse of flesh revealed when her shirt pulled free of her trousers. But what jammed his breath was her smile, as open and radiant as the delight dancing in her eyes, and the sound of her laughter when Conn licked her hand. Soft and supple, and husky enough to stir any man's senses . . .

"What are you looking at, O'Byrne?"

Slowly expelling his breath, Ronan met Triona's wary gaze. She wasn't smiling any longer, though it hardly mattered. She could be sticking out her tongue at him and grimacing and she'd still be one of the loveliest women he'd ever seen.

"Your bird," he lied, feeling distinctly uncomfortable and beginning to wish his new charge *had* been ugly as a hound. "Fine creature."

"Aye, so he is," Triona agreed, although she wasn't wholly convinced that Ronan had been staring at her falcon. Gripping the reins with one hand, she quickly tucked in her rust-colored shirt, a hot blush firing her cheeks when Ronan pointedly looked away.

Damn if she hadn't caught him watching her more than once during the past few days! she fumed, realizing just where his attention had been drawn. She had tried to avoid him, this unwanted guardian of hers, but that had been impossible in the somewhat cramped hall of Imaal. And then at her father's burial, when Ronan had stood right next to her, so close that their fingertips had brushed—

"Does your cat share as illustrious a name as Conn the Hundred Fighter?"

Triona met Ronan's eyes, feeling suddenly a bit too warm. "Of course she does!" she snapped, wishing that she had kept her mouth shut for the entire journey as she had planned. As far as she was concerned, she and Ronan had nothing more to discuss than raiding. Furthermore, as soon as their vengeance was won, she, Aud and her pets would be on their way. Not home to Imaal, where Murchertach now ruled, but someplace else. Just where, though, she wasn't yet sure.

"Well?"

Triona sighed with exasperation but decided to humor Ronan's attempt at conversation. If she satisfied his curiosity, maybe then he would leave her alone.

"This is Maeve"—she gave the drowsy cat a fond stroke—"and the falcon you were so admiring is Ferdiad."

For a fleeting instant Triona imagined she saw the barest hint of a smile on Ronan's face. But when he turned back to the mountain path, his striking features were as serious as ever. "Maeve the Warrior-Queen and her Connaught champion Ferdiad, friend and yet enemy of the mighty hero Cuchulain."

"Aye, and don't forget Laeg, here." Triona proudly patted her stallion's glistening reddish-brown neck. "He's as stout-hearted as they come. I knew his name should be Laeg the moment I first rode him."

"Cuchulain's stalwart charioteer, courageous and true. So you've named all your pets after Eire's ancient heroes. You must know your legends well."

"As should any good Irishman."

"Aye, and she can sing them well, too, Lord! Triona has a lovely voice," added Aud, close behind them.

"Aud!" Triona twisted around and gave her maid a quelling look, but the spare middle-aged woman simply nudged her spotted pony into a faster walk until they were riding three abreast.

Pleased to hear that Triona possessed at least one maidenly virtue, Ronan asked, "A lovely voice you say?"

"Oh, aye, Lord, as lilting as a lark," declared Aud, clearly eager to converse now that Triona had broken her silence. So eager in fact, that she leaned closer to Ronan, her large brown eyes animated and appearing even rounder in her small beak-nosed face. "Do you have a harpist?"

"Enough, Aud," Triona groused. She pulled up on the reins and fell back in front of the the four O'Bryne clansmen who trailed them, the winding mountain path only wide enough for two horses. "I'm sure the O'Byrne doesn't want to hear all of this—"

"Nonsense," Ronan interrupted, hoping to discover if there were more worthy womanly qualities to his reluctant charge than met the eye. "As your guardian, everything about you is of interest to me. Allow the good woman to speak." He turned back to Aud. "Aye, I've a harpist, one of the finest in Wicklow."

"He'd have to be one of the finest to match my sweeting's fair music," Aud chatted on proudly, listing the ancient legends that Triona could recite in song: the tale of the Red Branch Knights, Deirdre of the Sorrows, the Children of Lir and so many more.

"Jesu, Mary and Joseph," muttered Triona as she fell back even farther, embarrassed. Yet she should be used to such talk by now, and she knew her irrepressible maid meant no harm. Loyal to the bone, Aud had doted upon her since she was a wee babe. But Aud was also a meddler, forever hoping that somewhere there was a man Triona might accept. . . .

"Little chance of that," Triona breathed to herself, watching as Conn playfully lunged in and out of the trees. She doubted there was a man alive who'd take her just as she was—

"So Murchertach wasn't the first man that Triona spurned."

"Oh no, Lord, there've been plenty of others."

"Aud!" Wondering how the conversation had jumped from the legends of Eire to such a personal topic, Triona realized with growing irritation that she should have been listening to her maid more carefully. "That's enough talk about me!"

"But the O'Byrne was merely asking—"

"Too many questions!" Triona scowled at Ronan as she kicked Laeg forward, forcing Aud to shift places with her, the startled maid now riding behind. "If he must know anything else, then he can ask me himself."

"There is something," said Ronan, noting the inborn grace in Triona's gesture as she shoved an unruly shock of bright copper hair from her face. "Why have you rejected every suitor?"

"Didn't like them."

The truculent tilt of her chin told Ronan that the subject was a touchy one but he persisted, puzzled by her answer. "Nothing more than that?"

"She shot two of them with her arrows!" Aud interjected as if she couldn't help herself. "Such fine-looking young men, too, and of good family. One in the leg and the other—"

"I grazed him in the shoulder," Triona finished tightly.

"You shot them?" Frowning to himself, Ronan remembered with discomfort how close he had come to being skewered by one of her arrows. "Did they overstep their bounds? Touch you? Insult you?"

"No, just wouldn't leave me in peace."

"So you shot them."

"I said *grazed*, O'Byrne. It wasn't my intent to maim them. Their wounds were barely scratches. It was just enough to make them go away."

Ronan studied her, amazed. "And your father didn't object?"

"Why should he? He respected my judgment."

Now he'd heard just about enough, Ronan thought angrily, exasperated by her flippant answers. Not one of his men was half as wild. Her weapons had to go. And speaking of weapons . . .

"How did you come to be so skilled with the bow?" he asked, Triona immediately granting him a look of pure irritation.

"Have you wax in your ears, O'Byrne? I already told you, my father taught me."

"But surely that is an unusual thing for a man to allow his daughter, chieftain or no."

"Mayhap, but it seemed to give him the balm he needed after losing his only son. He had always loved to shoot targets with Conor, to hunt, to fish." Triona noted that Ronan's expression had darkened, his grip on the reins very tight, but she continued on. "I hoped it might cheer him—if I learned to shoot, and it did. By the time my mother saw how good I'd become, it was too late."

"Too late?"

"Aye. I never had to embroider another stitch, or bother learning about household things for that matter, and my father never forced me. He would have lost his best hunting companion, he always said."

Ronan made no comment to this last bit, his tight-lipped silence vexing Triona.

"Well, since we're asking questions of each other, what about you?" she demanded, her own curiosity getting the better of her. "You said you have no wife and no children, yet surely a renowned chieftain such as yourself has been offered many a pleasing bride."

"I've no time for marriage," came his gruff answer as he looked away.

"But if you don't mind me saying so, Lord, 'tis a shame, is what it is," Aud interjected in disbelief. "A fine handsome man like you."

"Handsome, aye, but I'd wager that stern expression you seem to favor has frightened away more than one maiden," Triona muttered loud enough for Ronan to hear. "If you think I'm not as I used to be, O'Byrne, neither are you. I remember you always laughing, always smiling and telling tales. I remember the serving girls fighting over which one would wait upon you, and how you would pull them onto your lap and kiss—"

"Then you were up far too late for your young age," Ronan cut her off, his stone gray eyes locking with hers. "People change, Triona. Enough said."

She stared back, momentarily silenced by the vehemence of his voice and the haunted cast to his eyes. Strangely he looked younger at that moment, as if the years had been stripped away, and she dropped her gaze at the sudden tugging in her chest, her breath stilled in her throat.

The sensation reminded her of when she used to watch him from a knothole in the kitchen, her father's hall resounding with merriment. When she used to watch Ronan's face, thinking him the most handsome of men with his midnight brows, lean, strong features and that devil-may-care smile. When she used to watch him kiss those giggling girls . . . knowing she shouldn't be there and yet unable to tear herself away, wishing that one day when she was older, Ronan O'Byrne might be kissing her—

"I said look to your mount, Triona. The path is steep here."

"W-what?" Flustered both by the turn of her thoughts as well as not hearing Ronan's warning the first time, she tightened her grip on the reins, preventing Laeg from dancing sideways. As they began to descend a sharp hill, the green wooded beauty of Glenmalure stretching out before them, Triona was grateful that she had the rocky path to occupy her attention until she regained her composure. A composure she resolved not to lose again.

"We'll be there soon," Ronan announced, taking the lead when the path once more grew level.

Gathering Maeve under one arm, Triona urged Laeg into a trot and caught up with Ronan; from his surprised expression, she guessed that he had expected her to stay behind with Aud. The command in his eyes told her that he wanted her to do just that, which she ignored.

His clansmen seemed to obey him without question, and she imagined she would, too, once they were out on a raid. Granted, she could see why Ronan had won such successes against the Normans given the unswerving obedience and loyalty of his men. But right now she had something important to discuss with him. She determinedly rode a little ahead of him, then declared over her shoulder, "I've the perfect plan to avenge my father."

"We'll talk of it later."

"Later?" Stunned, Triona yanked up on the reins and waited until his glossy black stallion was even with hers. "What do you mean, *later?* My father lies cold in his grave, dead by Norman hands, and . . . and you're saying that I must wait to discuss our plans for vengeance?"

Ronan passed her without answering, which infuriated Triona. Once again she caught up with him, her voice growing shrill as she persisted.

"But we know who those men were! The Normans who attacked my father bore the de Roche crest, a three-headed dragon! That accursed baron of Naas might well have been among them when my father strayed onto de Roche land—"

"De Roche land?" Ronan interrupted, his harsh tone clearly meant to rebuke her. "You mean stolen land, *O'Byrne* land and

Fineen, as my kinsman, had every right to be hunting upon it! And if your father's men hadn't been hunting elsewhere, but had kept him within sight instead of stumbling upon his attackers after it was too late, the O'Toole would still be alive. Murchertach told me there were three Irish for every Norman. That's why the yellow curs retreated without a fight. Three to one!"

"Aye, three to one," echoed Triona, the same sick feeling welling inside her that had plagued her since that day. Remorse, because like her clansmen she hadn't been with her father when he had ridden after that wounded buck. And crushing despair, when she had seen the bloody gash across his ribs, his right thigh slashed to the white bone, and guessed then that he would not survive . . .

"Enough, Triona, you cannot blame yourself," Ronan said grimly, her stricken expression cuing him to what she must be thinking. At once he found himself wishing he could be as charitable with himself, then he thrust his mind back to Triona. He had learned from Murchertach that she had accompanied her father on that fateful hunting trip, a harsh ordeal she would have been spared if not for Fineen's misguided indulgence. "As I told you, we'll talk of this later."

When she didn't answer, simply hugging her white cat closer to her breast, Ronan almost regretted what was to come.

Almost.

The resentful look she shot at him only heightened his resolve.

Chapter 4

TRIONA HAD EXPECTED Ronan's mountain stronghold to be as formidable as the man, and she was right.

They passed through two massive earthen ramparts before they reached the inner embankment, atop which was erected a timber palisade of stout red oak. As the final gates were opened for them, this last set so tall and heavy that eight strong men were needed for the task, she was certain that even if the Normans ever found this remote stockade they'd be hard-pressed to breach it.

"It's just as I imagined, O'Byrne." Triona looked around her at the rugged peaks towering above the glen, the mighty Lugnaquilla rising to the southwest. "Considering the rebel's price on your head, you couldn't have found a safer haven."

That Ronan gave no reply didn't concern Triona. From the set look on his face, she imagined he was already preoccupied with any number of the responsibilities that plagued an important chieftain.

As for herself, her thoughts were racing ahead to that first raid. Aye, she was good with weapons, but she'd never before ridden on such a venture. Her father and the Imaal O'Tooles had raided with other rebel clans in earlier days, but after Conor's death, Fineen had kept to the Wicklow Mountains. So she knew little of harrying Normans. She would have to watch and learn quickly from Ronan and his men, the better that she'd be prepared when they finally faced her father's murderers.

Anticipation filled her as their small band rode into the stronghold, Conn barking at the lead and Aud jouncing along on her pony behind Triona. The next time she passed these gates, she would be embarking on her plan to avenge her father. Aye, she could hardly wait!

"So you're back, brother!"

The welcoming cry came from across the yard as Triona reined in her mount with the others in front of the stable. Distracted by the smiling dark-haired young man striding toward them, she wasn't aware that Ronan had dismounted until she realized he'd come to stand next to her horse. At the same moment two of the O'Byrne clansmen who had accompanied them from Imaal walked up behind her and snatched away Maeve and Ferdiad, her cat yowling in surprise, her startled falcon frantically beating its wings. Outraged, Triona yelled out a curse that split the air, yet she had no sooner swung her leg over Laeg's neck when Ronan caught her around the waist, his expression determined.

"What . . . What in blazes are you doing?" she demanded, her face burning with indignation as she tried futilely to twist free of his grasp.

"I would think it plain enough. Helping a maiden from her horse."

"Maiden? Have you gone mad? You know well enough that I don't need your help . . . oh!"

He swept her into the air so suddenly that Triona threw her arms around his neck, then in the next instant her feet touched the ground. Horrified to find herself clinging to him, his hard, honed body pressed intimately against hers, Triona shoved away from him with such force that she fell backward . . . right into another pair of strong arms.

"Whoa, what have we here, Ronan? Spoils from a raid? I thought you'd gone to Imaal to see the O'Toole—"

"I've just come from Imaal," Ronan cut in, relieved that his younger brother had caught Triona yet oddly disgruntled at the sight of her in his arms. Shrugging off the feeling, he held out his hand to her. He wasn't surprised when she refused him by cursing him soundly as she thrust herself away from his brother.

"Spoils indeed! I'm Triona O'Toole!" came her affronted announcement as Conn trotted over and sat down beside her.

"Fineen's daughter," added Ronan in explanation, feeling the full force of her angry eyes upon him. "My brother, Niall."

"This is certainly a surprise," interjected Niall, his blue-gray eyes puzzled yet friendly. Then he suddenly sobered, asking Triona more than Ronan, "And the O'Toole?"

"My father is dead."

Her throat gone tight, Triona watched as the two men shared a glance. She knew Ronan had a brother, a younger sister, too, though she had never expected to meet them. Perhaps ten years Ronan's junior and not quite as tall, Niall bore the same powerfully sinewed physique. But while Ronan's hair was black as midnight and brushed his shoulders, Niall's shorter dark brown hair had strong glints of red.

And though both men were very striking in looks their features were different, she noted when Niall turned back to her, his eyes holding sympathy. Or perhaps it only appeared so because his face was more open than Ronan's, his expression kind whereas Ronan always looked so severe.

"My condolences, Triona," Niall offered, the sincerity in his voice touching her. Strangely, she did not feel the same animosity toward this man as she did for Ronan. Yet perhaps it was not so strange after all. Niall O'Byrne had had nothing to do with Conor's death. He had been a mere boy at the time.

"Thank you," she finally murmured, but before she could say anything more, Ronan took her arm. Firmly. She gaped at him in angry surprise but he ignored her, addressing Niall.

"Triona is now under my protection and will be staying with us for a time . . . at least until I find her a husband."

"Husband?" Triona had only to look at the hard line of Ronan's jaw and her momentary confusion vanished. Shocked, she jerked away from him as if he had set a blazing torch to her sleeve.

"Husband?" parroted Aud as Triona tripped over Conn in her haste to reach her mount. She fell to her hands and knees, scraping her palms, but quickly scrambled to her feet, cursing Ronan and his deceit every step of the way.

The bold liar! She would kill him! She would shoot him so full of arrows that he'd bleed like a sieve!

"If you're looking for your bowcase, I've had it locked away for safekeeping."

Breathless, Triona froze. A quick glance at the empty leather sheath strapped to Laeg's back confirmed the sick feeling in the pit of her stomach. Her bowcase was gone. Gone! Ronan's men must have taken it while she was being introduced to Niall. At once her hand flew to her waist, disbelief filling her when Ronan gestured to the hunting knife that was now sheathed in his belt. The wily wretch! He'd stolen her knife while he held her, his hand as stealthy and swift as any thief's.

"I can't have you wounding any prospective husbands, Triona. Word will fly through the glens and then no one will come to have a look at you for fear of their lives."

"To *look* at me?" Enraged, Triona rounded upon him. "What am I, O'Byrne? A milk cow for barter? A prize goat?"

"Now, sweeting, you might hear him out—"

"Silence, Aud!" Triona commanded over her shoulder, never having felt so furious in her life. "You tricked me, O'Byrne! I knew I should never have trusted you, but I thought because you were my father's godson . . . damn me for a fool! You lied—"

"Reasoned with you is more the truth of it." Ronan stifled unexpected regret at the pained outrage in her eyes. If he didn't take her in hand now, no one would want this hotheaded hellion for a wife. And what other destiny was there for a woman? "I could have brought you here by force, but I decided to spare you the humiliation."

"So you lied to me instead! Made me believe I'd be raiding with you against the Normans when all along you had other plans for me! Despicable plans!"

"I swore you no oath, Triona," said Ronan, uncomfortably aware that her loud accusations were drawing a curious crowd of his clansmen. "Yet I did swear an oath to your father to take you into my care, an obligation I've little time for but one I could not refuse. An obligation I intend to fulfill by finding you a husband. As your guardian, that is my right."

"And if I don't want to marry?" she flung at him, her fists clenched into tight balls at her sides.

"You've no choice but to marry someone, something your father should have said to you years ago instead of allowing you to run wild as a hare."

"A hare is it now?" she blurted, mocking him. "They're swift creatures to be sure but timid, and *that* I am not. I say take your rotten plans and eat them, O'Byrne!"

A muffled chuckle sounded somewhere behind Ronan, but it died abruptly when he shot a dark look over his shoulder. Then he turned his attention back to Triona, his body grown taut with tension. "Hear me well, chit. From now on, you will occupy yourself with maidenly pursuits and become the modest, obedient young woman any man would wish for in a bride—"

"I will not!"

"I think she means it, brother," Niall threw in to Ronan's mounting annoyance, an amused look on his face.

"I *do* mean it!" Triona seconded, her chin lifted defiantly.

This last outburst proved too much for Ronan, the blood pounding like thunder in his temple. By God, he would tame her, the quicker to be done with her! In three strides he had her by the waist. Before she could do more than gasp, he'd pitched her across his shoulders as a hunter might a felled deer, pinning her flailing limbs with his arms.

"How . . . how dare you!" shrieked Triona, her cheeks ablaze with embarrassment as laughter rippled across the yard. "Conn! Come help!"

She almost cried with relief as the huge wolfhound came bounding after them, growling ferociously, his long white teeth bared.

But her relief became utter frustration when Ronan wheeled abruptly. "Sit!" he shouted. Her dog dropped obediently to its haunches, cocking its head.

"He is well trained," came Ronan's stiff comment as he turned and set off with her again, great peals of laughter crescendoing around them. "But his loyalty I would question."

Triona was so incensed she could say nothing, her muscles beginning to cramp from the way he was carrying her, her tangled hair covering her face. She knew they had entered a building when it suddenly grew darker, heard his footfalls upon planked wood and smelled the musty smoke from a peat fire, until finally it grew bright again although not as light as outside.

"This apartment used to belong to my mother. I think you'll find it adequate to your needs."

With that Triona was dumped unceremoniously onto something soft but she bolted upright at once, sputtering and swiping away the hair from her eyes and mouth. Ronan was standing at the foot of a canopied bed, looking as stern as she had ever seen him.

"It occurred to me that Aud omitted a very popular legend from her list this afternoon, 'Cuchulain's Courtship of the Maiden Emer,'" he said in a low forbidding voice. "Do you know it?"

"Of course I know it!" she shot back, thinking his question more than odd as she glanced beyond him to the door, her nearest means of escape. "Hate it, too! It's a ridiculous story—"

"And one you shall sing for us after supper tonight," he cut in, his intense gray eyes daring her to make a move from the bed. "I want to hear every verse, Triona O'Toole, especially the ones about the six maidenly gifts of Lady Emer. Her beauty of person"—his disapproving gaze fell pointedly to her rumpled clothing, then he once more met her eyes—"her beauty of voice—"

"Oh, so you don't enjoy my screeching and shouting?"

"Her gift of music, her knowledge of embroidering and needlework—"

"You'll never see me stitching the day away and you can stake your life on that, O'Byrne!"

"Her gift of wisdom—"

"Thank you very much but I've my wits about me. Enough to know I was a fool to have ever trusted you."

"And the gift of virtuous chastity."

Taking immediate affront at the unspoken question in his eyes, Triona blurted indignantly, "I've that, too, not that it's any of your damned business! And I'll not be singing that silly poem tonight, you can be sure!"

"You will sing it, Triona, and you'll be wearing a maiden's gown and mantle when you do." His gaze swept her from head to toe. "You look to be close to my sister Maire's size, though she might be a bit taller. You can borrow a few gowns from her until I've some made for you."

"Don't trouble yourself for I won't be going near them!"

"You *will* wear them, woman," he countered, the dark warning look he gave her so ominous that Triona scooted back a bit on the bed. "You'll emulate *all* of Lady Emer's fine traits if you want your stay at Glenmalure to be a pleasant one. Do you understand me?"

Triona nodded reluctantly, swallowing the caustic remark that flew like lightning to her tongue. But when he turned his back on her to leave, she could no longer resist, her pent up fury overwhelming her.

"What of my father, O'Byrne?" she demanded, raising her voice even louder when he didn't stop. "Did you lie about him, too? About the vengeance you were planning?"

He paused then, his wide shoulders stiff with tension, although he didn't turn around.

"Baron Maurice de Roche of Kildare will pay dearly for your father's death. That I swear."

"But when?" she cried as he began to close the door behind him.

"It's no longer any of your concern. You've womanly things to occupy you now."

No longer any of her concern? Triona raged as the door was pulled shut with a dull thunk. Was he mad? She would not rest until her father was avenged. So she had sworn!

She vaulted from the bed and flung herself across the room just as a key grated in the lock. Stunned that Ronan could so cruelly confine her, she pounded upon the door with her fists.

"O'Byrne?"

She heard footfalls receding, and she pounded even harder. "O'Byrne!"

Still no answer and she knew then that he was gone. Just as she knew she would make him pay for deceiving her.

The blackhearted liar! Aye, he would pay, and in ways that would make him wish that he had held to his word!

Chapter 5

"BEGORRA, BROTHER, YOU'VE taken on quite a handful."

Snorting in assent, Ronan lifted his cup and took another draft of ale. The feasting-hall was abustle with preparations for supper but at least at this end near the fire, he and Niall had enjoyed a measure of privacy.

"The O'Toole's adopted daughter no less," Niall continued. "Probably the last request you would have expected."

"What I expected was a docile young woman who'd give me no trouble," said Ronan, throwing a disgruntled look across the table. "Find her a husband and be done with it, my duty ended. Or I'd never have sworn——"

"No, Ronan, you would have sworn either way. You'd not have let Fineen go to his death worrying for his daughter."

Ronan didn't answer, although Niall spoke the truth. Aye, he'd have taken Triona into his care even if she was twice the hellion—although that was difficult to fathom—but that didn't mean he had to like it. He didn't, and the sooner he found her a husband. . . .

Low chuckling drew Ronan's attention. He frowned at Niall's grin. "Something amuses you?"

To his surprise, Niall began to laugh in earnest, his mirth only fanning Ronan's irritation.

"I knew I've been too soft with you, Niall. Twenty-four years old, my Tanist, no less, and you're still unable to hold your ale——"

"It's not the ale," Niall broke in, his laughter abating but only slightly. "I was thinking of earlier this afternoon. You should have seen your face, Ronan! You usually manage to keep a tight rein on yourself, but when Triona stood up to you . . . just a wee bit of a thing, too, and spouted she'd have no part of your plans for her—"

"Something she'll not do again if she's wise." Ronan thunked his empty cup upon the table and gestured for a nearby servant. "She'll learn soon enough that my patience is very short when it comes to such willfulness."

"I'll say." Wiping the tears of laughter from his eyes, Niall shook his head. "I couldn't believe it when you picked her up and threw her across your shoulders."

"She deserved much more than that. That chit needs a good strong dose of discipline. She's lucky I didn't take her across my knee."

"You think that would make her change her ways?" Growing thoughtful, Niall waited until his own cup was refilled before adding, "Odd, a young woman not wanting to marry. Did you have a chance to ask her why?"

"Yes, but it doesn't matter. She'll relent and abide by my wishes soon enough."

"I don't know, brother. If she's always done exactly as she pleases. . . ."

"I said she will change. And quickly, for I've little time for her foolishness."

"Just as you've no time for a wife?"

Tensing, Ronan met Niall's eyes. "You know why I've never married."

"Aye, as you've said since I can remember, you've been too busy. Harrying the Normans, looking after the needs of our clan. But it's more than that, Ronan, and I'll not hold my peace any longer. Your guilt has consumed you! You've been doing penance ever since Conor O'Toole's death, denying yourself—"

"Enough!" Ronan thrust himself from the bench, giving no heed that his roar had caused all activity in the hall to cease. "I will hear no more!"

"Aye, the truth always stings deeper than any wound," Niall continued undaunted, rising to look Ronan squarely in the eyes. "If it's so important to make amends to the O'Tooles, mayhap instead of finding Triona a husband, you might think to wed her yourself."

Stunned, Ronan stared at his brother, his fury ebbing into sheer incredulity.

"Me, marry Triona O'Toole? Now I know you've drunk too much ale." He sat heavily, tunneling his hand through his hair. "With that insolent tongue and her willful ways, I'd never know a moment's peace. No, Niall, you've always been a more tolerant man. You'd sooner be the one to wed her."

"Don't think I haven't already considered it. You've long told me that I should settle down."

Again Ronan was stunned, this time by the strange cramping in his gut. The fierce grip on his cup amazed him, too, his knuckles gone white. And it was all he could do to mutter, "Go on, then, if you want her," before he downed half his ale in one swallow. Yet he scarcely tasted the pungent liquid, and when he lowered his cup, he found that same amused smile on Niall's face.

"No, I think I'll pass, brother. You know I've always favored blonds." Niall set his cup down and rose. "I think I'll go sit with Maire for a while. She was resting when I went by earlier."

Ronan set his cup down, too. "I'll walk over with you—"

"No, no, relax and finish your ale," Niall broke in, already striding away. "I've got to change clothes first for supper, so say I'll meet you over there. No hurry."

Odd, Ronan thought, shooting a narrowed glance over his shoulder as Niall left the hall. His brother already wore one of his finest tunics, made from green cloth stolen from a Norman merchant who'd given up his wares only too eagerly in exchange for his life. . . .

Ronan suddenly noticed that every servant in the hall was staring at him, standing stock-still as if their shoes had been bolted to the floor. "Go back to your work," he ordered them, angry with himself for exploding so violently at Niall.

That wasn't like him. He preferred to keep his emotions well in check. Had for years. He was a man of self-control. Strict self-discipline. It was safest that way. Yet it was clear now that these past few days had affected him, visiting Imaal and seeing Fineen again, bringing everything back, his memories of Conor more painful than ever. He felt taut as a drum, edgy, made all the worse by his new charge's willfulness. No wonder the servants were staring.

Pleased to see that the bustling activity had resumed, Ronan turned back around and lifted his cup to drink, his gaze drawn to the fire. As he watched the bright red-gold flames, it was unsettling how easily Triona's face came to mind.

Unsettling, too, the rousing memory of her in his arms when he had pulled her from her horse. It had been a long time since he had held a woman who felt as good as she, her firm breasts swelling against him, her slim hips snug with his—

"Lord! Lord, forgive me, but I must speak with you!"

Looking up from the fire, Ronan frowned at the young maidservant rushing toward him, one of the four women he'd sent to assist Triona. Already imagining what the girl had to say he had to gesture for her to speak up, his darkening expression clearly daunting her.

"I–it's the lady, Lord. She refuses to bathe . . . refuses to let us inside the room! She sent me to tell you that she'll ready herself for supper only if her maid, Aud, assists her. And she wants her pets, Lord, or else she'll not budge. And her door unlocked, so she doesn't feel like a prisoner."

Incensed by this preposterous list of demands, Ronan rose so suddenly from his chair that the poor girl jumped like a nervous doe. She didn't wait as he dashed the last of his ale into the hissing flames but scurried from the hall, Ronan following a few strides behind her.

Triona spun from the window as a key creaked in the lock. She raced at once across the room and lent her weight to the barricade she had erected. Her heart began to pound as someone tried to enter but when the door held firm, she laughed in triumph. Ha! She could just imagine the angry look on Ronan's face!

"So you got my message, eh, O'Byrne?" she taunted him, only to fall silent when a decidedly different male voice came to her through the door.

"Triona, it's Niall! Open the door and be quick about it! I just heard from the servants that my brother's on his way."

"Niall?" Astonished yet suspicious, she hissed through the crack. "What are you doing here? And how do I know Ronan's not standing out there with you?"

"I give you my word that he's not, because he doesn't even know that I'm here. Please, Triona, open the door, even if it's only a little. I've something to tell you."

"What in blazes?" she muttered, unconvinced. Yet remembering the kindness in Niall's eyes and how his offer of sympathy had moved her, she decided to trust him. Just because Ronan was a liar didn't mean the trait must run in the family.

"Triona!"

"All right, all right, I'll open it but just a bit." Leaning into the heavy oak chest, Triona moved it back a few inches. Then she cracked the door, meeting Niall's gaze. "Now you be quick about it. What did you want to tell me?"

"Just that I'm sorry my brother disappointed you. And I hope you go on standing up to him. I think you can earn his respect."

"Respect?" she snorted. "As if I need the respect of such an onerous man. I think if he smiled his face might crack," Triona groused, although she was secretly astonished that Niall had taken up her cause. Impatiently, she added, "I don't need you telling me what I should do, either. I've my own mind, never you fear."

"I never doubted it. I just hope that you're not planning to escape the stronghold."

"I could if I wanted to," she said honestly, looking to the three glazed windows on opposite walls. "It would be an easy matter, but why should I? Your brother needs to be taught a lesson. He deserves it, you know."

"Aye, so he does," Niall agreed, again to her astonishment. "And if you persist long enough, mayhap he'll relent and allow you to ride with us."

It was on the tip of Triona's tongue to tell him that she was already planning to accompany them on their raids, with or without Ronan's blessed permission, but she decided it wouldn't be wise to reveal too much. "You think so?" she asked instead, feigning a hopeful tone.

"It's possible. Just remember, Triona, if there's anything I can do to help you, you must let me know."

To help her? Now truly amazed, Triona was about to ask him why he was being so accommodating, but a sudden commotion caused her to slam the door and heave the chest back in place.

"Niall? I thought you'd gone to change your clothes. What the devil are you doing here?"

Ronan! Her heart hammering, Triona pressed her ear to the doorjamb and listened breathlessly.

"Nothing much, brother," came Niall's calm response. "I saw the servants running in and out, and thought I'd see what all the fuss—"

"Triona is causing the fuss, in case you haven't already guessed."

Hearing Ronan's determined footfalls approaching the door, Triona once again braced herself against the barricade. She heard the key turn, felt him test the door and finding it blocked, he warned through his teeth, "By God, woman, open this door or I'll break it down."

"Good, I hope you do! You'll have nothing left to lock and I'll have a nice breezeway! It's a bit too stuffy in here for my liking."

Triona grew tense when it became quiet outside the door . . . too quiet. She screamed in surprise when the chest began to move beneath her, Ronan shoving himself into the room as if her barricade had been no more substantial than a bag of feathers.

"Easy, brother, I heard she simply wants her maid," Niall's raised voice carried to her as she darted to the bed.

Whirling, she found the room suddenly full of people— Ronan standing at the front, his expression truly ominous to behold, the maidservants gaping at her as if she were mad and Niall in the background, smiling encouragingly. Daring to believe she had found a friend and ally, she threw her shoulders back and lifted her chin.

"That's right. I only want my own maid—"

"Bring in the tub."

Triona started at Ronan's grated command, then watched wide-eyed as the servants scuttled to do his bidding. It seemed no more than an instant had passed before a large wooden tub was being rolled into the room.

"And the water. Cold now, but she's only herself to blame. We'll dunk her if we have to."

Understanding dawned as brimming buckets were emptied into the tub, Triona walking backward from Ronan in disbelief. "You can't be meaning to . . . to make me. . . ."

"Exactly, Triona. I sent these women to assist you at your bath and I intend to stand here and see that they do. And if by some foolishness you still insist upon defying me, then be warned that I'm prepared to see to the chore myself."

Her jaw dropped. Glancing around her in desperation, she saw to her dismay that Niall had vanished. Oddly, knowing she was alone helped her to recover herself and bolster her courage. Aye, there were more than a few ways to taunt this overbearing lout.

"Very well, if you insist," she said pleasantly, fighting the urge to grin at the wary surprise in Ronan's eyes. After tugging off her leather shoes, she rolled up one trouser leg and dipped her big toe into the water. "Hmmm, just right. I've always loved cold baths. Just like swimming naked in the lough."

With that she shrugged out of her jerkin, her action greeted by shocked gasps from the maidservants as they glanced from Ronan to Triona.

She set to work at her trousers, undaunted. Keeping her eyes trained boldly upon Ronan, she dropped her belt to the oak floor with a plunk, and once again the women gasped, their faces turning bright red with embarrassment.

"May I ask you something?" Triona said, Ronan's resolute stare making her feel suddenly quite nervous as she began to slip her trousers over her hips. Thankfully her shirt was long and afforded her some cover, but when Ronan's gaze traveled with her trousers down her legs, she felt a bewildering flush of heat from her scalp to her toes.

Damn him, was he really going to watch her then? She would have thought he'd have left once she had proved she would honor his command. But he looked as if he had no intention of leaving. As he continued to stare at her, she began to feel even more flustered and unsure of herself.

"I said may I ask you—"

"I heard you the first time," Ronan interrupted, although in truth it was impossible to concentrate on anything being said with Triona stripping to the skin right in front of him.

He had thought himself provoked enough to make good on his threat, but now his anger was being replaced by something far more potent. It didn't help either that with her jerkin gone, her hardened nipples could plainly be seen beneath her shirt as well as the tantalizing outline of her breasts . . . high and saucy, and generous enough to fill a man's hands. . . .

A sudden splash jolted his gaze back to Triona's face as she sank with a sharp gasp into the tub, her trousers pooled on the floor where she had stepped out of them. Her eyes were very wide as she worked at the single tie at her throat with trembling fingers, the lower sodden half of her shirt floating around her.

"You can see that I intend to bathe," she said in a small voice that he'd never heard from her before. "But I'm not used to having so many servants around me. Is it possible that Aud . . . ?"

"I will consider it. And the return of your pets. But the door will remain locked until all six points we discussed earlier are satisfied. I will be obeyed, Triona. I think you can see that now."

She nodded, her hands gripping the sides of the tub. Then, as she inhaled raggedly, her beautiful eyes growing even wider, she started to lift her dripping shirt over her head. Ronan felt his body grow rigid as first her narrow waist was revealed, her bare flesh the color of sweet cream . . . then the lushly rounded undersides of her breasts.

"I'll see you at supper," was all he could manage before he turned and abruptly left the room, slamming the door shut behind him.

Triona slowly dropped her shirt as the key scraped in the lock. Her hands shaking uncontrollably, her flesh puckered with goose bumps that had nothing to do with the cold water, she waited until Ronan's footsteps had receded before uttering a blistering oath that made the servants gasp in shock all over again.

Chapter 6

"AH, SWEETING, YOU look so lovely! Like an angel!"

"Mayhap, Aud, but I feel like I'm being smothered," Triona grumbled as she entered the noisy feasting-hall, her loyal maid waiting by the doors to greet her. She tugged at the green silk sheathing her hips. "Ronan's sister must be thin as a pole—either that or I've forgotten just how confining these miserable things can be."

"You didn't like the last gown you wore either," Aud said with a wry shake of her head. "And that was ten years past. I can still see you stomping into the house, your gown ripped from hem to thigh to make room for your legs, and then you standing there and swearing you'd never wear another. The O'Toole was laughing and Lady Alice was arguing . . ."

"Until you spoke up like the good-hearted soul you've always been and offered to stitch me a pair of trousers," said Triona, remembering her elation when Lady Alice had thrown up her hands in defeat. "That put an end to the matter quick enough."

"Aye, your good mother lost all control of you then. After that, you were your father's daughter through and through."

Triona didn't reply, the fond recollection vanishing when she suddenly noticed the clansmen who'd escorted her to the hall had positioned themselves at the entrance. She glared at the two men and they stared stonily back, crossing their arms over their chests.

Obviously Ronan expected she might try to retire without his sainted permission, she thought irritably as she moved with

Aud away from the doors. "Are these O'Byrnes treating you well?" she asked, concerned.

"Aye, well enough. They gave me my own sleeping room in the servants' house and then sent me straight to work in the kitchen. But I'd rather be mending your clothes than chopping onions and turnips. I'd like to be with you, sweeting."

"So you shall," Triona muttered though she plastered a smile upon her face just for Ronan's benefit.

She could see him now at the head table, Niall seated to his left and an empty place at his right, and she could feel his eyes upon her like a disconcerting weight. Already he was watching her, searching for any hint of defiance.

But he'd see none tonight, at least not what he expected. She wanted that damned door left unlocked and the freedom to move about the stronghold at will. So for now, let him think that his rude bullying had left her more inclined to obey him . . . no matter how much it galled her.

"Come on, Aud. You're sitting next to me." Triona took her maid's bony arm but to her surprise Aud held back, her large dark eyes doubtful.

"I don't know if I should, sweeting. I want you to find a good husband, I've made no secret of that, but I've been thinking since we arrived and I don't like that the O'Byrne might force some man upon you. Your father wanted him to give you a home and protect you, not marry you off against your will! If I go up to that table, I might just tell him so!"

Amazed by this show of temper in a woman usually so good-natured, Triona gave her maid's narrow shoulders a reassuring squeeze. "Dearest Aud. Don't worry that Ronan will have his way. He won't, you know. If there's a husband for me, I'll find him myself."

"Aye, and you won't hear me defending him again, not after he hoisted you over his shoulders as if you were a sack of corn and not the daughter of Fineen O'Toole!"

Aud was right. Ronan wasn't just a murderer and a liar, but a damned tyrant. That was clear enough from the way he'd forced himself into her room and demanded that she bathe right in front of him. And how dare he insist that she conform to his bloodless idea of the proper Irish maiden? She wasn't wax to be twisted and pulled into any shape he fancied.

"I'll show him a proper maiden," Triona groused through clenched teeth, nodding for Aud to follow her. Aye, when she was done with Ronan, he'd wish he had never heard of Lady Emer and her six precious gifts.

That thought made it easier for Triona to smile; as demurely as she could she proceeded to the main table with her head slightly bowed.

She could feel everyone watching her—clansmen, wives, their children—all conversation momentarily suspended except for an occasional chuckle or whispered aside. Imagining that talk had flown about Ronan's humiliating treatment of her, she couldn't wait to give these O'Byrnes something to really set their tongues wagging.

But not yet, she told herself firmly. Ronan rose and came around the table to meet her. Amazingly enough, he had traded his black devil's garb for more festive wear. In fact, she wasn't prepared for how handsome he looked in a tunic as deep blue as the Irish sea, the color accentuating the steely gray of his eyes.

She wasn't prepared either for the familiar way his gaze moved over her . . . as if now he somehow knew her better. Vividly those heart-pounding moments in her room came back to her, the way he'd watched her every movement as she undressed, how breathless she had become, how strange she had felt—

"I see you chose to honor my command. Very wise."

Startled from her thoughts, Triona followed his gaze to her gown. How he must be gloating! Drawing a quick breath, she met his eyes, grateful for the arrogance in his tone. That proved more steadying than anything he could have said. "You approve?" she asked softly, fearing if she spoke any louder she'd scream.

Ronan ran his eyes over her again, thoughtfully.

If he had thought a maiden's garb would suit her, he could never have imagined how much. The shimmering emerald silk seemed woven just for her, the rich jewel-like color making her hair shine redder, her fair skin appear much more flawless, her stunning eyes that much greener.

Eyes whose mood did not match her carefully composed expression. Her resentment was clear and put him on his guard. He was not fool enough to believe that this hoyden would bend so easily to his will. Far from it. He'd heard the scathing curse that she had flung at him from the tub.

"Approve?" he echoed grimly. "My approval will be won when you accept the husband I choose for you. Now come. You've delayed our meal long enough."

Feeling her tense as he took her arm, Ronan knew she had been tempted to resist him. But she quickly collected herself, asking in a tone that this time held an undeniable edge, "Is there room enough for Aud? She's more a beloved aunt to me than a servant."

"Very well, she can sit beside you."

Anything to preserve some peace, Ronan told himself as he led Triona to her chair, Aud following behind. And if the talkative maid lent him some more useful information about his unpredictable charge, so much the—

"Oh . . . oh, no!"

"What the devil . . . ?" Ronan caught Triona just as she stumbled forward, grabbing her around the waist and hauling her against him. Looking down into her flushed face, he fought the urge to embrace her more tightly, her silk-clad body seductively warm and soft.

"I—I must have tripped," Triona lied, disconcerted by the strength of Ronan's arms. She had planned to fall flat on her face. Still determined to appear the clumsiest maiden in the land—so awkward and ungainly that no man would ever want her—she took a step backward in such a way that she trounced soundly on Ronan's toes. She had to fight not to smile when his startled expletive rose to the very rafters.

"By God, woman, watch what you're doing!"

"It's the gown! My foot is caught in the hem!" she cried as she feigned losing her balance once more, twisting at the waist so suddenly that her elbow jabbed him right in the ribs. As he exhaled in pain, she blurted in hasty apology, "Oh dear, I'm so sorry. Wearing a long skirt isn't anything like trousers. I can hardly move."

"So stand still!"

Triona froze, her ears ringing from his command, his grip bruising as he righted her. Yet any discomfort she felt at that moment was worth it. Ronan looked so exasperated that she was tempted to laugh. Delighted with her performance, she lowered her head so she wouldn't give her scheme away.

"Sit down. Carefully."

As she did what she was told, she caught Niall's amused wink out of the corner of her eye. She winked back as Ronan retook his seat, then she sighed loudly as if thoroughly disgusted with herself for creating such a scene. Lifting her eyes to look out across the huge room, she realized from all the stunned faces that she had indeed fooled them all, heightening her sense of satisfaction.

"Don't think this incident has changed my mind," Ronan added with finality. "You'll grow used to wearing gowns soon enough."

When goats fly, Triona thought smugly to herself as Ronan gestured for the servants to begin carrying in the meal.

"You may keep that gown, if you'd like," a sweet sounding voice said. "I think it looks far better on you than it could ever look on me."

Triona turned, focusing for the first time on the pale lovely girl seated next to Niall. She guessed at once that this must be Maire from her thick midnight tresses and gray eyes, so like Ronan's. Triona suspected, too, that she and Maire must be very close in age. Yet there all similarity ended. Triona had always prided herself upon being healthy as a horse, but this poor girl looked fragile enough to break.

"I hope you'll keep the others, too." A delicate smile curved lips the color of faded pink roses as Maire glanced fondly at her two older brothers and then back to Triona. "Ronan and Niall spoil me overmuch with so many gowns. I really don't need them."

Triona wanted to spout that she didn't need them either, but the offer had been made so generously, so graciously, she refrained. "You're very kind."

"Aye, she is," Ronan interjected tersely. He leaned forward as if to block Maire from her view, giving Triona the distinct impression that he didn't want the two of them to converse.

He must be afraid some of her bad unmaidenlike qualities might rub off on his dear sister, she thought, affronted. Just for that, she decided to spite him by inviting Maire to come and see her tomorrow. But before she could say a word, Triona felt a nudge to her arm as Aud leaned over to whisper in her ear.

"She can't walk, sweeting."

Stunned, Triona met Aud's eyes. Their conversation was masked by the mounting clatter in the hall.

"The O'Byrne carried her himself into supper. I talked to one of the servants while I was waiting for you at the door, and she said a terrible childhood fever was the cause. A shame, it is, too. Such a pretty girl."

A shame, indeed, Triona thought guiltily, glancing beyond Ronan to Maire's fine-boned profile. Shame on her for pretending to trip all over herself when two seats down from her was a young woman who couldn't walk at all. Triona flushed uncomfortably and looked down at the table.

Her wine cup was full so she lifted it and took a long sip, the amber liquid's cool sweetness improving her mood. She had never tasted anything so good; they'd never had wine as fine as this vintage in Imaal.

She noted for the first time, too, that her cup gleamed of silver, as did the plate set in front of her. In fact the entire table was set with silver: ewers, knives, spoons and bowls. Glancing around the hall, she saw to her amazement that most clansmen held mazers with bright silver rims or shiny cups like her own.

"Is this a special feast night?" she asked. When Ronan didn't reply, she added conversationally, "It surely must be. I've never seen so much silver. We had fine plate in my father's household, but only enough for his table. And we never used it except for the most important feast days."

"Believe me, Triona, your presence tonight is no cause for celebration," Ronan said stiffly, his ribs still smarting and his big toe throbbing. When she merely shrugged and looked away, he swallowed a deep draft of wine but it did little to soothe his foul mood. If he'd felt edgy earlier that day, now his carefully nurtured self-control felt in shreds.

Damn her, did she think that he could be so easily deceived? She had walked capably enough across the hall, her lithe grace capturing not only his attention but every other man's in the room. Graceful, that is, until she was close enough to do him bodily injury—

"I'd say your hospitality is sorely lacking, brother. If you don't care to converse with our beautiful guest, then perhaps we could exchange seats."

"You'll stay where you are." Ronan shot Niall a dark look. To his annoyance his brother speculatively raised his brow. Maire was looking at him oddly, too. Realizing how possessive he must have appeared, Ronan's vexation mounted.

By God, the last thing he wanted was for them to think that he held some genuine interest in Triona. Though he admitted he found her desirable, he found many women desirable, at least for a night.

"What are these?"

Ronan glanced at the steaming platter of chicken being held in front of Triona, her eyes fixed inquisitively upon the pear-shaped nuts studding the fragrant golden sauce.

"Almonds, a delicacy from the East. Compliments of the Normans . . . like the wine you've been drinking."

Impressed, Triona held out her cup. "This, too?"

Ronan nodded. "The silver, the linen tablecloths, the silk on your back, the rare saffron in that sauce, the meat roasting on our spits." He paused to drink, his eyes granite hard when he lowered his cup. "Anything they hold dear, we've taken. Their lives if they're fool enough to stand in our way."

Hearing the sudden harshness in his voice, Triona imagined that few Normans of sane mind would dare to raise their weapons against so forbidding an opponent as Black O'Byrne.

"Aye, Triona, we've even taken a cook," Niall said with a laugh.

"A cook?" Astonished, Triona glanced at Niall then back to Ronan. "How?"

He shrugged as if the incident had been of no consequence. "An unwise man left his manor too lightly guarded during supper. When we rode our horses into the knight's hall, our weapons drawn and ready, his cook threw down his ladle and begged to go with us."

"An Irishman," Niall interjected, clearly eager to tell part of the story. "Seamus was sold into slavery as a lad and cooked for Normans most of his life."

"Aye, though after his years with our foes he adds a bit of foreign refinement to our meals." Ronan's voice grew harsher. "It's well-known among our enemies that we Wicklow barbarians prefer our women filthy, our wine sour and our meat still warm and bleeding."

This comment brought great guffaws from the clansmen seated nearby, one man nearly choking, his mouth was so full of food.

"Our clever Seamus toiled for a time in an Irish kitchen as well, a MacMurrough's kitchen." Ronan's voice rose above the din. "For a wedding between Irish and Norman. And well we know that the MacMurrough clan's taste has long been for treason, and forming alliances with the French-tongued dogs who stole Kildare from its rightful owners, the O'Byrnes!"

This time the hall erupted in jeers, slurs and curses upon the name MacMurrough and all its descendants. The noise grew so deafening that Niall had to stand on his chair and roar at the top of his lungs for the harper, a lank, sallow-faced man who unfolded his gaunt frame from a nearby corner and came forward carrying his harp.

"I think the O'Byrne is in mind for a tune," Niall announced as Ronan pushed himself back in his chair, his foot braced on the table. "Play of Dermot MacMurrough, harper, and how that traitor, that accursed king of Leinster invited the Normans to our green isle!"

Triona became so caught up in the impassioned music leaping from the strings that she gave no more thought to her meal, the food growing cold upon her plate. She knew the words as well as anyone, the infamous story recounting Dermot's treacherous plea to the Norman King Henry to send fighting men to protect his Leinster kingdom from invading Irish clans. So the Normans came, forcing clan after clan to bow under their yoke while those who didn't bend were branded as rebels and burned from their homes.

The O'Byrnes were one of those clans. As the harper's high tenor voice soared into the air, his rusty hair and beard wild about his face as he sang, Triona wasn't surprised when everyone in the hall joined him.

Forty years had passed since the Normans had sailed across the Irish Sea and conquered much of Eire, but the O'Byrnes still had strong reason to hate the MacMurroughs. While the Irish traitors enjoyed the comfort of their lands around them, a reward for their devil's alliance, the O'Byrnes and the O'Tooles lived in the mountains where they had been forced to take refuge . . . their rich hereditary lands to the north overrun by men clad in shirts of mail.

"At least the O'Byrne didn't deceive us about the harper, eh, sweeting?" came Aud's sudden whisper. "The man plays as fine as you sing."

Startled, Triona almost hadn't heard her maid above the cascading strings. But before she could respond Triona felt a strong hand at her elbow.

"You will sing next."

Ronan's commanding voice sent a shiver plummeting to the pit of her stomach. She was suddenly so nervous that she almost abandoned her plan to sing poorly, displaying yet another lack in feminine graces. But one glance at Ronan's face made her resentment flare hot. His stone gray eyes held a clear warning, that to her, became a dare. Aye, she had been blessed with a crystalline singing voice, but she wasn't about to share her gift with him!

Triona rose as the harper's long yellow-nailed fingers sounded the last biting strains of Dermot MacMurrough's tune and then moved into the gentler courtship melody of Lady Emer and the legendary hero Cuchulain.

"Remember, Triona," Ronan warned her. "Every last verse."

In spite of her pounding heart and damp palms, she closed her eyes and breathed serenely. Her father had often chuckled at her made-up verses mocking the shy, self-denyingly noble, ridiculously perfect conception of maidenly excellence. Fineen had been proud possessing instead a daughter whose skill with the bow had matched his own.

"The song, Triona," Ronan prompted sternly, wondering if she planned to keep them waiting all night. He shot an impatient glance at Aud who smiled stiffly.

"As lilting as a lark, Lord, you will—"

The last of Aud's words were drowned out as Triona emitted the most grating, most shrill noise Ronan had ever heard in his life . . . so piercingly high that he clapped his hands over his ears while every face in the hall looked at Triona in horror.

"Woman!"

Chapter 7

TRIONA GASPED AS she was whirled around by the arm, coming face-to-face with a man she doubted could look more furious.

"Yes?" she asked Ronan innocently, blinking.

He was so enraged that he couldn't seem to answer, so she glanced at Niall instead. The younger man looked quite stunned. So did Maire, although she had the smallest of smiles upon her face.

"Oh dear, I started too fast, didn't I?" Triona prodded. "Too slow? Perhaps a bit too loud—"

"Enough!" Ronan's command made her jump, but she recklessly decided his eyes weren't yet furious enough.

"But if you'd let me begin again, I'm sure that I—"

"No more!"

"No more? But I just started. I thought you wanted to hear every verse . . . oh!" Triona was swung around so roughly that the room spun around her.

"Lilting as a lark?" Ronan demanded of the astonished openmouthed maid, his grip on Triona's arm so punishing that she winced. "Tell me, Aud. Did you not say that your mistress had a lovely voice?"

"Aye, Lord, that I did," Aud replied, recovering so quickly from her shock that Triona believed she couldn't have done any better herself. "A wee bit on the sharp side I must admit and perhaps a shade too breathy, but pleasant enough to listen to just the same."

"Then you must be deaf, woman, for if I've any hearing left after this night, I'll count myself fortunate. As for you"—

Ronan turned Triona roughly to face him—"you're blessed to have earned such loyalty. If Aud had been any less glib with her answer, you'd have found yourself locked in your room for a fortnight instead of a week."

Triona's eyes widened in disbelief. "What? You're going to lock me up for a week? After I did everything you wanted . . . spoke softly, acted agreeably, agreed to sing . . . wore this— this wretched gown?" She was so outraged that this time she gave no heed to Maire's feelings. Triona raised her hand to slap Ronan but he caught it, his strong fingers crushing hers in a punishing grip.

"Bruised ribs and a broken toe are enough injury for one night, thank you—" Ronan ducked just in time to miss her other doubled fist aimed right for his jaw. Uttering a low curse, he yanked her arms behind her back and then brought her hard against him. "You're a wild one, Triona O'Toole, but I'm faster than you. Now either you walk in as maidenly a fashion as you can stomach or I'll throw you over my—"

"I'll walk!" Triona declared, the muffled laughter rippling through the hall enough to convince her that she would not be the brunt of these O'Byrnes' amusement again.

Thinking that as soon as Ronan released her arms she would bolt for the doors, her hopes were dashed when he wrenched her silk mantle from her shoulders and wound it around her waist like a lead rope. Then he prodded her with his knee, ordering over the erupting guffaws of his men, "Move."

Her face burning bright crimson, she crossed her arms over her breasts and planted her feet firmly on the floor. "I will not! Not until you allow me to walk at will—oh!"

Triona rounded upon Ronan in horror, her bottom smarting where he had just pinched her.

"Now there was a pure bell-like tone if ever I've heard one," he said. To her surprise a trace of a smile was on his face. "Perhaps if I pinch you some more we might hear the fair music Aud told me so much about—instead of the noise you screeched just to spite me."

Triona moved then, closing her ears to the laughter that followed them past the crowded tables and out into the starlit night. She didn't stop until she had reached the dwelling-house, where she paused outside the door to catch her breath.

"Beautiful night."

Her breasts rising and falling from hurrying so fast, her humiliation so great she felt hot tears welling in her eyes, Triona glanced at him in disbelief. He wasn't watching her but looking up at the waning moon, his striking features awash in its light.

Her heart seemed to skip a beat and she hated herself for it, hated herself for thinking him handsome after what he'd just done to her. But she hated herself even more when he met her eyes, her heart leaping into her throat when he reached out and smudged away a tear with his thumb . . . his touch upon her cheek as soft as a whisper.

"Tears? You're more a maiden than you think, Triona."

Ronan knew he'd said the wrong thing the moment her fist connected with his lower abdomen. Exhaling in pain, he doubled over, not having seen the blow coming.

"And you're more the fool, O'Byrne, to think I'll become something I'm not to please the likes of you!"

She had slipped out from under her silken restraint before he could catch her, but to his surprise she fled into the lamp-lit dwelling-house instead of heading for the gate. Holding his stomach, he followed as she ran to her apartment and furiously slammed the door behind her. He listened for a brief instant and, swearing that he heard muffled sobbing, was stunned by how quickly his hand moved to the latch.

"May I go to her?" Aud, accompanied by one of his clansmen, was hurrying to the door.

Ronan spun, startled.

"She left the hall in such a rush I thought I should follow her, Lord," the older man began in explanation, gesturing to Aud.

"It's all right, Sean. She may enter but lock the door behind her."

Feeling Aud's anger, Ronan passed by her without another word. Yet his own anger that a servant would dare to censure his actions was soon overshadowed by keen regret that she'd come at all. A regret that sent him striding tight-lipped for the hall, more determined than ever that his recalcitrant charge

would be tamed, wedded and gone from Glenmalure before
the next waning moon.

"It's been three days, Ronan. Are you truly going to leave
her locked in there for a full week?"

Ronan gave his brother a hard look as he dismounted.
"I'd wager if we had returned yesterday, you'd have said
the same thing and then it would only have been two days.
And likewise my answer would have been the same. Triona
needs firm discipline. She stays."

"Then don't be surprised if she's twice the handful when
you finally let her out." Niall slid off his horse, his expression
exasperated as he tossed the reins to a waiting servant. "To my
mind, you're being too damned uncompromising."

"Very well, then," Ronan said tightly, wheeling halfway to
the stable door. "Since I can sense you're most anxious to tell
me. How should I be treating her?"

"Not like a stern taskmaster determined to break a young
mare! Since Triona came to Glenmalure, if you're not ordering
her about or making threats, you're humiliating her at every
turn. That stunt the other night when you made her look like
a stubborn filly at the end of a halter, tweaking her to get her
to go—"

"She would have run for the doors if I hadn't controlled
her," Ronan cut him off, waving from the stable the last of the
clansmen who'd accompanied them on their raid. In truth, he
regretted his callous behavior, but he didn't need his younger
brother, Tanist or no, berating him in front of his men. Only
when the servants had led their lathered horses away, leaving
him and Niall alone, did Ronan demand, "Since when have
you become Triona's champion?"

"I think you can guess, brother. Since she first stood up to
you—"

"And I told you I've no interest in taking her to wife!"

To Ronan's irritation, his vehement outburst was greeted by
a grin, Niall spreading out his hands.

"Who said anything again about a wife? All I'm saying
is that you might do better trying another tack with Triona
than forcing her to obey you. You want her to act the proper

maiden, Ronan, but how can she when you don't treat her like one? You certainly haven't given her any encouragement that it's something she might even want to try."

"I treated her well enough that first night—until the chit purposely shrieked in my ear."

Niall shook his head, clearly unconvinced.

"No? Then what's your estimation of my conduct?"

"You were brusque with her and inhospitable, and that's the mildest of judgments. Yet things could have gone differently, brother. Mayhap if you'd appealed more to her feminine nature, she might not have been so inclined to defy you."

"Feminine nature?" Ronan muttered, remembering Triona's well-aimed blow to his stomach. "Other than some tears, I've seen little evidence of that."

"Mayhap, but all women love compliments. You know how it pleases Maire when you praise her embroidery. Did you think to praise Triona's gown? Her hair? The beauty of her eyes?"

Ronan remained silent, remembering how he had thought Triona lovely, but said nothing.

"You see? A few well-chosen words might have swayed her temper. Did you suggest she try a particular dish? Did you ask her if the wine pleased her? If she might like a soft cushion for her chair?"

"So she could pummel me with it?" Shaking his head, Ronan turned and looked out onto the yard. "You're mad if you think this idea could work."

"Am I? I recall that you used to charm the wenches easily enough, Ronan, so much so that they would have done anything for you. I remember you and Conor always vying with each other over who could win the most attention."

Ronan stiffened, but didn't turn around. "That was a long time ago. You were only a boy—"

"But not so young that I didn't watch you and Conor in awe, hoping some day I'd find as much favor with the fairer sex. You both knew how to please them, how to tease them and make them laugh so even the plainest girls felt pretty around you. Now if you spend time with a woman, it's only to take her to your bed for a single night's tumble—"

"Are you done?" Ronan demanded, rounding upon him. "Because if you're not, little brother, I tell you now that I've heard enough!"

"Aye, I'm done." Sighing heavily, Niall brushed past Ronan. "Do what you will with Triona. You'll hear no more brotherly advice from me. But if I could venture one guess as to why she doesn't want to marry, *I'd* wager it's because she fears being wed to a man who'd treat her with as heavy a hand as you."

Niall was gone before Ronan could reply, his brother's long strides noticeably marked by weariness. They had scarcely slept these past two nights, having ridden deep into Wexford to steal cattle. A raid Ronan had called for after returning to the dinner, his gut still aching from Triona's unexpected blow.

And he was to appeal to her feminine nature? Ronan thought incredulously, heading for his dwelling-house.

Triona possessed a face and body beautiful enough to haunt any man's dreams, and a grace about her as natural as breathing, but there her resemblance to any woman he'd ever known ended. She would more likely be charmed by his complimenting a target hit dead-center than upon the color of her eyes.

Ronan paused at the door, a pang hitting him as he thought again of the tears he had seen.

Perhaps Triona truly was more a maiden than she appeared— though obviously from her reaction something she would have preferred to hide. By God, could she be hiding more from him as well? Might she simply be afraid to marry?

If that was so, perhaps he would have to temper his methods. She'd never accept a husband and marriage if he couldn't convince her that she had nothing to fear . . . from him or the man he would choose for her. And perhaps if he gave her a bit more freedom, she'd be less intent upon defying him.

"Anything's worth a try," he said to himself, turning away from the door. "But, little brother, you'd better be right."

"I'm going to scream." Triona threw a glance at Aud as she paced furiously around the large sunny room. "Scream I tell you, so loud and long it'll be heard all the way to Dublin!

Three days Ronan's been gone, and I've been stuck in here! Three whole days!"

"Stuck only because you won't break one of those windows." Aud looked up from the borrowed linen gown she was shortening. "You could do it easily—"

"And have that tyrant extend my sentence by another week? I've already told you a hundred times, Aud. I will not give him the pleasure!"

"But he wouldn't be able to force you to stay in here even an hour longer than you wanted to if you left Glenmalure altogether, now would he?"

Triona stopped, sighing with exasperation. "Aud, for the last time, that's just too easy. First of all, I'd never leave here without you and all of my pets. And secondly, I've a few things to do before I bid this miserable place farewell."

"Aye, so you've said."

Hearing the uneasiness in her maid's voice, Triona went to her side. "What's this now? You don't believe I'll find a way to join Ronan when he rides against Maurice de Roche? I will, you know, and one of my arrows will send that baron straight to hell for what he and his men did to my father."

"Aye, I don't doubt you could do it, Triona, and that's why I grow more worried every time I hear of your plans. I already told you of the strange dream your father had just before the O'Byrne arrived at his deathbed—how he was tossing and moaning and saying first your name and then the baron's—"

"And I said then that I've no fear of dreams, Aud."

"No, but I do! And it gave me a chill just to hear him, as if an evil hand had passed over my heart. I think your father was trying to warn you away from avenging him, sweeting, and if you'd heard him cry out your name as I had . . . as if he saw you in the clutches of the devil himself—"

"Aud, this is nonsense." Triona settled her arm around her maid's shoulders but to her surprise, Aud shrugged it off as she twisted around to face her.

"And mayhap it isn't! I told myself when you agreed to leave Imaal with the O'Byrne that I shouldn't worry. He would protect you if the need ever came. I'm certain that's why your father summoned him at the end, that, and knowing this place was safe. But the O'Byrne deceived you, and when you ride with him now he won't even know you're among his men to protect you! So I'm asking you as sure as I love you, Triona, give up this idea of seeking revenge for your father!"

Sighing to herself, Triona sank to her knees beside the chair. "You know I can't, Aud. I swore—"

"Aye, you can, just as easily as you could break one of those fine glass windows and find a way out of this stronghold, out of this glen and to the west coast of Eire if you have to. Far enough away for you to be safe."

"And leave you here? I already told you I wouldn't—"

"Your father didn't cry out my name, sweeting. You're the one in danger."

"For the last time, Aud, I'm not in danger!" Triona rose, annoyed with her maid's stubborn insistence. "It would take more than a dream for me to believe that. We're staying, I tell you. After my father is avenged, and after I teach Ronan a lesson or two about betrayal we'll leave Glenmalure. But not a day sooner."

While Aud sighed heavily, shaking her head, Triona moved to the nearest window. She'd just have to wait until the spawn let her out of here, no matter how much it made her feel like screaming.

She stared sullenly outside, wishing she had more of a view than the oak palisade. But at least she had a view. The few small windows at her father's stockade had been so thick and grainy that seeing anything through them had been impossible; these windows couldn't be clearer.

"More compliments of the Normans, no doubt," she said dryly to herself, yanking at the tight collar of her gown. It was amazing to her that she was still dressing herself in the damned things after the other night when she'd stormed in here and slammed the door in Ronan's face.

She remembered swearing a dozen times into her sodden pillow that she didn't care what he did to her anymore, she'd never wear another gown or pretend a moment longer that she intended to obey him. Not after the humiliation she'd suffered at his hands.

But her angry tears had soon given way to cold reason. She could do nothing until that door was left unlocked, and it wouldn't be unlocked until she convinced Ronan that she was at least willing to play the maiden—

A throaty bark beyond the door made Triona whirl from the window, her eyes meeting Aud's.

"That sounded like Conn! Conn!"

Triona's cry was greeted by another bark that became frantic whimpers, heavy paws scratching at the door. A key had no sooner grated in the lock than a huge furry flash burst into the room. Triona was thrown laughing against the bed as Conn jumped up on his hind legs and pounced upon her, whining and licking her face.

"Oh, Conn, I've missed you! My brave Conn!"

Triona was soon able to calm him by rubbing his wiry coat, the panting wolfhound flopping to a sitting position in front of her. It was then she spied Ronan standing in the doorway, a sleepy-eyed Maeve draped comfortably over his arm.

"I thought you might like the company of your pets."

Astonished, Triona sank down on the mattress while Ronan came over and deposited Maeve beside her, but not before giving the purring cat another good scratch behind the ears.

"Curious creature. She spit like a serpent until I gave her a stroke or two, then she didn't seem to mind my picking her up."

"Aye, she's like that sometimes," Triona murmured as Ronan gave Conn's head a rough pat. Conn seemed to be enjoying every moment, even going so far as to lick Ronan's fingers.

"Ah, your Ferdiad is well and roosting with the other falcons. You are free to visit him whenever you like."

Triona met Ronan's eyes, shocked anew. "Free . . . ?"

Ronan nodded as he turned to leave.

"You mean I can come and go as I please?"

Again he nodded, then he was gone, the door left open behind him.

Incredulous, Triona gaped after him. "Jesu, Mary and Joseph . . . O'Byrne, wait!"

Chapter 8

CONN BARKED EXCITEDLY as Triona ran from the room, her gown hiked up above her knees.

"O'Byrne—oh!"

She stopped short, surprised to find Ronan leaning against an opposite doorjamb as if he had fully expected her to fly after him. Following his gaze, she felt her cheeks flare and she quickly dropped her gown to cover her legs, her bare toes peeking from beneath the silken hem.

"You've no slippers to wear . . . ?"

"Aye, I've slippers," she mumbled, strangely flustered at seeing him adopting such a casual stance, his arms crossed loosely over his chest.

Or maybe she was disconcerted because he wasn't glaring at her sternly. She'd never seen his expression more relaxed. Or because he'd spoken to her evenly instead of giving her a blunt command. Suddenly she grew wary.

"Are you feeling well?"

He didn't smile, but his eyes held a hint of something quite unusual. *Amusement?* Her suspicions mounted.

"Quite well. Why?"

"You're acting very . . . unlike yourself. Did you take a bump on the head during your raid?"

"No bumps." His expression tightened a little, but he didn't alter his stance. "Who told you we'd been on a raid?"

"The servants who brought Aud and me our food made no secret of it." Triona eyed him narrowly, his sudden caginess making her all the more wary. "You did go raiding after cattle, didn't you?"

62

He nodded, and she relaxed a little. So he hadn't ridden out yet to avenge her father. Now if he would only explain why he was being so damned—*nice* to her.

"It pleases me that you're still wearing gowns, Triona. I thought I might find you in trousers again, especially after upsetting you the other night."

"You didn't upset me." Triona lifted her chin. "Made me furious is more the truth of it. After I'd done everything you wanted—"

"I know, and I owe you an apology. I shouldn't have expected so much from you, especially that first night. Change takes time, and I've granted you precious little. I plan to amend that."

Triona knew she must be staring at him, but she couldn't help herself. An apology . . . from Black O'Byrne? The man who had done nothing but bully her and make her life miserable since she'd come to Glenmalure? She scratched her palm with her fingernail, hard, just to make sure she was awake.

"That's why I've decided to leave your door unlocked—unless of course you give me serious reason to confine you again. But I believe you and I have finally come to an understanding, haven't we, Triona?"

So, he thought he'd already won, she thought angrily even as she gave him a short nod. Ha! Now that she was no longer a prisoner, she'd won, and he didn't even realize—

His fingers cupping her chin made her start, her eyes flaring in surprise. The warmth of his touch was almost as disconcerting as the way he was looking at her, his gaze intense and searching.

"You've no reason to fear the marriage I plan to arrange for you. I would never wed you to a man who'd mistreat you."

Bewildered, Triona parroted, "Mistreat me?"

He stroked her jawline with his thumb, adding, "I've Niall to thank for helping me understand what's been troubling you. It is all clear to me now . . . why you claim you don't want to marry, why you've long acted the hellion—"

"I don't want to marry!" Triona blurted out heatedly, growing all the more confused when instead of becoming angered by her outburst, Ronan touched his finger lightly to her lips.

"So you say," he said in a low husky voice that made her heart do the strangest flip-flop. "Just as you told me you've spurned your every suitor because you didn't like them."

"I didn't! Those blessed louts were all the same, just like you! They all wanted to—"

"Triona, you can't hide behind your argumentative tongue and hotheaded willfulness forever. Surely you can see that lashing out at your suitors and chasing them away with arrows is not the answer. Marriage may seem frightening, but to the right man—"

"There is no right man!"

Shoving away from him, Triona almost tripped over Conn. Regaining her balance as the wolfhound sprang to his feet and began playfully wagging his tail, she whirled back to Ronan. "You must have taken a blow to the head because you're making little sense! Now if you don't mind"—she gestured to Conn—"I'd like to go outside with my dog."

Ronan sighed heavily, trying to muster all of his patience. Obviously Triona's fears about marriage were more deeply ingrained than he had imagined.

"Go on, then. I'd accompany you, but I haven't gotten any sleep since—"

"I'd rather go by myself, thank you."

Ronan felt a muscle twinge at his jaw, but he held his peace and turned into his room.

"Where are you going?" Triona asked.

"To lie down," he said over his shoulder, working at his sword belt.

"But surely you don't mean in there."

Ronan looked back at her as he dropped the belt with a heavy clank onto a low table. "Why shouldn't I? This is my room, my house—"

"Your house?"

"Aye. My parents' before me and now mine."

She didn't reply, glancing nervously from her open doorway to his. Only a short few feet separated them.

Imagining the direction of her thoughts, Ronan wondered if he should offer to reside elsewhere during the remainder of her stay. But something made him hold his ground; perhaps his presence might deter her from doing anything foolish. Although he now felt he understood her better, she was still unpredictable.

"I thought you were going outside," he said. Her eyes were upon him as he hauled his tunic over his head, but when he looked again, she was gone.

"He's mad," Triona muttered with certainty, squinting in the bright morning sunshine as she hastened from the building. "Touched in the head. One too many raids, too much strain, too many responsibilities." She threw up her hands as Conn bounded along barking in front of her. "He's gone mad."

And she was mad to have stood there like a gaping fool as he undressed, she berated herself, her heart still beating a little too fast.

She'd seen men before without their shirts, but no one who looked as powerful as Ronan. She had felt how rock hard his abdomen was beneath her fist—both times!—and she was not surprised after seeing his sharply defined muscles. He had the honed, lean look of a man who'd worked his body long and strenuously, and she could just imagine what the rest of him. . . .

"Triona!"

Shocked by the turn of her thoughts, Triona was grateful for Niall's interruption. She waited for him to catch up to her, a joint of beef in one hand and a brimming cup of ale in the other. His grin stretched from ear to ear as if he couldn't have been happier to see her.

"You're outside!"

Smiling wryly at his obvious observation, Triona picked up a stray stick of birch kindling and tossed it for Conn. "So I am, and it's about time, too." She sobered, glancing at Niall. "Why aren't you resting like your madman of a brother?"

Niall shrugged, though his smile, too, faded. "I lay down, but my stomach was grumbling so loudly I decided I should fill it first. If he is so sensibly resting, why is my brother a madman?"

"Because he's proved it to me!" Triona swept up the slobbery stick that Conn had dropped at her feet and threw it farther this time. "I was surprised enough when he brought me my pets and said from now on I could come and go as I pleased, but when he started talking to me so nicely—"

"He did?"

Hearing the amazement in Niall's voice, Triona nodded. "I thought that was strange, too. But then," she paused, "then he apologized to me."

"Did he now, the devil."

Grabbing Niall's arm, Triona yanked him to such an abrupt halt that ale sloshed down the front of his shirt. "I don't like the way you said that, Niall O'Byrne." She studied him suspiciously. "Are you and Ronan plotting together? He said he had you to thank for telling him what's been troubling me."

"Troubling you?"

"Aye, you heard me!"

Niall stared at her as if confused. Sighing with exasperation, Triona prompted, "He seems to think I'm afraid of marriage, afraid of being mistreated. Did you tell him this swill?"

Understanding now shone in Niall's eyes as he murmured, "Not exactly . . . but I imagine that's it, isn't it?"

Now Triona was stumped, her temples beginning to pound.

"I can't think of any other explanation why a beautiful young woman like yourself wouldn't want to wed."

Ignoring his compliment, Triona was tempted to tell him that she wasn't afraid of anything, least of all marriage! If only these dense men had bothered to ask *her* why she didn't want to marry instead of reasoning it out so neatly for themselves! She could have told them that she'd bind herself to no man unless she found one who'd want and respect her just the way she was. Respect her without changing her. Instead they'd gotten it all wrong. . . .

Triona glanced down at the ground, fighting the sudden urge to grin. *They had it all wrong!* Oh, it was too perfect! Why hadn't she realized before that she now had full license to act exactly as she pleased?

"I've upset you."

Meeting Niall's eyes, Triona had all she could do to feign irritation. "Aye, you've upset me! I don't want to talk about this anymore!"

"Then we won't," Niall said quickly, lengthening his strides to keep up with her as she set out at a brisk pace. Conn trotted along beside them. "Let's talk about supper the other night and how wonderful I found your singing."

This time she couldn't help smiling, although only a small one. She was supposed to be upset, after all. "You said you hoped I'd stand up to your brother, so I decided to oblige you."

And now she could continue to do just that, Triona thought smugly as Niall chuckled to himself. Since Ronan was so concerned about her fears he'd think twice before punishing her for any lapses she might suffer. . . .

"I'd say you sounded like a lark," Niall commented wryly, "but a very big one."

"A giant crow is more the truth of it," Triona countered, deciding there was little harm in playing along.

This reply drew a hearty laugh from Niall, who slowed down before a stout wooden structure.

"Your house?" At his nod, Triona added, "A good rest to you." She began to walk away, then stopped and glanced back at Niall. "Whatever you said to Ronan, it's clear I've you to thank for my freedom."

He shrugged lightly, looking around them to make sure no one else was near. "I told you I'd help you any way I could."

"A strange thing, you have to admit, Niall O'Byrne." Triona searched his face. "I doubt your brother would be pleased to know you'd sided with me against him . . . if indeed that's what you've done. I've been meaning to ask you why—"

"You're a hard one not to help." Niall laughed as he glanced down at his sodden shirt. "This place hasn't been so lively in years."

"Aye, and I'm not finished yet," she said without thinking. She clamped her mouth shut as Niall sobered, although his blue-gray eyes still shone with humor.

"Not finished? Is there the slightest wee bit of a chance that we've read you wrong, Triona O'Toole?"

She didn't answer, changing the subject instead. "Where's my falcon?"

"Over there. That small building by the stable."

Triona smiled her thanks and set off before he could speak again. "Come, Conn! Let's see how Ferdiad has been faring, and then we'll go visit Laeg."

Yet she didn't get far. Curiosity overcame her when she spied the serving woman who'd brought her Maire's gowns stepping from the adjacent dwelling-house.

"Does Maire live here?"

The older woman, a plump kindly-looking soul, eyed her carefully. "Aye."

Did everyone protect Maire so diligently? Triona wondered, gesturing to Conn to sit and wait for her before glancing back at the woman. "I'd like to greet her if I may."

There was a weighty pause, then the serving woman nodded. "She's at her sewing in the back chamber."

As the woman moved away, Triona headed to the door. At least Niall must trust her with his sister, she thought, noting that he'd already gone into his house.

She, too, went inside, the smell of wild roses greeting her. She saw at once that fresh bouquets of pink and yellow blossoms were placed here and there, their lush fragrance adding to the air of femininity that permeated the large room. A room that was filled with fine things, beautiful things, unlike any place Triona had seen before.

Hangings of painted cloth graced the walls, richly colored woven carpets covered the floor. Delicately wrought candle holders, made of gold, gleamed in the light cast by glowing ivory candles. An embroidered cloth of startling white was spread upon a table, rose-colored cushions with gold tassels upon the chairs. An elegant jewel chest, decorated with enamel of many hues, was placed upon a smaller table. Triona could only guess at the wonders it must hold—costly spoils taken on a raid. She had no doubt that many of these things had once belonged to Normans.

"Ita, is that you?"

Once more Triona was struck by the sweetness of Maire's voice; she felt chagrined that she hadn't announced herself sooner.

"No, it's Triona." She went at once to the back room, an equally well-appointed bedchamber, stopping in the door.

Maire was sitting at a recessed window seat that must have been built especially for her. The bright sunlight poured in upon her fragile beauty. And upon her face was a smile of such welcome that Triona could not help but smile back.

"I'm so pleased to see you. Come and sit by me, Triona. There's more than enough room for two."

Triona obliged, noting the soft fur blanket draped over Maire's legs and the embroidery lying idle in her lap. Triona noticed, too, as she sat down opposite the young woman, how translucent Maire's skin appeared in the sunlight, almost as white as milk. She found herself thinking that Maire could use some wind and fresh air upon her cheeks to add some color, then wondered if Maire had ever been atop a horse. Probably not. . . .

"I was hoping you might visit," Maire's gentle voice broke into Triona's thoughts. "I'm glad that Ronan decided to let you out of your room. I told him the other night that I didn't think it was fair what he did to you."

Had she another ally among the O'Byrnes? Triona wondered, looking at Maire with surprise. But before she had a chance to reply, Maire added softly, "I'm glad to see that you're walking more ably in your gown, too."

"I've been practicing," Triona murmured, her lie making her feel uncomfortable. Her face growing warm, she looked out the window, cursing again her unintentionally thoughtless stunt.

"Triona."

She started, meeting Maire's eyes.

"You don't have to say you like the gowns for my sake. I should have known better than to push them upon you." Another smile curved Maire's pale lips. "Actually, the few times I've tried to use that crutch over there, my gown has proved a nuisance. Mayhap I should try a pair of trousers."

"Oh, Ronan would love that," Triona muttered to herself, relieved that Maire seemed to understand about the gowns.

Maire laughed delicately. "I imagine that my wearing trousers *would* make Ronan a bit unhappy."

"A bit?" Triona let out a snort at the thought of Ronan's face. "He would think I had tainted you for sure. He didn't even want me to talk to you at supper, and if he knew now that we were sitting here together—"

"You must come to see me whenever you wish," Maire broke in, her lovely features grown sober. "Ronan has always been very protective, mayhap more than he. . . ." She didn't finish, uttering a soft sigh as she looked down at the embroidery in her lap. Only after a long moment did she glance up again, her gray eyes wistful. "It must be a wonderful thing to be able to wed. You're so fortunate, Triona."

Triona immediately bristled, not so much at Maire but the unpleasant topic she'd raised. "Fortunate? To have your brother threatening to force some man upon me?"

"Aye, that isn't right, but at least you're so healthy and whole no man would ever refuse you." Then, shaking her head as if angry with herself, Maire's tone gentled. "Ah, it's better this way. It wouldn't be fair to burden a man with an invalid, and surely no man would ever want one for a wife. . ."

For a moment Triona felt as if she'd been forgotten, Maire was so lost in her thoughts. But it gave her a chance to think, too, astonished as she was by what Maire had revealed. They couldn't be more different, Maire appearing more the mythic Lady Emer than any woman Triona had known, generous, sweet-natured, self-denying, and surrounded by beautiful things that held little interest for Triona. Yet they were uncannily alike, too. Both of them wishing for acceptance . . . for the world to be different.

Pity washed over Triona, but she knew that wasn't what Maire needed. "You say you've tried that crutch?" she asked, glancing at the polished piece of hazelwood resting against the wall.

Maire looked up as if startled. "Aye, now and again this past year. I was feeling a bit stronger, and I thought mayhap it might help my legs so Ronan agreed to have it made for me. But he had me swear I'd never attempt to use it alone, fearing I'd fall and hurt myself. Ita usually helps me, but never for as long as I'd like."

Aye, her wary Ita probably feared she'd hurt herself, Triona thought, rising to fetch the crutch. No doubt Maire had received little encouragement from all of her well-intentioned protectors, their concern making them believe Maire's efforts could only make her worse. Thus no horseback rides, little fresh air from the looks of her, and few words to inspire her. Triona could just imagine the sheltered life she'd lived, poor girl, with that stern-faced Ronan in charge.

"Well, Maire O'Byrne, Ita isn't here, so it's my turn to help." Triona held out the crutch. "And we'll go for as long as you want."

Maire stared at her, clearly stunned. "Truly?"

Triona nodded. "I'm not as big as Ita but I can support you well enough, and besides, you look to weigh a good bit less than me. Oh aye, and while I'm asking, have you ever ridden a horse?"

Maire shook her head, her eyes growing wider. "Ronan's never allowed me to."

"The tyrant," Triona muttered with a frown.

"Oh, no, it was only because he feared—"

"I know. That you might be hurt. But I'm not afraid because I think walking and riding is exactly what you long to be doing, not sitting here all alone." As tears glistened in Maire's eyes, Triona felt something swimming in her own as she bent down to help Maire to rise. "Come on, now. We'll start slow, and work at it every day if we can. The riding might have to wait until we can show Ronan you're making some progress—aye, and what we're doing will have to be a secret."

"Our secret," Maire murmured, gritting her teeth as she stood shakily.

Chapter 9

IT WAS LATE afternoon when Ronan entered the stable, his instincts telling him where Triona might be found. But he didn't see her readily, at least not until he heard spirited humming—a hunting tune—coming from a middle stall. And then he spied only the top of her head and the vigorous stroke of her arm above the wooden siding as she brushed her tall stallion Laeg's back.

"I could swear that's not the same voice I heard the other night," he said dryly, not surprised when the singing stopped. He heard a low curse, then Triona was peering at him over the stall, clearly standing on tiptoes.

"That's because it always sounds better when it's not so loud."

"Ah, I see."

"Truly! If you'd like I could show you the difference—"

"Spare my ears, Triona." At once he saw her eyes narrow, and he realized he had probably spoken too sternly. Reminding himself of his new mission, Ronan moved to the stall entrance, adding in a more pleasant tone, "Why don't you come out? Laeg looks well groomed enough for three horses."

He fell silent, presented for the second time that day with the enticing sight of Triona's bare legs as she obligingly left the stall—her apricot-colored gown tucked up between her thighs like trousers.

"I hope you don't mind, but it was impossible for me to move about until I raised the skirt."

Pleased as much by her handiwork as with the tightening of Ronan's jaw, Triona hooked her thumbs on the belt she'd fashioned from rope to hold everything up. She'd been imagining this moment, ever since she'd come to the stable. She could see that Ronan was trying to hold onto his patience, and she hoped she didn't appear too smug. Aye, spiting him was going to be such fun!

"I do mind, but I suppose I can see the purpose in it," came his careful answer, his voice not quite as agreeable as a moment before.

"Well, you can see I'm still wearing a gown, and that's what you wanted, isn't it?"

He nodded, his gaze sweeping over her again. Except this time his appraisal took longer, much longer, until Triona began to grow uncomfortable. His expression had changed, too, from displeasure to something . . . something else. From the way he was staring at her, one would think he'd never seen a woman's legs before!

"Is it warts you're searching for, O'Byrne? If so, I don't have any, or hairy moles, or any blemish for that matter!"

"Actually"—his slate gray eyes lifted to hers—"I was going to say your legs are very lovely."

She gaped at him, completely taken by surprise. "You—you were?"

"Aye. Slim and lithe . . ."

"Lithe?" Triona's heart began to pound, Ronan's gaze wandering down her thighs again as if to emphasize his every word.

"Very lithe. And sleek. Like the silk of your gown, I would imagine, soft to the touch—"

"Touch?" The spell shattered, Triona took a stumbling step backward, her eyes narrowing at Ronan. "Don't you even dare think of touching me, O'Byrne! Don't you even dare!"

"I thought no such thing," Ronan lied, trying to tell that to the heat blazing in his loins. His sudden decision to test Niall's advice had succeeded more than he could have imagined possible, painfully so for him. As for Triona, he'd swear she had been no more thinking of defying him a moment ago than running away. By God, had no man ever complimented her before? From the startled look she'd given him, he doubted any had.

"If anyone touches you, Triona, it will be your husband," he continued as she began to wrench the skirt from the improvised belt at her waist, appearing almost frantic to cover herself. "Yet you can hardly blame me if I commented on what you so freely displayed."

"I wasn't displaying anything!" Triona's temper flared as hot as her face. "Least of all to you, Ronan O'Byrne!" Yanking her wrinkled gown over her legs, she straightened to find that same unsettling glint of amusement in his eyes. "If you've found something funny in this—this latest outrage, I can tell you that I have not!"

"I'm only wondering how you're going to mount your horse. It might have been easier before . . ." Glancing at the rope belt she'd flung atop a pile of hay, he shrugged. "I'm sure you'll manage. I came here to ask if you might like to join me on a ride—"

"A ride?" Instantly, Triona knew she had found the perfect way to retaliate. "Across the glen?"

"If you wish."

Still unused to his acquiescence, Triona turned her back on him and seized Laeg's bridle from a peg. "You're damned right I'll manage. Watch me."

He was watching her, too. She could feel it, and she hoped he couldn't see that her fingers were trembling. They hadn't stopped since he'd said her legs were . . . Oh, begorra, why was she wasting time thinking about it?

"I could help you with that bit."

"I don't need your help," she snapped, although Laeg didn't seem to agree. The stallion was bobbing his finely sculpted head as if to tell her to mind what she was doing. "Easy, Laeg, I'll get it right," she assured him as she settled the bit in his mouth and then backed him from the stall.

"We've some sidesaddles the other women use."

"Ha! That's the last thing I need," Triona scoffed. "Just like you, O'Byrne, and most Irishmen worthy of the name, I've never used a saddle in my life—*any* kind of saddle." She grabbed onto Laeg's thick black mane and pulled herself onto his back. Except then she was stuck, like a plank of wood across his back, unable to sit astride him. She swore she would burn the gown to cinders as soon as she had the chance.

"Mayhap if we rode together, I could hold—"

"You've your own blessed horse to ride!" she cut in, know-ing she must look awkward as she balanced precariously on one hip and then flopped over, raising herself to a sitting position. A position that to her fury had both her legs dan-gling over one side, something she hadn't had to endure since childhood.

"Well done."

She turned to find Ronan already astride his huge black stallion, the muscular animal snorting belligerently at Laeg as if offering a challenge, its glossy neck arched and its nostrils flared. But she and Laeg could never hope to win any race with her barely able to keep from sliding off. . . .

That thought decided the matter. Her scowl daring Ronan to say a word, Triona pulled up her gown as modestly as possible and threw her bare leg over Laeg's neck. With a toss of her head, she was out the stable door and heading to the gates, not caring in the least if Ronan was following her.

He was, only a few paces separating them.

"Easy, man," he told himself, tempted to haul her back to the stable and command she ride in a more maidenlike fashion. He didn't appreciate the stares she was drawing, her creamy thighs hugging her mount a sight to leave any man agog. But at least she was still wearing a gown. One concession might soon lead to others if he managed to keep his mission in mind.

"What's wrong with your men, O'Byrne? Why won't they open the gates?" she demanded as he drew alongside her. "Surely they can see that I'm not trying to ride out alone."

"Too busy gawking," Ronan muttered to himself, throwing a dark look at the guards manning the gates.

Immediately the way was opened, Ronan not surprised when the same thing happened at the two outer gates. But the last set had no more than swung open when Triona kicked her steed into a full gallop. Ronan found himself pelted with clods of earth as she flew ahead of him.

"Come on, Laeg! Let's show Black O'Byrne what it means to ride!"

Her mood lightened by the wind whipping at her hair, Triona
waved her arm and whooped at the top of her lungs. The sheep
grazing at the bottom of the hill scattered, bawling, and the
clatter of the bells around their necks filled the air. She glanced
over her shoulder to see that she held a good lead over Ronan
though his stallion was lunging hard.

"Faster, Laeg!" she cried, hoping Ronan was angry, no, furious. As furious as his brazen compliments had made her. How
dare he comment upon her appearance as if he had the right!

She raced on past rough pasture and ever-thickening forest
that stretched far up the surrounding mountainsides, her head
bent low against Laeg's powerful neck as the stallion thundered beneath her. Whenever she ventured a quick glance
behind her, Ronan remained a good twenty lengths away,
making her triumphant smile stretch all the wider.

She had shown him! He wouldn't dare to ask her to ride
with him again out of sheer embarrassment!

"Have you had enough?"

Startled that she could have heard Ronan calling to her so
clearly, she shot a look over her shoulder to find that her lead
had shrunk to less than five lengths.

"I said, have you had—"

"I heard you!" she shouted back to him, urging Laeg with
a firm squeeze of her knees to go faster. "*You* should be the
one asking yourself if you've had enough! Are you blind,
O'Byrne? I've been holding the lead since—"

She didn't finish, glancing behind her again to see that
Ronan had fallen back . . . to the same twenty lengths. And
when she saw him shrug, sitting fully upright as if he didn't
care that such a posture might slow him down, a realization
dawned on her that churned her stomach. The spawn! He
wasn't trying to catch her. He was letting her win!

Triona yanked up on the reins so suddenly that Laeg snorted
in surprise, the stallion rearing and jabbing at the air as she
wheeled him around. She had to wait only a moment before
Ronan had drawn alongside her, to her annoyance his powerful
stallion appearing to have barely worked up a lather.

"Have you been enjoying yourself?" she demanded, rubbing
Laeg's sweat-glistening neck to calm him.

"I was going to ask the same of you," said Ronan, struck more than he wanted to admit by the emerald fire in her eyes.

He had never known a woman who could look so beautiful when angry, her cheeks flushed pink from her ride, her lush coppery curls wild and billowing around her face. And her lips were as red as ripe berries as if the wind whistling down from the great Lugnaquilla had chafed them.

"Now what are you staring at?"

"You," Ronan admitted. As her eyes flared in surprise, he added quickly, "You've got straw in your hair."

"I do?" She raised her hand to check, then just as suddenly retook the reins, exhaling with exasperation. "You've got a fine way of changing the subject, but it won't work, O'Byrne. Why didn't you try to catch me?"

"Begorra, now, is that what you wanted me to do?" Her lips drew into a tight line, and Ronan found he was enjoying teasing her, something he hadn't done to anyone in years. "I thought you were merely giving Laeg a good run. If it was a race you wanted, you should have said so . . . though I doubt it would be a fair one."

"Oh no?" Triona tugged sharply on the reins to keep Laeg from dancing sideways. "What are you saying, O'Byrne? That my Laeg can't hold his own against that . . . that disagreeable black beast of yours?"

"This so-called disagreeable beast comes from the finest racing stock in Eire," Ronan said calmly.

"So does Laeg! Do you think as the daughter of Fineen O'Toole I'd ride anything less?" Triona suddenly smiled at him archly. "I know why you won't ride against me, and it has nothing to do with Laeg."

He remained silent.

"It's because I'm a woman, isn't it? You truly don't think I could beat you, so you're not even willing to let me try. Are you afraid you might lose, O'Byrne?"

She knew she'd hit her mark from the anger now glinting in his eyes, but to her surprise his reply was remarkably steady.

"Do you see that cairn in the distance?"

She nodded, tense excitement gathering inside her.

"I'll give you a five-length lead . . . so whenever you're ready . . ."

She didn't wait to hear more, her heels digging into Laeg's sides.

"Fly, Laeg! Fly with you!"

She'd never felt such exhilaration as they plunged at a full canter toward the cairn, nor did she waste a moment to glance behind her. She knew Ronan was riding hard and fast to catch up with her, her taunting challenge no doubt burning like fire in his veins. Just as she burned to beat him.

"Come on, Laeg! Come on!" The world around her became a blur as she focused every ounce of her will upon the cairn that loomed ever larger. The pounding of hooves rang like thunder in her ears, a thunder that grew more deafening as Ronan's black stallion appeared like an ominous cloud out of the corner of her eye . . . drawing closer and closer until horse and rider were lunging right alongside her.

"Laeg, run! Run!" They were almost there, the circular pile of stones only a mere ten lengths away . . . so close, so close—

Triona gasped as she was suddenly swept from her horse, Ronan's powerful arms encircling her as both steeds forged past the cairn. She was so stunned that she could only gape at him, her breath snagged in her throat, his embrace so tight that she swore she could feel his heartbeat through her back.

It seemed to take forever for them to stop. Even when they finally did, Ronan's mount heaving beneath them, Triona could not speak.

Had she been in some danger? Immediately her gaze flew to Laeg; she was relieved to see that he was safe and drinking from a stream. Then why . . . ?

Ronan saw the question in her eyes, but in truth, he wasn't sure what madness had spurred him to grab her from her horse. And now that he held her so close, her taut bottom wedged between his thighs, her very nearness wreaking havoc with his senses, he felt decidedly reluctant to let her go. By God, what was this wild hoyden doing to him?

In the next instant her elbow ground into his ribs, hitting the same spot she'd jabbed once before.

"Damn you, O'Byrne, what were you thinking? I could have been killed! You could have dropped me! I . . . I could have been trampled!"

"You said you wanted me to catch you," he said through clenched teeth.

"You spawn, not like that!"

Her outrage like a dousing of cold water to his inflamed senses and his reason, Ronan nonetheless tightened his hold in spite of her wriggling, pinning her arms against her body.

"I could have won if you'd left me alone! I was ahead and you know it. You couldn't bear the thought of losing!"

Ronan didn't point out that their horses had been nose to nose. She would never believe him.

"Very well, I'll grant that Laeg was ahead . . . barely. You would have won."

Since Triona could not raise his ire that way, she changed her tack. "All right, O'Byrne, enough! Let me down!"

Renewing her struggles, she sharply inhaled when one of his arms wedged beneath her breasts. She'd no more opened her mouth to protest when he said huskily against her ear, "What's wrong, Triona? You don't find it pleasant to be held by a man?"

She froze, stunned.

If she had been trying to ignore the disconcerting sensation of his arms around her, she was acutely conscious of it now. But that wasn't all. As he shifted, she felt his hard thighs rubbing against her hips, the heat of his body and his warm breath upon her neck making her stomach feel all aquiver.

"I think you *do* find it pleasant," came his whisper as his arm slid gently along the undersides of her breasts. "Probably more than you would have ever imagined. Have you ever allowed a man to hold you like this before?"

"N-no." Triona felt her flesh burst into goose bumps as Ronan drew her even closer against him.

"Do you like it?"

Like it? Triona could hardly speak for the fierce pounding of her heart, his embrace conjuring vivid memories from long ago. Memories of watching him hold other women as he was doing to her now, holding them and caressing them as they laughed and sighed and offered their willing mouths for him to kiss . . . Jesu, Mary and Joseph, was he going to kiss her?

"I said do you like it, Triona?"

"Aye," she heard herself reply as if from a great distance, an incredible yearning overwhelming her. "It's very nice . . ."

Ronan knew from his slamming heartbeat that he'd gone far enough, and he reluctantly began to release her. "Then you can see you have nothing to fear. One day soon your husband will hold you like this and you'll like it as well— by God, woman!"

Ronan cursed as his horse suddenly bucked wildly beneath them, Triona giving the animal's ear a second sharp yank as she shoved Ronan backward with all her might. The next thing he knew he had hit the ground, hard, while Triona grabbed the reins and expertly wheeled around his stallion.

"Are you deaf, O'Byrne? I told you many times I want no husband and I meant it! But mayhap a good stretch of the legs might better convince you!"

Roaring in fury, Ronan lunged to his feet but she was gone. And he had no sooner glanced at Laeg when a shrill whistle sent the huge bay galloping after her, his black tail flying. Ronan had to throw himself aside as the whinnying animal almost ran him down.

"Triona!"

Spitting out grass as he picked himself up for the second time, Ronan stood silently for a long moment before uttering an oath he hoped she'd hear all the way across the glen.

Chapter 10

TRIONA WAS SURROUNDED by shouting O'Byrne clansmen before she reached the gates, several riding out after Ronan when she angrily gestured where they could find him. Even Niall came running at the sound of the commotion, but she rode past him, ignoring his openmouthed astonishment at seeing her astride Ronan's horse, Laeg trotting behind.

She went right to the stable, dismounting and tossing the sweaty stallion's reins to a gaping servant and then leading Laeg back into his stall. She would have seen to his care, too, if her hands hadn't been trembling so badly.

After giving another servant the necessary instructions, she left, scarcely able this time to summon a smile as Conn bounded across the yard to greet her. All she wanted to do was escape to her room where she could scold herself soundly for being a fool.

Aye, and what a fool! How could she have thought for a moment that Ronan might want to kiss her? He wasn't the least bit interested in her . . . not in *that* way. He simply wanted to ease her supposed fears so he could marry her off and then forget about her, his obligation fulfilled.

But what made her even angrier as she stormed into the dwelling-house was that she had wanted him to kiss her.

Ronan O'Byrne!

Her brother's murderer!

And even if there wasn't that foul blood between them, Ronan was only another man who would not accept her as she was, just like Murchertach O'Toole. Not that she'd ever wanted to kiss that brawny oaf. Or for him to kiss her. Shoving open the door to her apartment, she grimaced.

"Triona, what happened to your gown?"

As Aud hastened toward her, Triona glanced down at the rumpled garment that reeked decidedly of horse sweat. "Nothing that burning won't cure."

"Burning! Surely a good washing will do. And your hair could use one, too, sweeting. You've some straw—"

"So I was told," she groused, about to run her fingers through her hair until she spied the jumbled assortment of bound chests and furnishings that had been stacked against one wall.

"Your things finally arrived from Imaal," Aud said, following her gaze. "Didn't you see the wagon outside? They just finished unloading. Made quick work of it, too."

"There was no wagon," Triona replied, at least none that she remembered. But she'd been so furious, she wasn't surprised she'd overlooked it.

"Then they must have gone to the kitchen for some food before the journey back. The O'Toole's men apologized for the delay."

"No doubt caused by Murchertach," Triona said under her breath. It was very hard to hear him addressed as chieftain instead of her father. But seeing her inheritance stacked in her room was even harder. The trunks and treasured objects had once belonged to her parents, had once graced their home. It was all she had left from her years in Imaal. Murchertach as her father's successor had gained all else.

"I'll call for some hot water so you can bathe . . . unless you'd rather not be alone, sweeting."

"I'll be fine, Aud." Triona walked over to a table and ran her palm across the finely carved wood.

She knew when the door shut softly that her maid had left, but she didn't look up. Instead, she skimmed her hand over a sturdy-backed chair, one of four that had always held a place in front of the hearth. Touching the smooth wood, she could almost hear again her father's laughter as he listened to some tale . . . hear his snores resounding through the dwelling-house whenever he fell asleep in front of the fire.

Sighing, Triona moved on.

There was an oaken headboard, too, richly carved by Irish craftsmen during the reign of King Brian Boru two centuries before the Normans had come to Eire. Reaching over a stack of chests so she might trace the intricate filigree patterns, Triona cursed when her arm hit the topmost coffer, accidentally knocking it to the floor with a crash of splintering wood.

"Begorra, you clumsy . . ." Triona recognized the small brass-fitted chest as one that had belonged to her father.

She knelt and righted it, relieved to find upon first inspection that the sturdy coffer appeared sound. She popped the latch and tilted back the lid to look inside at the masculine array of items: a neck torque of twisted gold, a huge pair of winter gloves lined with marten, cloak-pins, heavy silver brooches . . .

A fresh pang caused Triona to slam down the lid. Her anguish was heightened by anger that nothing yet had been done to avenge her father's death.

"Damn you, Ronan, you'd better not have lied about making that Baron de Roche pay!" she muttered fiercely as she rose, bringing the chest with her. Or so she thought she had. To her surprise, the wooden bottom suddenly gave way with a sharp crack and fell to the floor, barely missing her toes. As had the jeweled dagger lying glittering at her feet.

"Dagger . . . ?" She had seen no dagger inside the coffer— and why hadn't everything else fallen out, too?

Holding fast to the lid, Triona upended the chest. There had been two bottoms, the space between them just big enough to hold the dagger. But why would her father have hidden such a thing?

Her thoughts scattered as approaching footfalls sounded from the outer room, their course so ominously determined she could swear she felt the floor shaking beneath her feet. She knew it wasn't Aud hurrying back to tell her that her bathwater would soon be ready.

Her heart racing, she snatched up the dagger and the splintered piece of wood, doing her best to replace them before hastily setting the chest back on top of the stack. Then she plopped down on the nearest chair, waiting nervously for Ronan to explode into the room.

Except he never did. The footsteps stopped just outside her door, no sound coming at all for the longest moment.

A moment in which she realized with the most unsettling stab of disappointment that Ronan must truly be anxious to see her wedded if his newfound patience could stretch this far. Well, fine with him! She'd be gone from Glenmalure soon enough, but not before she'd turned that midnight dark hair of his a nice shade of gray!

As he retreated toward his own room, Triona vaulted from the chair, startling Maeve who yowled and disappeared back beneath the bed. Ronan was just shutting his door when she knocked boldly, lifting her chin as he pulled it open.

"You and I must talk, O'Byrne—" She stopped, a smile spreading across her face in spite of herself, a giggle welling in her throat.

"Something amuses you?" Ronan asked tightly, wrestling all over again with barely controlled anger that still threatened to explode. By God, turning away from her door had been hard enough without her coming now to taunt him!

"I-it's your chin," she said, clearly trying not to laugh. "There's grass . . ."

She couldn't go on, her husky giggles overwhelming her as Ronan swiped his hand along his jawline. But he must have missed the grass because she only laughed harder.

"However did you . . . ?"

"Your damned horse nearly trampled me." Ronan took another swipe at himself, exhaling heavily when Triona merely shook her head and grinned as she pointed now to the left side of his face. "At least I didn't end up with a mouthful of dirt."

This comment brought forth a fresh peal of laughter. Ronan was amazed to feel his irritation subsiding.

If he had thought Triona beautiful when angry, words couldn't describe how lovely she appeared when smiling, her incredible green eyes alight as he'd never seen them. Recalling all too vividly the enticing feel of her in his arms, he wondered what she might have done if he had kissed her, something he had been more than tempted to do—

"Here, let me get it."

Ronan started when Triona's fingers brushed across his cheek, her unexpected touch arousing within him a longing as acute as any he'd known. Without thinking, he took a step toward her only to have her retreat in surprise, her smile gone, her eyes suddenly wary.

"I was only going to return the favor," he said quickly, more stung by her wariness than he wished to admit. Reaching out, he gently pulled a golden wisp of straw from her hair and handed it to her. "There are a few more—"

"Aud can help me later," she cut him off, jerking her head away. Her tone was no longer light but as determined as it had been when she first knocked upon his door. "We must talk."

"So you said." Ronan turned and walked back into his room.

Her reaction to his embrace had convinced him to stay his course, though he had burned to throw her over his knee for knocking him from his horse. Convinced him, too, that the sooner he calmed her fears about marriage, the better. He wanted her gone from here . . . especially now that he knew part of him—insanely enough—was beginning to want her to stay.

"Come and sit down," he said as he poured two cups of scarlet-colored wine.

"I'd rather stand." Triona did not want to step any farther into his room than she must. Her heart was still racing from a moment ago; she couldn't believe how easily she'd lost sight of why she'd come to speak to him. And all because of a wee bit of grass!

"Suit yourself, but you must want something to drink." He walked over to her and handed her a cup before she could decline. "I know I do. There's nothing like a good stretch of the legs to build up a man's thirst."

She met his eyes and saw no humor there, only a look as wry as his tone. Then he left her, sinking into a chair placed at the foot of the bed and stretching his long legs in front of him.

She took a sip, before blurting, "My things came today from Imaal—"

"So Niall told me. Arrived just after we left for our ride . . . or should I say, race."

"Aye, well, it's made me think about my father—"

"As I imagined it would."

"Are you going to stop interrupting me?" she demanded, propping her fist on her hip.

This time Triona swore she saw amusement lighting his eyes. She took another steadying sip of wine as he nodded an apology and gestured for her to continue.

"Very well, then. I came to ask you what's being done to avenge my father."

"Everything that can be done, for now."

Vexed as much as unsatisfied with his terse answer, Triona said sarcastically, "And how shall I interpret that bounty of news?"

Ronan gave a low sigh of exasperation. "I already swore that Baron de Roche of Naas would pay for your father's death. That should be enough for you—"

"It's not enough!" Triona forgot she held a cup of wine as she rushed farther into the room, spilling some. Yet she paid little heed to the dampness now soaking her gown. "He was my father, O'Byrne! Aye, mayhap not of blood but I knew no other. Damn you, I loved him! Surely that should warrant some consideration from you!"

As the room fell silent, Triona could not tell from Ronan's stern expression if he was going to answer her or not. But when he sighed again, this time resignedly, she knew she had swayed him.

"Men have been sent north to Kildare to keep watch and ask questions of the tenants who work the baron's land."

The bitterness in Ronan's voice was understandable. The fertile plains Baron de Roche claimed had once belonged to the O'Byrnes. "What kind of questions?" she asked in a quieter tone.

"About the baron's comings and goings. It is my plan to capture him by surprise, but with as few of his knights around him as possible. I'll not have any unnecessary shedding of my people's blood, none if I can prevent it."

"And after you capture him?"

"He will hang."

Triona exhaled with impatience, wondering how long it would take for Ronan's men to return. A few days? A week or more?

"Surely there must be a quicker way," she murmured half to herself. She lifted her gaze to find Ronan watching her closely. "The plan I had in mind was for some kind of ruse, something to draw that bastard from his castle. What if a fire was started in the fields, or an outbuilding set ablaze?"

"Such a commotion would only draw much of his force with him. There is an order to these things, Triona. Recklessness only breeds injury"—he paused, his jaw growing tight—"or worse. I told you I'd not needlessly risk my men's lives."

"But you wouldn't have to! All it would take is one well-aimed—" Seeing Ronan lean forward in his chair, Triona abruptly fell silent, biting her tongue.

Jesu, Mary and Joseph! Was she mad? She had nearly given away the heart of her plan.

"You're right, of course," she amended hastily, backing herself out of the room. "I wouldn't want any O'Byrne's death added to my father's." She glanced down with feigned dismay at her gown. "I should go . . . take a bath, I mean. I must look a sight . . . smell horrible, too. Horses, spilt wine . . . aye, and straw in my hair—"

"Aye, you're indeed a sight," Ronan interrupted, rising from his chair. "Even if you went to supper just as you are, Triona O'Toole, you'd still outshine any other woman there."

Triona was so startled by his unexpected compliment that she backed right into the door.

"Th-that's very kind of you to say . . ." she began lamely, unable to wrest her eyes from his as he walked toward her.

"Not kind at all. It's the truth—"

"Sweeting, they're coming with your bathwater. Are you still dressed so I can let them in to fill the . . . Triona? Triona, where are you?"

"In here, Aud!" Triona gestured over her shoulder as she blurted to Ronan, "I—I should go."

And she did, flying out the door and past a wide-eyed Aud into the safety of her own room.

Chapter 11

TRIONA DIDN'T ATTEND supper. Not after she heard from Aud that the O'Toole clansmen who'd brought her belongings to Glenmalure would be at the feasting-hall. Ronan had invited them to stay the night.

She didn't want those O'Tooles to see her. She could just imagine how Murchertach would gloat if he discovered she had been reduced to wearing gowns, just as she imagined Ronan would boast to his astonished guests that his firm hand had forced her compliance. But there would be no boasting or gloating because she wasn't stepping foot from this room until the O'Tooles left for Imaal.

So after her bath—made more pleasant, she had to admit, by some violet-scented soaps Maire had sent—Triona sent Aud to the hall with her excuses, instructing her to tell Ronan that she had retired for the night, simply too tired even to eat. Of course, that could be a problem because she was starving, her belly alive with grumbling noises. But one night without food was not a tragedy.

Besides, it would help keep her mind clear and she needed to think, Triona told herself as she doused every lamp save the one by her bed. After giving a drowsy-looking Conn a fond pat on the head, she climbed under the covers. Maeve, already curled into a tight white ball atop the other pillow, didn't so much as twitch a muscle as Triona made herself comfortable, propping her arm beneath her head.

She still couldn't believe how flustered she'd become by Ronan's bold compliments. Aye, she could have kicked herself when she got back to her room. Of course he didn't mean any of those fine flattering words. So why couldn't she just ignore them instead of becoming all quivery inside, or worse yet, gaping at him like a landed fish?

"Must be those damned eyes of his," she muttered, yanking the covers over her breasts. Gray as twilight but with a hard glint of silver in them. Any woman might find them compelling. Certainly enough of them had back in Imaal.

A soft rap at the door made Triona grip the covers tightly. Conn perked up his ears as he growled low in his throat. But both she and the wolfhound relaxed when Aud peeked inside the room.

"I saw your light and thought you might still be awake, sweeting. I brought you some bread."

"Oh, Aud, you've saved my life!" Triona eagerly threw back the covers as her maid hastened to the bed. "You must have heard my stomach growling all the way to the hall."

"Well, not that far, but I can hear it rumbling now. Here you go, and a nice wedge of cheese, too. It's all I could grab from the servants' table without the O'Byrne noticing."

Triona bit hungrily into the crusty bread, asking with her mouth full, "He was watching you?"

"I think so. Especially since I'd told him you were too tired to eat. From the look he gave me, I'm not sure if he believed me." Aud's plain face lit into a smile. "But then again, he probably thinks he has good cause to be wary. I imagine he hasn't forgotten how I defended your fine singing."

Triona smiled, too, smugly remembering.

"Oh, aye. Those O'Tooles were sitting right beside him, sweeting, just as you expected."

Snorting in comment, Triona split the pungent yellow cheese in half and tossed a chunk to Conn. "Poor dog. He won't get a proper supper tonight, either."

"Don't be worrying about Conn," Aud said with a chuckle. "He was feasting well enough when I went to the kitchen to see about some hot water for your bath. That cook Seamus has taken quite a liking to him, which is a wonder. He's a grouchy one, always complaining about this pain or that, either his heart or his innards. Doesn't seem to like much of anything save for food and from the looks of him, he's eaten more than his fair share."

"I wish you'd told me Conn had made such friends with the cook before I'd given him half my supper," Triona said, reaching down to rub behind Conn's ear.

"I could try to get you some more—"

"No, Aud, I was only jesting." Triona tore off another chunk of bread and popped it into her mouth.

"Well then, I suppose I'll head for my room and slip into a warm bed myself—"

"No, no, wait! I've something to show you first." Hoisting her white linen sleeping gown above her knees, Triona climbed out of bed and ran across the room. "I accidentally knocked over this chest and guess what fell out of the bottom? A false bottom, Aud!"

"A trinket?" Aud ventured uncertainly as Triona ran back to the bed with one of her hands behind her back. "Some coins?"

"No, something better. Look!"

Producing the dagger, Triona was so fascinated by the bloodred rubies and crystalline diamonds glittering round the silver hilt that she didn't notice Aud had turned very pale.

"Beautiful, isn't it? I haven't been able to place the design. I've never seen anything to match it. But that hardly matters. I couldn't have found it at a better time, especially since Ronan has locked away my bowcase. I only wonder why my father hid the dagger . . . but mayhap because it looks to be so costly—" Triona stopped, realizing that Aud had remained oddly silent. "Aud? Is something wrong?"

"Wrong?" As if snapping out of a daze, Aud shook her dark head. "No, nothing at all, sweeting . . . just a little tired—"

"But you seemed fine a moment ago," Triona interrupted, growing concerned. "You look so wan all of a sudden. Are you not feeling well?"

"I told you I'm tired, Triona O'Toole, and there's nothing more to it than that!"

Startled that Aud had spoken so sharply, Triona shrugged. "All right, Aud, if you say so—"

"Aye, I do, and it's time now that I went on to bed." Then, as if to make amends, Aud leaned forward and brushed a kiss on Triona's cheek. "Good night, sweeting. Sleep well."

"And you," Triona murmured. Only after the door had closed behind Aud did Triona drop her gaze to the wolfhound lying beside the bed. "What do you make of that, Conn? I've never seen her act so strangely."

As Conn thumped his tail upon the floor, Triona lifted the dagger to the lamp so she could inspect it better. Slim-bladed and light, it seemed to fit her palm perfectly as if fashioned for a woman's smaller hand. And it would be easy enough to conceal. . . .

Her gloating smile quickly faded. Mayhap that was why Aud had become so moody. Seeing her again with a weapon in her hand must have reminded her maid of Triona's determined plan for vengeance. And her dear superstitious Aud had already made it quite clear how she felt about—

Conn's sudden growling made the hair prickle on the back of Triona's neck.

"What is it, Conn?"

The wolfhound just as abruptly ceased his growling as if recognizing the approaching footsteps, his tail thunking a friendly welcome against the floor.

Triona didn't hesitate. She shoved the dagger under the mattress, blew out the lamp and dove under the covers. She listened breathlessly as Conn got up and trotted eagerly across the room.

"Easy, Conn, it's me."

The spawn! What was Ronan . . . ?

Triona squeezed her eyes shut, her heart thumping in double time with Ronan's footsteps as he approached the bed. But her heart jumped to her throat when she suddenly felt his hand sliding along her thigh. Gasping, she bolted upright, scaring Maeve with a wild howl from her pillow, Conn sent into a fit of barking by the door.

"You . . . you—" Triona sputtered, outraged. "Just what do you think you're doing?"

"Checking," came Ronan's disembodied voice in the dark, its deep huskiness sending shivers racing through Triona in spite of herself.

"Checking? What, if I might ask? If I'm too plump or too thin?"

"That you're where Aud said you'd be. Sleep well, Triona."

"That's all you have to say for yourself? Sleep well?" Her voice rang shrilly as he left the room. "I hope you don't!"

Just as she doubted she would now, Triona fumed, falling back onto her pillow. Obviously he must suspect that she was plotting, and for that she had her own loose tongue to blame. If she was going to be able to seize her chance, she would have to be very careful of everything she said to him from now on. . . .

"Aye, you may capture our Norman quarry, O'Byrne," Triona whispered vehemently to herself. "But he'll be dead of an arrow long before you find a tree to hang him."

Determined to think of nothing but revenge, she tossed onto her side and tugged the covers up to her ear.

But to her dismay when she closed her eyes, all that came to mind was the unsettling memory of Ronan's hand upon her thigh.

It was still dark outside when Triona awoke with a start, her stomach yowling so hungrily she swore it was soon to devour itself. Even Conn must have heard it because he was standing beside the bed, his head cocked as another loud rumbling sounded.

Jesu, Mary and Joseph, she'd never last until the morning meal! Throwing back the covers, Triona knew she had to get something to eat or she wouldn't get any more sleep either, her vow to stay in her room be damned.

"Come, Conn. Let's find the kitchen."

As she stole out the door, Conn tagging after her like a four-legged shadow, Triona knew it must be early. The peat fire in the hearth was very low, casting a dim orange glow over the vast outer room. She paused as she passed Ronan's room, but thankfully she didn't hear a sound. Lifting up her gown, she ran on tiptoes to the main door. She breathed a sigh of relief as soon as she stepped outside.

The yard was dark. A few scattered torches sputtered about the stronghold. She imagined there must be guards on patrol, but she hoped she wouldn't run into any of them.

"Quiet, Conn." She tapped his nose once as she'd trained

him so he wouldn't growl or bark. "Like we're hunting."

Stealthily, they made their way across the yard; although she'd never been to the kitchen, she was certain it must be near the feasting-hall. Conn did know the way. Every few steps he sniffed the air, his tail wagging faster and faster as they drew closer to a low wooden building flanking the hall.

Triona, too, smelled the unmistakable fragrance of honey glazed pork as they approached the door, and she wondered as her stomach grumbled painfully if that's what she had missed for supper. Damn those O'Tooles! Why couldn't they have packed a meal and left for Imaal yesterday instead of leaving her to starve?

Her mouth began to water as they crept inside the building, Conn's wagging tail becoming a blur. The yeasty scent of rising dough hung in the air, the morning's bread waiting to be baked. That mingled with the pungent smells of spices and salted meats was so deliciously unbearable, Triona was certain she had died and gone to heaven. Or at least her stomach thought so.

She wished she had a candle, but once again, her eager wolfhound seemed to know the way. And there were a few coals still glowing beneath the iron roasting spits lining the walls that cast a bit of light. She grabbed Conn's ruff, allowing him to lead her deeper into the room past hulking cauldrons and long trestle tables—until he stopped abruptly.

"In there, Conn?"

His scratching at the low side door was her answer; she knew they'd found the room where the evening's leftovers must be kept. Yet her attention was drawn to a row of oblong tarts on the table just ahead, the crusts gleaming eerily in the meager light. Oh, she loved fresh baked tarts, especially ones made of berries!

"Stay, Conn," she ordered, as she hurried to the table.

She knew it was a piggish thing to do, but she was so hungry. She dipped her hand into the nearest pastry, the fragrant aroma of wild raspberries topped by a buttery crust overwhelming her senses. But she had no sooner taken a bite than Conn broke from his sitting position—no doubt tempted beyond endurance—and bumped impatiently against her, causing the tart to slip through her fingers and tumble down the front of her sleeping gown.

"Oh, Conn," she whispered with exasperation, wiping her chin and licking her fingers. If she had looked a mess earlier that day, she could just imagine how she appeared now with bright red berry filling staining her face and clothing.

Beckoning for Conn to follow her, Triona led him back to the larder and let him inside, knowing he'd soon find something to satisfy him. As for herself, she hurried back to the tarts but it was so dark that she snagged her foot on a table leg, crying out as she barely managed to catch herself from falling.

"All this trouble for a wee bit of something to eat," she grumbled, testing her weight on her aching ankle just as a door slammed nearby.

"Who's there? Who's in my kitchen?"

Triona froze, not knowing which way to run. Someone with a candle came rushing toward her. The next thing she knew the light was thrust in her face, then a horrified scream rent the air. She stared back in astonishment at a stout, florid-faced man who appeared to be choking, his plump hand pressed to his chest, his pudgy cheeks growing redder and redder.

"God help me . . . Lady Eva! Bloody . . . back from the grave. Saints protect me!"

"No, no, I'm Triona O'Toole!" she cried even as a terrible rattling noise came from the man's throat, the candle tumbling from his hand. She had no sooner stomped out the flame when he pitched forward, almost knocking her down as his bulk crashed to the floor.

Stunned, Triona stood there for an instant, not knowing what to do. She should send for help . . . She should—

"See if he's breathing," she told herself shakily, falling to her knees beside him and pressing her fingers to his throat. Yes, that's what she should do! See if he was . . .

Gasping, Triona thought her own heart was going to stop. Jesu, Mary and Joseph, she had killed him! Or something had killed him. Panicking, she lunged to her feet and began to run, paying no heed to the sharp pains shooting through her ankle.

"Conn! Conn!"

She had only reached the front door, when she ran straight into something hard that seized her by the arms and shook her.

"By God, woman, now what have you done?"

Chapter 12

IN THE NEXT instant, several guards running up behind him with blazing torches, Ronan felt the color drain from his face as he spied the bloody splotches staining the front of Triona's gown. He didn't wait for an explanation, but swept her in his arms, shouting to his clansmen, "Fetch the healer! Run with you! Go!"

"But Ronan—"

"Sshh, you must keep still, Triona," he bade her, holding her tightly against his chest as he ran with her toward his dwelling-house. His heart was pounding. His stomach cramped in gut-wrenching knots.

By God, what terrible thing could have happened to cause such wounds? Had she been attacked? If so, he would throttle the wretch himself with his bare hands!

"Ronan . . . !"

"I said keep still, Triona," he repeated firmly, surprised that she would have the strength to wriggle so strongly in his arms after losing so much blood. Or maybe she was growing delirious, her injured body going into spasms. He had seen such a thing before. . . .

"Where is that damned healer?" he roared into the night as he neared his dwelling-house. By now, clansmen and their wives were running from their homes, crying, bewildered children stumbling at their heels. Everywhere people were shouting for the healer as fresh torches were lit, the stronghold ablaze with light and confusion.

Ronan kicked in the door, swallowing hard at the stickiness between his fingers as he rushed toward Triona's room. She had ceased her struggling, an ominous sign. God help him, he would never forgive himself if he had failed in his oath to Fineen to protect her! Never!

"Lie still, Triona," he commanded softly, a catch in his voice as he lay her gently upon the bed. "The healer will be here soon, but you mustn't move. It will only make the bleeding worse, the pain worse—"

"But I'm not bleeding! That's what I've been trying to tell you! It's tart filling. Raspberry tart filling!"

In shock, Ronan had no time to reply as the room was flooded with bright torchlight, the balding healer's eyes very round as he was practically carried to the bed by two strapping clansmen. Spilling behind them came more clansmen, Niall among them. Shoving her way through them all, her knobby elbows jabbing and poking, came a stricken-faced Aud.

"Out of my way! My sweeting needs me! Out of my way, I tell you!"

"Aye, I want everyone to step back!" demanded the healer, apparently having recovered himself from his rough handling. "Step back so I can see what needs to be done—"

"Silence!"

Triona started as all faces turned in astonishment to Ronan.

It had been an amazing thing to watch his expression grow more thunderous by the moment. She was all the more anxious because she knew his mounting fury was directed toward her. She could just imagine what he was thinking, that once again she had roused his people into chaos and commotion. And he didn't even know yet that—

"Make way, make way! I must speak with the O'Byrne!"

Triona sank back upon the pillows, wishing desperately that she was a thousand miles away as a flush-faced clansman pushed his way to the front of the room.

"Lord, I've terrible news! It's Seamus, the cook! He's dead!"

"Dead?" Ronan's voice was so ominously low that Triona felt a chill plummet down her spine.

"Aye, Lord, we found him in the kitchen! There's no mark upon him, but his face . . ." Shuddering, the clansman continued in a hushed voice, "His eyes were wide open, Lord, as wide as they could be—like something had frightened the wits from him. I've never seen such a look upon a dead man's face . . . as if . . . as if . . ."

"As if what?" Ronan demanded when the man fell silent. Everyone in the room was listening intently.

"Why, Lord, as if he'd seen a ghost."

As shocked gasps filled the air, a few clansmen hastily crossing themselves, Triona blurted out, "It was me, not a ghost! I was going to tell you what had happened, but then you thought I'd been wounded and you wouldn't listen—"

"You killed my cook."

She gaped at him, stunned and actually hurt that he would accuse her of so cold-blooded a thing until indignation bubbled up to save her. "I did not kill him! Mayhap if you'd allow me to explain instead of interrupting me . . ."

"Then explain, Triona, and quickly."

Glaring at him, she continued. "I was hungry so I went to the kitchen, and there were these fresh tarts—"

"Raspberry." Ronan's gaze fell to the bright red splotches on her gown, then to the fingers of her right hand which were practically stuck together from the sweet stuff, his expression growing even darker.

"Aye, raspberry. But I tripped and Seamus must have heard me because he rushed into the kitchen, and the next thing I knew . . ." She paused, shaking her head. "I don't know what he thought, but he screamed and then he was dead. Just like that."

"Just like that."

She bristled at his scathing tone. "If you don't believe me, then fetch a priest and I'll swear to him that what I've told you is the truth. I don't know what else I can do but to say I'm terribly sorry. All I wanted was to get a little something to eat and then come right back to bed. If I'd known that Seamus was so superstitious, I'd never have gone to the kitchen . . . at least not at night."

Regretting now that he'd ever unlocked her door, Ronan could think of a hundred ways to make her feel even sorrier. He was just about to name one when Aud piped up.

"Aye, Lord, it's a terrible thing that's happened, but you

cannot blame my poor sweeting. I heard Seamus say more than a few times that he'd been feeling ill of late."

Ronan shot a look at the older woman. Aud met his gaze with fire in her eyes, reminding him of a mother hen ready to peck at him to protect her chick.

"I'm sure Triona's suffered quite a shock herself," Niall said calmly. "As would any young woman if in her place. Mayhap if the room was cleared so she might rest . . ."

Tempted to say she deserved the double shock of finding herself once more a prisoner in her room, Ronan resisted the impulse. Such a move would only undo any progress he'd made with her. If indeed he'd made any at all.

But progress or not, he'd wait no longer to invite potential husbands to Glenmalure. He'd lost all control of himself tonight and he didn't like it—by God, his emotions running amuck since Triona had come to his stronghold. His relief that she hadn't been injured was still so intense that even now it threatened to overwhelm him.

"Go back to your homes," he commanded, his gaze sweeping his clansmen's faces. "Calm your wives and children." Then he turned to Triona, saying as evenly as he could, "I trust that other than the obvious damage to your gown, you've suffered no injury."

"Except for my ankle," Triona admitted, thinking that she'd never seen Ronan's eyes so stormy. "I must have twisted it when I tripped in the kitchen."

"See to it, healer." With that, Ronan left the room, Niall throwing her a reassuring smile as he followed after his brother. Within a moment, there was no one left but herself, Aud and the healer who gingerly examined her ankle.

"Ouch!"

"There is much swelling, lady, but thankfully nothing is broken. I must go and make you a plaster."

As the healer hastened out the door, Aud shook her head, tears glistening in her large brown eyes. "You near scared the life from me as well, sweeting. When I heard that you'd been hurt—"

"But I wasn't, Aud, as you plainly see." Hoping to make her maid smile, Triona quipped, "Too bad all this wonderful

raspberry filling ended up on my gown instead of in my
stomach. It's still growling."

Aud began sobbing, sinking down on the bed beside her.

"Now, now, Aud, I'm fine," Triona insisted, throwing her
arm around her maid's quaking shoulders. "I believe I gave
Ronan a scare, too, but look how quickly he recovered."

Funny, Triona thought as Aud wiped her face with her
sleeve. Until she had just now said it aloud, she hadn't really
considered Ronan's feelings.

She had been so frustrated that he wouldn't listen to her,
she'd scarcely considered that he must have been terribly concerned. At least when she ran everything back in her mind, his
actions would lead her to think so. And his voice had caught
so strangely when he had laid her upon the bed. . . .

"Aye, I'm better now, Triona." Aud's bony shoulders were
no longer shaking. "That's enough worrying about me. I should
be worrying over you and not the other way around. It must
have been an awful thing to have Seamus fall dead in front
of you."

"It was awful," Triona said softly, shuddering. "That clansman of Ronan's was right, you know. I think Seamus truly
believed he was looking at a ghost. He seemed to know me,
Aud, though I'd never met him before."

Aud reached over and squeezed her hand. "Now why would
you say that, sweeting?"

"He called me by a name . . . Eva, I believe it was. Lady
Eva."

Feeling Aud's grip suddenly tighten, Triona glanced at her
in surprise. "Aud?" But instead of answering, her maid rose to
her feet and busied herself with pulling a fresh sleeping gown
from the chest at the foot of the bed, her expression decidedly
tight-lipped.

"Aud?" Triona repeated, perplexed.

"Here you go, sweeting. Let's have you changed before the
healer returns with your plaster."

Shrugging, Triona kept silent. But as Aud helped her from
the bed and then lifted the soiled gown over her head, she
decided that she'd never experienced so much strangeness in
one day's time.

Yet at least she could easily reason through Ronan's odd behavior tonight. That he had once again contained his obvious anger was proof enough of his desire to make her biddable enough to marry her off.

"Bastard," she muttered once she was settled again in bed. Aud plumped the pillows.

"Aye, it's a good thing that he's dead."

"What was that, Aud?"

Appearing startled that she had spoken aloud, Aud added hastily, "Only that it's a good thing no bones were broken. You should be up and about in no time."

So she would, Triona vowed, cursing her clumsiness. She would allow nothing to stop her from gaining her father's vengeance. Nothing.

"Aye, brother, he does look like he saw a ghost."

Ronan said nothing. He dropped the blanket over Seamus's stricken face.

"I've already sent men to Glendalough for the priest," Niall added, following after Ronan as he made his way back through the kitchen. "They should be here by midmorning."

"Good. Tell the rest we'll be riding out after Seamus's burial."

"Another raid, Ronan? We just got back from the last one."

Ronan spun, some of the emotion he had bridled for so long spilling over. "Thanks to Triona, little brother, we're in need of a new cook. But if you'd rather stay here and keep her company, by all means—"

"Easy, Ronan. I didn't mean to make it sound as if I don't want to ride with you. It's just that this is the second time Triona's antics have spurred you into calling a raid."

"I said nothing about a raid." Ronan left Niall to stride after him as he stepped outside into the faint morning light. "I've decided to pay the O'Nolan in Carlow a visit. He might be more than willing to trade his cook for a copper-haired bride."

"The O'Nolan?" Niall caught Ronan by the arm and pulled him to a stop. "You can't be serious. The man's already outlived three wives and he's more than twice her age!"

Ronan stared at his brother, never having felt so tightly wound. It was all he could do not to shove Niall into the dirt. "The O'Nolan's hale enough. Still hunts. Raids. And he's a genial man. Mayhap he's of the mind that a spirited young wife might add some amusement to his days. I only wish I'd considered him *before* Triona frightened my cook to death."

Ronan yanked his arm free and stalked across the yard. But he hadn't gone far before Niall was dogging him again.

"This has nothing to do with Seamus, Ronan, and you know it! But it has everything to do with Triona. You're beginning to care for her, aren't you? Aye, and it's tearing you apart, making you crazy. I've never seen you like this! You want her, but you think you don't deserve her—think you don't deserve even a moment's happiness! So now you're going to foist her off on the O'Nolan—"

"If he's willing to put up with her, he's welcome to the task," Ronan cut in, ignoring the bulk of Niall's words.

"And if he isn't willing?"

Not wanting to consider that possibility, Ronan growled, "Then I will proceed as before but only"—he rounded upon Niall so suddenly that his startled brother fell back a step— "*only* if you cease badgering me. Triona *will* wed. If not the O'Nolan than some other man I choose for her. By God, Niall, are we understood?"

"Aye, brother. Couldn't be clearer. How long shall I tell the men we'll be gone?"

Surprised Niall had given up so readily, Ronan wondered if he had actually convinced him to put the whole unsettling matter of Triona to rest. "A few days. Mayhap longer if we see any Norman manors that look tempting and not too well guarded."

"They'll be ready."

As Niall strode away, Ronan resumed his own course. He had to change clothes before anything else could be done. Yet he wasn't prepared upon entering his dwelling-house that the scene from only an hour past could come back to him with such gripping force.

He had heard Triona leave her room with Conn, and he had taken only a moment to wrench on some clothes before following after her. But by the time he was outside she had disappeared. Suspecting she might be plotting some mischief, he had gone first to check the stable.

Then that terrified scream had split the air. He had run to the kitchen only to have Triona rush headlong into his arms. And when he saw the blood upon her gown . . .

"Raspberries," Ronan muttered, wondering how he could have been so fooled even as his stomach twisted painfully. "Damned raspberries."

Chapter *13*

"JESU, MARY AND Joseph!"

"It still hurts that much?" Aud asked as Triona sank back down upon the mattress, swearing in frustration.

"Aye, and when I see that Ronan O'Byrne again, I'm going to tell him that his healer is no more worthy of the title than a goat! It's a good thing I wasn't truly bleeding, otherwise I'd probably be dead!"

"Now, Triona, the healer's done everything he knows to help you. Mayhap it will just take a little more time—"

"A week isn't enough? I've done everything that balding buffoon asked of me—stayed in this bed though I nearly died of boredom—"

"But you've had Maire's visits to cheer you."

"Aye, Aud, but that's not the point. I've also had to endure that healer's smelly lard plasters and his foul-tasting herb potions because he insisted they would make my ankle like new. But they haven't, so I say no more! If I'd been walking on my ankle all along, I'm certain I'd be doing much better."

Pulling herself up with the aid of a bedpost, Triona winced. But she was determined to both ignore the pain and prove that her theory was correct. She managed to limp around the room, although she had to call Conn to her side once when she almost lost her balance.

Her poor wolfhound had had a miserable week, too, after eating practically all the leftovers in the larder. No wonder he hadn't come running after her when she had called for him, the glutton. When Aud had finally found him snoring atop a pile of hay in the stable, she said he looked a bitch ready to birth pups from the bulging size of his stomach.

"There, this works very well," Triona said, patting Conn's head after she'd circled with him again. "I'll just keep him near me until I'm walking without this limp."

"I'm afraid that won't be possible."

Triona spun to face Ronan, almost toppling over until she grabbed Conn for support. At the same moment Ronan's strong arms flew around her, easily lifting her back to a standing position.

"Do you always make a habit of startling people, O'Byrne?" she demanded. She hoped her irritable tone would cover her amazement at seeing him again. The devil take him for being such a handsome man! It was astonishing how good he looked to her after his being gone a week, no matter the serious look on his face. She was grateful when he released her, the strength of him making her heart thump all the faster.

"It wasn't my intent to startle you. It's just that Conn won't be able to accompany you today. I can't have him scaring away our guests."

"Guests?" Triona found it difficult to concentrate upon what Ronan was saying with his still standing so close to her. "You call your new cook a guest? At least that's what the servants told me you'd gone to do . . . find a cook, I mean. It must have been difficult if it took you a full week."

"I had other things to do," he answered cryptically, his jawline tightening. "But aye, I've a new cook. He's already hard at work in the kitchen . . . preparing a feast in honor of the chieftain who's come all the way from the Blackstairs in Carlow to meet you."

Ronan's last statement took her completely by surprise.

"To meet me? Why would a chieftain . . . ?" She gaped at Ronan, suddenly comprehending.

"Taig O'Nolan's an honorable man, Triona. A good-hearted man. I wouldn't have allowed him to come if I thought he was anything less than the husband you deserve—"

"So you finally brought someone here to take a look at me, did you?" Triona cried, backing away from him. "Just like you said that first day I came to Glenmalure!" She would have run if she could, but her twisted ankle was still sore. She turned her back on Ronan but he caught her and swept her fighting and cursing off her feet.

"Calm yourself, Triona. I told you I'd never wed you to a man who'd mistreat you. The O'Nolan may have had three wives—"

"Three!"

"But they were happy with him, each one. He was a broken man when his last wife died just this winter."

"I don't care if he wanted to climb into the grave with her!" Triona shrieked as Ronan carried her from the room. "Damn you, O'Byrne, let me down! Let me down!"

"Aud, see that Conn does not escape," came his stern reply. Triona's ranting and struggling clearly did not daunt him.

He didn't seem daunted, either, when people stared at them outside, Triona wriggling like a worm and uttering every curse she'd ever heard. Even when she caught him in the chest with her elbow, Ronan merely grunted and said, "You will meet the man, Triona, and you will see you've nothing to fear. He may be a bit older than your other suitors—"

"Older?" she echoed, falling still to catch her breath.

"By more than twenty years"—Ronan's grip only tightened as Triona resumed her struggles in earnest—"but if you look upon the difference as wisdom garnered that he will share with you—"

"He could be a drooling idiot for all I care, O'Byrne! I won't be marrying him—"

"If he wants you, you *will* marry him. I'd prefer that you meet the O'Nolan with dignity, but if I must, I'll carry you like a spoiled child into the hall. The choice is yours."

Triona went limp as they neared the gabled building, her mind racing over what Ronan had just said. *If he wants you . . .*

Aye, she'd see that the O'Nolan wanted something, but it wouldn't be her. When she was finished with this aging chieftain from Carlow, he'd want to be heading home to the Blackstairs Mountains without a bride!

"I'll walk," she muttered.

"Wise choice," said Ronan, breathing a bit easier now that she had ceased her wild flailing. But he was no less wary.

"The O'Nolan's anxious to meet you. He's brought gifts," he continued. Somehow his thoughts centered on the last time he'd held Triona. Then he'd thought he might lose her and now, he had no doubt of it. Once the O'Nolan saw her, he wouldn't be able to resist taking her for his wife.

Ronan cursed the unreasoning sense of possession that swept him. By God, it was time he released her! Her closeness was torture, the warmth of her body scorching him through her yellow gown. And the way her generous breasts were pressing tightly against her silk bodice, her nipples hard and roused . . .

"Enough," he muttered, not surprised when Triona met his eyes. His breath caught at the emerald beauty of her gaze. The slow-burning outrage reflected there pained him as he recalled her smile days ago when she'd laughed at the grass on his chin.

"Talking to yourself, O'Byrne?"

He frowned, amending, "I meant I've carried you far enough." He set her down carefully, but kept a firm grip on her elbow. "If you find your ankle is paining you, don't hesitate to lean—"

"Thank you, but I won't be needing your assistance," Triona said tartly, wrenching herself free.

As the hall doors were thrown open for them, she took a moment to shake out her gown. The skirt was twisted around her hips from the way Ronan had been holding her. Before she even lifted her eyes she knew he was watching her, and when she did look up, the sarcastic remark she'd planned to fling at him was stilled along with her breath.

Why was he staring at her so? she wondered, his eyes a deep brooding gray. But her heart had no more begun to pound again when Ronan resolutely looked away, gesturing for her to walk in front of him.

"Tyrant," she muttered. But he didn't frown, once more exhibiting the forced patience that she was coming to hate. It couldn't be more clear to her that he was eager for the O'Nolan to whisk her away to his damned mountains. Ha! Soon Ronan would find he was stuck with her for a while longer.

"The O'Nolan's waiting, Triona."

"I can well imagine," she said bitterly, entering the hall with Ronan just behind her.

The first man she noticed was Niall as he rose from a chair facing the huge hearth. Still dressed in dark riding clothes like Ronan, she imagined they hadn't been back long at the stronghold and again she felt a rush of fury. Obviously Ronan hadn't wanted to waste any time before dragging her here to meet his special guest.

"So where is he—" she began, only to stop dead as a stout, curly bearded man rose beside Niall, a toothy grin splitting his face from ear to ear.

"That's the O'Nolan?" As Ronan nodded, Triona thought her stomach might turn over. "But he's so fat!"

"Sturdily built, Triona. Healthy as a bull."

That comment made her feel sicker. No wonder he'd outlasted three wives, and Ronan wanted her to be this man's fourth! It was enough to make her retch.

Triona jumped when the chieftain clapped his beefy hands as if he had spotted his next meal. The next thing she knew he was bearing down upon them, apparently unwilling to wait any longer for them to approach. She practically fell back against Ronan as the O'Nolan stopped right in front of her, planting his big fists on his hips as he looked her up and down.

"Aye, Ronan, you're a man of your word. She's a beauty. And that copper hair! I've never seen any brighter. You can come a wee bit closer, Triona. I don't bite—"

"But mayhap I do!" She wished her ankle was better so she could have ground her heel into Ronan's toes for even considering her as a match for this large gray oaf. "And just in case the O'Byrne didn't inform you, I'll not be marrying you or anyone else, Taig O'Nolan!"

The hearty shout of laughter that greeted her declaration took Triona by surprise. For a man supposedly heartbroken over the death of his last wife, he seemed very merry.

"Aye, you said she was high-spirited, too! Just like my first wife, God keep her."

"And you should be ashamed for thinking to wed again after losing your third wife only this past winter!" Triona scolded him. To her relief, the chieftain sobered if only a little.

"It's a bit soon, I admit, but I've never been one to enjoy living alone. And I've a curious affliction. I fall in love a bit too easily. But I'm loyal as a hound once I do, so don't let that trouble you." Another wide grin stretched his face, his ruddy features neither handsome nor unattractive but somewhere solidly in between. "You seem like a young woman who'd keep me well entertained, Triona O'Toole. Now come and see what I've brought you."

Before Triona could protest, her hand was locked in his huge one, but he didn't drag her across the room as she had feared he might. Instead he seemed most solicitous of her injured ankle, walking slowly with her despite his eagerness to show her his gifts, and even asking her if she wanted a cushion for her foot after she'd sat down.

To her amazement, she even began to feel a bit guilty for thinking of him so unkindly when he laid two small bundles in her lap, one wrapped in blue silk and the other in purple.

"I've always believed any woman of mine should have pretty things. Especially one as beautiful as you."

Although flattered by the sincerity of his compliment—aye, Ronan should take lessons!—Triona shook her head. "I'm not your woman and I don't want your gifts," she declared, but not as sharply as she might have a few moments ago. "You'd do better to save them for someone else—"

"At least open them, Triona."

The man looked so damned earnest she couldn't find it in her heart to refuse him. But she wasn't going to keep them, whatever they were, she thought determinedly, unwrapping the smallest of the two packages. She would just look at them—

Triona's low gasp brought a grin to the chieftain's face as she held up a delicate gold arm-ring that glittered and sparkled with precious stones of scarlet, green and blue.

"It's beautiful," she murmured, glancing up to find Ronan with the strangest look on his face . . . almost as if he were somehow displeased with her reaction. As for Niall, he looked both confused and concerned as if he couldn't quite believe what he was seeing.

"I can't keep this," she said firmly, as she held out the arm-ring to the O'Nolan. "Besides, I've never worn such ornaments."

"All the more reason why you must keep it," the chieftain insisted stubbornly, folding her fingers around his gift. "Now unwrap the other one."

Sighing, she did, but she told herself it was only to humor him. And again she gasped as Maire would surely have done when Triona revealed a necklace of glistening pink pearls.

She thought of yanking it apart right then as her instincts were telling her to do—as Niall was gesturing that she do!—but she had the notion that the O'Nolan would merely laugh, gather the pearls from the floor and present them to her again.

Damn Ronan for bringing a man to Glenmalure who was just as good-hearted as he had claimed! She wanted no part of this chieftain or his gifts, but neither could she envision herself being deliberately cruel. She wasn't a banshee!

Her dilemma only worsened when the feast began a short while later. The hall was filled to capacity with O'Byrnes and O'Nolan clansmen who'd accompanied their chieftain. Maire was there, too, oddly looking as concerned as Niall. They seemed to grow even more concerned as the evening wore on.

When the mutton soup was passed, Triona could have dumped a steaming bowlful into the O'Nolan's lap but she didn't. She could have "accidentally" stabbed his leg with her cutting knife, splashed wine into his beaming face, shrieked in his ear . . . anything instead of allowing him to serve her himself, always filling her plate with savory morsels before his own.

Anything instead of finding his lively stories so funny that she laughed until tears came to her eyes.

Anything instead of being convinced by the end of the night that Taig O'Nolan, chieftain of the Blackstairs O'Nolans, was so kind, attentive and good-humored that it was no wonder his three wives had been happy. But she wasn't convinced enough to be the next one!

At last Triona could stand it no longer. Her head spun from searching for a solution.

It hadn't helped either that Niall had been staring at her all night as if trying to tell her something, his frown growing as deep as Ronan's. And she couldn't imagine why *Ronan* was looking so angry when she was behaving so well. It must seem that his matchmaking was proceeding as planned.

"Forgive me," she finally interrupted the O'Nolan just as he was about to launch into another tale. "I'm so tired . . . and my ankle is aching terribly. I'd like to retire—"

"I'll help you, Triona," Niall interjected.

"Sit, little brother. Keep our guest company while I escort Triona back to her room," Ronan announced to Triona's greater astonishment. He'd hardly said a word all night to speak up now?

She *knew* he was going to try to convince her to announce a betrothal as he walked her to her room.

"Actually," she began, "I'd like the O'Nolan to accompany me."

"An honor," the chieftain enthused, though he seemed concerned by the sudden scowl on Ronan's face. "Unless you object?"

"Not at all," came Ronan's gruff response. "Your cup will be filled and waiting for your return . . . which I trust will be soon."

Hearing the hard edge to his voice, Triona imagined that was his way of warning her against trying any tricks. How he'd gloat if he knew she hadn't thought of a single one!

As she and the chieftain left the hall, Triona managed to catch Aud's eye. "My maid," she hastily explained when Aud rose from the servants' table to walk behind them.

"Aye, it wouldn't be proper without her," the O'Nolan agreed.

Even now he was only thinking of what was best for her, Triona marveled, aware that a lesser man might have seized an opportunity to be alone.

Suddenly likening the O'Nolan to her father, she wondered if he might accept that as an excuse for why they couldn't marry. Surely it wouldn't be right for her to wed a man that reminded her so strongly of Fineen. . . .

"I'm only surprised Ronan isn't following us as well," the chieftain added, his voice grown philosophic.

Chapter 14

TRIONA STOPPED TO stare at the O'Nolan, confused.

"I'm sure that Ronan trusts you," she began. Then, embarrassed, she added, "I mean . . . that you wouldn't have—"

"Taken advantage of you?" the chieftain finished for her, gesturing for Aud to catch up to them. "I may have seen many winters come and go, Triona O'Toole, but that doesn't mean my blood doesn't grow warm at the sight of a fine woman like you. But there's a younger man whose blood is boiling hot as pitch right now, though I doubt he'd ever admit it."

"I—I don't understand—"

"Ronan. He wasn't himself tonight, well, not that he hasn't been the same since . . ." The O'Nolan didn't finish, clearing his throat instead before adding, "He's been scowling all night, not like him at all. Aye, I'm not blind. He may have brought me here to wed you, but it's clear he wants you for himself. And I'll not stand in his way."

Her heart suddenly pounding, Triona knew she must be gaping at the man.

Ronan . . . want her? Of course that couldn't be true. If he'd been scowling when they'd left the hall, it was only because he probably suspected she had some wild plot brewing.

"Ronan doesn't want me!" she finally managed to blurt out even as she realized with horror that the O'Nolan had given her the escape route she needed and now she was refuting him. "At least I don't think he does," she quickly amended. "He claims he has no time for a wife."

"Aye, so he's long said. But his words ring false." Signaling for Aud to come take his place beside Triona, the chieftain said

112

to her, "You've a fine mistress here. . . ."

"Aud, Lord."

"Aud, is it? Begorra, now, that was my second wife's name. I've always loved the sound of it."

Triona couldn't believe her ears when Aud actually giggled. And she was looking so queerly at the O'Nolan. . . .

"T-thank you, Lord. That was very kind of you to say."

Triona glanced at the O'Nolan to find him grinning again, and it made her glad that he didn't seem heartbroken at all that she would not be his bride. In fact, he was fairly beaming at Aud . . . and in the torchlight, Triona could swear her maid was blushing!

"Aud, my ankle's feeling much better. I think I'll walk the rest of the way by myself. Why don't you accompany the O'Nolan back to the hall?"

As if her suggestion had burst a spell, Aud was suddenly at her side, her hands slightly trembling as she took Triona's arm. "No, no, sweeting, I'll help you."

"Aye, you shouldn't be walking alone," interjected the chieftain, although he sounded disappointed.

"I'm fine," Triona insisted, gently breaking free of Aud and walking a few steps just to prove to both of them that she was practically no longer limping. "See?"

"Are you sure, sweeting?"

Triona's answer was to turn back around and keep walking, smiling to herself when a moment later she heard another giggle followed by a burst of robust laughter. She didn't look over her shoulder until she reached the dwelling-house. By then, there was no sign of Aud or the O'Nolan.

Triona laughed, suddenly quite pleased with herself. Now she felt like the matchmaker! But it didn't take her long to sober when she thought of how angry Ronan would be when he learned she'd not be going to Carlow. Yet it was his own fault for scowling so much and giving the O'Nolan the wrong impression!

She shrugged. Let Ronan do what he would. He was proving his own worst enemy, which was fine with her. At this rate he'd not be done with her until *she* was ready to leave Glenmalure.

*   *   *

"Where the devil is he?"

"You brought the O'Nolan here to woo Triona, brother. Mayhap that's exactly what he's doing."

Ronan thrust himself back in his chair, bracing his foot on the table as he glared out over the boisterous hall. At first he had attempted to appear unconcerned that the chieftain still hadn't returned; now nearly a full hour later he could barely contain himself.

"If you're implying what I think you are, Niall, then you're wrong. Triona would never let him near her . . . at least not so soon."

"No? She seemed to enjoy his company well enough tonight, laughing at his stories, eating the food he set on her plate—"

"Drinking the wine he poured for her." Maire's normally sweet voice was edged with a hint of reproach.

"Aye, so she did," Niall agreed as he glanced at his sister. "But then, mayhap Ronan didn't notice—"

"I noticed." Seeing Niall's slow smile—and the curious light in Maire's eyes—Ronan angrily added, "I noticed that all was going as it should be. If I'm any judge, Taig has found himself another wife."

"Then drink with me, brother!" Not smiling any longer, Niall raised his cup. "Your duty to Fineen O'Toole will soon be ended! That's what you wanted, isn't it?" When Ronan didn't respond, Niall leaned over in his chair and said in a low aside, "Don't concern yourself with the O'Nolan's absence. He and Triona are probably playing chess."

Ronan slammed his cup upon the table, scarcely noticing that the hall had suddenly become less noisy. Many of his clansmen turned his way as he rose while Niall looked up at him in mock surprise.

"You didn't like my toast?"

"Stay here with Maire, little brother, and tend to our guests. I don't want to cause an alarm."

"If you're going to search for the O'Nolan, you might find that he won't welcome the intrusion."

"I'll take that risk. Better that than to find him dead like Seamus."

At least Ronan tried to tell himself that was his reasoning for leaving the hall. Yet something else was driving him, something he didn't want to name. By God, here he was incredibly hoping that Triona had made some drastic move and he wouldn't find her with the O'Nolan!

"Get hold of yourself, man," Ronan muttered, scanning the darkened yard for any sight of the chieftain. Surely if his guards had seen anything suspicious, they would have reported to him immediately. And since they hadn't, the feast continuing undisturbed, that could only mean . . .

It seemed Ronan was at Triona's door in a moment's time. His jaw tightened painfully as he forced himself to knock rather than kicking it down. No answer came so he knocked again, louder. He heard Conn growling, then a sleepy voice calling, "Aud? Is that you?"

At least Triona was in her room. But alone?

Ronan's breath jammed as he thrust open the door, his eyes adjusting to the faint light cast by a flickering oil lamp. Conn lay on the floor, his tail thunking heavily, while Triona bolted upright in bed, the covers clutched to her breast.

"Ronan?"

"Where is he?"

"Who?"

"Taig O'Nolan, woman!"

"Why, in the hall with you . . . isn't he?"

Ronan's fierce relief was short-lived as fury swept him. "No! He never returned!"

Triona gasped as Ronan was beside the bed in two strides. Suddenly she was wrenched from beneath the covers to her knees, Ronan's fingers biting cruelly into her arms.

"I said the O'Nolan never returned," he repeated, his voice ominously low. "You will tell me what happened from the moment you left the hall, Triona." He gave her a rude shake. "Do you hear me?"

"Nothing happened!"

"Something did or the O'Nolan would have come back to the hall. Did he try to kiss you? Is that what happened? He tried to kiss you and you somehow retaliated, knocked him over the head, kicked him, punched him—"

"Why do you care if he kissed me?" Triona demanded, growing furious at his rough handling. "That's what you would have wanted him to do, isn't it?"

"I could not care a whit if he did, I just want to know what happened afterward—"

"Damn you, O'Byrne! I've never been kissed so obviously that didn't happen, or I'm sure I would have known about it!"

Her outburst hung in the air as the room fell silent, Ronan's eyes narrowing in disbelief.

"You've never been kissed?"

The huskiness of his voice sent shivers spiraling from her stomach to her toes. Suddenly acutely aware of how closely he held her, his silvery eyes blazing into hers, Triona found she had only a bare whisper of voice to answer.

"No. Nev—"

His lips came down upon hers before she could pull away, Ronan's arms enveloping her so tightly that she feared for a fleeting moment she might be crushed. But her fear disappeared when his mouth began moving over hers, slowly at first as if sampling the taste of her, savoring the warmth of her, the feel of her . . . then more hungrily as if he liked very much what he'd found and meant to devour her.

And she was certain she was being devoured when his tongue suddenly swept deep into her mouth, one hand plunging through her hair to tilt back her head while the other drew her that much closer . . . so close she could feel his heartbeat thundering against her breast. Or was it hers to match the blood pounding in her ears?

Within an instant, the sound had grown to a deafening roar, her fingers clutching wildly at his tunic as a raging heat suddenly engulfed her from head to toe. Yet no sooner had her tongue begun to spar with his in a thrilling dance that sent her senses spinning and her insides melting then she heard him groan, his body tensing.

"By God, woman, if you'd been kissed before you would have saved me a lot of trouble."

Triona's eyes shot open as Ronan lifted his head away from hers though he still held her tightly around the waist . . . as if reluctant to let her go. But when he spoke again his voice was no longer husky.

"I'd wager if you'd known how much you would like a man's touch, you would have married long ago."

She slapped him across the face almost before she was aware she'd raised her hand. Her body trembled in outrage and chagrin that she could have so wantonly lost all control of herself.

"Is that the kind of retaliation you meant, O'Byrne? A blow? Or perhaps something harsher?"

He dodged to the side before her doubled fist could slam into his stomach, catching her as she almost toppled forward from the bed. In the next moment, her arms were pinned painfully behind her back, his face only inches from her own.

"You will tell me what happened to the O'Nolan. . . ."

"I don't know!" Triona cried, tears smarting her eyes from how fiercely he held her. "When I saw him last he was walking back to the hall with Aud!"

"Aud? You set your maid to do your devious bidding?"

"Of course not! He seemed to have taken a liking to her after he told me he didn't want to marry me."

Ronan released her so suddenly that she fell back onto the mattress, almost landing on Maeve who screeched and jumped to the floor. Conn had long since risen to his feet, his big brown eyes looking uncertainly from Ronan to Triona as he began to whine.

"Now you've upset everybody!" she blurted, tears to her dismay tumbling down her cheeks. "Why don't you just leave—"

"Not until I find out why you've concocted such a lie."

"It's no lie! Find the O'Nolan and ask him! He told me that he wasn't going to stand in your way . . . that he could see plainly that you wanted me for yourself. I tried to tell him he was wrong . . . and he even said that you've long told him you've no time for a wife—"

"Aye, and I meant it," Ronan cut in, more deeply stung by Triona's tears than he'd ever admit. "I don't want you. I don't want anybody! The only thing I want is vengeance . . . vengeance and if God is merciful, some peace."

He stopped as his throat tightened, realizing he had given voice to things never before said. Without another word he headed for the door, not surprised when Triona shouted after him, her voice strangely ragged, "I don't want you either, O'Byrne! You're the last man I'd ever think to wed!"

"You will wed, Triona. That I promise." Ronan swallowed hard against long pent-up emotion that threatened to overcome him as he faced her from the doorway. "And rest assured, it won't be me. When I convince the O'Nolan of that, you'll be journeying to Carlow as his bride."

He ducked out, slamming the door behind him just as a pillow came hurtling through the air.

Chapter 15

"AT LEAST THE rest of your evening was more enjoyable than mine," Triona muttered, staring out the window at the rain coming down in sheets.

"Aye, well, it was until the O'Byrne came crashing at my door." Looking up from her mending, Aud shook her head. "Taig wasn't at all pleased, I can tell you."

"Taig is it now?" Triona couldn't help smiling as she glanced over her shoulder, for the moment her mood feeling a little brighter. She wasn't surprised to see Aud blush. Her maid had been doing it all morning.

"Aye, he told me it was only fair since he was calling me by my given name." As Aud smiled, some secret memory making her plain face look younger than her thirty-nine years, Triona heaved a sigh.

"You should have gone with him to Carlow, Aud. Far away from this miserable place."

"And leave you here all alone with that—that Black O'Byrne? No wonder they call him by such a name! It would surely describe his mood when Taig said he was no longer looking for a bride . . . at least not one with coppery hair, if you don't mind me saying so."

"Why should I mind?" Triona traced her finger over the foggy patch her breath had left on the window. "You've always wanted me to be happy. Why wouldn't I want the same for you?" Suddenly she cursed, realizing she had written Ronan's name on the glass.

"Triona?"

"It's nothing, Aud." Triona swiped across the window with

her palm; she wished she could just as easily erase the memory of Ronan's kiss from her mind.

She had scarcely slept last night thinking about it, that, and everything he'd said to her, the spawn. At least one thing hadn't changed since she'd left Imaal. Ronan wanted nothing to do with her and she wanted nothing to do with him.

A sudden pang made Triona curse again as she shoved away from the window.

"Your ankle, sweeting?"

"Aye," Triona lied, not wanting to tell her maid what was really plaguing her. It was all so absurd. One kiss shouldn't have caused this hollow ache deep inside her. Not even a kiss as wonderful, as dizzyingly hard to forget as Ronan's.

"Ha! It wasn't that incredible," she groused to herself as she plopped onto her bed and toyed absently with Maeve's switching tail. And, of course, she had nothing to compare it to. The whole experience could have been quite ordinary.

She sighed, not believing that thought for a moment as she flipped onto her back.

"Sweeting, whatever is troubling you? You're as restless as I've ever seen."

"Nothing, Aud." Although once again she had lied. *Everything* was more the truth of it!

"Well, you may be saying so, but I hope you're not fretting because I didn't go to Carlow. If Taig O'Nolan's as fond of me as he claimed, he'll wait as long as he has to—"

"But the two of you shouldn't have to wait!" Triona broke in vehemently, grateful for something to distract her. "You've the right to live your own life, Aud. You're not a slave, but free to come and go as you choose."

"And I choose to stay here with you! From the moment your father laid you in my arms, aye, no matter that you were wailing like a banshee, your little face as red as could be, I swore to protect you. Swore on a crucifix, and that lightning should strike me to the ground if I ever failed you! So until you're gone from this place, sweeting, I'll be by your side."

"Oh, Aud." Triona thrust herself from the bed and rushed over to give her maid a fierce hug. "I only wish I knew when that might be. I never asked Ronan yesterday if he'd heard any news yet from Kildare, and I doubt now if he'd tell me anyway." Suddenly, she brightened. "Niall might know—if I can find him alone to ask him."

"You think he'd tell you if they'd heard anything?"

"I hope so." Triona went to her clothing chest and pulled out a pair of trousers and a shirt. The rain and mud were as good an excuse as any to wear her favorite clothes again rather than silk or fine linen. As she shed her light blue gown, she said almost to herself, "At least Niall's told me twice he'd help me if I ever needed it."

"A strange thing, if you ask me."

Triona dressed hurriedly, impatient to be on her way. "I thought so, too, but I suppose I'll find out today if he really meant it."

"You might discover more than you want if the O'Byrne sees you in those trousers."

"He won't," Triona said confidently, slipping on a pair of hard-soled leather shoes. "My brown cloak will cover everything. Besides, it's raining too hard. A gown would just trail in the mud." Ready at last, she wadded the gown into a ball and tossed it to Conn. To her delight, the wolfhound caught it between his jaws and shook the garment ferociously. "Good Conn! That more than matches my feelings!"

"But not mine when I'll have to mend it again," Aud chided as Triona rushed to retrieve the sodden garment.

"Too bad you didn't do the same thing to Ronan last night," she said softly, rubbing Conn's ears. "But you've taken a liking to him, only the saints know why."

"Here you go, sweeting."

Triona hurried back to Aud and shrugged into the cloak, then settled the hood over her hair. "I'll be back soon. And don't forget to keep Conn here with you. He'd lead Ronan right to me."

"Aye, it wouldn't be wise for you to be found consorting with the O'Byrne's own brother, now would it?"

Triona shook her head, gave Aud a peck on the cheek and then flew out the door. Luckily, there was no sign of Ronan as she passed his room, though the door was open, the interior dark and silent. Praying she wouldn't encounter him, she drew the hood more tightly around her face as she stepped outside.

If it had been raining in sheets a short while ago, now it seemed that the boiling gray sky had opened up with a vengeance, the downpour a deluge. But Triona wasn't daunted as she lowered her head and hurried toward Niall's dwelling-house. She loved storms, the louder the thunder the better.

"You there, out of the way!"

"What . . . ?" Glancing up, Triona barely had a moment to dodge the two riders bearing down upon her. Mud splattered her from head to foot as their horses galloped by. Realizing that they must have just ridden through the gates, she grew tense with excitement.

Might they have come from Kildare? From their urgency, her instincts were telling her that it must be so. Seeing that they had dismounted and rushed into the hall, she imagined they had gone to report to Ronan. She hurried across the yard, unable to run because of her sore ankle, but so excited she hardly noticed.

She was grateful when several other clansmen joined her at the entrance, apparently having seen the riders as well. As they all hastened inside, stamping their feet and shaking the rain from their cloaks, Triona kept to the back, using their bulk to conceal her presence. Thankfully no one was paying her any heed. All eyes were trained to the front of the hall where Ronan had stood to meet the riders, all ears listening to the breathless announcement.

"Lord, news from Kildare! Maurice de Roche has left his castle with a small force to journey southward. He goes to meet the Norman King John who landed in Waterford with his forces only two days' past."

"So it's no longer a rumor," one of the clansmen standing in front of Triona commented gruffly to his neighbor. "That bastard has finally come to Eire to crush the rebellion among his own vassals."

"Aye, may they all butcher each other!" hissed another man as Ronan's commanding voice carried to them.

"A small force?"

"Aye, Lord. Ten knights. The rest will join the baron when King John's army arrives in Dublin—"

"So they think." Ronan's tone had grown harsh. "But their liege lord is a dead man. King John will find a nice Irish welcome waiting for him on his march north . . . eleven Norman corpses swinging from a tree."

Triona ducked as Ronan suddenly looked out across the hall at the men surrounding her.

"Arm yourselves and prepare to ride! Tell the others to meet at the gates as soon as they're ready. Now go! If we're to catch de Roche, we've no time to waste."

Triona gasped as the clansmen who'd served as her shield seemed to lunge as one body for the doors, leaving her to scramble after them. But Ronan had already turned his attention back to the exhausted riders. And thanks to the pouring rain, none of the men wasted a glance on her as several ran for the stable while others branched out to pound upon doors and raise the alarm.

Triona, too, headed for the stable. The day had come! She had hoped to prepare, knowing little of Normans, but she would just have to rely on the skills she already possessed. First she needed a horse, but she couldn't ride Laeg. Ronan would surely recognize . . .

Suddenly she stopped, realizing that Ronan might very well come to check on her before he left the stronghold, despite his call for haste. If she wasn't there, he might guess her plans. He already suspected her.

"Ninny," she grumbled, quickly making her way back to her dwelling-house. Just in time, too. Shooting a glance over her shoulder just before she went inside, Triona felt her heart jump as she saw Ronan leaving the hall.

She ran to her room, cursing the lingering pain in her ankle as she shoved open the door with a crash.

"Saints preserve us, Triona, you startled me!"

"Tell Ronan I'm resting, Aud. Nothing more!" Muddy cloak, shoes and all, Triona dove into the bed and pulled the covers to her ears, then rolled over so her back would be facing the door.

"Oh, sweeting, I just changed those sheets! And you've tracked water all over the floor—"

"I did?" Sitting up to look, Triona felt her heart sink. It was dark enough in the outer room that Ronan might not notice the floor was wet but in here, with all the windows . . . "Aud, do something! If he sees the mess—"

"Lie down!" Aud commanded sharply, her maid using the very garment she had been mending to quickly wipe the floor dry. "And that goes for you, too, Conn!"

"Aye, lie down, lie down!" Triona whispered, her wolf-hound nudging her fingers with his cold nose as she signaled to him to drop. Pitching back onto her side, she heard a heavy thunk as Conn's elbows hit the floor and she knew he had obeyed.

Only when she heard Aud's chair creak, her maid humming softly as she resumed her needlework, did Triona breathe a sigh of relief. The picture of quiet serenity that she wanted Ronan to see had been restored. But she froze when she heard his approaching footsteps. Her rampant heartbeat was anything but serene as she listened to his hand turn the latch.

"She's resting, Lord," Aud murmured, Triona not moving a muscle as she felt Ronan's suspicious eyes upon her.

"This early in the day? Is she ill?"

"No, Lord, just weary from last evening. She told me she didn't sleep well last night."

That was true enough, Triona thought, forcing herself to breathe steadily and slowly though she felt as if she couldn't breathe at all. But she wished Aud hadn't told him!

"She's not alone in that," came Ronan's terse response just before he closed the door.

Triona smiled in triumph. She wished she could have seen the look on Ronan's face when Taig O'Nolan told him that he could keep the new cook but the chieftain no longer had any interest in taking a bride. Aye, she hoped Ronan would lose many nights of sleep over that news! But her smile faded when she heard a key grind in the lock. She flung aside the covers in outrage.

"Why that—"

"Sshh, now, he'll hear you!"

At that moment, Triona almost didn't care. Almost. In the next instant, she was across the room and listening at the door. Listening and waiting, her cheeks hot and her pulse racing. When she was certain Ronan had left the dwelling-house, she returned to the bed and retrieved her dagger from beneath the mattress.

"What are you doing, sweeting? Why do you need—"

"My chance has finally come, Aud." Triona secured the weapon in her belt.

"Chance?"

"To avenge my father." Seeing the stricken look on Aud's face, Triona spared a moment to give her a reassuring hug, then she went to one of the sturdy-backed chairs that had once belonged to her parents. Thankfully, it wasn't as heavy as it appeared.

"I don't know how long I'll be gone, Aud, so you'll have to help Maire exercise her legs as you did this past week while I was abed. Aye, and you'll have to hang something to keep the rain out." With that, Triona swung the chair at the nearest window, averting her eyes as the fine Norman glass shattered.

"Sweeting!"

Triona heard the anguish in Aud's voice but she didn't allow herself to look back as she climbed out the window. Pulling the hood of her cloak back over her hair, her only thought now was that somehow she had to find a horse and join Ronan's men before they rode out the gates.

She ran to the stable. She gave thanks again for the relentlessly pounding rain that leant her anonymity as she hurried across the yard. That and the fact that the stronghold resounded with commotion, thunder booming overhead, clansmen shouting to each other, horses whinnying, wives and children calling their farewells from doorways.

The stable, too, was in a furor as servants and clansmen rushed to and fro; she barely had entered the dim interior when Ronan rode right past her on his snorting black mount. But if she had escaped *his* notice, she almost was unmasked when she slipped on the morass of mud and horse dung that the dirt floor had become. A clansman reached out to grab her just before she went facedown into the stinking muck.

"My—my thanks," she said as gruffly as she could manage, keeping her head lowered. But her voice must not have been gruff enough. Strong fingers lifted her chin.

"Triona?"

She gulped, looking straight into Niall's eyes.

"Good God, what are you doing here?"

"Please, Niall, you must help me!" she said in a desperate whisper, risking everything on the hope that he would understand. "I must ride with you . . . after de Roche! If he's to hang, I deserve to be there!"

"But, Triona, it's too dangerous. And if Ronan discovers—"

"He won't! Not if you don't tell him. Now we haven't any more time! I need a horse." Seeing him still undecided, she added, "You told me if there was anything you could do to help me, I had only to ask! Well, damn you, I'm asking! Are you a liar, then, just like your brother?"

Niall pulled her over so sharply next to a nearby stall that she gasped in surprise.

"Ronan is no liar, Triona. He's a good man. An honorable man who goes now to avenge *your* father. Remember that! Now take that horse over there. His owner is abed with fever."

She gulped, nodding, then caught Niall's sleeve as he began to walk away. She wanted to say that she needed her bowcase but the frown on his face—so like Ronan's—made her hold her tongue. Obviously he was not convinced that he'd made the right decision. She would have to content herself with the dagger; luckily, her aim was as good with knives as with arrows.

"Thank you, Niall," she murmured.

His frown only grew deeper. "Save your thanks, Triona. We've a long journey ahead of us and if Ronan spies you . . . " Niall didn't finish, shaking his dark head as he went to an opposite stall.

Triona shrugged off his chilling words and quickly bridled her mount. The animal, a reddish brown gelding with a star on its forehead, looked to be strong and healthy, but certainly not anywhere as magnificent as Laeg. She cast a longing glance at her stallion. His ears swiveled with interest at all the commotion, his low nickering telling her that he sensed she was near.

"Are you coming?"

She started, glancing up as Niall rode past her. She didn't want to be the last one from the stable, so she pulled herself onto the gelding's back and followed after Niall, grateful when several other clansmen rode out with her at the same time.

She saw to her relief as she rode toward the gates that she needn't have worried Ronan might notice her. He and most of his men were already galloping from the stronghold, leaving her, Niall and a dozen others to bring up the rear.

Except she didn't wait for Niall. Fearing he might still change his mind, she kicked her mount into a canter and bolted through the gates.

Chapter 16

RONAN SQUINTED AGAINST the cold drizzle slashing at his face, his thoughts once more consumed by Triona despite his determination to keep his mind upon the Norman quarry he and his men had been pursuing half the breadth of Leinster.

So she hadn't slept well last night. Well, neither had he, damn her.

By God, he should never have kissed her! Then he wouldn't have been tormented with burning memories he would sooner forget . . . how incredibly soft her lips had been, how sweet she had tasted, how good she had smelled . . . and how damned close he had come to losing all command of himself when she began to kiss him back—

"Leave it!" he muttered, forcing his thoughts instead to the curses she would hurl at him when he returned with the news that Baron Maurice de Roche had eluded him. Cursing himself, Ronan could no longer deny that to continue this chase would be sheer folly.

At first the trail had looked promising, the baron and his ten knights holding no more than a few miles' lead. But their pace had never slackened as Ronan had hoped, de Roche clearly anxious to meet up with his king.

Now it was almost dark. If the baron stopped for the night at all, he would no doubt do so in Kilkenny. And that Norman-held town lay too close to King John and his approaching forces to risk venturing there. Ronan had his men's safety to consider; he would take no reckless chances. He had learned that lesson years ago. God help him, he had learned.

Ronan held up his arm and reined in his mount, the powerful animal's increasing exhaustion another factor. As his sixty-odd clansmen slowed their horses to a halt behind him, he raised his voice so all could hear.

"We've ridden hard, men, but we'll go no farther south. Kilkenny may already harbor some of King John's army. We'll return to the River Barrow and make camp for a few hours so the horses may rest, then ride for Glenmalure."

So far to the rear that she could barely make out Ronan's face in the gathering dusk and drizzle, Triona couldn't believe her ears.

Go no farther? Was he mad? Surely they must be close to Baron de Roche and his men or they wouldn't have pursued them for this long. Yet they were giving up the chase?

She wasn't giving up! Triona fumed, swiftly making her own plans. She might never have another chance. Yet as everyone wheeled their horses around, she had no choice but to follow suit. To draw attention to herself at this point would gain her nothing.

But as night settled even deeper around them, she began to deliberately slow her mount until once more she was riding at the rear, her heart thundering as Ronan passed her without a glance. And if Niall had been keeping watch on her, he was lost now in the surge of clansmen that had become no more than fuzzy shapes in the gathering darkness.

Finally Triona veered her mount off the road altogether and into the trees where she waited breathlessly for the thundering sound of hooves to fade. Only when she was certain that she was alone did she venture out into the open.

It was growing so dark that she could barely see the road, but thankfully a bright quarter moon was peeking from behind translucent clouds that appeared to be lifting. She took a moment to wind her sodden cloak more tightly around her, doing her best to ignore the chill seeping into her bones, then she dug her heels into the gelding's flanks.

"On with you now. To Kilkenny!"

Ronan dismounted, grateful that the cursed rain had finally stopped. But the day had hardly ended as he would have liked.

Now Fineen's revenge would have to wait for weeks, maybe even months depending upon how long this King John remained in Eire. No doubt the loyal Baron de Roche would not stray far from his king's side, making it virtually impossible to capture him by surprise.

"More good news for Triona," Ronan groused, imagining again the ruckus she would raise. First she would call him a coward for not having pursued the baron into Kilkenny, then accuse him of being unfit to lead his men if he couldn't have pushed them harder, and finally, end by declaring she could have done better herself.

"Ronan!" Niall called.

He spun, frowning at the agitation in his brother's voice as Niall rushed toward him. "Where the devil have you been these long hours? Usually you ride at the front with me—"

"She's gone, Ronan!"

He tensed, something telling him that this day was not destined to improve. "Do you mean . . . ?"

"Aye, and I knew it was the wrong decision from the first. But she said she deserved to be there if de Roche was going to hang so I—"

"By God, Niall, have you gone mad? You allowed Triona to ride with us?"

As Ronan's incredulous roar echoed around the clearing, every clansman fell still where he stood. But Niall rushed on as if he'd fully expected such an outburst.

"I couldn't believe it when I found her in the stable. You'd told me that you had locked her door."

"Little good it did," Ronan muttered, imagining all too well how she had escaped. "So you say that she's gone?"

"Aye. I kept close watch on her, too, riding well to the back with her until we stopped a while ago. I thought she was still with me, but it got so damned dark—"

"The fool woman's gone to Kilkenny."

Niall didn't reply, his expression as grim as Ronan's in the moonlight.

"Did she have weapons? Her bowcase and hunting knife are locked away, but she might have stolen—"

"It's possible, Ronan. She was wearing a heavy cloak that could easily have hidden—"

"All the damned weapons she needed." Ronan's insides were churning as he went to his stallion and vaulted onto the animal's back. "As my Tanist, you're in charge, Niall."

"But, Ronan, you can't go there alone! The town is surely overrun with Normans and you've a price on your head. At least take some men with you!"

"And risk their lives as well?" Ronan gathered the reins and swung his horse sharply around. "At first light lead the men back to Glenmalure. Don't wait for me. King John's forces might have come to fight their own kind, but that doesn't mean they wouldn't enjoy whetting their swords upon a band of Wicklow rebels."

As Niall swore in frustration, Ronan plunged his stallion back onto the road, daring to hope he might catch up with Triona before she reached Kilkenny. Even if he didn't catch her, maybe once she saw that the odds were so slim of her finding Maurice de Roche in a town filled with Normans, she'd realize the insane folly of her plan and turn back.

Now Ronan swore.

Triona O'Toole, admit she'd taken on more than she could manage?

The sheer absurdity of that idea made him ride all the harder.

Triona was amazed at how easily she gained entrance into the walled town of Kilkenny.

Even at this late hour, the road was crowded with wagons and carts bearing all manner of foodstuffs she imagined would be needed to feed King John's army. Incredibly enough, she had only to dismount and lead her horse through the gates, the distracted guards paying her no more heed than they were to the squawking chickens and squealing pigs.

Taking care to note the direction she took so she would be able to find her way out again, Triona was also careful to keep her hood pulled down over her hair. If she appeared a youth, she'd be much less noticeable. The last thing she wanted was to attract any undue attention.

She'd never seen so many Normans before and for that matter, she'd never visited one of their towns.

She decided quickly that she didn't like the place, the noisy streets narrow and overcrowded with pedestrians, animals and all manner of creaking transport, the houses cramped-looking and ugly, the air rank with foul smells and ringing with the babble of voices. And the inhabitants were so rude.

No one seemed to give a mind to their neighbor, which in her situation was a very good thing. But she'd never experienced such jostling and shoving. And, of course, the men were all so much taller than she it was difficult to see where she was going without having to keep an eye open for any sign of Maurice de Roche's coat of arms.

Aye, that bloodred three-headed dragon was emblazoned forever upon her mind. She, Murchertach and some twenty O'Toole clansmen had come upon the horrid sight all at once . . . her father lying brutally wounded upon the ground as six Norman knights rode into the trees, their painted shields glistening in the sun.

One of the Normans had glanced back at them, the dark-haired man riding at their lead. He had been too far away for Triona to see his face, but she had heard him laughing, a cruel sound, a cold sound. Even now the memory made her flesh crawl. Aye, she would never forget that day.

"Stand aside! Make way for the king's men!"

Triona was barely able to pull her horse clear before three mailed knights rode past on their spirited steeds, all of them laughing raucously to see people scrambling to move out of their way. But they didn't go far, dismounting in front of some sort of public house, servants rushing out to lead their horses to the stable next door. A brightly painted sign hung out over the street showing a brimming cup of ale and a platter of steaming food, while ill-kempt women loitered near the doors.

"You look to be men who could use some feminine company," taunted one, a big-boned Irishwoman with dark tangled hair. Bending forward so they might better view her ample breasts, she added with a seductive smile, "See anything that pleases you?"

To the woman's delight, one of the knights grabbed her round the waist and half-carried her into the public house.

His companions each likewise chose a willing female before entering, the men's coarse laughter ringing out as they soundly swatted the women's bottoms to make them hurry.

"What are you gaping at, boy?"

Triona swung around, meeting the light blue eyes of a Norman knight across the street who was leaning upon his shield. A glistening black shield with a scarlet three-headed dragon at its heart. Seeing it, she nearly choked.

"N-nothing," she somehow managed, hastily leading her horse away.

"Good idea, boy. Better run home with you. And don't tell your mother what you've been drooling over or she'll cuff your ears!"

As his loud chuckling followed her down the street, Triona felt her blood begin to boil.

Aye, she'd like to cut off *his* ears! Surely that knight had to be one of de Roche's men. He must have been left to stand guard in the street while the baron caroused indoors.

Triona quickly turned into a side alley where she tethered her horse to a post. She had no idea if the gelding would still be there when she returned, but she'd have to take that chance. She imagined leaving him at the stable would require payment, and she had no coin.

"I'll not be gone long," she promised, the gelding nickering to her as she hurried back out onto the crowded street.

She was immediately pleased to see that the knight was no longer alone; two brightly dressed women were vying for his attention. Hoping that they would divert him, at least until she could get inside the public house, Triona hurried toward the doors, her heart beginning to race.

At last she would have her revenge! She had sworn that the Normans responsible for her father's death would feel the sting of her arrows, but the jeweled dagger would do just as nicely. She would just have to get as close to the baron as possible so her aim would be sure. . . .

"Hold there, boy! Where do you think you're going?"

Triona gasped as the blue-eyed knight shoved his way through the women and came barreling toward her, but luckily he was a big man and slow on his feet. She ducked inside the doors.

Immediately she felt as if she'd been blinded, the noisy room so crowded and poorly lit that she stumbled headlong into another knight, the man cursing vehemently as he spun to take a swing at her. She dodged him, too, only to feel someone grab her cloak.

"God's blood, you're a slippery little fish! Get your Irish arse out of here, boy!"

Feeling herself being tugged backward by the same knight who'd rushed inside after her, Triona panicked and snatched the dagger from her belt. The next thing she heard was a sharp intake of breath, then the man bellowed out a curse.

"He's cut my hand, the bugger!"

Suddenly the room resounded with jeers and laughter, one man's rising above the rest. Triona felt her blood run cold as she spun, her gaze falling upon a dark-haired knight seated at a distant table, a plump female on his lap.

"God's teeth, William! If you can't best an Irish stripling, what good are you to King John? Ten shillings to the man who catches the little bastard! He'll know not to raise a weapon to his betters once he's hanging dead from the rafters."

"No . . ." Triona breathed in horror as a half dozen Normans suddenly lunged for her at the same moment someone wrenched her violently backward. As the men fell into each other, crashing to a heap on the floor, she was propelled bodily toward some nearby stairs.

"Go! Now!"

Triona dazedly obeyed the hissed command, scrambling up the wooden steps as she was pushed from behind. She was pushed and shoved down a dark corridor until they came to an open doorway.

"In there!"

Blindly she ducked into the pitch-dark room only to have it suddenly flooded with torchlight from the street below as the shutters were kicked open. Stunned, she gaped at Ronan, but had no more focused on the Norman mailshirt he wore when he wrenched off her cloak and threw it under the bed. Then he grabbed her by the shoulders and ripped downward, tearing away her shirt until it hung in tatters from her waist.

"How . . . how dare—"

"Say nothing if you want to live!" He shoved her down upon the stained mattress, taking only a moment to wrest a smelly blanket over them before he covered her with his body. "By God, Triona, say nothing!"

She couldn't have spoken even if she had wanted to, his mouth crushing hers in a kiss that stopped her breath. He didn't stop kissing her even when heavy footsteps came storming down the hallway, doors opening and then slamming one by one while women's startled screams and male cursing filled the air.

Ronan didn't stop even when their door was kicked open though she started in surprise beneath him, much in part because he'd begun to grind his hips against hers.

"God's blood, the little bugger's gone! Must have jumped out the window there . . . while these two kept right on—"

"Can you blame the man, William? Look at her! Would you come up for air if you had a red-haired wench as fine as that spreading her legs for your pecker?"

Coarse laughter rang out and the door slammed shut, leaving Triona and Ronan alone.

Chapter 17

EXCEPT RONAN DIDN'T stop kissing her, though his hips slowed to a rhythmic thrusting as his tongue plunged deeply into her mouth. And this time it was Triona who moaned as her hips rose to meet Ronan's, craving some answer to the heat suddenly building inside her . . . some answer to the insistent tug deep down where his body was bulging rock hard against hers.

"Woman . . . you're going to be the death of me yet," came his ragged whisper, his warm mouth lifting from hers even as his lower body pressed her deeper into the mattress. Then with a low vehement oath he was gone from her, pulling her so abruptly to her feet that she gasped in surprise, shocked back to reality. He shoved her toward the window.

"We'll have to jump."

"Jump?" She snatched her torn clothing in front of her as she realized almost stupidly that she was naked from the waist up.

"Those idiots might not have seen me helping you up the stairs when they collided into each other, but someone else probably did. I'll wager they'll be back when they realize they've been duped—"

A roar of outrage suddenly carried to them from downstairs, Ronan once more shoving Triona toward the window.

"But we'll break our necks!"

"You'd rather stay here to see them stretched?"

Triona gulped as she looked down at the street. "All right, all right, then, I'll do it!"

"You never had a choice, woman."

Ronan grabbed her beneath the arms and swung her feetfirst through the window, lowering her as far as he could before he let go. Triona had no chance to shriek before she landed hard on her bottom, dazed yet unharmed. Clutching her shredded shirt to her breasts, she scrambled out of the way just as Ronan leapt from the window, landing on his haunches beside her.

"Is there a fire?" blurted a startled passerby.

Ronan ignored the shocked stares all around him and helped Triona to her feet.

"God's blood, man, why else do you think we jumped?" he answered, giving his best imitation of a Norman accent. He was pleased when his announcement sent people screaming in all directions for water, the ensuing confusion providing the perfect cover.

Triona, however, appeared astounded, her eyes very round as Ronan swept her into his arms. "Where did you learn—"

"Later." It took only a quick glance around him for Ronan to realize the "borrowed" steed he had ridden into Kilkenny must have been taken to the stable. There was no time to retrieve the animal. Instead he held Triona close and ran toward the alley that he'd spied her hurrying from earlier, ruefully wishing he'd been close enough then, to grab her. But at least her horse was still tethered where she'd left him.

"But, Ronan, how did you know—"

"I said later, woman!" He lifted her onto the gelding's back and mounted behind her. "Hold on!"

They burst from the alley at a full gallop, veering down an opposite street and away from the bedlam in front of the public house. To Triona it seemed only an instant had passed before they were almost to the town gates. She tensed when she saw that the well-armed guard had more than tripled.

"Jesu, Mary and Joseph, they'll surely stop us!"

"A mailed knight?"

"But you're riding without a saddle, Ronan. They'll know you're Irish!"

"Not if you fight me." He jerked her closer, her bottom wedged between his hard thighs. "Not if you scream. That's what these raping dogs are more than accustomed to hearing from Irish women."

Triona began to struggle but it was difficult since she was also trying to hold onto her clothing.

"Not good enough, Triona. You'll have to do better if we're going to distract them."

She gasped as Ronan suddenly wrenched away the remnants of her shirt and flung the tattered garment into the air. But she screamed in outrage when his hand went for the waist of her trousers, fighting him in earnest as she heard an ominous ripping sound.

"You—you spawn! I'll have no clothes left! No, damn you! No . . . !"

She had never felt so humiliated as they thundered past the guards, all of them gaping at her bobbing breasts. Gaping with eyes full of lust as Ronan groped her, her indignant screams only making the guards laugh uproariously and elbow each other.

But as soon as they were safely past the gates and careening out into the dark night, Ronan wound his arms tightly around her, murmuring in her ear, "Forgive me, Triona."

It was enough to stop the hot tears welling in her eyes, the sincerity of his apology striking her more deeply than she could have imagined possible. And the incredible warmth of his arms kept her from trembling though the night was cool, the air still smelling of rain and wet earth.

They rode silently for long moments, the lights of the town fading behind them. At last it seemed as if the nightmare of Kilkenny was only that, a bad dream, and one which she knew could have been far worse if Ronan hadn't found her. He must have read her thoughts. Again he spoke in her ear, slowing their mount to a trot so she could hear him. "You saw de Roche?"

"Aye." She shuddered, remembering the man's harsh laughter. "At least from a distance. I only wish the place hadn't been so dark so I could have taken a good look at his face."

"And you had hoped to fell him with this dagger?"

Triona was stunned when Ronan pulled the weapon from his belt, the rubies and diamonds sparkling brilliantly in the moonlight. "I thought I'd lost it downstairs in the public house. Where did you—"

"In the bed." He shoved the dagger back into his belt. "I spied it just before I jumped from the window."

She fell silent, her cheeks burning as she remembered all too well what they'd done in that bed. Suddenly she felt that same disconcerting tug deep down below her belly, and she quickly forced herself to focus upon another sensation, the smooth chain mail rubbing against her bare back. But before she could ask where he'd gotten it, Ronan once again seemed to have read her mind.

"A few miles outside of Kilkenny—we're almost to the place now, I came across a drunken knight wandering lost who was only too willing to exchange his life for his horse and armor. He'd come to join his king, or so he said right before he passed out, the old fool."

"You let him live?"

"Aye. I'm not one to kill defenseless men, Triona. And if I hadn't come across him as I did, things would have gone far differently for you tonight. While you somehow stumbled upon de Roche, I was taken for a knight and directed straight to where he was lodging—"

"With that fine Norman accent of yours," Triona cut him off, growing irritated by his lecturing tone. "I'm surprised that you would stoop so low as to imitate your hated enemy."

"It has served me well on more than one occasion, woman, even saved my life." His arms tightened punishingly around her. "And to answer your earlier question, it was Seamus who taught me. He'd spent so many years among Normans that he could speak like one himself. But of course, neither of us can thank him now for what ultimately saved *your* life, can we?"

"For the last time, O'Byrne, I already apologized for what happened to Seamus!" Her face flushed hotly at his fierce embrace. "But if you're expecting me to say I shouldn't have gone into Kilkenny, don't be holding your breath—"

"You will apologize." Ronan drew her so roughly against him that she exhaled in surprise. "Not to me but to my men who are wondering even now if their chieftain is alive or dead. And to Niall because you lied to him. You never intended to stand by and watch while we hung de Roche from a tree, but instead to pursue your own reckless course. No matter how many of my men were placed in jeopardy."

Triona clamped her mouth shut, refusing to say another word. She imagined that Ronan had wanted to berate her the entire journey back to where his men were camped.

And to think she'd allowed herself to be lulled for even a moment by an apology she suspected now had been as false as his Norman accent! No doubt they could have gotten through those damned gates without his rude handling, but he couldn't resist teaching her a lesson she'd never forget!

Suddenly she froze, wondering if he planned to make her ride back half-naked to Glenmalure to complete her humiliation. Aye, he had purposely embarrassed her before! But she had just opened her mouth to accuse him when he sharply veered their mount toward a thick stand of trees.

"I left my horse here," Ronan explained tersely, hearing his stallion whinnying to him as they approached. And a damned good thing he and Triona would soon be riding separately, too!

Tonight she had given his emotions a wild ride he doubted he'd ever forget: from fury over her foolhardiness to relief as acute as any he'd known when they had ridden safely through the town gates. And though his ire was mounting again that she could be so stubbornly unrepentant after her escapade, it paled beside the desire ripping through him.

Desire so damned intense that her every bouncing movement against him was excruciating, his efforts to focus on anything else but on her scantily clad form becoming impossible.

If he had thought that kissing her again had nearly undone him, nothing could have prepared him for the translucent beauty of her bare skin in the moonlight and the provocative swell of her breasts against his arms. Certain that he might explode if he held her a moment longer, he couldn't dismount fast enough when they reached his stallion.

"You can wear my cloak," he said, gathering up the clothing he had left beneath the oak where his horse was tethered. "It's damp but—"

"I'm surprised you're allowing me to wear anything at all," Triona interrupted tartly, dismounting and crossing her arms over her breasts.

She couldn't see his expression in the dark, the canopy of leaves overhead blocking out the moonlight, but she sensed his eyes upon her. Shivering, she considered darting around the gelding to afford herself some extra cover. But before she could move, Ronan was walking back toward her, his silhouette tall and broad and overwhelmingly powerful.

"You truly think I would have done that to you?"

Again she shivered, but this time at the husky anger in his voice as he drew closer. "Aye, just to teach me another one of your crude lessons, you would. You've deliberately humiliated me before, O'Byrne. Why should this time be any different?"

"If you're referring to what I did in Kilkenny, Triona, it wasn't meant to embarrass you. But I thought my apology—"

"Convinced me that you were forced to paw at me like a wild animal? You've forgotten that I know you as a liar, O'Byrne. I don't trust your apologies any more than I've believed any of your fine compliments! Now I'll take that cloak. It's cool out here. . . ."

Triona fell silent as Ronan whirled the heavy garment around her shoulders but instead of letting go, he used it to suddenly draw her against him. "What—what are you doing?"

"I've never wantonly mistreated any woman, Triona." His voice had grown angrier, huskier. "I'll not have you saying that when we return to Glenmalure."

"Al-all right," Triona stammered, the incredible heat of his body scorching her right through the chain mail. "Mayhap I spoke too hastily—"

"Aye, you did," Ronan cut in, knowing that he shouldn't be holding her so closely but unable to help himself. "If there's any lesson to be taught here, it's that I don't *paw* at women," he added pointedly, his hand sliding between them to cover her breast. "I caress them . . . like this. . . ."

Triona inhaled in surprise as he gently stroked her, his warm fingers closing over her roused nipple. Stunned, she thought immediately to pull away—the spawn!—but the sensation was so wonderful that she leaned into his touch in spite of herself.

"Do you call this coarse, Triona? Crude?" came his taunting whisper as his hand slid slowly to her other breast, his circling palm huge and warm and altogether arousing.

"No . . ." she said finally, gasping when he squeezed her. She went mute, her breath snagged, her body beginning to tremble.

"Aye then, woman, what of this?" Ronan demanded, laving her lips with his tongue before plunging into her mouth to savor the sweetness that had haunted him for hours.

He felt her start, but it didn't take long before she melted against him as if surrendering to his kiss. He groaned when her tongue met his and began to tease and cavort, Ronan warning himself through the desire clouding his brain that this little lesson should go no further. But she was so warm and willing, he told himself that he would allow himself just this one kiss, then he would stop.

"Would you say now that my touch offends you, Triona?" he demanded hoarsely against her wet lips, drawing her even closer, his hands sliding down to cup her taut bottom. In answer, she moaned softly into his mouth, a low husky sound, a thrilling sound.

"Can you tell me, then, that you don't believe me when I say your lips are the softest I've ever known?"

"No, I believe you . . ." Triona whispered dazedly as his kiss once more deepened, becoming so possessive that she felt as surely as the other night that he would devour her.

And she found she wanted to be devoured, opening her mouth to him as hungrily as he delved his tongue inside to taste her. Her hands moved with a wildness over his chest, her palms, her fingertips pressing urgently against cold hard metal as that same burst of heat suddenly overwhelmed her, driving her to cling to him as if his very nearness could answer the incredible craving building inside her.

Just one more caress! Ronan warned himself again when her arms flew unexpectedly round his neck to hold him tight. Just once more to feel the silky splendor of her skin, its softness its tantalizing curves and hollows. Then he would stop! By God, he would stop!

Ronan slipped his hands between them and worked fever ishly at her leather belt until it dropped with a thud at their feet. Then he was sliding her torn trousers from her hips, the garment no sooner pooling around her ankles before he lifted her and crushed her lithe body against him. She felt like flame in his arms, her skin so sleek, so hot . . .

Suddenly something snapped inside Ronan, a great shuddering coming from deep within him as he carried her out from beneath the tree and into the moonlight.

He wanted to see her, to see all of her. He pulled the cloak from her shoulders and flung it out over the ground. Her body was creamy white perfection as he knelt and laid her down, the lush triangle at the crown of her thighs and the deep hue of her nipples the only contrast to her fair coloring.

"If I said I've never seen a woman as beautiful as you, would you believe me, Triona?" he demanded hoarsely, bending over her to capture a hard swollen peak in his mouth.

She couldn't answer, her back arching as his tongue swirled round and round her nipple, his hands sweeping over her body as if he wanted to touch every inch of her. But she froze when his strong fingers found the place where she was burning . . . where that same insistent tug had become an ache like nothing she had ever known.

"Ronan!"

Her wild impassioned cry was answered as his powerful body came down upon hers, the smooth links of his mailshirt pressing into her breasts as his fingers slipped deeply inside her and then out again, teasing and circling until she thought he'd go mad. From some distant dizzying place she heard him groan, felt his weight lift from her for only an instant, then his hips settled heavily over hers once more, his knee spreading her legs wide.

But it wasn't his fingers that returned to torment her. She gasped as a hard bulging heat suddenly thrust into her flesh . . . crying out when she felt a blistering pain.

"Oh God, Triona," Ronan said hoarsely, her outburst shattering the haze that gripped him. But he couldn't stop the fierce pounding of his blood, his loins, his heart any more than he could undo the damage already done. Instead he thrust inside her more deeply, commanding in a ragged whisper as she cried out again, "Do what I do, Triona! I promise . . . it will ease the pain."

Desperately she obeyed him, meeting his quickening thrusts with her own as his body seemed to expand to an even greater fullness inside her. And she had no sooner begun to do so than the sharp stinging swiftly receded, becoming no more than a wisp of memory and then, not even that as a sensation far more compelling overwhelmed her.

It was both heat and fire, that mysterious ache growing so powerful she was trembling to her toes. She threw her arms around Ronan's broad back and held on to him, certain if she didn't she would die right then from the sheer intensity of her pleasure.

And when he suddenly tensed, his body growing rigid but for the fierce throbbing at the very core of her, she thrust her hips upward one last time, crying out at the glorious height of her climax.

Crying out Ronan's name until his mouth captured hers . . . her ecstasy echoing all around them.

Chapter 18

BUT RONAN DIDN'T kiss her long. When he lifted his head a moment later, his sated body still buried inside her, the full weight of what he had done hit him more forcefully than any blow.

It must have struck Triona, too, for suddenly she grew very still beneath him, her eyes large dark pools in the moonlight as she stared up at him. It seemed as if she were waiting for him to speak with held breath. But he had no words to express the depths of his sudden self-loathing.

By God, he was her guardian! Sworn to protect her! Instead he had ravaged her, stealing not just an embrace, a kiss, a caress, but the one thing that should have been reserved for her husband. Muttering a low curse, he withdrew from the tight sheath of her body and rolled from her, adjusting his trousers as he rose to his feet.

Triona was stunned, watching him. She felt like bursting into tears. "So your little lesson is over?" she asked bitterly, feeling more crushed than she could have ever imagined. He had left her so quickly. If she had dared to hope for even an instant that what had happened so unexpectedly between them might mean he truly wanted her for himself after all, she knew now that she was wrong.

Triona yanked the cloak around her naked body when Ronan made no reply, flinging at him as he went to collect the horses, "I suppose you'll want me to keep silent about this deed as well! We can't have the next man you bring to Glenmalure thinking that his intended bride is damaged goods!"

"There won't be a next man," Ronan muttered far too low

for Triona to hear, the pain in her voice making him that much more furious with himself.

If she had disliked him before, she must hate him now. He wasn't so deluded to think that she would have given herself to him if he had granted her a choice. Instead he'd forced himself upon her so suddenly that she had had no chance to protest.

"Damn you, O'Byrne, I can't find my trousers!"

Hearing her frustrated tears, Ronan wanted to go to her and crush her in his arms. But certain that would be the last thing she wanted from him, he swiftly found her belt and trousers and took them to her, not surprised when she snatched the clothing out of his hand.

"You blackhearted spawn! Of course you would know right where to find my things since you're the one who stripped them from me!"

He said nothing, returning to the horses. Nor did he say a word when she approached, swathed in his heavy cloak.

She asked him for no assistance as she mounted the gelding and he didn't offer to help her, knowing that he would be refused. Nor did she wait for him as he mounted beside her, but kicked her horse into a gallop.

He had been expecting as much, deciding it was a very good thing he carried her dagger in his belt. He caught up with her on his superior animal and took the lead. If she had the dagger, he knew he might very well have found the blade sticking in his back.

"No wonder she was so quiet when you returned to the camp. The ride home, too. So what are you going to do with her now, brother?"

Ronan stared into the flames, his throat so tight that he could barely swallow his ale.

He had asked himself that same question all the way back to Glenmalure, Triona's sullen silence haunting him every interminable mile. Even when they had arrived at the stronghold, the warm midday sun already high above the mountains, she had refused to say a word to him or anyone else. Instead she had headed straight for her room while Ronan had gone to the hall, a grim-faced Niall striding after him.

"Ronan?"

Exhaling heavily, he met Niall's eyes. "She'll be welcome at the convent in Glendalough. I plan to escort her there in the morning."

"A convent?" Clearly stunned, Niall leaned across the table. "This is madness! First you tried to foist her off on the O'Nolan and now you want to exile her. By God, brother, why won't you just admit that what happened was because you want Triona? At the very least you should be offering to marry her—"

Ronan slammed his fist down so hard that the female servant stoking the fire jumped, dropping the poker with a clatter to the floor.

"Marry the woman, Niall? Against her will? That's the only way I'd ever have her now, and I'd say I've already made her life enough of a hell. At least in Glendalough she'll be safe and still have exactly what she wants, to remain unmarried and . . . to be far away from me."

As the hall fell silent, Niall stared at him with amazement. "What in blazes are you gaping at?" Ronan demanded.

"So you have considered marrying her."

Ronan snorted. "That surprises you? Do you think I'm some kind of a callous lout? It was my first thought after—" He didn't finish, staring into the flames again.

Nothing was said for a long moment until Niall gave a low whistle. "Begorra, brother, there's hope for you yet. I was beginning to believe the day would never come, but that damned guilt of yours is finally loosening its devil's hold. Triona's broken through, hasn't she? You're smitten with her."

Ronan looked up to find Niall grinning from ear to ear as if quite pleased with himself.

"Smitten? I recognize my responsibility if that's what you're implying."

"Oh aye, your responsibility. I suppose we can call it that until you're ready to admit you're as entitled to some happiness as anyone else. So why, then, are you sitting here talking about taking Triona to a convent when what you really think you should do is wed her?"

Again Ronan's fist hit the table, his roar filling the hall.

"Damn you, Niall, didn't you hear me? I already told you she'd never marry me willingly—"

"And reasoning with her hasn't helped you in the past? Or have you forgotten how you persuaded her to come to Glenmalure in the first place? You accomplished that feat easily enough."

Ronan lunged from his chair so suddenly that the poor serving woman stoking the fire whirled in surprise. But Niall didn't appear at all startled, his grin grew all the wider.

"In a hurry, brother?"

Ronan didn't bother to answer, nor did he turn around when Niall shouted across the hall after him, "If I were you, I'd say nothing about any convent. It's just one less choice to give her!"

Ronan didn't need the advice. He'd already decided that he would offer no choice at all.

Triona laid her head against the tub's hard rim, willing herself to relax. But if the steamy bathwater was proving a balm for her aching muscles, it was doing nothing to improve her mood. She felt as tightly strung as a bow. It wasn't helping either that Aud was hovering over her, clucking her tongue indignantly.

"Look at those scratches on your skin! He's a beast is what he is! Saved you from that Baron de Roche only to . . . to—"

"I already told you they're not scratches, Aud." Exhaling heavily, Triona sank farther into the tub. "They're red marks from his damned mailshirt."

"Scratches, red marks, it makes no difference to me, Triona O'Toole! They shouldn't be there!"

"But they are, and there isn't anything I can do to change that except wait for them to fade."

"Aye, and I'm glad that we won't be waiting here! I'm just sorry that it took something like this to make you come to your senses, sweeting. Sorry more than I can say."

"That makes two of us," Triona muttered as Aud went to the clothes chest and pulled out a sleeping gown. Aud had already insisted a half dozen times that Triona should at least try to rest after riding all night, but right now she was no closer to wanting to sleep than being able to relax.

She already knew that Ronan wasn't resting. Aud had just checked and informed her that his room was still empty. No doubt he was at the feasting-hall, downing ale and wondering who among his clan alliances wouldn't mind wedding a tarnished bride. But they'd find no bride waiting at Glenmalure. She and Aud and all of her pets would be leaving this wretched place as soon as Ronan and his men rode out on their next raid.

Triona hoped that blessed opportunity would come tomorrow. She couldn't bear the thought that she and Ronan would be sleeping tonight under the same roof after . . .

She splashed water on her face, but it did little to cool the sudden flaring of her cheeks. Nor did it chase away the heated memories, making her swear once more that there couldn't be a bigger fool anywhere in Eire than her.

How could she have surrendered to Ronan so wantonly? It wasn't as if she cared about him—impossible thought! Knowing what he had done to her brother, how could she? And he certainly didn't care about her.

"Someone's coming, sweeting."

Someone? Triona knew immediately it was Ronan, recognizing those determined footfalls. "My robe, Aud. I don't want to be sitting here like a turtle in this tub!"

She had no sooner risen and wrapped the garment around her, the light wool sticking to her skin since she'd had no chance to dry herself, when Ronan knocked heavily. She nodded, imagining her eyes were as wide as Aud's as her maid went to open the door.

Her heart was hammering, too, breathlessness, panic and fury seizing her all at once. She pressed her hand to her breast to steady herself, lifting her chin.

Yet no amount of steadying could have eased her hurt when Ronan suddenly was facing her. It was almost as if she were reliving how wretched she'd felt when he rolled from her so abruptly, refusing even to speak to her. She had to fight hard to keep tears from blurring her eyes.

"I'd expected you would be coming to tell me your plans for me, O'Byrne, but so soon?"

The bitterness in her voice hit him like a slap. Ronan, however, remained resolute.

Aye, she hated him. That he could tell. But even so, she would still have to listen to reason.

Seeing her now, her damp robe clinging provocatively to her body, her beautiful face the very picture of outrage, he knew that he wanted her. Needed her was more the truth of it, Niall's words haunting him as much as the stirring memory of her passion.

He needed her as desperately as a drowning man grabbing for a branch that could save him, though he knew that would give her no consolation. Yet he hadn't come to console . . .

"We must talk, Triona. Alone."

"Ha! You're mad if you think I've any desire to be alone with you." She gestured for Aud to stay. "There's nothing you could say to me that isn't fit for my maid's ears as well."

"Aye, if my sweeting wants me to stay, I'll not leave her!"

Seeing the anger in Aud's eyes, Ronan knew then that Triona must have confided in the woman. Sighing, he decided not to argue.

"Very well." He met Triona's eyes. "I want you for my wife."

"Your wife, Lord?" Aud exclaimed before Triona could utter a word. But it was just as well so she had an instant to recover herself. Her heart felt lodged in her throat, her breath gone altogether.

He had just said he wanted her, hadn't he? Jesu, Mary and Joseph! Could she have possibly been wrong about last night?

Triona started at the hard nudge in her ribs, realizing Aud had hastened to her side.

"Sweeting, are you just going to stare at the man? The O'Byrne has asked you to marry him! You must answer!"

"Think of the babe that may have been planted in your womb before you say anything, Triona." Ronan's slate gray eyes burned into hers. "We've both a duty now—"

"Duty?" Triona blurted, feeling as if her whirling emotions had suddenly hit the ground with a terrible thud.

"Aye. I've a duty to you as well to take you for my bride.

Last night should never have happened but since it did, we must wed. I'll not turn my back on what is right and neither should you."

Fool, fool, fool! Triona cried to herself, a familiar ache welling inside her. *Duty? Obligation?* She hated those words! That's all she had ever been to him, an unwanted burden, a heavy stone around his neck, an oath given that he wished he'd never sworn.

"You've a very short memory, O'Byrne," she heard herself finally say when Aud nudged her again. "I told you from the first that I don't want a husband."

"Things have changed now, Triona. But if it is your fears about marriage that are clouding your judgment—"

"I never had any fears about marriage!" Her face burning, Triona clutched her robe more tightly around her. "You and Niall, aye, and I suppose Maire as well may have thought so but you were all wrong! If you'd only asked me you would have known sooner that I'll never marry until I meet a man who'll respect me as I am! I'll never give up my freedom for anyone and lastly for you, Ronan O'Byrne! You more than anyone else have tried to make me something I'm not—the dutiful maiden who would be more than content to be the dutiful wife. But I'm not Lady Emer and never will be, so clearly we're not suited!"

"Then rest assured I will take you just as you are," Ronan said as vehemently, so determined to have her that he was willing at that moment to thrust aside his better judgment. "You can do what you like, be as you like. You can even ride with my men and me on our raids if you've a mind to."

"Ride with you?" Her incredulous laugh echoed around the room. "Do you think I'm such a simpleton that I would fall for your lies again?"

"It's not a lie, Triona. As soon as we're wed, you will see that this time I speak the truth."

Incensed that he would so blatantly try to deceive her to satisfy his own damnable sense of duty, Triona was tempted to tell him exactly what she thought of his promise. But suddenly another idea struck her, an idea that almost made her smile in spite of her fury.

Why not deceive him as well? She had long wanted to teach him a lesson and now he deserved one more than ever.

If she could win herself some time by leading him to believe there was a way she might wed him—even though nothing could be further from the truth!—just think what she could do to frustrate him before she left Glenmalure altogether.

"Mayhap I'd be more inclined to consider your marriage offer, O'Byrne, if you were willing to first prove to me your good intentions," she challenged him. "But since I can't imagine that you would ever agree to such an arrangement—"

"Agreed."

She was stunned by how readily he had answered, her heart beating faster at the determined look on his handsome face. For a man who was offering to marry her solely out of obligation, he seemed bent upon . . .

Triona followed his gaze, horrified to see that her hardened nipples were plainly visible beneath her sodden robe. Suddenly realizing what he must be thinking, she flushed from head to toe.

So lust was driving him, the spawn! Obviously since he'd taken advantage of her once, why should he bother now to control his baser instincts? She met his eyes, growing even more flustered when she saw the heat smoldering in those flint gray depths.

"You—you understand, of course, that just because we've already . . . well, it doesn't mean that—"

"I won't force myself on you again, if that's what concerns you," Ronan said tightly, regretting the concession immediately.

Yet he wouldn't wait forever. A few weeks should be more than enough time to convince her that he'd meant what he said about taking her just as she was—sheer madness though it may be.

"Get some rest, Triona. We'll be planning our next raids in the morning. With so many Normans flocking to join King John, there should be manors aplenty left poorly guarded and ripe for plundering. De Roche's castle in Kildare could even become a target—"

"De Roche?"

"Aye. He may have escaped our vengeance until King John sails back to England, but at least we can ravage the bastard's home—*if* enough of his men leave for Dublin and make the risk a small one."

Triona was so astonished that Ronan was already including her in his plans, she said nothing more as he left the room. It was Aud who finally broke the stillness.

"So we're staying, sweeting?"

Triona shot her a frown, hearing little disappointment in Aud's voice. "For a time. But don't fire your hopes just because Ronan mentioned marriage. He's still a beast, just as you said. Nothing has changed."

Except that now she would finally be able to repay him for all the torment he'd caused her.

"You'd turn your back on him even if there's a babe?"

Triona hesitated, feeling a pain in her heart. But she had only to remember the hated word *duty* upon Ronan's lips, and she squared her shoulders. "Aye, Aud, even that couldn't make me marry him."

Chapter 19

A BRILLIANT SUNNY morning greeted Triona as she left the dwelling-house. Conn trotted at her side, and the stronghold was already alive with the sounds of children laughing and playing, dogs barking, and people going about their work.

"Go, Conn." She gestured to the dogs chasing each other near the kitchen. "Go and play, too."

As the wolfhound bounded away, Triona flung her arms over her head and stretched. She had slept much later than she had planned. Surprising considering she hadn't expected to sleep at all after Ronan had left her. But exhaustion had overcome her.

She felt fine now, though. Well rested, well fed, a hasty breakfast of oat bread and honey warming her stomach. And she was more than eager to exercise her newly regained freedom. She had even gone to Ronan's room to enjoy the reaction her leather jerkin, shirt and trousers might have upon him, but he wasn't there.

Nor had his monstrous bed looked slept in, making her wonder if he had stayed up all night drowning his misery in ale. No doubt since he had asked her to wed him, that stone around his neck had grown all the heavier.

"I hope it chokes him," she muttered, making her way to the feasting-hall where she imagined Ronan and his men were gathered. Aye, if he thought her a burden now, just wait . . .

"Triona!"

She tensed as Niall left the hall and made straight for her. She suspected he might be angry with her over the other day, but he was smiling broadly. In fact, his eyes were fairly dancing.

"You look well this morning, Triona."

"And you look very pleased about something, Niall O'Byrne."

"Can't I look pleased to greet the woman my brother has asked to wed?"

Triona didn't know why she felt so stunned. Of course Ronan would have told Niall. Probably Maire, too. Yet it made her feel more than a bit embarrassed.

"Ronan asked me, but that doesn't mean I've accepted," she said stiffly, deciding she'd say no more on the unpleasant topic. She brushed past Niall, but he caught up with her and fell in step.

"That's true, indeed, Triona, but at least you finally have your wish. I heard that you might be riding with us."

"Might?" Triona shot him a sharp glance. "I fully intend to. Is that brother of yours in the hall?"

"Aye, with our clansmen. He asked me to come and fetch you. He thought you might want to hear our plans."

"So I do, but I'm amazed Ronan can consider strategy at all after drinking through the night."

"Drinking? What makes you think he—"

"His bed wasn't slept in, Niall. Not even touched. Where else could he have . . . ?" Suddenly she stopped cold in her tracks, a fierce pang ripping through her. Niall had the most curious smile on his face.

"There's no other woman if that's what you're thinking, Triona. Ronan's moved into another dwelling-house. He thought you might prefer that for now—given everything that's happened."

Her cheeks flaring hotly, she couldn't answer; she stormed instead for the hall.

Of course she didn't care in the least if Ronan had another woman . . . ten woman! Twenty women! It would be a good thing if he did. He might have said he wouldn't force himself upon her, but that didn't mean she believed him. She'd seen that hungry look in his eyes—

"Triona, wait!"

She paused at the doors as Niall again caught up with her. He wasn't smiling anymore, his expression very serious.

"I just want to warn you that not everyone is pleased you'll be riding with us. Ronan has always allowed his men their fair say in clan matters, and this time is no exception. Many of them are arguing that raiding is no fit calling for a woman, but home and hearth—"

"You think this is something new to me, Niall? I may have been Fineen O'Toole's daughter, but I had to prove myself first to his clansmen to ride with them. Hunt with them. Why should things be any different here?"

She turned around and shoved through the doors, not surprised when the boisterous din of laughter and conversation abruptly ceased. Her eyes swept the large room. She spied Ronan almost at once near the fire, his dark riding clothes and his black hair impossible to miss. And though her heart had begun to beat faster, she squelched the tingling of excitement just at seeing him again.

Boldly Triona proceeded to the front of the hall, ignoring openmouthed stares and grumbled asides as she reveled in the freedom of movement her trousers gave her. If there had been a crucifix handy she would have sworn before them all that she'd never wear another gown, not if she had anything to say about it!

She saw that Ronan was frowning, too; she supposed he had guessed her thoughts and it made her smile. Her smugness seemed to irritate him. But when he spoke, his voice was calm. Almost too calm.

"I'm pleased that you've decided to join us, Triona. But I regret to say that my view is not shared by everyone."

"Aye, Lord, it's not a woman's place to be adding her voice to our plans!"

Triona spun, facing a carrot-haired giant who'd hauled himself from his seat to challenge her. "I'm sorry. We haven't had the pleasure of meeting . . ."

"Flann O'Faelin, miss, and it's no insult I'm giving you to say you're not welcome among us."

"Then take it as no insult, Flann, when I remind you that there are women warriors aplenty in the ancient tales—"

"Aye, but you don't look to me like a warrior, a wee thing like you," added another brawny clansman who thunked down his cup of ale as he arose. "A woman as fair as you would only be a distraction."

Triona snorted. "You might serve the O'Byrne better to stay at home, then, if you're so easily bewildered."

Robust laughter erupted around the hall. Triona saw that Ronan's frown was as deep as ever.

"Mayhap you O'Byrnes might do better if you told me why you really don't want me to join you," she continued, undaunted though every eye was upon her. "You've said it's not a woman's place, that I'm too small, I might distract you—"

"All that, and we'd be worrying for you every step as if you were a wife or a daughter!" interjected a stout, full-bearded clansman. Many others seconded his outburst with resounding "Ayes!"

Triona, however, wasn't perturbed by the noise. "Well, it's flattered I am that you'd be concerned for me, but I've already proved I can ride as long and as well as any of you." Feeling her face growing warm, Triona quickly decided not to elaborate. "And I'm fully capable of taking care of myself—"

"Like you did in Kilkenny?"

She whirled to face Ronan, his eyes burning like quicksilver into hers.

"I thought you agreed that I have a right to be here!" She was furious, though not surprised, that his true colors had won out after all.

"I did, Triona. But if a serious error in judgment was made, I think it would be wise that you admit it now. It could help."

Aware that the hall had grown very quiet, Triona decided at least this once she would trust Ronan at his word.

"Aye, then, I'll admit that I might have been reckless in going on to Kilkenny," she announced, "but only because I wasn't better armed. Things would have gone far differently if I'd had my bowcase with me instead of a small dagger. I could have avoided putting myself in danger, and stayed at a safe distance. My father's death would have been avenged rather than us having to content ourselves now with raiding de Roche's castle—"

"*Us* she says!" Flann O'Faelin broke in, his voice thundering around the hall. "As if she truly thinks she'll soon be riding with the Glenmalure O'Byrnes! As if we're to believe this wee bit of bluster can wield a bow just as she claims!"

Triona's face burned as guffaws rang out all around her.

"Triona."

She barely heard Ronan's voice over the boisterous laughter, but she felt the gentle nudge at her back. Her eyes widened in amazement as he held out her bowcase. Struck by the warmth in his gaze, she almost smiled at him, but she caught herself just in time.

Aye, he was clever, she thought angrily, realizing how skillfully he had engineered this entire confrontation.

"Flann O'Faelin, I seem to have found my bowcase."

"Indeed, miss." The big Irishman propped his fists at his waist, a look of pure condescension on his face. "I don't suppose there's a chance you've even the know-how to string the bow?"

Triona had to fight the overwhelming urge to send a missile streaking right past his huge bumpy nose, opting instead to have a little fun. "Oh, my father showed me a time or two."

"Aye, the O'Toole was a renowned bowman to be sure, but that doesn't mean—"

"Is this right, Flann?" Purposely, Triona came very close to stringing the bow only to let it clatter to the floor as she pretended that she'd tweaked her finger. "Begorra, the damned thing!" Sighing with frustration, she picked up the bow as if to try again, but the Irishman rushed forward and took it from her hand.

"Now, now, miss, it's easier than it seems. See?" In an instant, the bow was strung and handed back to her.

"You're right, Flann, that did look easy. And it's such a pretty thing, too," she said, turning the bow back and forth as she admired it. "The wood looks so smooth and shiny."

"She called it pretty!" a clansman shouted scornfully, his guffaws joining those of his neighbors. "A damned bow!"

"Deadly, too, I would imagine," she added, glancing behind her to find Ronan watching her intently, the barest hint of a smile on his face. Feeling a shiver, she quickly looked away.

"That is, deadly if I could only learn to shoot straight." She set an arrow to the string so suddenly that Flann gaped at her in surprise. "Is this how I aim?"

She pointed directly down the center of the hall, twenty startled clansmen diving for cover as the arrow zinged over their heads to embed harmlessly in the opposite wall.

"Begorra, now, that wasn't very good, was it? I'll try again. Mayhap I can hit something more interesting this time."

The arrow had no sooner touched the string than it flew right past the brawny clansman who'd claimed she might distract him, the poor fellow dousing himself with ale as he lunged beneath a table.

Triona sighed, shaking her head. "Only a chair that time." Expertly stringing the bow once more, she smiled at Flann, his face fast becoming as red as his hair. "Do you see that wooden cup in Niall's hand?"

Flann looked to where Niall was standing near the back of the hall, nodding as he glanced back at Triona.

"Niall O'Byrne, might you finish your drink so you can throw your cup into the air for me?"

"My pleasure, Triona." He obligingly downed the contents, then saluted her with the empty cup just before tossing it high over his head. There was a whizzing sound followed by a thunk, Niall grinning broadly as he swept up the skewered cup. "Aye, I'm glad you warned me first. It would have been a waste of good ale."

Smiling back at him, Triona still wasn't satisfied. "Mayhap one more shot, wouldn't you say?" she asked Flann, who had sunk onto a bench.

Just to show him that she could do it, she deftly restrung the bow, another fletched missile zinging across the room before the poor man could even nod. She wasn't surprised at the astonished shouts, clansmen rushing to see where this last arrow had shattered the one already embedded in the wall.

"Aye, Flann, my dear father showed me a time or two."

"So it seems," the big Irishman agreed, shaking his head as he began to chuckle. He pointed to the clansmen emerging from beneath tables and benches and his shoulders began to quake, a great bellow of laughter rending the air. As others joined him, Triona glanced at Ronan only to feel her heart seem to stop.

He was smiling, too, perhaps not as devil-may-care as she remembered from all those years ago, but smiling just the same. And in his eyes was something so unsettling she forced herself to look away, focusing instead on the crowd gathered around the rear wall. But she barely saw the clansmen, she was so stunned by the admiration she'd glimpsed in Ronan's gaze.

Had she truly impressed him? Yet she just as quickly dismissed the thought, telling herself it hardly mattered. Anything Ronan said or did was only part of his plan to deceive her, and she'd do well not to forget it. She started when his voice sounded above the din, his tone so commanding that she didn't need to look at him to know that he was no longer smiling.

"Enough, men, we've raids to plan. That is unless any among you still hold reservations about Triona O'Toole riding with us?"

She waited, holding her breath, but there were none.

Chapter 20

TRIONA LOOKED OUT over the silent manor, Ronan crouching so close to her in the dark that she could feel the warmth of his body through her clothes. Flushing, she shifted a few inches away from him.

Jesu, Mary and Joseph, was he going to hover around her all night? Just because this was her first raid didn't mean she needed a personal escort. And why were they just waiting around? They'd been atop this hill for what seemed an eternity, waiting . . . waiting . . .

"Are you always so cautious?" she hissed, glancing from Ronan to the double row of neat cottages and the huge manor house that was surrounded by a timber palisade. "Surely everyone must be asleep by now and the guards are so few—"

"Quiet, Triona."

She glared at him, his tone silencing her more than his command. Stern, severe, aye, just like the tyrant she knew him to be. Yet in the next instant he leaned over to her, his hard thigh brushing her leg.

"Aye, I'm cautious, when my men's lives are at stake," he said in a very low voice that didn't sound half so stern. "Your life, too."

Triona swallowed. His eyes were glittering silver in the moonlight. Annoyed by the flush creeping once again over her face, she whispered back, "Don't be worrying about me! I'm not Lady Emer, remember? I can take care—"

"I know, I know. You can take care of yourself." Her indignation did little to ease Ronan's mind.

His clansmen might have claimed to be worried for her safety yesterday morning, but none could know the depth of his concern. Even assigning Flann O'Faelin and his second cousin, Sean O'Byrne, to watch out for her under the guise of showing her how things were done had given him no peace.

At least Triona was good with the bow, Ronan tried to assure himself, staring at her exquisite profile. By God, she was good with the bow. He hadn't been pleased when so many of his men had spoken against her, but she'd quickly proved herself. He needn't have worried his plan to win her might be thwarted.

"Ronan, the men have taken up their positions," came Niall's whisper behind him. "They await your signal."

Ronan gave a nod, his thoughts snapping back to the danger at hand. "Triona, stay close to Sean and Flann. Keep your eye on them. Do what they do. Remember. We've only a few moments to accomplish our aims. Arklow Castle is no more than a mile from here. If word somehow gets to them that the manor is under attack, help would come quickly. We ride in, take what we want, then ride out. Do you understand?"

A tart comment flew to Triona's lips that of course, she understood, she wasn't an idiot, but she merely stuck out her chin. Ronan was in command, after all. She did respect order. If she had been a new male member of these O'Byrne rebels, she imagined she would have heard much the same lecture.

And now was certainly not the time to thwart him. As Ronan had said, lives were at stake, hers as well. Any slip could mean death. But there would be no slip, at least not on her part.

She watched in silence as Ronan gave a sharp signal to the clansmen who'd already crept down the hill to the palisade. As they began to hoist each other up and scale the timber walls, she, Ronan and the rest of his men moved stealthily back to the trees and remounted their horses, the animals so well-trained that they'd made scarcely a nicker.

There they waited, the night silent around them but for the wind whooshing through the branches, thin clouds moving swiftly across the starry sky.

But they didn't have to wait long. Triona's eyes widened as the palisade gates suddenly swung open, the manor's guards clearly having been subdued. She didn't have even a moment to wonder about their fate as Ronan raised his arm and kicked his horse into a gallop, the rest of the O'Byrnes following him as they swooped like a dark thundering wave down the hill.

The commotion was immediate. They careened through the gates, Irish tenants rushing screaming out of their small wattle cottages only to fall silent and huddle together after one look at the legendary Black O'Byrne and his men. Ronan had told her that the common folk who worked the land for their Norman overlords rarely took up arms against Irish rebels. With Flann O'Faelin and Sean O'Byrne flanking her, Triona rode hard for the manor house, Ronan and a phalanx of his men already crashing through the doors.

She dismounted and rushed inside, her bow drawn, an arrow set to the string, only to be greeted by a scene of controlled chaos. As house guards were overcome by clansmen, other O'Byrnes were rounding up terrified servants and herding them like sheep into the hall. Still other clansmen searched for the family of the house, Ronan among them, the crying women and children in their fine white sleeping gowns being driven into the hall at sword point. An old couple was among them, too. Triona felt a tug of pity for their bleary-eyed confusion.

As the Normans were commanded to drop to their knees, the women weeping loudly as they clutched their children to their breasts, it became clear that the men of the house must have gone to fight with King John just as Ronan had suspected. Only a handful of house guards had been left to protect the family, and they had proved as helpless as the rest.

Helpless, that is, except for one foolish man who somehow wrested a knife from his O'Byrne captor. Another clansman skewered him in the stomach with his sword, the Norman crumpling to the floor, his lifeblood a scarlet pool around him. At once the women began to scream and wail, their fear like a cloying smell in the richly appointed room.

"Silence!"

Triona jumped. Ronan's harsh command seemed to shake the very rafters. At once the crying became frightened whimpers, all eyes upon the tall, black-garbed, black-maned Irishman who stood at the center of the hall.

"Who is the lady of the house?"

Ronan's demand was greeted by a sharp intake of breath, an older dark-haired woman rising shakily to her feet. But she fell to her knees when Ronan strode toward her, tears choking her voice.

"Please, sir, please do not molest us. It is only my dear parents here, my three daughters . . . and—and their children—"

"We do not rape women or kill children." Ronan's voice did not lose its cold edge. "*Unlike* your accursed kind, woman. Now where are your jewels?"

"In—in the coffer"—the Norman lady pointed with trembling fingers to a doorway leading from the hall. "My bedchamber—"

"Show me."

As the woman rose and hastened to obey, Ronan striding after her, the three daughters began to cry noisily until he shot them an ominous look. At once they fell silent, their drawn faces grown nearly as white as their sleeping gowns. Before Ronan left the hall, he commanded his men, "Take what valuables you want, but do it quickly."

Immediately O'Byrne clansmen went scrambling about the hall and into adjoining rooms, stuffing silver candlesticks, plates and other fine things into cloth bags, while some remained behind to guard the prisoners. Triona, too, held her ground, her bowstring kept taut, while Sean and Flann had their swords at the ready beside her. She glanced at the Norman lying facedown, swallowed hard and then looked away, straight into the stricken face of a young boy whose wide brown eyes were full of tears.

"Jesu, Mary and Joseph," she breathed to herself, feeling another strong wave of pity. A terrible business, raiding. Terrible. It would be one thing if they'd come upon armed knights spoiling for a fight, but innocent women and children?

"You'll grow used to those tears, miss," Flann murmured, the huge Irishman clearly sensing her thoughts. "Just remember one day that Norman whelp will wear armor and fight against us, rape our women, rape our land. Unless we can drive the spawn back across the water, saints help us."

Triona said nothing, looking away from the boy. Instead she focused upon the door where Ronan had disappeared, wondering what was keeping him so long. Struck by concern more acute than she could have imagined, she glanced at Flann. "Mayhap we should go after Ronan . . ."

The clansman's nod made her look back at the door, relief flooding her as Ronan strode into the hall, the pale lady of the house rushing ahead of him to embrace her sobbing daughters. But Triona's relief became alarm when a Norman guard suddenly appeared upon the balcony and aimed his crossbow right at Ronan.

"Ronan, duck!"

Triona released her bowstring at the same moment Ronan fell to his haunches, the Norman's arrow skimming over his head to embed with a sickening thunk in the wood floor. The Norman wasn't so fortunate. A terrible gurgling noise came from the man as he clutched at the arrow sticking from his throat. An instant later, he slumped dead over the railing as the women below began to scream at the blood dripping down upon them.

"Out of here! All of you!" Ronan roared to his clansmen, his eyes burning into Triona's as he straightened. "If that guard escaped our notice, then others could have gone to alert the castle! Move!"

Triona wanted to run, but her feet were stuck to the floor as if in warm pitch. She stared at the Norman, at his thick fingers twitching even in death. She had never before killed a man. Deer, wolves, waterfowl, but no, never a man . . .

She scarcely blinked when Ronan jammed her bow back into its leather case and then swept her into his arms, running with her from the hall. Only when she was hoisted with a jolt onto Ronan's stallion, Ronan mounting behind her, did she rouse enough to murmur, "Where's Laeg?"

"Flann has him."

No more was said as Ronan wrapped his arms around her and kicked his horse into a hard gallop. The air was filled with the wild thundering of hooves as threescore O'Byrne clansmen burst through the gates, the night wind whistling around them.

They rode and they rode, for how long Triona couldn't say. But at last Ronan drew his heaving stallion to a stop, waving his men to continue on without them. Triona reasoned they must be at a safe distance from the manor or else Ronan would never have done such a thing. It was her last thought before she began to retch, Ronan dismounting and dragging her from his horse's back so she could vomit upon the ground.

When she was finished, she felt weak. She just sat there, doubled over, her forehead on her knees. Until she felt Ronan gently lift her to stand beside him, his arm supporting her around the waist.

"Can you walk, Triona? There's a stream . . ."

She nodded, setting one foot shakily in front of the other as he led her to the water. Then he helped her once more to sit, leaving her for only an instant to soak one end of his cloak before returning to her side.

"Here. This will help."

Triona felt him lift her chin, the wet cloth cool upon her skin as he wiped her forehead, her face, her mouth. Gradually, she began to feel better, except for the pain in her abdomen from retching.

She began to grow embarrassed, too; aye, and angry for reacting as she had . . . more like a Lady Emer than the strong, clearheaded woman she had always prided herself to be. She pushed away from Ronan, imagining he must be gloating. She had fallen apart at that manor, no more able to take care of herself than a mewling kitten.

"There's no shame in what happened tonight, Triona. Many have suffered so after killing a man . . . some more than others."

Astonished that Ronan could have read her thoughts, Triona was struck, too, by the heaviness in his voice. But instead of being soothed by his words, she bristled.

"I suppose now you'll suggest that I shouldn't raid with you anymore since I can't hold my own—"

"No, I was going to thank you for saving my life."

Struck dumb, Triona could only stare at him, his handsome face half-cloaked in shadow, the moonlight glistening off his midnight hair.

"If you hadn't reacted so quickly, I would have been dead. You've instincts that any man would envy, aye, and an aim as true as I've seen."

Triona couldn't believe her ears. Ronan had complimented her . . . not on her appearance, her eyes, her legs, but on her skill! Her instincts! She was so stunned, she didn't know what to say. She—

She was being a blessed fool, is what she was being! Triona scolded herself, suddenly understanding exactly what he was doing when Ronan reached out to touch her hair. How could she have so easily forgotten that she couldn't believe anything he said or did? He was only telling her what he knew she wanted to hear, to trick her, to deceive her. As soon as his warm fingers grazed her cheek she was on her feet and backing away from him.

"I—I'm pleased that I could help, but I would have done the same for any O'Byrne. That Norman just happened to be aiming at you." She turned and pulled herself onto Ronan's horse. "We should catch up with the others. I'm fine now."

She heard Ronan's sigh in the darkness as he got up and walked toward her; she held her breath as he mounted behind her and thrust his arms through hers to take the reins. But he said nothing more, their ride a silent one all the way back to Glenmalure.

Chapter 21

RONAN'S WEARINESS WAS great, but it was nothing compared to his frustration. He rolled onto his side and stuffed his pillow beneath his head.

Four damned weeks! Almost an entire month now he had waited for some sign that Triona might be growing more inclined to wed him, certainly twice as long as he had ever intended. But he would swear she was no closer to accepting his offer of marriage than he was to regaining his own bed. By God, and it didn't help that this was the lumpiest mattress he had ever slept upon!

Ronan thrust himself onto his other side, this time jamming the down pillow against the headboard with such force that tiny white feathers burst from one corner. But he barely noticed them drifting around him, his frustration become like a raging fever.

Aye, even calling for three times as many raids had done him little good!

He had told his men that it was because they might never have a chance at such rich pickings again once King John quashed the rebellion among his subjects and left Eire. Even now the Norman army was still waging battle far to the north while to the south lay countless manors so poorly guarded they were like chickens waiting for the slaughter.

Yet behind that sound explanation lay the fact that he'd wanted to prove to Triona that he meant to stand by his word. And what better way than to raid so often that there had been barely time between to catch a few hours' sleep before they were up and riding again.

Or so he had thought. But obviously it hadn't worked for here he was, still sleeping alone while the woman he wanted no doubt hated him as much as before.

Ronan lunged from the bed, cursing his foolishness.

Damn her, he should have forced her to marry him. He would have forced her to marry the O'Nolan if the chieftain had wanted her. So why, then, hadn't he spared himself this torment?

Ronan thrust his legs into a pair of trousers, giving up for the moment any notion of sleeping. Instead he went outside.

The night was warm. A light breeze ruffled through his hair. He doubted a walk would help, but it was worth a try. He turned and headed away from the dwelling-house where Triona was sleeping—his own damned house!—deciding it was best not to go too near. It was dangerous, given his mood.

"Lord?"

"Aye." Ronan said no more to the guard who'd approached him, pleased to see that his men were being vigilant about their duty.

He walked on, nodding to the clansmen standing at their posts, their numbers doubled of late. It was unlikely that any Normans would dare stray into Glenmalure, the cowards preferring to fight their battles on the open plains. But he and his men—and Triona, had stolen some MacMurrough cattle a week past, and though Ronan was certain much of that traitorous clan had ridden north to join King John, it never hurt to be cautious.

"Brazen wench," he muttered, remembering how fearlessly Triona had plunged Laeg into that herd even as arrows had been flying all around her. Mayhap recklessly was a better word, his gut cramping at the memory.

His concern had hardly lessened over these past weeks, in fact, it had grown worse. Yet time after time, Triona had proven that she could look out for herself as well as his men. He had only to think of how narrowly he had escaped death thanks to her quick instincts to know she had earned her place among them.

Aye, he could not deny it. Triona O'Toole was a wonder, as courageous and adventuresome as any man. Yet he couldn't allow her to go on raiding forever. One day there might be children who would need their mother with them. Maybe there was even a babe now. *His* babe . . .

Ronan's low oath rent the night silence, his frustration hitting him again with violent force. Deciding that Triona was as much a woman who could drive a man to drunkenness, he turned around and strode for the hall. But he hadn't gone far when a stirring sound carried to him, lilting and yet huskily soft. He realized it was coming from the stable, dim light shining beneath the doors.

"The woman should be abed," he bit out, though his heart had begun to pound. Wondering what Triona might be up to at this late hour, he drew closer then stopped altogether, listening just outside the doors to the bewitching sound of her singing.

Aud hadn't exaggerated. Triona had the most beautiful voice he'd ever heard. As her song of ancient heroes spun out into the night, he felt his throat tighten.

Conor's little sister.

How could he have known this bold hellion would give him hope where only gnawing emptiness had been before? That she could make him feel as if there were a chance the terrible weight he'd carried for so long could be lifted?

Aye, he could still force her to marry him. But what would she think of him then? By God, he didn't want her hate! He wanted her—

"Is there anything wrong, Lord?"

Ronan swung to face the guard who had come up behind him. "No, nothing. I was listening . . ." He didn't finish, realizing Triona's singing had stopped. She must have heard their voices. His voice. Pained, he waved the guard away as he shoved open one of the stable doors.

The interior was full of shadows and warmer than outside, the still air smelling pungently of hay and horses. His gaze immediately went to Laeg, the magnificent animal swinging his great sculpted head to look at him. But Ronan didn't see Triona, and he guessed she must be hiding. That pained him, too.

He slowly approached Laeg's stall, searching the shadows, his senses alert for any clues that might give her away. He even stopped twice just to listen. But still he saw nothing, heard nothing. It wasn't until he was almost to the stall that he caught a flash of movement, lunging just in time to grab the back of her shirt as she darted from behind a stack of hay.

"Let me go! Damn you, let me go!" Triona demanded, flailing her arms wildly and on purpose as she tried to free herself. She felt her fist connect with Ronan's ribs, his sharp intake making her swing at him all the harder. "I'll tell the O'Byrne, I will! I've a right to be here if I want—"

She gasped as she was suddenly spun around to face him, his hand sweeping the tousled hair out of her eyes. "It's me, woman! Ronan!"

"What?" She blinked. "I—I thought you were one of the guards come to make me leave the stable." She dropped her gaze to where Ronan was rubbing his side. "Begorra, I hope I didn't hurt you," she said, feigning dismay.

"Would it have made any difference if you had?"

Triona didn't answer, disconcerted by the searching look in his eyes as well as the steely pressure of his arm locked around her waist. He was bare-chested, too, a heart-stopping sight she'd only seen a time or two, which didn't help matters.

Jesu, Mary and Joseph! Here she had managed since that first raid to avoid getting too close to him . . . to avoid being left alone with him only to find herself once more in his damnable embrace. Grateful when he released her, she immediately went to Laeg's stall, putting a good safe distance between them.

"If you were worried about the guards finding you then you shouldn't have been singing."

Triona shrugged as she picked up a brush and set once more to grooming Laeg's back. "It wasn't that loud."

"Mayhap not but it carried all the same. And fair singing it was, too. The prettiest I've ever heard."

Triona's hand fell still for a moment. An unexpected compliment. She flushed to her toes, wishing in spite of herself that he might have meant it.

"You're up late tonight," she said stiffly. "I would have thought you'd gone to bed hours ago."

"I could say the same for you, Triona."

Bristling, she glanced over at him. He'd come no closer, but now he was leaning against a timber support post, his arms folded over his chest swelling all too noticeably with hard muscle. He looked to her annoyance as if he fully intended to stay.

"You gave me the right to do as I wish, did you not?"

"Aye, four weeks ago."

Though his expression had hardly changed, Triona felt her cheeks begin to burn. "Has it been that long?" she said lightly, hoping to cover her sudden nervousness. "We've been so busy raiding that it's been hard to keep track of the days—"

"I haven't lost track."

This statement was more vehement than his last. Triona braced herself for the worst. Now it seemed the freedom she had been flaunting in front of him had forced his true colors after all.

"You must know by now if you're with child."

The brush fell still again as she stared at Ronan, but not because she was surprised by his words. It was the way he'd said them. His voice had softened, almost as if he were hoping . . .

"I'm not," she said bluntly, angry with herself for even thinking that he might have wanted there to be a babe between them.

"You're sure?"

"Of course I'm sure! My proof came two weeks' past—" She didn't elaborate, blushing.

"You could have told me sooner, Triona."

Incredibly, the man sounded wounded that she'd failed to share with him what to her had been a relief—which made little sense. She had actually avoided saying anything to postpone a disagreeable confrontation for as long as possible, but there seemed no way to dodge it now.

"Aye, I'll admit I should have said something, but it's not as if we've ever had much chance to talk with all the raiding . . ." She didn't go on, deciding she'd explained herself enough as she resumed grooming her horse.

Ronan, however, was stunned.

By God, had he heard correctly? Was she trying to tell him that she might have liked to spend time with him rather than raiding so much? If that was true, maybe these past weeks had helped to soften her hatred after all. Even a little would be a start.

"Have you decided where we're riding next?" Triona asked.

"We'll be staying in Glenmalure for a few days. My men need time with their families."

"Aye, poor Flann's been complaining that his wife will soon forget his name if he doesn't get a few nights at home with her."

As she smiled to herself, Ronan envied that one of his men had conjured what he had done so rarely. But more and more, he was taking heart. "So you don't object?" he said softly.

"Why should I?" Deciding that Ronan was looking at her very strangely, Triona did her best to keep focused upon her task. "Everyone could well use the rest. And mayhap when we're ready to ride again, we could head for Kildare. Surely we can think of a way to rout the men who stayed behind to protect de Roche's castle."

"Mayhap, Triona. We'll talk of it tomorrow."

She was astonished that Ronan was willing to discuss something that he had determined weeks ago to be far too risky. Yet nothing could have surprised her more than what he suggested next.

"Mayhap you might enjoy some hunting later in the morning? Wild boar? You could join me if you like."

"I'd rather not," she began, not wanting to go anywhere alone with him. But before she could utter another word, she was taunted by his sudden challenge.

"Don't tell me you're afraid I could do better than you."

"Better? You don't even wield a bow, O'Byrne. How could you ever hope to best me?"

His expression momentarily darkened, but then he shrugged. "Join me and find out."

He was gone from the stable before she could answer, leaving Triona to wonder what the devil he might be up to now.

Chapter 22

"HOW MUCH LONGER will you play this spiteful game, sweeting? To my mind, we should have left weeks ago if you've no intention of marrying the O'Byrne."

"It's not a game, Aud," Triona said tersely, fastening her leather belt around her waist. She glanced over her shoulder to where her maid was plumping a pillow with extra vigor this morning. "And I don't see what I've been doing as spiteful. I'm teaching Ronan a lesson, is all."

"And why, might I ask? Because the man chose to do the honorable thing in saying he'd wed you?"

"No, because he damn well deserves it!" Triona rounded upon the older woman, exasperated. "He deserves it for lying to me!"

"But I've seen no evidence that he's lying about letting you do as you like—"

"How could you when you've been defending him since the word marriage first tumbled from his mouth? It's blinded you, Aud. I remember when you told me you'd never defend him again after he lied to me that first time. For days you had nothing good to say about him—even calling him a beast!"

Aud sighed, but she didn't look at all daunted. "Aye, that name would have justly suited him if he'd come to say he still planned to force some man upon you. Or if he'd forced you to wed him. But there's been no forcing of any kind, sweeting. None at all. I have to tell you I've been wondering if you might have even exaggerated about that night—"

"I never said he forced me," Triona cut in, her face growing uncomfortably warm.

"No, that's true. Just that he took advantage of you."

"Which he did! One moment he was gathering up some clothes for me to wear, then the next he was . . ." She blushed in earnest now, the warmth spreading like wildfire throughout her body. "It all happened so fast . . . too fast. There wasn't anything I could do."

"Aye, I suppose not."

Triona stared incredulously at Aud, not liking at all her dry tone.

"There wasn't, Aud."

"I believe you, sweeting."

Then why was Aud fighting hard not to smile? Triona observed indignantly. "He's much bigger than me."

"Aye, that he is."

"And stronger."

"No doubt of it."

"And he was furious at me, too."

"Aye, I can just imagine what you said to bring that out in him."

Triona exhaled in a rush, growing twice as exasperated. "Even if I'd kicked him, or struck him, or scratched him, it wouldn't have made a bit of difference."

"So you didn't."

"No, I—" She stopped, her eyes narrowing. "What are you trying to make me say, Aud? That I might have wanted Ronan to do what he did?"

"Of course not, sweeting. Never entered my mind. Don't you think you should be on your way? I thought you and the O'Byrne were going hunting." With that, Aud immediately resumed tidying the room as if she hadn't expected an answer.

Not that Triona felt like giving her one. She gestured to Conn who'd been lying patiently by the bed, the huge wolfhound a shaggy blur of energy as he raced ahead of her out the door. After grabbing her bowcase Triona was close on his heels, her face still burning.

Of course she hadn't wanted Ronan to make love to her! How could Aud have even suggested such a thing? Aye, she'd be a liar not to admit that she'd given in easily enough to his caresses and his kisses, unbelievable as it still seemed to her. But she hadn't expected him to . . .

"Just pretend it never happened," she said firmly to herself as she left the dwelling-house and headed for the stable, Conn running in excited circles around her.

Yet little good it did. She had repeated those same words a thousand times during the past weeks, even last night when once again she hadn't been able to sleep. Damn him, it made no sense that she'd been thinking about what had happened more and more instead of the other way around! It's not like she wasn't trying to forget.

"I'll just refuse to go hunting with him," she muttered, throwing her bowcase over her shoulder. Aye, she'd visit Maire instead. She'd been gone raiding so much that their times together had been few, Aud helping Maire to exercise her legs whenever Triona couldn't.

It was still a secret. Nobody knew, not even Ita, Maire's overprotective maid. And Maire was growing stronger, too, her cheeks not half so pale. She still couldn't walk unassisted with the crutch, but maybe in a few months . . .

Triona frowned. Of course, she wasn't going to be here in a few months. But what would happen to Maire after she and Aud left Glenmalure? Would Maire keep trying to walk on her own? Aye, she really should visit her, if only she wasn't so curious about what Ronan was up to.

"I'd say it's far too fine a day to be frowning, wouldn't you?"

Triona glanced up to see Niall just leaving his house; she slowed her pace until he caught up with her. She was tempted to tell him she had every reason to be sullen with Ronan so much on her mind, but she held her tongue. She wasn't really sure where Niall stood with her anymore. Not since he had seemed so pleased that Ronan has asked her to wed him.

"If I'm frowning, it's only because your brother and I are getting too late a start to have any luck at hunting—"

"Hunting?" He sounded surprised.

Triona nodded.

"I'm almost envious of you. Ronan and I used to do a lot of hunting together before . . ." Niall had sobered, sighing. "Well, he's always been so busy with everything else. I suppose that means we won't be setting out on any raids today."

She shrugged. "Your brother is of the mind that his men need time with their families—or so he told me last night."

"I see."

She shot Niall a sideways glance to find him smiling to himself as if he knew some secret. "See what?"

She didn't get an answer, Niall jutting his chin instead. "There's Ronan now."

Triona looked to the stable, suddenly feeling nervous as she watched Ronan lead their prancing horses out into the yard. So he had been expecting her, the spawn! But her agitation was nothing compared to the breathlessness that swept her when she met his eyes. There was a stirring warmth in those silver-gray depths that could not be denied.

Begorra, was she mad? Why the devil had she allowed herself to be goaded into hunting with him? The last thing she wanted was to be alone . . .

"Niall, you must join us." She looped her arm through his before he could answer, tugging him along. "You said yourself that you haven't been hunting with Ronan for a while and I'm sure he wouldn't mind—"

"Niall has other things that demand his attention today," Ronan interjected, clearly having overheard her. "Don't you, little brother?"

"Aye, that I do."

Before Triona could blink, Niall had disengaged himself from her grasp and stepped aside, leaving her standing awkwardly in front of Ronan.

"But . . . but surely there is nothing so important . . ." she began, only to switch to another tack when Ronan firmly shook his head. "I—I can't go. I don't feel well."

"You look fine to me. Never lovelier."

Growing flush-faced in spite of herself, she snapped, "Just because I look fine doesn't mean I feel fine, Ronan O'Byrne. I'm sorry but you'll just have to go by yourself."

Ronan sighed. He could see now that he must have jumped to conclusions last night. But if challenging her had brought her this far, it could work again.

"Enough of this nonsense, Triona. Our quarry will be napping safely in its den if we delay any longer and then neither of us will have a chance at bringing home the prize. Unless of course you're truly worried that I might do better—"

"Better, O'Byrne? With those unwieldy javelins?"

Ronan followed her skeptical gaze to the leather spear case strapped to his mount. "They fly straight if aimed well."

"Mayhap, but I don't see why you won't use a bow. It's much more efficient—"

"I prefer javelins." Ronan's tone had grown stiff, some of the light gone from his eyes. "They've been known to bring down a wild pig or two."

"Well now, that would be an amazing sight to see. But what a shame we won't because my arrows will win the day long before you ever think to throw one of those things!"

As she grabbed Laeg's reins, Triona noted that Ronan looked pleased now and she suddenly realized what he was up to. She mounted her horse, fuming.

Too bad Aud hadn't witnessed this little exchange. Aye, it was clear that he was so sure of himself that he didn't think he had to impose his will.

What a witless impressionable dolt he must think her! A few weeks of raiding, a little hunting, and she might come to think it was worth it to marry him just to enjoy such freedom. . . .

"Tell the cook we'll have wild boar for the spit tonight," Ronan called out to Niall, jolting Triona from her thoughts.

"Aye, that I will, brother. Enjoy the hunt, Triona!"

"I intend to," she said through clenched teeth as Ronan drew his horse alongside her, the spirited black beast trying to take a nip out of Laeg's neck.

"Did you say something?"

Attempting with little success to ignore Ronan's thigh rubbing against hers, Triona somehow managed, "Just that Conn must come, too. He's a good nose for wild beasts."

Except when it comes to you, she thought resentfully as Ronan signaled for her dog to come before she had a chance to, Conn bounding after them out the gates.

* * *

"This looks like a good place to leave the horses," Triona said as she slowed Laeg to a halt.

Ronan glanced wryly at Triona, trying very hard to stifle his mounting annoyance. "Are you sure? I'd swear it looks much like the last three clearings I suggested."

"Absolutely sure. This is the perfect place."

"As you say." Ronan threw his leg over his stallion's neck to dismount when suddenly he heard an exasperated sigh.

"On second thought, mayhap Laeg would be happier if there was just a wee bit more grass. We should look some more."

Easy, man, Ronan warned himself, turning away from her so she wouldn't see him frown. Four weeks of constant raiding and he'd almost forgotten how easily this woman could rile him. And he suspected that was exactly what she was trying to do, which was all the more reason to tread lightly. He wanted to endear her to him, not drive her away even further.

"Very well, we can move on if you wish."

Triona sighed again, but this time out of sheer frustration.

"No, no, this place will do fine."

"You're sure?"

In answer, she slid from Laeg's back and tethered him to a birch, Ronan dismounting just a few feet away from her. He was so close in fact, that she couldn't resist taking advantage of the opportunity by shrieking at the top of her lungs, "Conn, where are you?"

"By God, woman!"

She grinned as Ronan grabbed for his stallion's reins, the huge animal rearing and snorting in fright. Yet by the time he had controlled his horse and spun to face her, Triona had recovered herself, hoping she appeared suitably contrite.

"I'm sorry. Truly."

"I thought you said Conn knew to come at a single command?"

Oh, he was irritated now, she thought smugly, his eyes a deep stormy gray. "He does, it's just that . . ." She shrugged, raising her hands as Conn came crashing through the woods toward them. "I wasn't thinking, I guess."

"No, you weren't. We'll be lucky if we find any prey now for miles."

"Well, my father always said I had lungs like a banshee when I was a babe. It appears I still do."

Ronan seemed ready to make a comment, but then he must have thought better of it. He turned to pull two javelins from his spear case. Triona concentrated upon her weapons as well, shouldering her bowcase and then checking to see that the jeweled dagger was sheathed securely in her belt. She hadn't had to ask Ronan to give the weapon back. He'd returned it along with her hunting knife the same day as her bowcase, though she preferred carrying the dagger since it reminded her of her father.

More of Ronan's false gestures of goodwill, she thought, feeling a cold nose nudging her hand.

"Are you ready to hunt, my brave Conn?" she murmured, dropping down on one knee to give him a hug. "But you must be careful. I'll not lose you to some wily old pig."

"We should set out, Triona. The day is slipping away from us."

She looked up to find Ronan watching her, the familiar warmth returned to his eyes. Quickly she rose, regretting once more that she was alone with him in these woods—thank God at least she had Conn—but determined to make the best of this chance to spite him.

"You should lead," she suggested, not liking the thought of him following her, his gaze roaming where it would.

"Very well, but stay close to me," he said to her surprise.

"Why should I do that? I'm not some helpless maiden lost in the forest, O'Byrne. I know its dangers."

"I'm aware of that, Triona." His voice had lowered to a husky timbre. "But there may be others in these woods besides ourselves. As a precaution, just humor me."

"MacMurroughs?" She noticed for the first time that Ronan also wore his fighting sword.

When he nodded, she found herself warmed that he would be so concerned for her safety, but she did her best to shrug it off just as she often had done during their raids. Yet some of the pleasant feeling still remained as they set off through the thick trees, Conn already forging ahead with his nose to the ground.

As they proceeded in silence, Triona found, too, that her spirits were buoyed just by being out walking in the wild again.

She loved the pungent earthy smell of moss, loved its soft sponginess beneath her feet and the swish of filmy ferns against her legs. She loved the way the sunlight was filtering through the lush canopy of leaves overhead, narrow shafts bathing the forest around them in hazy gold. It was so magical, it was easy to imagine impudent wee fairies watching them from beneath creamy toadstools and behind ivy-covered rocks, the occasional rustling breeze through the trees masking their merry whispers.

"Begorra, it's beautiful out here."

She'd spoken in a mere whisper herself, but Ronan stopped and looked around him.

"Aye, I've always loved these woods. When I was a boy, I'd roam about for hours—well past dark, until my father would come hunting for me."

She nodded, understanding his passion. "I did the same thing in Imaal. It used to give my mother a fright—she feared wolves so, but my father didn't mind." She sighed softly. "He didn't mind anything I did."

A long silence fell, Triona gazing at the bluebells and wood sorrel nestled at the foot of a towering oak.

"Fineen must have been very proud of you."

She looked up in surprise, but she saw no mockery in Ronan's face. "Aye, so he often told me."

"I can understand why. Your courage and skill during our raids these past weeks have more than shown that you were deserving of such praise."

Truly stunned, Triona had never wished more fervently that Ronan's words were sincere. Nor had she ever felt so flustered. She quickly sought to change the subject back to the trees, the leaves, the moss, anything but to talk more of her. "Just—just look at this place, Ronan. It's so green it hurts your eyes."

Ronan was looking, but not around him anymore. His heart was slamming in his throat, the way she'd said his name, so soft and husky, touching him deeply.

"And over there—the way the sunlight is shining through those trees. Like gold mist spilling from the sky. Have you ever seen anything more wondrous?"

He didn't want to break the spell, it was so sweet, every part of him wishing that things could always be like this between them. But finally he spoke, his eyes upon her face. "No, Triona. I've never seen anything more wondrous . . . than you."

She started as if stung and met his gaze.

He stared back, daring to hope . . .

A distant frantic barking made Ronan turn his head just as Triona opened her mouth to speak, but whatever she might have said was lost as she shouted, "That's Conn! He must have found something!"

They both began to run, Ronan with a javelin in each hand while Triona deftly pulled out her bow.

Her heart was racing, but it wasn't because of her exertion. She couldn't forget the burning look in Ronan's eyes even as she told herself fiercely that his flattering words meant nothing to her. Nothing! She damned well would have told him, too, if Conn hadn't—

A shrill yelp rent the air, Triona feeling the blood drain from her face.

"Conn! Oh God, Conn!"

Chapter 23

NO BARKING CAME back to her, only the nervous chattering of birds overhead as she and Ronan plunged onward, dodging trees and jumping over fallen logs. But they didn't go much farther before Ronan came to a sudden halt, his breathing as hard as hers as he gestured for them to split up.

"Go that way, Triona, there! Call me if you find him and I'll do the same." Then he was gone, wending through the trees as swiftly and surely as any man she'd ever seen while she veered off to the right.

She was almost to the rise of a hill when she heard Conn's barking, her relief intense that it sounded hale and strong. Wondering if Ronan might have heard it, too, she shouted his name as she burst into a small clearing, an arrow set to the bowstring and ready to fly.

"Conn . . . what in blazes?"

The frantic wolfhound, reared up on his hind legs, barely gave her a glance, his full attention focused upon the spitting creature he had cornered high in a tree. Cautiously Triona approached, keeping her arrow trained upon the large, wicked-looking wildcat just in case it decided to spring.

"Conn, back! That's not a pig."

Still barking, Conn obediently retreated a few feet only to rush forward again when the cat swatted at the air with its paw. Triona edged closer herself, more than anything to get a better look.

She had seen only a few of these rare dangerous creatures and this cat was by far the largest, probably three times the size of Maeve. Triona shivered as the animal fixed its yellow eyes upon her, yet she was awed by its wild beauty. No wonder such creatures had been immortalized in Eire's ancient legends.

"Conn, no. I don't want to shoot him, so back away. Back!"

This time the wolfhound retreated to her side, whining in frustration. Probably a bit of pain, too, Triona realized after risking a glance and seeing the bloodied claw marks alongside his snout. The cat had taken a good swipe at him, but fortunately it appeared only a minor grazing.

"Aye, I know you'd like to get back at him for spoiling your handsome face, my Conn, but trust me," she said in a low steady voice, her bowstring still pulled taut as they backed out of the clearing. "You're no match for such a creature. And Ronan's cook would hardly want a wildcat in his kitchen."

Triona fell silent, wondering suddenly what had become of Ronan. He must have heard her shout, and Conn's barking had been loud enough to summon the saints.

Confident that she had retreated far enough away from the wildcat to venture a glance around her, Triona scanned the forest. It had grown darker, the patches of sky visible through the trees heavy with clouds, the sun disappeared. She felt another shiver, unease gripping her.

Ronan should have been here by now.

After he'd made it a point to warn her to stay close to him, surely he wouldn't have wanted them to be apart for this long . . . there might be some MacMurroughs.

"Jesu, Mary and Joseph," she whispered, her eyes darting all around her as she half crouched beside a broad tree trunk. Tapping Conn's nose in a command for him to keep silent, she thought back over the last few moments.

If there had been fighting, she would have heard the melee. Shouts, the clang of swords. Unless the weapons used had been arrows, the attack having come so swiftly—

"Oh, God. Ronan."

Swallowing hard, she shoved away from the tree and began to cut stealthily through the woods, her path the one Ronan should have taken. Her heartbeat was drumming so loudly in her ears it was almost impossible to listen for anything else, her eyes cutting to the left and right. But she saw nothing out of the ordinary, finally daring to send Conn ahead of her with a vehement whisper, "Find Ronan, Conn. Go!"

She followed him, her legs beginning to ache from all the running. She wanted to shout Ronan's name but she didn't dare. If enemies were near, that would only bring them down upon her. Yet she was almost to the place where they had separated earlier and still there was no sign of Ronan.

"Conn? What the devil . . . ?"

The wolfhound had veered so abruptly that Triona almost stumbled trying to follow him, his agitated tail-wagging making her breath freeze in her chest. Then Conn just as suddenly came to a halt near what looked to be a sharp dip in the earth and began to bark frantically. Only when Triona drew closer could she see that the dip was no natural depression but a yawning pit, remnants of a sod and bramble covering scattered around its rim.

A deer trap.

The kind that often bore a sharpened stake at the bottom, pointed upward, a cruel instrument of death for whatever hapless animal tumbled inside.

Triona's stomach pitched; she came very close to becoming sick all over herself. She was so shaken that she could barely bring herself to look down into the deep round hole.

"Ronan . . ."

He was there, lying facedown and ominously still atop what was left of the sod covering.

She jumped before she even knew what she was doing, landing hard on her haunches beside him. He was still breathing. Her relief was so intense that her eyes blurred with tears. Then she saw the shattered stake lying crosswise beneath him, clearly having been broken by his fall.

"Lucky, lucky spawn," she said hoarsely, smoothing the midnight hair out of his face with trembling fingers. He looked almost as if he were asleep, which made her fear then that he must have severely knocked his head.

Triona flung aside her bowcase and shifted to her knees. She managed to roll Ronan over but only after a good bit of effort. He was so much bigger than she, and heavier, that she was astounded she could have lain beneath him when he made love to her and not been crushed.

"Ninny, this is hardly the time to think of such things," she chided herself, swiping aside chunks of broken sod and dried brambles as she scrambled to lift his head into her lap. His handsome face was so pale that she felt her throat tighten; she desperately wished that there was something else she could do for him. But she was no healer.

Dirt raining down upon her made Triona look up, amazed to see Conn digging furiously at the sides of the pit.

"Conn, no! That won't help us. Go home! Go find Niall!"

Whining, the wolfhound stubbornly dug some more, a large dirt clod barely missing Triona's head.

"No, Conn, no! Go find Niall! Go!"

More earth sprayed down upon her as the wolfhound suddenly spun and retreated, Triona wondering if he had obeyed. But after long moments had passed and he still did not reappear, she dared to hope that he was on his way back to the stronghold.

Even if Ronan soon regained his senses, she doubted they'd be able to climb out of this pit without assistance. The earthen walls were at least seven feet high and slanted inward, which would make them almost impossible to scale.

Triona's gaze fell once more to Ronan's face. Gently she brushed away the dirt from his cheek. At least his breathing seemed normal, a promising sign. Without thinking, she traced his warm lips with her finger, remembering with a jolt the first time he had kissed her . . . how wonderful his mouth had felt upon hers, how incredibly overwhelming—

"Aye, and don't forget what he said about not wanting you, Triona O'Toole," she muttered to herself, tears welling in her eyes. She didn't try to stop them, indulging herself for the first time in weeks.

Damn him, why shouldn't she cry? No man had ever hurt her like this one. And no man had ever made her care before like Ronan, which almost seemed worse. Closing her eyes, she leaned her head against the dirt wall and let the tears come.

"Conor, look out behind you! Conor!"

Ronan sat bolt upright, grimacing at the pounding pain in his head. His heart was pounding, too, phantom visions crashing around him. The silver flash of mail in the moonlight, swords ringing, arrows flying, men screaming . . . God help him, men dying. He clamped clammy palms over his ears to block out the terrible sounds, squeezing his eyes shut, clenching his teeth—

"Ronan!"

He felt someone grab him by the shoulders and shake him. "Ronan, can't you hear me?"

It was a voice he knew, a woman's voice bringing him back from the edge. But when he opened his eyes and saw only high earthen walls around him, he feared for a fleeting moment he was in his grave. Until a face appeared in front of him, the face of an angel . . . a coppery-haired, green-eyed wild angel who shook him again, calling his name.

"Ronan O'Byrne, if you don't answer me right now—"

"I hear you, woman. You don't have to shout."

Triona stared at him indignantly, snatching her hands away. Talk about true colors! Here she had spent the last hour worrying if he was ever going to wake up and then, when he finally did, he had the nerve to be surly.

"I wasn't shouting. You were the one who was shouting. You scared me, sitting up so sudden."

"I'm sorry." He slowly rubbed his hands over his face, then met her eyes. "I must have been having a dream—"

"You mean a nightmare." Now that he was awake, Triona shifted to an opposite wall. "You've a good bump on your head that was probably the cause of it."

"That dream has nothing to do with any bump," Ronan said under his breath, gingerly touching the swollen lump on the side of his head. He sucked in his breath as pain shot through his skull.

"Aye, I can tell it hurts, but hopefully help will come soon." Ronan glanced up at Triona. "Help?"

"I sent Conn after Niall. At least I hope that's where he went and not after that wildcat again. Someone's got to help us out of this damned deer trap."

Ronan was stunned, staring around him almost stupidly at the circular dirt walls. Then his gaze fell upon the splintered stake only a few inches away from his hand. By God, had he come that close . . .

"You're a lucky one, O'Byrne. Conn and I didn't know what we were going to find when we came upon this hole."

He glanced back at Triona, her voice having grown strangely quiet. "You could have gone after help yourself."

She shrugged, looking away as thunder rumbled overhead. "I suppose so, but . . . well, now we're both stuck . . . and with a storm brewing, too. It's been thundering for a while now."

A strong gust of wind suddenly whistled into the pit, bringing with it the first few cool drops of rain. Yet it could have been bucketfuls for all Ronan would have noticed. He was staring at Triona, amazed.

She had jumped down here to be with him.

"I owe you my thanks, Triona."

The huskiness of Ronan's voice took her by surprise, Triona meeting his eyes. The warmth she saw there undeniably thrilled her, as well as put her on her guard.

"If you mean for my deciding to stay with you—"

"Aye."

She swallowed nervously, the pit suddenly appearing much smaller to her and Ronan sitting decidedly too close. "You were my father's godson, O'Byrne. As if I could just leave you here, not knowing if you were alive or dead."

"That's the reason?"

"Of course!" she snapped, growing increasingly uncomfortable at the direction of their conversation. "What other reason could there be?"

He sighed heavily.

She rose and began to pace.

"Where the devil can they be? Conn should have reached the stronghold long ago."

"Mayhap we won't have to wait for them."

Triona spun to see that Ronan had risen, too, although he staggered a bit as he moved to a wall.

"Ronan?"

When he glanced at her, she immediately wished she hadn't sounded so concerned.

"Come over here, Triona."

"What?"

He held out his hand. "Please."

She looked from his outstretched hand to his face, jumping as a deafening thunderclap sounded above them.

"Woman, if we have a chance to get out of here it will have to be before the rain starts in earnest. Otherwise you'll have nothing to grab onto but mud when I boost you up—"

"Boost me . . . ?"

He lunged and grabbed her arm before she could dart away, easily dragging her against him. Astonished, she stared up at his face, her hands pressed to his chest, his heart beating in hard steady strokes beneath her palm. But in the next moment, he whirled her around so her back was against his chest.

"When I crouch down, I want you to climb onto my shoulders. Are you ready?"

"But, Ronan, your head. You're not feeling well. Should you—" She didn't have a chance to say more, gasping as he went down on his knees behind her and grabbed her hips. Before she could blink she was sitting astride him, her fingers laced around his forehead as he rose with her to his feet.

"Triona, you'll have to lift your hands a bit or I won't be able to see."

For some strange reason that made her grin, imagining how ridiculous they must look. "Of course, Ronan. I'm sorry." Obliging him, she took care, too, not to apply any pressure to the bump on his head.

"Good, that's better. Now grab onto anything up there that looks sturdy enough to hold you, sod, a tree root, then pull yourself up."

"But what about you?"

"Just concentrate on yourself for the moment, Triona. I'll stand as close to the wall as I can."

Her shoulders now level with the rim of the pit, Triona threw out her arms and grabbed for something, anything that might sustain her weight. But the sharp inward slant of the walls wasn't making her task any easier, her back aching at the unnatural angle. And when she lunged a second time, she only succeeded in dragging with her chunks of sod and prickly brambles, much of which rained down upon Ronan.

"What in blazes . . . Ouch!"

"Ronan?" She glanced down as he began to cough from all the dust and dirt; she smiled in spite of herself at the dried grass littering his hair. "Are you all right?"

"Fine. Just try again."

She did, trying hard, too, to suppress the husky giggles welling in her throat. But after another unsuccessful lunge, Ronan's coughing and sputtering only growing worse as she dragged more dirt and debris into the pit, she began to laugh in earnest.

"By God, woman, are you trying to bury us alive? Grab onto something!"

"There's nothing to grab, Ronan!"

"Well, if you'd stop laughing—" He gave a low curse, stepping with her away from the wall. "You're doing this to try me, aren't you?"

Before Triona could answer, he grabbed her round the waist and lifted her above his head as if she weighed nothing, then plunked her down right in front of him. She was spun to face him, her eyes widening at the sight that greeted her. If she'd thought for an instant that he might be angry, she began to giggle afresh at the lopsided grin on his face.

"Laugh if you will, Triona O'Toole, but I'm not the only one who looks a mess. You should see yourself."

Indeed, she was covered in a fine layer of dirt, with brambles and broken ferns sticking to her clothes. But Ronan looked as if he had been rolling happily as a pup on the ground, his hair, his brows, even his eyelashes a dusty shade of brown.

"You might want to brush yourself off a bit," she suggested, her playful swipe at his tunic only making her cough as a cloud of dust rose between them.

"When we're out of here. I'd wager we'll only get dirtier. Are you ready to try again?"

She nodded and Ronan hoisted her onto his shoulders. She was still giggling but she couldn't help it, Ronan looking so funny as he tried to keep his stance steady while she lunged and flailed her arms. She was so busy glancing down at him that she gave little heed when she suddenly caught something in her hand, but it wasn't a tree root squirming between her fingers. Looking up, she shrieked, an ugly green forest toad staring at her with bulging eyes.

"Let me down! Oh, God, Ronan, let me down!" She didn't wait, twisting off his shoulders in such haste that she lost her balance and tumbled backward, Ronan barely catching her as he fell, too, right on top of her.

"By God, woman, what . . . ?"

Triona shrieked again, the toad having toppled into the pit to land with a loud plop on Ronan's shoulder. It stared back at her, wet and slimy and covered with bumpy warts and only inches from her face.

"Get it away from me! It's on your shoulder, Ronan—oh!" She froze as the toad took a hop toward her. Triona's voice rose to a desperate squeak. "Ronan, please . . ."

As his low chuckling began to fill the pit, Ronan looked unbelievingly from the wiggling toad he had captured in his hand to Triona's stricken face. "You're afraid of this little thing?"

"Little? It's huge! Throw it out of here! Throw it out!"

Still chuckling, Ronan obliged her, though he didn't throw the poor creature. Instead he rolled off Triona and went to the pit wall, where a single jump enabled him to deposit the toad beyond the rim of the pit. Hoping for the creature's sake that it didn't hop back inside—Triona might squash it!—Ronan turned back to her, shaking his head as he held out his hand to help her to her feet.

"The courageous Triona O'Toole, afraid of toads?"

"Hardly afraid," she countered, glaring at him as she arose without his assistance. "I don't like them, is all—"

She gasped as Ronan caught her, dragging her into his arms. "You were afraid, woman. Admit it," he said huskily, a teasing smile on his lips. "All I'm wondering is what happened to make you—"

"I'll tell you what happened!" Triona blurted, shuddering at the memory. "I was only thirteen at the time. Murchertach O'Toole hid a whole bucketful of those—those disgusting things in my bed and when I crawled in—" She couldn't go on, grimacing as goose bumps puckered her skin. But when she looked up, she began to giggle in spite of herself at the endearing grin on Ronan's face. Yet still she tried to remain indignant. "It was a terrible thing he did."

"Aye, I'd agree with you there."

"I didn't talk to him for weeks."

"As he well deserved. A good reason, too, not to marry the man."

"Aye, it was one of them." Triona's giggles faded as she stared up at Ronan, discovering that he had sobered, too. "You know the other."

"So I do," he said in a half whisper, gently wiping across her cheek with his knuckles. Suddenly he seemed to grow tense, his gaze lifting to search her eyes. "Strange, these tracks on your skin. If I didn't know better . . ."

Triona half turned before he could finish, her hands flying to her face. "They're nothing . . . the rain."

"But so far it's only sprinkled, Triona."

"Aye, but it poured while you were lying senseless."

"That's not possible. Our clothes would be wet."

She didn't know what to say, she'd become so flustered. She tried to turn her back to him, but he caught her by the shoulders and brought her around once more to face him. As he lifted her chin, his eyes burning intently into hers, she didn't think she'd ever felt her heart beating so hard.

"Were your tears for me, Triona?"

Chapter 24

HER BREATH GONE still, she couldn't speak, but Ronan didn't wait for an answer. His mouth came down upon hers at the same moment agitated whining sounded above them, followed by a bark more startling than the thunder booming across the sky.

"Damn."

Ronan's low oath did more to bring Triona back to reality than Conn's continued barking. She shoved herself out of his embrace so abruptly that she stumbled and fell hard on her bottom—an added jolt she needed to calm her rioting senses.

"No, no, I can get up by myself!" she insisted as Ronan took her arm to help her. Wrenching herself free, she clambered back to her feet. "Just stay away from me, O'Byrne! Stay away—"

"Good God, are you two all right?"

"Never better," Ronan said tightly, glancing up at Niall's worried face as more clansmen gathered around the pit. "Get us out of here."

Within moments, the task was accomplished, Ronan and Triona brushing themselves off as Niall shook his head.

"You can imagine the commotion when Conn came tearing back to the stronghold without you. I've never heard such barking. I feared some MacMurroughs had dared to trespass on our land."

Ronan was acutely aware that Triona had remained silent, doing her best to avoid his eyes. But she did bend down to give her dog a fierce hug, probably more out of gratitude for

Conn saving her from Ronan than anything else. Pained, he
turned back to his brother.

"The MacMurroughs would be fools to come to Glenmalure,
and why should they? They've a rich Norman king to replenish
their herds. All the more reason to steal more of their cattle
before they return from the north." Ronan glanced at Triona
to find her shouldering her bowcase, and this time, she'd been
looking at him as if listening intently. "That is, after the men
have enjoyed a few more days' rest. Triona and I've yet a boar
to snare."

She gave no answer other than the stiff jutting of her chin,
then she turned and walked away.

"You mean a wife to snare, aye, brother?" Niall said in a
low aside, jabbing Ronan's ribs not-so-subtly with his elbow.
"The two of you all alone in a deer trap. I hope progress was
made."

"I'd like to think so," Ronan murmured, the salty taste of
Triona's lips haunting him. "But who can say."

"I was so worried for you and Ronan, Triona. When Ita
brought me word that you were safe, I wanted to grab my
crutch and find you, but that would have surely spoiled our
secret."

Triona kept her silence, knowing Maire wouldn't have gotten very far on her own. Not yet. But even now, as she
helped Maire walk across the bright candlelit room, the crutch
thunking alongside her, Triona could tell it was only a matter
of time before Maire would need no assistance.

Maire was so determined, her fair brow knit in concentra-
tion as she placed one foot fearlessly in front of the other,
fighting the stiffness in her legs and the pain of working
muscles long unused, that Triona was able to swallow some
of her regret that she wouldn't be here to see that day. Maire
would be all right without her. Aye, Maire would be all
right.

"A deer trap, too. It must have been terrible to see Ronan
lying down there."

"Aye, it was," Triona admitted, but she decided she would
say no more on the matter.

She'd forgotten herself entirely in that damned pit, giggling like a ninny with Ronan, teasing him, enjoying those lighthearted moments as if there could be more of them. But there wouldn't be, so she didn't want to build any false hope in Maire, especially when the younger woman—only by a year, Triona had discovered—had expressed several times how much she wanted Triona to be happy here at Glenmalure. Happy with Ronan. But thankfully Maire had never pressed too hard and she didn't now, as if sensing that Triona was anything but happy.

"I think I've had enough for today, Triona. Aud was here earlier, so I've had more than my share of walking. You've both been so good to me."

Triona shrugged as she helped Maire to settle herself at the window seat, big drops of rain drumming against the Norman glass. "And you've been braver than any woman I've known—"

"Few women could be braver than you, Triona," Maire cut in gently, picking up her embroidery after she'd draped the fur blanket over her legs. "To jump into that pit after my brother. Niall told me how deep it was."

Niall again, Triona thought with an exasperated sigh. It seemed he had been apprising Maire of every detail for weeks. But then Triona supposed he didn't want Maire feeling left out of the goings-on about the stronghold. Aye, that wouldn't be fair.

"I'd . . . I'd rather not talk about it," Triona said stiffly. "I should go."

"Oh no, Triona, sit with me for a while." An understanding smile lit Maire's face. "I know it's been a trying day for you, so we don't have to discuss it anymore. Here, I could show you a few embroidery stitches."

Triona gave a wry laugh in spite of her dark mood, imagining what Ronan would think if he ever found her with a needle in her hand. He would tease her, taunt her, just as he'd done with that damned toad. But she sat down anyway.

She had come here to visit Maire, but she had also wanted to take her mind from her own troubles. And Maire's goodhearted kindness always helped her to feel better. And if talking about sewing would hold her unsettling thoughts of Ronan at bay, aye then, she would do it.

Late in the night, Triona burrowed deeper under the covers as lightning lit the room, the rainstorm that had been raging for hours only making it that much more difficult for her to fall asleep. But she supposed it could have been a calm night, and she'd still be fighting the same familiar battle. There'd be no escaping her thoughts now.

Were your tears for me, Triona? How could she have allowed herself to become so weak-kneed and rattled?

"Mayhap I *am* an impressionable dolt," she muttered, throwing aside the covers in frustration. She heard a muffled yowl and quickly flipped them back, smiling apologetically as her cat darted to the safety of a pillow. "Sorry, Maeve."

Her smile didn't last long. As lightning flashed, the rain drumming even harder now upon the roof, Triona sighed with resignation and climbed out of bed.

A pity it was pouring so viciously or she could have gone to the stable. Yet with her luck Ronan might be there, and she'd already taken supper alone with Aud rather than at the feasting-hall just to avoid his company. Maybe if she sat for a while by the hearth in the other room, she'd grow drowsy. It had worked before.

Triona whisked a robe over her thin sleeping gown, pausing to pat Conn's head before she went to the door. The poor dog was so exhausted that he didn't try to follow her. And what a loyal day's work, too. Who knows what Ronan might have done if Conn hadn't brought help when he did?

Her flesh dimpling, Triona railed at herself again for being a fool as she left the room.

"Begorra, did I wake you? I was trying to be quiet," said a familiar male voice.

Triona stopped short, staring openmouthed at Ronan. She barely noticed the fire already stoked and blazing in the hearth as a blush raced across her cheeks.

Jesu, Mary and Joseph! With only that linen towel slung around his hips, the man was standing there practically naked! Astonished, she swept him with her eyes; she'd never seen so much of him before. And never that midnight line of hair trailing down a lower abdomen as magnificently honed and hard-muscled as the rest of his body.

Triona felt her face burn all the brighter. It didn't help when she met his eyes to find he was appraising her as well. Instinctively, she drew her robe more tightly around her, not knowing her action only accentuated the generous outline of her breasts.

"What . . . what are you doing here?"

"I was wondering when you were going to ask," he said, his tone as warm as the look in his eyes.

"Aye, well, you can imagine that I'm surprised to see you," she replied indignantly. "You're supposed to be staying at that other dwelling-house—"

"The roof sprang a leak. Right over the bed, in fact."

"Then why didn't you just move the bed to another part of the room?"

"The mattress was already soaked, Triona. Sleeping in it tonight would have been akin to swimming."

"But—"

"This *is* my house," he broke in, his voice firm. "Actually, I'm enjoying being back. I never liked that other bed."

"Aye, you look to be enjoying yourself," Triona said stiffly, noticing the brimming cup of wine set near a chair that had been drawn closer to the fire.

"I was just drying myself," Ronan continued. "I got a bit soaked running over here." He toweled his hair for a brief moment, then flung the drying cloth over his shoulder. "That should be enough."

Her pulse thrumming crazily as he took a draft of wine, Triona hoped so. The devil take him. With his thick black mane damp and tousled, he had a wild look about him that she found all too compelling. Dangerously so.

"I . . . I think I should go back to bed."

"Should? I hope not on my account. This house is as much our home as it is mine."

Now what did he mean by that? Triona wondered, then she just as suddenly stiffened.

There it was again, that blessed cocksure attitude. Ronan must truly believe she was close to marrying him, especially

after she'd been fool enough to let him kiss her again. And now
here he was planning to sleep in the next room. She doubted
that the roof had sprung a leak any more than he was innocently walking around with only a towel draped around him!

"Well then, since you've put it so graciously, mayhap I'll
join you for a while," she said, deciding she'd be damned if
she would allow him to intimidate her. "I was having trouble
sleeping anyway."

"You were?"

"Aye, the thunder and lightning."

"Oh."

Taking gleeful note that he seemed disappointed, she hoped
she'd pricked his overweening confidence. The arrogant, pride-
ful spawn!

"Actually, the storm isn't the full reason I couldn't sleep.
I've been thinking about what happened in the deer trap."

Ronan had been pouring her a cup of wine, but he stopped to
look at her. She quickly rushed on, grabbing at a topic that she
had, in truth, been wondering about, but which had nothing to
do with tears or kisses.

"That bad dream you had today. You shouted out my brother
Conor's name, you know. At least I think that's who you
meant."

Ronan's grip had tightened around the cup, but he willed
himself to stay calm. Triona had a gift for taking him by
surprise, but he should have expected one day she might wish
to discuss Conor.

"You might be more comfortable if you sat down," he suggested, pulling another chair next to his own. "Here, near the
fire. You look chilled."

"Very well."

She sat, accepting the wine. But she didn't drink. Ronan
could feel her watching him as he stood staring silently into
the flames, a painful lump welling in his throat.

God help him, even though this moment had come, that
didn't make it any easier. Just thinking about that terrible
day made him feel as if he were reliving the horror. But
finally he faced Triona, her beautiful eyes wary, her lips
drawn together.

"You know your father forgave me for Conor's death."

She frowned, visibly stiffening. "Aye, but that doesn't mean I've forgotten—"

"Nor have I forgotten, Triona. Even without that dream to haunt me, I could never forget that it was my arrow that killed him."

"Murdered him, you mean."

Ronan wasn't surprised by the vehemence in her voice, but her charge cut him to the quick. "Is that what you truly believe? By God, woman, Conor was my closest friend! I would never have deliberately done anything to hurt him."

"But you did that night! My father rarely spoke of you after Conor's death but the few times he did, he said your recklessness killed my brother. You knew the Norman manor was heavily guarded, but you went ahead all the same, your hotheaded lust for vengeance overwhelming your reason. If that wasn't deliberate, leading Conor and the rest of your men into certain danger with your eyes wide open, I don't know what else you'd call it!"

"It was a mistake," Ronan murmured, the lump in his throat almost choking him, his palms gone clammy. "A horrible mistake."

"Aye, a mistake that was paid for with Conor's life when the Normans mounted a counterattack."

"I was aiming at the man behind him," Ronan said hoarsely, staring past Triona and her accusing eyes to a memory that had leapt to agonizing life in his mind. "I was trying to save him. A Norman was bearing down on Conor, his sword raised to strike. I shouted a warning, Conor ducked, but another Norman's horse slammed into his mount, knocking him back into my range of fire. My arrow struck him. . . . God forgive me, it happened so fast." Remembered rage filled Ronan. "They came after me next, laughing and taunting me for slaying one of my own . . . but they weren't laughing when I sent them both to hell."

Triona shuddered, Ronan's expression so tortured that she wished now she'd never mentioned his nightmare.

She regretted it even more when he hurled his cup at the wall, bright red wine splattering the whitewash. Yet when he fixed his gaze upon her once more, her chest grew tight at the despair in his eyes. And, glistening there, were tears.

"You'll never see beyond this, will you? You'll never see me as anything other than the man who killed your brother. By God, Triona, do you hate me that much?"

She didn't know what to say, utterly stunned by this side of him. It was as if he had laid himself bare to her, the emotion in his voice like an open wound, bleeding and raw. Then he just as suddenly turned from her, his face inscrutable.

"Leave me."

"Leave . . . ?"

"Go, damn you!"

She fled, his tone grown so ominous that she upset the chair in her haste to reach her room.

Chapter 25

TRIONA AROSE THE next morning before Aud had even come to wake her. Not that she would have needed rousing.

When she had finally closed her eyes in the wee hours of the night, exhaustion conquering her, she had slept hard. But only for a short while. A pale dawn was barely streaking the windows as she dressed, her mind once more consumed by Ronan.

Yet that was nothing new. He had plagued her thoughts since she'd come to Glenmalure. But this morning there was a marked difference. For the first time, she wasn't angry that she could think of little else but him. She was angry at herself for thinking of him so unfairly.

Aye, she'd been a banshee, saints forgive her. Mean and hateful and cruel. And if Ronan never spoke to her again, she'd deserve it. Especially after last night.

She remembered wishing as a girl that she hoped Ronan was suffering over her brother's death, just as she and her parents had suffered. But if time had healed her grief, it was clear Ronan was tormented still. Horribly.

Why hadn't she seen it before? All along, it had been as plain as the red of her hair.

No wonder Ronan wasn't the devil-may-care young man she could recall so clearly, but stern and sometimes forbidding—aye, as he'd been to her those first few days at the stronghold—and cautious almost to a fault. Conor's death had changed him.

Ronan had virtually told her that himself the day he came to Imaal, saying he no longer used a bow. Yet according to her father, Ronan had been one of his finest students. And when they'd gone hunting yesterday, Ronan had claimed he preferred javelins. Why else would he have abandoned the bow if not because of what he'd done to Conor?

"But of course, you weren't listening to him—only thinking of yourself." Triona shoved on her shoes, disgusted.

Just as she hadn't listened during their journey from Imaal when she'd asked him why he didn't laugh anymore or smile. He'd offered no explanation other than that people change. Aye, even then she hadn't understood.

He'd claimed that he had no time for marriage, too, Triona pondered as she hastened to the door, Conn padding along behind her. Yet she'd given that statement no special consideration either, as if it were a common thing for a man not to want a wife and family. Might his reluctance also have something to do with Conor's death?

Triona sighed as she left her room, so much still making little sense to her. Especially that Ronan had seemed to care so deeply about what she thought of him.

Her gaze flew to the hearth, the fire died down to glowing embers, her chair still overturned. Flies buzzed around the wine cup that she had no recollection of dropping, while Conn sniffed curiously at the opposite wall streaked with red.

Triona felt a rush of remorse, remembering Ronan's tormented face when he'd flung his cup across the room. Torment she'd only compounded with her cruel accusation of murder.

Aye, she owed Ronan an apology. She would have done so last night, but she doubted he would have wanted to talk to her further, he'd been so angry. She couldn't blame him. At least now after some rest she hoped that he might be more receptive to listening to her.

Triona went to his room and took a deep steadying breath as she raised her hand to knock. But she'd barely touched the door when it drifted open, apparently not closed all the way.

"Ronan?"

No answer came. She wondered if he was sleeping so soundly that he hadn't heard her. She stepped inside, her heart immediately sinking. His bed was empty, clearly not even slept upon.

Why would the man want to sleep under the same roof with a shrew like you? Triona scolded herself as she hurried from the dwelling-house.

Conn bounded after some sparrows, but she headed in the opposite direction, avoiding puddles from last night's storm as well as curious glances from the guards standing sentinel around the stronghold. She didn't stop until she'd reached the small building where Ronan had been staying; once inside, she was surprised to find only one room. And there, at the far end, stood a bed that she could see even from the door was a sodden mess, water still dripping from the beams overhead.

"So he hadn't lied," Triona breathed, wondering how many other times she had misjudged him over the past weeks.

"Looking for the O'Byrne, miss?" said a man's voice from behind her.

Triona spun, startled to see that a clansman had walked up without her even hearing him. "Aye, have you seen him?"

"He left the stronghold several hours ago, miss."

"Left?"

"Aye, by himself, he did. Wouldn't take any of us with him. Said he was heading for the Blackstairs in Carlow."

"But that's where the O'Nolan . . ." Triona didn't finish, outrage sweeping her. Jesu, Mary and Joseph, here she was ready to apologize and he'd ridden off to Carlow, probably to try and talk Taig O'Nolan into wedding her again!

"The O'Byrne didn't say anything more than that, miss, but he spent some time with his brother just before he left. Mayhap Niall could tell you—"

Triona had heard enough, brushing past the startled clansman without another word.

Saints deliver her, the spawn! Ronan must have been angry, all right. Angry enough not to want to play his deceitful games anymore, but instead to rid himself of her accusations forever. And if he failed with the O'Nolan, no doubt Ronan planned to ride the length of Leinster until he found someone to take her off his hands. Why be plagued by a

woman who insisted upon reminding him of something he'd
rather forget?

Triona was so incensed that she didn't bother to knock at
Niall's door, but stormed inside. "Niall O'Byrne?"

She stopped short as Niall looked up from his chair near the
hearth, his expression broodingly pensive for all she'd taken
him by surprise.

"Triona, I'd have thought you abed—"

"I just heard that Ronan has gone to Carlow. Is this true?"

"Aye. To see the O'Nolan."

Triona threw up her hands in exasperation. "The O'Nolan,
did he? Will that fine brother of yours never cease trying to
direct my life? He knows damned well I'll never consent to
marry that chieftain, and Taig told Ronan that he doesn't want
me anyway!"

Now Niall looked startled, his dark brows knit into a frown.
"Who said anything about your marrying the O'Nolan?"

"That's why Ronan's gone to Carlow, isn't it? I suppose he
told you what happened last night—that we talked about my
brother, Conor, and now he can't wait to be rid of me because
I accused him of—"

"Aye, I heard what you spewed," Niall cut in, his deepening
frown so reminiscent of Ronan's as he lunged from his chair to
face her. "It's a heartless, unjust charge you've made, Triona
O'Toole. Do you think your father would have given you over
to my brother's care if he truly thought Ronan was a murderer?
I only wish the O'Toole would have forgiven him years ago
and eased some of my brother's misery. And now you've gone
and made things worse!"

"I've made things worse?" she spouted, surprised that the
man she had once thought her friend and ally was attacking
her so harshly. "What of Ronan's behavior? Damn him, he's
on his way to Carlow—"

"To arrange for the O'Nolan to take over your guardianship,
Triona. I told you before that my brother is a man of his
word, but he can't bear that the oath he made to your father
has caused you such unhappiness. Ronan would rather you
make your home with someone you respect than a man you
despise."

Stunned that she had so easily misjudged Ronan again, Triona nonetheless could not help grumbling, "For a man of his word, Ronan hasn't shown as much when it comes to his dealings with me."

"Why? Because he had to reason with you once to spare you humiliation before your clan? Even then he was thinking of what was best for you."

"Oh, and I suppose his wanting to make me into the proper Irish maiden was best for me? Obviously you didn't think so, Niall O'Byrne, or you wouldn't have taken my side, helping me—"

"I had good reason for helping you, but clearly I was wrong." Niall turned away from her, staring into the fire. "A damned good reason . . . gone to ashes."

Niall sounded so disheartened that Triona couldn't help softening her tone. "What reason was that, Niall? If you recall, I asked you this once before—"

"Aye, the day Ronan released you from your room. Hardly the time to let you know that I hoped one day you'd be marrying my brother." Niall gave a heavy sigh. "I should say *we* hoped. Maire has been wishing the same thing, too."

Triona was so astonished that she couldn't speak.

"I saw the difference in Ronan from the moment he brought you here, as if you'd set a fire under him. Maire saw it, too, that night at the feast. We knew then that if anyone could help bring our older brother back again, it was you."

Triona finally managed a whisper. "Bring him back?"

"Aye, Triona, to make Ronan want to find joy in life again. Do you think you're the only one who lost a brother the day Conor died? I lost my brother, too, as surely as if that arrow had pierced Ronan through the heart. We used to hunt together, laugh together, but no more. He's closed himself off from us for years, hiding his hurt behind a strict code of discipline, his guilt eating away the man that the O'Byrnes of Glenmalure once knew—that Maire and I once knew and loved. Until *you* came along, driving him out of himself with your fiery hair and your spirit to match. Why else do you think I hoped you'd stand up to him?"

Shocked, Triona sank onto a bench. Given what she had seen last night with Ronan, much of what Niall was saying made perfect sense. Yet there was still so much . . .

"You and Maire might have wanted Ronan to marry me, Niall, but he swore he didn't want a wife—"

"Aye, because the man believes he has no right to happiness! Don't you see? Then he wouldn't be paying for Conor's death. So he's been punishing himself for years, allowing no woman a place in his heart . . . until you, Triona."

Her heart was suddenly pounding, but Triona shook her head. "How can that be true? I'm not anything like the woman Ronan could be happy with . . . as—as far away from his precious Lady Emer as a fish to a goat!"

"If you'd been any different, Ronan would never have given you a second glance. Do you think a modest and dutiful mouse could have broken through such pain? You made him feel as if he had a chance, Triona. A chance at happiness, if only he could somehow make you hate him less—"

"I never said I hated him!"

Niall looked as startled as she was for having shouted.

"You don't?"

She didn't answer, looking down at her hands.

"Triona . . ."

"Of course I don't hate him," she finally mumbled, glancing up to find Niall watching her intently. "But I should for everything the man's done to me!"

"Aye, he wasn't exactly hospitable to you in the beginning. Plain unreasonable at times."

Triona snorted. "At times?"

Her outburst brought a reluctant grin to Niall's face. Yet he quickly sobered, saying gently, "I know Ronan felt terrible about what happened between the two of you . . . after he helped you escape from Kilkenny."

"As well he should!" Triona blurted, her face growing uncomfortably warm that Niall would even mention that night.

"He believed you truly hated him, telling me that he'd made your life nothing short of hell. He even talked of escorting you to a convent—"

"A convent?"

"That's what I said, but he seemed to think you wanted only to be far away from him."

"He was right," she muttered, remembering how she'd planned to leave Glenmalure as soon as Ronan left on his next raid. But only because he didn't want her, not because she despised him. And if what Niall was telling her was true—that Ronan had wanted her all along . . .

"Your brother didn't offer to send me to a convent, though," she added. "He offered to marry me out of duty as if . . . well, as if that were a fine enough reason to wed!"

"So you're saying you might have accepted him if he'd told you then that he cared?"

"Aye, I might have—" Triona clamped her mouth shut, her eyes growing wide at what she'd just revealed. Niall, meanwhile, had such an array of emotions passing over his face that it was an amazing sight to see: astonishment, delight, and finally, confusion.

"Yet you didn't outright refuse him, either. You said you'd consider his offer if he first proved that he was willing to take you as you are."

"Aye, why not lead him on a fine chase to repay him for some of the pain he's caused me!"

This time she glared at Niall. In truth, though, she felt relieved that she'd finally gotten it off her chest. And Niall no longer looked confused as he uttered a low whistle.

"So that's what it's been all along. A deliberate game . . . though I can understand why."

"Now you're sounding like Aud," Triona muttered as she rose from the bench. "For your information, Niall O'Byrne, I was planning to apologize to your brother this very morning. I can admit when I'm wrong. But when I heard Ronan had gone to see the O'Nolan, you can well imagine what I thought, after everything . . ."

Niall nodded, searching her eyes. "You mean after all the heartache he's caused you. Aye, you can tell me the truth, Triona. For surely you wouldn't have been feeling so much pain over my brother if you didn't care about him, too."

She couldn't answer, a lump rising in her throat that felt big enough to choke her. But her silence seemed enough to convince Niall, for he came over to her and squeezed her hand.

"It's all right, Triona O'Toole. I'm not the one who should be hearing those words, anyway. But if you've a mind to travel, we could be at the O'Nolan's by nightfall."

The idea roused her spirits, but Triona still was doubtful. "Mayhap we should give Ronan a few days. I've hurt him so badly . . . and you said yourself, I've only made things worse."

"Aye, he was in a terrible way when he left, I'll not deny it. But I can't believe that once he sees you, he'll be able to ignore why you've come."

Triona suddenly felt quite nervous as she mustered a small smile. "All right then, we'll go."

"Begorra, you can do better than that, girl! You've a smile that could charm the very sun to shine. I only hope I'm as lucky as Ronan to find a woman like you."

Flushing warmly, Triona obliged him with a grin, but in the next moment she was racing for the door.

"Pack a few things and then meet me at the stable," Niall called after her. As for Triona, she couldn't run to her dwelling-house fast enough, almost colliding with Aud who was just stepping outside.

"Saints preserve us, sweeting, where've you been? I went to wake you and you weren't in your bed—"

"I'm going to Carlow, Aud," Triona broke in, breathless. "After Ronan."

"He's not here?"

She shook her head, gesturing for Aud to follow her. "I'll explain everything while I pack, but I've got to hurry."

"You don't have to explain things to me, sweeting, I can well imagine what's happened," Aud said, not budging from the front door. "I'm just glad to see that you've finally come to your senses about the O'Byrne. You want the man, don't you?"

Already halfway to her room, Triona spun. "How . . . ?"

Aud's soft chuckle came to her from the threshold. "You forget I've known you since you were a wee babe,

Triona O'Toole. Not much escapes your Aud. Now on with you and get your things whilst I go pack you some food."

After throwing Aud a smile, Triona did as she was bade, her nervousness returning with a vengeance as she passed Ronan's room. One glimpse at that huge bed and she bolted for her door, her face burning hot as flame.

Chapter 26

"MORE WINE, RONAN?"

Ronan didn't have to answer, Taig O'Nolan seeing to it that his cup was refilled to the brim. And it wasn't just any cup either, but a huge silver chalice that matched the one in Taig's beefy hand.

Stolen from a wealthy Norman merchant, the chieftain had informed him proudly. Sizeable enough for brave thirsts, and in the morning, monstrous headaches. But the morning was still a long way off and Ronan planned to make damned good use of his cup before the night was done. Draining it in two drafts, he thunked the empty vessel onto the table.

"At that rate we'll soon be carrying you to your bed," Taig said, the concern in his eyes belying his grin. Gesturing for a servant to pour Ronan more wine, he added, "Aye, but mayhap that would be a good thing. At least you'd get some sleep. I have to say, Ronan O'Byrne, you've looked better."

"Felt better, too," Ronan said tightly, surprised that his words weren't slurred. Nor was the wine having much effect on the pain gnawing at his gut. But give him time. He shoved away his untouched plate and took another long draft.

"Aye, man, drink up. Food won't help what ails you."

Nothing could help what ailed him, Ronan thought bitterly, glancing around a packed hall that had yet to show any signs of blurring. Even drinking himself into the ground would only prove a temporary solution. Come morning, he would be hit again by the realization that Triona would soon be leaving him forever.

"Good riddance to her," Ronan muttered vehemently, the boisterous clamor drowning out his words.

And pity the O'Nolan who would soon have that coldhearted chit under his roof. The chieftain had readily agreed to take Triona into his care, though Ronan suspected it was more that Taig was eager to see Aud again. The O'Nolan had asked after Aud before Ronan even had a chance to say why he'd come to Carlow.

Then the O'Nolan had tried to convince him to give Triona a little more time to come around to the idea of marrying him.

A little more time!

To torture himself?

To torture her, when she clearly wanted nothing to do with him? She might as well have cut out his beating heart and thrown it into the fire, so fierce was her contempt. And after he had laid himself open to her as he had done to no other...

Grimacing at the pain cramping his insides, Ronan made short work of emptying the chalice. Taig, meanwhile, seemed deep in conversation with a clansman who'd suddenly come up to him. Ronan took it upon himself to shout for wine. And this time his words were slurred a bit, which perversely pleased him.

"More guests?" he bit off to the servant who hurried to fill his cup, Ronan noting that several places were hastily being set along the table. As the woman nodded, he realized that the O'Nolan had risen from his chair.

"Ah . . . Ronan."

He turned, puzzled by the curious expression on Taig's face. The stout Irishman looked highly distracted, almost as if he didn't know whether to grin or frown.

"If I've given offense by ordering my own wine—"

"No, no, no offense was taken. We've visitors, Ronan."

"So I gathered," he said, his voice grown dark with sarcasm. "You might do well to warn them that I'm not the best of company this night."

"Mayhap they're already aware—" Taig didn't finish, saying simply as he left the table, "I must greet them."

Ronan focused back on his cup, wondering at the O'Nolan's cryptic words. Who might already be aware?

A sudden giggling nearby made Ronan raise his head, his gaze falling upon a pretty blond serving girl who was whispering to another servant. She giggled again when she realized he was staring at her, her cheeks reddening at his attention. But she soon looked crestfallen when he looked away, her high-pitched tittering annoying him.

Instead he found himself longing for another woman's soft, husky laughter, though he'd heard it far too rarely. And not the sight of blond hair but bright copper red, riotous with curls, and eyes as emerald green as Eire itself.

"Damnit, man, it's done!" he raged to himself, remembering how Triona had merely stared at him last night as he waited for what had seemed a lifetime for her to answer. Waiting as all hope within him died.

Feeling suddenly as if he couldn't breathe, Ronan lurched to his feet, the overheated hall grown close and stuffy. Or maybe the copious wine he'd drunk was finally affecting him, his vision grown blurred. He needed fresh air. Aye, that would help him.

Ronan half stumbled in his haste to leave the table, but fortunately few seemed to have noticed as he made his way out of the hall. He knew it had been a sound move as soon as the balmy night air hit his face. Leaning his shoulder against the timber wall, he drank in deep breaths.

"Brother?"

Ronan spun so fast that the world swayed around him, but nothing could have brought things more sharply into focus than the sight that greeted him. Astonished, he gaped at Niall, who was flanked by the O'Nolan on one side and Triona on the other, her eyes large and luminous in the torchlight.

"What in blazes . . . ?"

"Our visitors," Taig began, but Ronan didn't let him utter another word, bitterly exploding.

"So you couldn't wait until I got back to tell you the fine news, could you, Triona? You had to pull it out of my all too unsuspecting brother and then demand that he bring you here at once. Well, enjoy your new home! The O'Nolan is more than happy to have you—ah, and don't worry that your father won't be avenged. I honor my obligations—"

"Ronan, enough," Niall interjected. "If you'd only take a moment to hear what Triona has to say—"

"We haven't a damned thing to say to each other." Ronan roughly brushed past Niall when his brother made a move to block him. "By the way, little brother, there's plenty of good wine left in the hall. I didn't drink it all."

"I fear he's drunk," Taig murmured as Triona watched Ronan disappear into the shadows, his vehement verbal attack confirming the mounting nervousness she'd felt during the entire journey.

"Aye, I've never seen him like this before," Niall said, sounding shaken. "Ronan's never been one to drown himself in drink, even after Conor—"

"It's my fault," Taig broke in. "I encouraged him. I thought it might help—at least tonight. . . ."

"You're a good-hearted man, Taig O'Nolan, and this isn't your fault," Triona tried to reassure him. "It's my fault. I'm the only one who can mend this mess."

"Not now you won't," Niall objected, grabbing her arm as she started to go after Ronan. "He's furious and drunk, Triona, you heard the O'Nolan. You'd do better to wait until morning when Ronan's more likely to listen to reason—"

"I can't wait, Niall! If he's sotted, it's because I drove him to it. I must try to talk to him."

Triona twisted away from Niall before he could reply, Taig firmly admonishing him as she hurried across the sloping yard.

"Let her go, man! Can't you see she's right? There's nothing else you and I can do."

Triona heard no more. The moon was full and bright, lending ample light, but her spirits began to sag when she saw no sign of Ronan. Stupidly she'd failed to ask where he'd be sleeping the night, but she couldn't go back to the hall. Niall might again try to stop her—

Triona gasped as someone suddenly grabbed her and pulled her into the shadows. Strong fingers funneled through her hair to yank her head back as she was enveloped in a steely embrace.

"So you're following me, woman? Come to taunt me further with your adder's tongue?"

"Ronan," she rasped, feeling as if her hair might be pulled from its roots. "Please . . ."

To her relief, he eased his fierce hold but only slightly, his hot wine-scented breath fanning her face.

"Keep away from me, Triona. Do you hear? Go back to the hall and drink a fine toast that you're finally free of me and the oath I should *never* have sworn."

He thrust her away from him so roughly that she fell to the ground with a sharp intake of breath, and this time, he made no motion to help her to rise. Instead he stepped over her sprawled legs, staggering a little as he strode into the moonlight.

"Oh no, you won't, Ronan O'Byrne," Triona muttered, picking herself up and setting out after him. "You're not going to chase me away that easily."

She kept well to the shadows as she followed him, surprised when instead of turning into one of the dwelling-houses along the way, he made his way to the stable.

Was he thinking of riding back to Glenmalure? she wondered as he disappeared inside the gabled building, slamming the door behind him.

Triona suspected as much when she eased open the door and peeked around it. Ronan was fumbling with a bridle that, in his inebriated state, he couldn't seem to untangle. If the situation weren't so grave, she might have giggled. Truly, he looked so frustrated. Her heart going out to him, she slipped through the door.

"Do you need some help?"

She'd clearly startled him because he dropped the bridle into a ripe pile of horse dung, his fierce oath ringing from the rafters.

"By God, woman, I told you to go back to the hall!"

She shrugged, imagining it would only infuriate him further but unable to help herself. "There's nothing in the hall that interests me. I'd rather be with you."

Again she seemed to have caught him off guard as he stared at her for a moment, but in the next instant his eyes narrowed suspiciously. "You're a coldhearted wench, Triona O'Toole. Always eager to twist the knife deeper. But you'll forgive me if I don't stay to humor you."

As he turned to wrest another bridle from the wall, nearly staggering into another smelly dung pile, Triona ventured closer.

"Going riding?"

"No, I plan to flail myself with the thing!" he shouted as he rounded on her, his handsome face a mask of fury.

"I was only—"

"Of course I'm going riding, woman. To get as far away as I can from you! At least you've saved me the task of escorting you here to Carlow, and for that, you've my thanks!"

Stung, Triona nonetheless remained undaunted. "You're hardly in any shape to stand let alone ride, Ronan. Mayhap if you sat down for a while, we could talk."

Again he seemed taken by surprise, but it was short-lived.

"We've nothing to discuss," he said in a voice grown so low that it seemed strikingly more ominous than his belligerent ranting. "As I told you to stay well away from me, Triona. I've no stomach any longer for your spiteful tricks or accusations."

"What if I haven't come to accuse?" she asked, stubbornly standing her ground no matter that his eyes were blazing into hers like silver fury. "What if I told you that I've come to apologize? I wanted to last night, but you were so angry. I've been wrong about Conor. To blame you, I mean. I can see now how much you've suffered. And—and I don't hate you, Ronan."

He gave no answer, a muscle flashing at his jaw. Taking that as a much hoped for cue he might be ready to listen, Triona opened her mouth to say more only to have him suddenly lunge for her. She stumbled backward in surprise, but there was nowhere for her to go as she crashed up against a stall. The next thing she knew she was pinned there by the shoulders, Ronan's face mere inches from her own.

"You don't listen to warnings, do you? You persist in torturing me, taunting me—"

"It was no taunt!" His grip hurting her, Triona tried to twist free. "Niall was right! You're too drunk to listen to reason. But like a fool I said I couldn't wait—"

"No, you couldn't wait to show me one last time how much you truly despise me. Well, go on, then! You have my full attention—as much as a goodly intake of wine will allow, and I'm within range as I'm sure you wanted. Scream your taunts in my ear, stomp on my toes, strike me, slap me like the wild hellion you are, but have done, woman, and then leave me in peace!"

As Ronan released her shoulders, Triona wasted no time. She rose on tiptoes and Ronan seemed to brace himself, but his eyes widened when she flung her arms around his neck.

"So now you're going to throttle—"

He was silenced as she pressed her lips against his, hoping desperately that if he wouldn't listen to her words at least he would understand her kiss. She exulted when his arms flew around her to crush her body against him, a ragged groan breaking from his throat. But when he lifted his mouth from hers, breathless moments later, his eyes held even more pain.

"Witch. I should have known you'd strike at me with the cruelest trick of all. To tease me so wantonly with what I can never call my own . . ."

Triona was stunned, tears leaping to her eyes. "You . . . you think I'm just playing some spiteful game?" She was so hurt that now she did try to stomp on his toes, but before she could prove successful he'd swept her into his arms. "No, let me down! Coming here was a mistake. Let me down!"

He didn't answer, carrying her kicking and struggling to the back of the stable where it was dark.

"Ronan? Ronan, what are you doing?"

She got her answer when she was dumped onto a soft pile of straw, Ronan pinning her down with his powerful body before she thought to try to flee.

"Ronan—"

His lips were brutal as they captured hers, his mouth hot and tasting of wine. Lying stiff as a board beneath him, Triona nonetheless gave up any notion of fighting him when his kiss deepened, his tongue lashing wildly at hers. Soon everything felt hot, so hot, until she felt, too, as if she were melting into the straw. She began to kiss him back, her eager response making him groan and lift his head.

"Aye, woman, if this is how you wish to taunt me then we will play it out. We will play it out!"

He said nothing more, his mouth devouring her as his hand slipped between their bodies. Triona felt a sharp tug, but his ravaging kiss kept her so preoccupied that she had no notion that her trousers were being dragged from her hips, or that the hard bulge pressing so insistently between her thighs had sprung free of its restraint.

She knew it, though, when his hot turgid flesh slid easily into hers, Ronan grasping the balled fists her hands had become and pushing her even deeper into the straw.

"Aye, taunt me," he said into her mouth, his voice low and raw as he sank into her deeply, so deeply, then withdrew with agonizing slowness. "Tease me, woman." He sank into her again, and Triona could not help but moan. "Ah, that's it. With your hips, your beautiful body, with your soft taunting mouth, so hot . . . so wet . . ."

He barely had begun to thrust faster when Triona cried out, her body growing rigid as her climax burst upon her with lightning swiftness. But it was no more sudden than Ronan's, his shattering release nearly causing him to black out.

And when he did try to lift his head long moments later, he felt such a streak of pain that he moaned aloud. As dizziness crashed over him, he rolled onto his back, throwing his arm over his eyes. It was then that he heard ragged sobbing, the sound carrying straight as an arrow to his wine-dazed brain.

By God, what had he done? Triona . . .

He reached for her, but she was gone.

Chapter 27

"TRIONA!"

His hoarse shout greeted by nervous neighing, Ronan swiftly fastened his trousers as he lurched to his feet, rising just in time to see Triona scrambling onto Laeg's back. He began to run, pitching crazily, but he was so far to the rear of the stable he had no chance to stop her. She veered her stallion out into the moonlit yard before she even got to the doors.

And when he lunged outside, he couldn't believe that the O'Nolan's men opened the gates for her, but they did, no doubt fearing she would have crashed into them if they hadn't. Now Triona was truly gone, careening wildly out into the night. And it was his fault! His damned fault!

As shouts went up, the commotion raising an alarm, clansmen began to pour from the hall, the O'Nolan and Niall among them. But Ronan paid them little heed as he rushed back into the stable, willing himself to think clearly despite the wine still dulling his senses.

Within what seemed no more than a moment's time, he had bridled his stallion and led the snorting animal out into the yard. Only to come face-to-face with Niall who bore down upon him, his eyes ablaze.

"What's happened? Damn you, Ronan, what have you done?"

His tense silence seemed to confirm Niall's worst fears. In the next instant, Ronan felt a shattering blow to his jaw that felled him.

"Stay off of him, man!" roared the O'Nolan to Niall as Ronan staggered to his feet, grimacing in pain. "He's your brother, aye, but he's your chieftain as well!"

"Chieftain or no, he deserved it! The woman came all this way to apologize to him. All this way!"

Ronan faced Niall, his brother being restrained with great difficulty by three strapping clansmen. "Release him."

"Aye, I'm not finished with you!" Niall shouted, although the O'Nolan gestured for his men not to abandon their hold in spite of Ronan's command. "Another good crack and mayhap you'll see that you've just chased away a woman who wants to be your bride, only the saints know why!"

Triona's sobbing coming back sharply to haunt him, Ronan had never felt so wretched. "She said this to you?"

"Not to me, brother, because she wanted to tell you herself! She couldn't have been more eager to see you—aye, nervous, too, because she knew how badly she'd hurt you. But when we saw that you'd been drinking, I told her she should wait until morning. But she couldn't wait, Ronan! She couldn't wait to tell you how sorry she was for accusing you so wrongly about Conor. Couldn't wait to tell you how much she cares!"

Ronan could say nothing, his throat was so tight. God help him, he deserved that Triona would never come back to him. After what he'd done to her—

"Aye, it's hitting you, isn't it? As well it should! And you know what's the most ironic thing of all, brother?"

Ronan met Niall's eyes.

"All along when you thought Triona hated you? She was only acting as she did because she thought you truly didn't want her. Aye, you heard me. She thought she was nothing but an obligation to you—that if she ever wed you, you'd go right back to trying to make her into something she wasn't just as you did when she first came to Glenmalure."

"I do want her," Ronan said in a fierce whisper. "I love her."

"Aye, well, you've done a fine job of showing it!"

"Then get out of my way, damn you, and let me find her!" His jaw still throbbing, Ronan vaulted onto his stallion's back and gathered up the reins.

"Triona can't be thinking to ride far, brother," Niall said, his voice now not half so angry. "At least not tonight. She wouldn't run Laeg that hard after riding all the way to Carlow without a stop."

Without a stop? Ronan once more felt his throat tighten as he looked down at his brother. "I owe you much, Niall O'Byrne."

"Tell me that after you've found her, Ronan. And if she'll still have you. Now go on with you!"

He did, galloping toward the gates as Taig O'Nolan shouted after him, "Aye, and we'll be searching, too! My men know the Blackstairs like the palm of their hands. We'll send up a shout if . . ."

Ronan was already well down the hill, the O'Nolan's words lost to his mount's pounding hooves.

Triona didn't know where she was riding. All she knew was that she had to escape. Her eyes blinded by tears, she was grateful that Laeg was so surefooted for she wasn't doing a very good job of guiding him.

She was grateful, too, for the full moon shining over a wholly unfamiliar glen. She pressed on past densely wooded hills that rose sharply into peaks that weren't as high as those of Glenmalure but just as rugged-looking. But when Laeg's gait began to grow labored, she knew that she couldn't push him much farther. They would have to stop and rest, at least for a few hours.

Then what? Triona asked herself, veering her exhausted stallion into the forest to lessen the chance that anyone would find her. She dismounted and began to lead Laeg almost aimlessly through the trees, each step giving her no answer to her question other than that she never wanted to see Ronan again.

Fresh tears burned her eyes as she remembered what he'd called her.

A witch.

And worst of all he had forced himself upon her, after he'd said he would never do so again. Aye, she may have given in to him, but if she'd fought him tooth and nail, would it have made any difference?

Triona nearly bumped into a gnarled oak, she was so ravaged by her thoughts. Sighing, she decided this place was as good as any to rest for a while but when she tried to tether Laeg, he tossed his head at her and kept walking.

"What is it, Laeg?" She followed after him, not surprised that her voice had gone hoarse. It seemed she'd done enough crying within the past few days to last a lifetime.

Laeg's high-pitched whinny sent a chill racing through her. Triona lunged for the reins as the frightened animal suddenly bolted.

"Laeg, no! Wait!"

She was too late, snatching at nothing but air and losing her balance in the bargain. She hit the ground so hard that the wind was knocked with a painful whoosh from her lungs, but she didn't lie on her stomach for long. An ominous howl coming from somewhere not too far behind her made her scramble to her feet, her eyes darting all around her as she set off at a desperate run after Laeg.

Jesu, Mary and Joseph! She had to find her horse! If there were wolves following their trail she would need weapons, but her bowcase was still in the leather sheath strapped to Laeg's back.

Another chilling howl made Triona run harder, but the trees were so thick that she had to weave in and out—which served only to slow her down. And nowhere did she see any sign of Laeg, not that she could have spied him so easily. The forest had grown almost as black as pitch, very little moonlight filtering through the abundant summer leaves.

Foolish ninny! Triona paused a brief moment to catch her breath and get her bearings. She should never have strayed so deeply into the woods. If she hadn't been so preoccupied with Ronan, she would have been thinking more clearly and paying attention to what she was doing.

A terrified whinny suddenly sounded in the distance, Triona fearing in that moment for her stallion's life. Oh God, if the wolves had found him . . .

"Run, Laeg! Run!" she shrieked at the top of her lungs, hoping her voice would carry through the trees. She bolted herself when she saw a dark skulking shape out of the corner of her eye, her heart hammering wildly.

She shrieked again, this time in a desperate attempt to

frighten away the demon dogs she sensed like an evil wind were following her. She pulled her jeweled dagger from its sheath, grateful she had at least something to use against them. Hoping that Laeg had found his way safely out of the woods, she headed herself in a direction that she prayed would take her back into the open.

Her heartbeat pounding in her ears, she kept shouting as she ran, shouting and waving her arms. She even glanced behind her once, but what she saw made her not want to turn around again. She'd spied at least five wolves gliding like hungry wraiths in her wake, so close to her now that she could see the fearful yellow glow of their eyes.

Helplessness filled her. She would never be able to fight them with one small dagger. Somehow she had to elude them; she began to search desperately for a tree she could climb. But the lowest limbs were well over her head, and when she heard a low growl off to her left, she knew with horrible certainty that the wolves were circling around her.

A moment later she heard another feral growl no more than fifteen feet in front of her. She began to laugh giddily, for the first time in her life her fear so great she could taste it.

She stopped and pivoted in place. There was nowhere else she could go. Again she shrieked as loud as she could, but her ploy didn't daunt the stealthy creatures. She saw a dark flash as the nearest wolf lunged for her, screaming in earnest as she somehow managed to dodge its lathered jaws and yet swipe across its belly with her dagger.

She heard a shrill yelp, praying that she'd injured the creature severely enough to fell it. But then another wolf came at her, this one much bigger than the last. Before she could lunge out of the way, the hellhound's weight knocked her hard to the ground, her dagger flying from her hand. Yet she felt no fanged teeth sinking into her flesh, the night creature slumping lifelessly across her legs, its warm body twitching.

Stunned, Triona saw the fletched arrow sticking from its ribs at the same moment someone yanked her bodily to her feet and thrust her against a tree.

"Don't move!"

She couldn't have if she had wanted to, tears coursing down her cheeks as she was shielded by Ronan's body, his back wedging her in place. She heard him curse as another wolf lunged at them . . . heard the zinging arrow find its mark, the vicious growls abruptly falling silent. Thrice more it happened, Ronan finally stepping away from her to pull her roughly into his arms.

"By God, woman, you've never been one to make things easy on a man."

She wasn't going to make it any easier now, either, no matter that Ronan had just saved her life. Balling her fists, she pounded upon his broad chest, his arms, his shoulders, though her heart was screaming to her to throw her arms around him and hold him tight. But if she wouldn't, he did, crushing her against him, his voice raw and impassioned.

"Tell me it's not too late for us, woman! Tell me that you can forgive me . . . that you might still want me."

She squeezed her eyes tight against scalding tears that would not stop, his rampant heartbeat thudding in her ear. "How can you ask that of me when I'm nothing to you? A duty, an obligation . . . a—a witch!"

"No, Triona, you're an angel. My angel."

His warm lips covered hers, drawing her breath from her in a kiss more passionate than any that had gone before. Yet it was achingly brief as Ronan pulled away from her to sweep his weapons from the ground. He found her dagger, too, the diamonds sparkling in the dim moonlight, and returned it himself to the sheath at her belt.

"Many are looking for you, Triona. They must know that you are safe."

He lifted her into his arms before she could say a word, and hugged her close against his chest. "Thank the saints that you've the lungs of a banshee. Else I would never have found you in time . . ." He didn't finish, brushing a kiss to her temple as he set off with her through the woods.

"But, Ronan, the arrows. You used a bow."

"Aye, so I did," he murmured, kissing her hair. "Anything for you, Triona, *anything*, though the bowcase is yours. Laeg burst from the woods just as I reached the tree line. I had only to whistle as you do to bring him back."

"Then he is safe?"

"Aye. Like you."

His voice gone hoarse, Ronan said no more for he could not.

Triona, meanwhile, for once held her tongue that she was perfectly capable of walking. Instead, she threw her arms around his neck and buried her face against his shoulder.

Chapter 28

IF RONAN HAD had his way, he and Triona would have been married that very night.

But the O'Nolan voiced at once that no man should go into his wedding other than stone-cold sober, while Triona insisted they must wait until they got back to Glenmalure so Aud could be present. After all, it had been her maid's long held hope that one day Triona would find a man she could accept as her husband.

Triona's argument won easily over Taig O'Nolan's, for Ronan had been dead sober from the moment Niall had slammed him on the jaw. But now as he watched her being hustled away by a bevy of women who'd been charged to see that Triona was fed, bathed, and put to bed for a good night's sleep before their long ride home tomorrow, Ronan felt like getting drunk all over again.

"Aye, I know what you're thinking, man, and impetuous thoughts they are, too!" Taig bellowed, slapping Ronan on the back. "You've only made it worse for yourself by sampling a time or two what should have waited for the wedding."

Ronan felt a stab of remorse, determined that the next time he and Triona made love he'd show her just how good things could be between a man and a woman. God knows, he hadn't given her the best impression so far. And he'd hoped it would be tonight, but obviously he was going to have to wait.

"Come on, Ronan. You owe me a toast."

Ronan glanced at Niall, not surprised that his younger brother was grinning.

"I do?" he tossed back, discovering it suddenly wasn't so hard to grin himself. Clearly pleased, Niall's smile grew all the wider.

"Aye, I'd wager you didn't know your own Tanist was a fine matchmaker as well."

"That I didn't." Ronan rubbed his jaw, which if the truth be known, still ached from Niall's well-deserved blow. "Nor that you've a fist of iron. I guess I'll not be calling you 'little' brother anymore."

"That sounds fine with me and just so you know, Ronan, Maire helped, too. She wanted you and Triona to be together as much as I. She already loves her like a sister."

"Enough of these revelations, come on the both of you!" Taig interjected, the talk of a toast apparently having whet his thirst. "One good drink and we'll call it a night. The soon-to-be groom needs his rest as much as the beautiful bride, if you catch my meaning."

Ronan did, once more casting a glance toward the dwelling-house where Triona had disappeared.

"Impetuous, didn't I say?" the O'Nolan said with a hearty laugh, grabbing Ronan's arm.

"Aye, it's damned good to see," Niall replied, pulling Ronan along by the other.

Ronan wanted to be back at Glenmalure before dark, so he, Triona and Niall left early the next morning.

"Now don't be forgetting to tell Aud that I hope to see her soon after you're wed!" Taig called out as they walked their horses through the gates, Triona twisting around to reassure him.

"I won't, but I'm sure she'll be making a journey to Carlow without a word from me!"

Triona smiled at Taig's pleased grin. After waving to him one last time, she faced front, blushing warmly when she saw that Ronan was watching her.

Which was nothing new. He'd been staring at her ever since she'd left the house where she spent the night, almost as if he couldn't believe that everything had worked out so well between them . . . much as she had been doing to him.

"It seems we've more than one matchmaker in our midst, aye, Niall?"

"So it does, brother."

Enjoying their bantering tone, Triona shot a sly glance at Niall. "Aye, you'd better watch yourself, Niall O'Byrne. A fine handsome man such as you can't go much longer without being snared."

"I'd submit to being snared any day if I could have a woman as fair as you," he began, only to quickly amend as Ronan raised a black brow. "Except she'd have to be blond, of course. It's no insult to you, Triona, but redheads come with fearful tempers and the most stubborn natures. Wouldn't you agree, Ronan?"

Triona glanced at him, the teasing warmth in his eyes making her insides feel all aquiver.

"Aye, but that makes the winning of one all the sweeter."

His husky tone flustering her even more, Triona decided she needed a diversion—fast.

"Speaking of winning," she said playfully, looking out over the deep green glen that stretched before them. "How about a wee contest this morn? Say, to the other side of the glen? At this snail's pace, we'll never reach Wicklow by dark."

She didn't wait to hear their answers, spurring Laeg into a canter. But from the pounding of hooves, she knew Ronan and Niall were hard behind her which only made her ride faster.

She laughed, too, like she hadn't since she could remember, exhilaration sweeping her. It was such a rare wonderful thing to be in love. And she was, she knew that now, as surely as the sun was shining down upon them.

That thought sobered her a little; she hadn't yet told Ronan that she loved him. She hoped they would find a moment alone soon where she could do just that. She had been whisked away so abruptly last night at the O'Nolan's command, the women who accompanied her well-meaning but not the company she craved. And this morning there had been so many people hovering around. . . .

"You're going to lose if you persist in daydreaming!" Niall called out as his horse lunged past hers, Ronan already a length ahead of them both. Yet she could tell Ronan was purposely holding his powerful stallion back as if he didn't want to be too far away from her, his protectiveness warming her.

She leaned down low to hug Laeg's neck so she could catch up with Ronan and there she stayed, at his side, the two of them letting Niall win by ten lengths. And even when they slowed their pace Triona never strayed far from Ronan, remaining either alongside him or directly behind when their route north through the mountain passes grew too narrow to ride abreast.

They stopped briefly in the early afternoon for a meal, the moments filled with light ribbing between the two brothers. Niall had never seemed merrier, Ronan never more relaxed.

It was just as Niall had hoped, his older brother becoming carefree. Triona hadn't thought it possible that such a change could happen overnight, but with each passing hour she was seeing more of the man she remembered from her childhood.

When Niall made a jest about Ronan perhaps cutting his hair a bit so he wouldn't look so wild, Ronan's laughter was resonant and deep, the sound thrilling Triona. But his easy smile made her heart stop, as close as he had come yet to the devil-may-care grin that had haunted her since he was a girl. She realized then that she must have loved Ronan for years, though even a few short days ago she would never have admitted it.

"I don't know, Niall. I like Ronan's hair just the way it is."

And she meant it, too, recalling with a shiver how untamed he'd looked after toweling dry his thick mane. But she shivered all the more when Ronan smiled at her, offering her a piece of the rosy apple he was cutting.

"You see, brother? Already my soon-to-be bride defends me."

She smiled back at him, her heart racing as she bit noisily into the sweet fruit.

Soon-to-be. Tomorrow? It couldn't be any earlier, for a priest would have to be brought from Glendalough. Even if some of Ronan's clansmen left tonight, they wouldn't return until morning, which meant she and Ronan must spend another night away from each other.

"Is something wrong?" he suddenly asked her, searching her eyes. "You look flushed."

"No—no, nothing's wrong," she stammered, blushing all the more when a slow smile spread over Ronan's handsome face. Why, he was teasing her! He knew full well what she'd been thinking! Trying hard not to smile herself, she threw the last bit of her apple at him and rose to her feet.

"I'd say we should be going," Niall said wryly, glancing from her to Ronan. "I'm beginning to feel like the third wheel on a cart that needs only two."

"Begorra, don't be silly," Triona chided him, although in truth, she wondered if when they drew closer to the stronghold, Ronan might suggest Niall ride ahead so at least they could enjoy a kiss. But one look at Ronan and she mounted quickly, the smoldering heat in his eyes telling her that if his thoughts matched hers, a kiss would hardly satisfy him.

Their pace was a swift one for the next few hours, the sun just beginning to settle into the trees when they finally reached Glenmalure. But Ronan didn't say a word until the stronghold could be seen in the distance, and then he pulled his lathered mount alongside hers.

"Something you said a while ago still haunts me, Triona."

He looked so serious that Triona grew concerned, reining Laeg into a trot. "I've said a lot of things, Ronan. Some of them not so pleasant."

He shrugged off that comment, the roguish spark in his gray eyes reassuring her. "You were readying yourself for a bath, as I recall. A cold bath. You said you loved them . . . hmmm, you said it was just like swimming naked in the lough."

She softly drew in her breath, barely noticing that Niall had turned his horse around to wait for them. "Aye, I remember."

"Is it true, then?"

"What? That I like cold baths?"

Ronan smiled at her teasing. "No, woman, it was the other I've been wondering about."

"Well, to tell you the truth, I've enjoyed a swim or two when there's been nothing between me and the water . . . but only when I've been alone."

"That I'm very glad to hear. I wouldn't like to know that any other man might have seen you—"

"Unless, of course, someone might have been peeking at me behind the bushes. I've heard that men do such things now and again."

Now Ronan was frowning, but before Triona could tease him further she was interrupted by Niall.

"Are the two of you going swimming or not? You've still an hour or so of daylight, and the lough's just over that rise."

"Damnit, man, I was getting around to it," Ronan groused to his grinning brother, though he wasn't really angry. He forgot about Niall spoiling his surprise altogether when Triona gave him a sly smile.

"Aye, I might agree to go with you, but only if you don't peek."

As she suddenly urged Laeg into a gallop, Ronan could see that she hadn't expected an answer. Nor would he have agreed to such a preposterous demand. But before he set off after her, he turned once more to Niall.

"The priest—"

"I know, brother. I'll send for him as soon as I reach the stronghold. Enjoy your swim."

"I intend to." Ronan left Niall and galloped up the rise, his blood beginning to heat at the chase. He saw that Triona had already disappeared into the thick stand of fir trees that sheltered the lough so he rode faster, the roar of the waterfall that fed the mountain lake growing ever louder.

She was swimming by the time he burst through the trees, her scattered clothes showing how hastily she had stripped. Laeg, too, was enjoying himself, the bay stallion knee-deep in water and drinking contentedly. As Ronan rode down to the grassy bank, Laeg swung his sculpted head to look at them, snorting an invitation to his sweaty mount.

"Aye, why don't you let that poor beast of yours have a drink, too?" Triona called to him, treading water some thirty feet away.

Unable to take his eyes from her, Ronan dismounted and gave his horse a sound smack on the rump, the steed eagerly joining Laeg. The water was murky from the recent rain, but

Ronan could see Triona well enough. And the sight of her bare creamy skin made him want to join her all the more quickly. Wasting no time, he shed his sword belt and then tugged his tunic over his head.

"That's my horse's name, you know. Beast."

Remembering with a pang how she had once considered Ronan just that, Triona decided he still had a savage look about him, his midnight hair all tousled as he tossed his tunic to the ground. Suddenly growing nervous when his hands went to his trousers, she spun in the water so her back was facing him.

"I didn't say *you* couldn't peek, Triona."

Her cheeks flaring hot as fire, the water did nothing to cool her skin even when she sank under the surface for a brief moment, smoothing back her wet hair when she came up for air. Daring a glance over her shoulder, she was surprised to see that Ronan hadn't yet removed his trousers.

"Are you afraid to look upon the man you will soon wed, woman?"

Chapter 29

SHE KNEW HE was teasing her, but Triona felt apprehensive although she didn't want Ronan to know. After all, she'd boasted enough times that she wasn't afraid of anything . . . well, except for warty toads.

Yet she couldn't help being anxious after what had gone before. They'd been intimate together, but she still felt uncertain. She'd certainly never seen him fully unclothed. Growing more nervous, she grasped for the perfect excuse.

"I-I'm not afraid. I'd just rather wait for our wedding night if it's all the same to you. To—to see you, I mean."

"Then I'll honor your request."

She heard a splash, spinning half around to see Ronan wading past the horses toward her. He was still wearing his trousers, which were now soaked past his thighs and sticking to him like a second skin.

"It's a fine soft day for swimming, wouldn't you say?" she asked rather lamely, finding that she was still nervous just at the sight of his magnificent chest. The water was up to his hips now, which drew her gaze to his honed belly and that fascinating trail of hair descending from his navel.

"See something that interests you?"

She sucked in her breath, meeting his eyes. She saw humor there, gaze laced, too, with a heat she'd glimpsed before.

"I . . . I was thinking you're . . . well, very fit."

"Funny, I was just thinking the same of you." He dove before she could sputter a reply, resurfacing only inches away from her. Shaking the water from his hair, he added roguishly as he tread water, "Funny, too, Triona, that you didn't at least wear your shirt. But mayhap you don't mind that I'm seeing you before our wedding night."

His deep laughter rang out as she splashed him, then dove to get as far away from him as she could.

If she'd known her tactic had given him a fine view of her bare bottom she probably would have swum away, but she wasn't thinking too clearly anymore. Suddenly she felt very much like the little fish with a very big fish eyeing her for its supper. Resurfacing briefly, she looked for someplace to hide.

She dove again, swimming underwater with an agility borne from long hours spent enjoying the loughs of Imaal. She kept going until she thought her lungs might burst, right through the wild tumult of current and foam created by the waterfall.

When she finally broke through the surface, gasping for air, she was right where she wanted to be. Hoisting herself onto a rock ledge, she looked around her at the dripping cavern formed from centuries of cascading water. She had been in such places before but none as lofty as this one. As white water crashed in front of her, cool spray stinging her face, she shielded her eyes and looked out over the lough.

She saw Ronan at once, diving again and again in a manner that could only be described as frantic.

With a pang of guilt, she suddenly realized he must be very worried about her. Jesu, Mary and Joseph, perhaps even thinking the worse—that she might have drowned. But before she could try shouting to him, he just as suddenly began swimming toward the waterfall with furious strokes. Triona's heart pounded almost as fast as she watched him. She had no sooner retreated to the back of the cavern where the tumbling water didn't seem half so loud when Ronan launched himself onto the ledge, his relief plain to see.

"Damnit, woman, are you trying to age me overnight?"

"I'm sorry, Ronan. I wasn't thinking . . ." Her voice trailed away as his gaze swept her. She wished then she had worn her shirt. Yet it made little sense that he should make her feel so nervous. Ninny, he was soon to be her husband! But she jumped all the same when he straightened and came toward her, her reaction causing him to stop just within arm's reach.

"Triona, you've nothing to fear—"

"I'm not afraid!" she cut in, though Ronan didn't appear convinced.

"Then come to me," he dared her, stepping closer so she wouldn't have that far to go although he kept his hands to his sides.

Triona was shivering, and it wasn't just because the air in the cavern was cool. With her arms crossed over her breasts, she took a small step, then another, until she and Ronan were standing only inches apart. Yet still his eyes beckoned to her. With a ragged sigh, she slowly dropped her arms to her sides.

His hands were waiting for hers, so warm and sure, their fingers lacing together. Without touching her anywhere else, he bent his head to her ear.

"I love you, Triona O'Toole. I would never do anything to hurt you. Never."

She felt chills plummet all the way to her toes, and when he drew back to look into her eyes, she knew she had found the moment.

"And I love you, Ronan O'Byrne. More than you'll ever know."

She saw tears cloud his eyes, felt him shudder as he clasped her hands all the harder, but still he seemed to be waiting. Unlacing her fingers, she reached up and cradled his face with her hands, standing on tiptoe as she pressed her mouth tenderly to his.

"I love you, Ronan—"

His arms closing around her fiercely stole her breath, but she wound hers around him just as tightly, clinging to him as he kissed her with a passion as fervent as his embrace. She couldn't say how long they stood there, nor did she care, her nervousness blessedly vanished.

She wasn't chilled anymore, either, his powerful body hotter than flame. It was the first time she'd ever felt his bare skin next to hers, her nipples rubbing against his chest, and she found herself craving more of the wondrous sensation. She blushed furiously when he pulled away to search her eyes, the scorching heat reflected in his gaze telling her that their thoughts were one and the same.

"I want you, woman, but this time the choice must be yours. If it is your desire to wait until our wedding, I'll honor—"

He was silenced by her kiss, Triona in that moment feeling altogether brazen and bold. She wanted him as badly, and just to show him, she ran her tongue teasingly over his lips, her wanton gesture rewarded by a groan.

But she didn't stop there, darting her tongue inside his mouth while she ran her fingernails up his back . . . startling him, startling even herself, as if she knew instinctively how to please him.

"I always knew you were a wild one, Triona O'Toole," came his husky voice against her lips. "But let's see if you'd go so far as to undress me."

Her eyes flared in surprise, but seeing his taunting smile, she eagerly accepted the challenge. Yet she also began to tremble as she slid her hands over his flat brown nipples and down his chest, her palms lingering to explore the rock hard contours of his abdomen before straying to the leather cord at his waist. She glanced up to see that he wasn't smiling any longer, his eyes burning into hers, the intent look on his face making her fingers shake twice as badly.

"I . . . I can't get the damned thing untied," she finally said after a moment's flustered fumbling. Ronan's hands replaced hers to see the matter quickly done.

"Dare you finish the job?" he taunted, taking another moment to seize her and ravage her lips before allowing her to answer.

Triona felt as if her head were spinning after that kiss, but somehow she managed to nod. And that wasn't all she managed, hooking her fingers inside the waist of his trousers and then tugging the sodden garment downward over his lean hips . . . yet slowly just to tease him.

"Woman . . ."

"Sshh," she bade him, dropping to one knee as she continued to tug.

Her heart began to slam against her breast as more and more of that seductive line of hair was revealed, and she couldn't resist leaning forward and tracing it with her tongue. At once Ronan caught her by the shoulders, his voice gone hoarse.

"Enough, Triona. I will finish the undressing."

"Why?" she asked honestly, surprised that he'd made her stop. "Have I displeased you?"

He groaned, shaking his head as he looked down at her. "You please me too much. Your boldness—"

"Is a thing of love, Ronan." Suddenly very much aware of her seductive hold upon him, Triona gave another small tug to his trousers. "You challenged me to a task, did you not?"

"Aye."

"Then I would like to finish it."

He exhaled brokenly, but offered no further resistance as Triona resumed stripping the wet garment from his body although in truth, her face couldn't have been burning any hotter. Especially when that tempting streak of hair became a midnight thatch, her breath jamming in her throat when his thick swollen flesh finally sprang free.

"Triona . . ."

Again Ronan took her by the shoulders, his hands shaking as she instinctively reached out to stroke him.

Her hands were trembling, too, a flush racing from her scalp to her toes that she could be so daring, but nonetheless she wrapped her fingers around the full-grown silken length of him. Ronan's sharp intake of breath told her that he liked very much what she was doing, yet something told her there was another way she could please him.

Her heartbeat hammering like thunder in her ears, she brushed her lips to him first, then swirled her tongue around his hot smooth flesh . . . once, twice, tasting a pungent wetness. Yet she had no sooner drawn him more fully into her mouth and begun to caress him with her tongue, her lips, when Ronan's wild groan filled the cavern.

The next thing she knew he had pulled her back up against him, freeing her only an instant to kick off his trousers before locking her once more within his arms. Now Triona felt all of him pressing against her, his chest, his lean belly, his hips, his hard thighs flush with her own. And pushing at that sensitive place between her legs, that fascinating part of him which she'd so eagerly caressed . . .

"Did I meet your challenge?" she somehow managed when he bent his head to nuzzle at her throat, the heat of his palm easily rousing her nipple to a tingling nub.

"Aye, woman, but now it's my turn to please you—"

"But you already have," she broke in, her breath catching as he gently bit her shoulder, then soothed the place with his tongue. In truth, the aching pressure between her thighs was already stoked to such heights that she thought she might burst from wanting him so much.

"No, Triona, not enough yet to make amends for . . ." He didn't finish, dropping to his knees in front of her and taking first one hardened nipple into his mouth and then the other, massaging and squeezing her breasts by turns.

The feel of his hot tongue flicking at her flesh was so delicious that she leaned into him, tunneling her fingers through his wet hair. Yet nothing could have prepared her for the path he chose next, his hands grasping her bottom to hold her close as he mimicked what she had done to him only moments ago.

His tongue forged a scorching trail to her navel only to linger there to dip and play, then traveled down her belly to the tuft of copper curls nestled at the crown of her thighs.

"Ronan . . ." Already she was shaking, but when he kissed her there, burying his face, then his tongue in her female-scented depths, she thought for certain she would die. Soon she learned that exquisite pleasure could be like pain, too. She moaned wildly when his tongue speared into her again and again, savoring, exploring, until she felt her knees collapse from under her.

"Ronan!"

He caught her so suddenly that she gasped, Ronan carrying her with him as he rose again to his full height.

"Hold me, Triona. Wrap your legs around me!" came his hoarse command, and she obeyed him, crying out in surprise as she sank onto hard flesh poised to meet her.

But her cry became breathless whimpers at the power of his thrusts, her back pressed to the cold cavern wall while the front of her body was on fire. Her lips were on fire, too, his kiss impassioned, their tongues entwined, their hips fused as if each were desperately striving to become part of the other.

And they did finally at the same moment, their shared climax so shattering that neither moved at the end for the throbbing spasms washing over them. A climax so intense that when it was done, Ronan collapsed with her against the cavern wall, his face buried in her hair as he fought to catch his breath.

To his amazement Triona began to giggle, brokenly at first as she labored for breath, but with that wonderful huskiness he so loved.

"I'm . . . I'm beginning to think you and I have little use for a bed, Ronan O'Byrne."

He laughed, too, hugging her fiercely as he sent a prayer of thanks to the merciful God who'd seen fit to bring him and this incomparable woman together. Longing all the more for that moment when he and Triona would become husband and wife, Ronan noticed that the cavern was growing dark. Regretfully, he eased his body from Triona's and set her down, though he still held her very close.

"The day is closing around us, Triona. We should get back to the stronghold."

"Oh no, let's stay," she murmured, brushing the sweetest kiss against his lips. "We're alone . . . no one can find us . . . no one."

"Mayhap, woman, but this wet cavern won't seem so pleasant when the night air grows cooler." He playfully smacked her bottom. "And you've not a stitch with you to keep you warm."

"Ah, but you'd keep me warm, Ronan. I know it."

Though sorely tempted, he shook his head, not quite the romantic that his wild angel appeared to be. "We can come back, I promise you. But I'm sure Niall has ordered a feast, called for the wine casks to be tapped, assembled my clansmen—"

"All right, all right," Triona murmured, disappointed that their interlude should end so soon yet eager to share her wonderful news with Aud, aye, and Maire, her sister-to-be. "But first another kiss, Ronan, that hopefully will last me until the priest comes."

"You'll be getting kisses aplenty, woman, whether the priest arrives in Glenmalure tomorrow or no. That, too, I promise you."

She giggled again, her languid feeling returning as Ronan captured her lips in a kiss that drove the breath from her body. But to her dismay, it hardly lasted long enough. With another good smack on her bottom, Ronan steered her toward the waterfall, the cascading tumult bringing a sly smile to her lips.

"You forgot your trousers, Ronan."

He laughed, caressing her cheek. "That would be a fine sight to see, wouldn't it? The O'Byrne returning to his people clad only in his tunic . . ."

He left her to retrieve his trousers, and Triona seized her chance.

"Race you to shore!"

She was gone before he could catch her, Triona diving from the ledge into the frothy lough. But when she surfaced, she heard loud splashing behind her and knew Ronan was swimming hard and fast in her wake.

And when she rose breathless and laughing from the water, he was right at her side, catching her in his arms and carrying her the rest of the way up the bank.

Chapter 30

A DEEP GRAY dusk had settled over Glenmalure by the time Ronan and Triona left the lough. Ronan cast a wry glance at the woman who'd proved far too great a temptation for him to resist making love to again. But they no sooner cleared the fir trees, riding at a hard gallop toward the stronghold, when he sensed suddenly that something was wrong.

Even from here, a good distance still remaining for them to cover, Ronan could see that the stronghold's stout outer gates were yawning open.

Triona had noticed, too. She glanced at him questioningly, shouting above the pounding of their horses' hooves, "Do you think it's because they're expecting us?"

Ronan didn't answer, his eyes on the line of glowing torches that was fast approaching the stronghold from the southeast. He counted thirty altogether, and now he could hear horses neighing and men calling out to those who were spilling from the gates with more bright torches.

Relief filled him, his hand moving away from his sword hilt. The large band of riders were his own clansmen. Yet he bade Triona all the same, "Stay close to me!"

They rode at a breakneck pace toward the stronghold, shouts of alarm going up as they approached—all the more strange to Ronan since his people should have known from Niall that he was soon to return. Fearing his men might not recognize them in the gathering darkness, Ronan had Triona rein in sharply beside him several hundred feet from the gates, a distance well out of range of any arrows.

"Name yourselves!" came Flann O'Faelin's great bellowing voice, the fierce command evidencing that Ronan had correctly judged his wary clansmen.

"The O'Byrne of Glenmalure!"

Immediately the host of riders came barreling down the hill, their blazing torches held high, Ronan and Triona soon encircled as they kicked their horses toward the gates.

"Why the commotion?" he demanded at once of Flann, who had whirled his mount sharply alongside him.

"Your brother was attacked, Lord—"

"Niall?" Triona blurted, her face gone pale in the torchlight.

"Aye, as he was riding to the stronghold," Flann continued grimly. "The men saw everything from the gates—rushing out as quickly as they could before the bastards had a chance to finish the job."

"How is he, man?" Ronan roared, a sick feeling welling inside him when Flann shook his head.

"Not good, Lord. He took an arrow clean through his right shoulder, and another caught him in the thigh. Not fatal of themselves, so the healer told us, but he's lost much blood. Nor has he regained his senses. He fell hard as a stone from his horse—"

"How could this have happened?" Triona cut in shrilly, her gaze jumping from Ronan to Flann. "It was still daylight!"

"Mayhap the MacMurroughs thought Niall was the O'Byrne and decided they'd rather slay a chieftain than wait for nightfall to steal back their cattle."

"MacMurroughs?" Ronan interjected.

"Aye, Lord, a dozen or more. We managed to bring down one of them with a spear, the wretch dying with the foul name of Dermot MacMurrough on his lips. We gave chase after the others but—"

"So it was from that you were just returning?"

"Aye, we lost them over the pass, the dogs."

Ronan was silent for a moment, his gut churning. Aye, it could have been him those devil's spawn had brought down, and Triona as well if they'd ridden on with Niall.

"See that the guard is tripled, Flann. I leave you in charge since my brother—" Ronan couldn't finish, his eyes meeting

Triona's. She looked as stricken as he felt, her expression pleading with him to say it was nothing but a terrible dream. "Come. We must see him."

They set off together through the gates, Ronan's men closing grim ranks behind them.

Triona wasn't surprised to find Aud sitting beside Niall's bed, her faithful maid having helped her through enough childhood illnesses to know a fair amount of remedies herself. Maire was there, too, her face ashen, her eyes brimming as she sat holding Niall's limp hand.

On the other side of the bed, intently mixing a strong-smelling herbal paste to serve as a poultice for Niall's wounds, was the bald healer. He was sweating profusely, clearly hard at his labors, the sickroom reeking of sour wood sorrel and the juice of overripe mashed apples. Triona hoped the man knew what he was doing. After his cures had had so little effect on her ankle, she prayed fervently he'd have better luck with Niall.

"How is he?" she asked of the healer while Ronan stared silently at Niall's white face as if he couldn't believe what had happened to his brother.

"No better, no worse."

"Can't you tell us anything more than that, man?" Ronan suddenly exploded, his voice resounding in the large room.

"It will be a long night, Lord," Aud interjected calmly as the healer gaped like a startled owl at Ronan, the man clearly too astonished to speak. "The bleeding has long since been stopped, a good sign. And the swelling on his head has grown no larger—that, too, a promising sign."

"Has he said anything?" Ronan asked in a much quieter tone, Triona hoping that Aud's soothing words had reassured him.

"No, Lord. Not yet."

Triona was warmed when Ronan took her hand and clasped it tightly as if to seek comfort from her, their fingers lacing. Aud must have noticed the intimate gesture, for suddenly her eyes were full of tears, a trembling smile on her lips. Yet she quickly recovered herself when the healer bade her to lift the cloth dressing covering Niall's upper thigh so he could slather fresh poultice on the wound.

"Damn those MacMurroughs to hell!" Ronan muttered fiercely as the angry red hole was revealed, Triona feeling sickened at the sight. Maire began to cry silently, her maid Ita hugging her delicate shoulders. But when the healer pressed gingerly around Niall's wound, a trickle of bright scarlet blood oozing forth, Ronan's vehement curse made all of them jump. He stormed from the sickroom, Triona following after him.

"Ronan?"

He seemed not to hear her, his clansmen surrounding him as soon as he stepped outside Niall's dwelling-house into the night. There were so many men gathered that Triona couldn't begin to push through them, and before she could try again to gain Ronan's attention, Flann's voice carried above the crowd.

"Word came from Kildare earlier this day, Lord. King John has triumphed over his vassals. His army still lies far to the north, but those who went to join him have been granted leave to return to their homes or journey with him back to Dublin."

"Then now is the time to strike," came Ronan's harsh reply, his men loudly voicing their assent. "Those accursed MacMurroughs must pay for their deed, and before their clansmen return to swell their numbers. You will remain here, Flann, with enough men to protect the stronghold, but the rest of you prepare to ride south to avenge my brother!"

As Ronan's clansmen hastened to obey him, the night suddenly exploding with their clamorous shouts for revenge, Triona at last was able to elbow her way through the rapidly thinning throng. To her dismay Ronan was no longer standing where she'd last seen him, but now striding across the yard with Flann.

Stung that he had forgotten about her, she ran after him, knowing that to try and shout above the din would be futile. But he must have seen her because suddenly he turned around, catching her by the shoulders as she nearly slammed into his chest. Her heart sinking, she knew what he was going to say the moment she looked into his eyes.

"You must stay here, Triona. This is no well-planned raid where we've enjoyed the element of surprise. Dermot's kin will probably be waiting for us—"

"My place is with you!" she insisted stubbornly even as he shook his head.

"And I'm telling you this time you *will* stay. Do not push me, Triona. If I have to lock you in your room just to know that you're safe, I will do it!"

Incredulous, Triona felt tears stinging her eyes but she angrily swallowed them down. "You . . . you would imprison me again?"

"Not imprison you, Triona. Protect you—"

"As if I haven't shown you enough times that I can damned well take care of myself?" Furious, she wrenched herself free. "Don't bother to send for the priest when you return, Ronan O'Byrne, for I'll not be marrying a tyrant such as you! And don't be surprised if I'm not here when—"

He lunged for her so suddenly that she gasped, his embrace as fierce as any she'd known.

"Cease your hot-tempered spouting and hear me, woman! The thought that any harm might have come to you drives me mad! If we'd continued with Niall instead of going on to the lough, that could have been you lying there in that bed, or worse."

"Aye, or it could have been you!" Her chest tightening painfully, Triona searched his eyes. "Let me go with you, Ronan. If we're both watching out for each other, then surely nothing could happen—"

His kiss silenced her, so impassioned that she felt herself melting against him. But again, it was achingly brief. When he pulled away to look at her, she knew that she hadn't changed his mind.

"Humor me this once, Triona. I want to ride out tonight knowing you're safe. Stay with Maire. She's so fragile. She could use your company. And I know my brother would want one of us beside him when he wakes . . . God willing that he wakes."

He kissed her again before she could answer, and then he

was gone, mounting the fresh horse that had been brought for him.

As he issued final commands to Flann, once more Triona felt as if she'd been forgotten. Yet Ronan's eyes were riveted upon her when he spun his horse around, though she could tell from his harsh expression that his mind was already consumed by revenge.

Strangely enough, she almost felt sorry for the Mac-Murroughs at that moment to have such wrath soon to descend upon them. But remembering Niall lying so still and pale in his bed, Triona cursed herself for such foolishness as Ronan and his men rode out the gates.

"Triona . . ."

She awoke with a start from her half sleep, lifting her head from her crossed arms to find Niall watching her. Immediately she thought to fetch the healer, who had gone to lie down for a short nap in the next room. Then she would have to alert Maire, who'd reluctantly agreed to get some rest. But Triona no sooner rose from her chair when Niall caught her hand.

"No. Stay."

She obliged him, so relieved to see Niall conscious again that it was a good thing she'd sat back down. Her knees had gone a bit wobbly.

"You and Ronan . . . You're both sound? Safe? I feared when that first arrow struck me that they might find you, too."

"No, no, we're fine," she assured him, touched that Niall would be so concerned for their welfare when he'd been the one attacked. "Ronan's just not back yet—"

"Back?"

"Aye, he and his men went after the spawn who did this to you. MacMurroughs from the sound of it."

Niall gave a low, very weak whistle. "So they ventured into Glenmalure after all." Before Triona could stop him, Niall tried to sit up only to slump back to the mattress, groaning in pain.

"Jesu, Mary and Joseph, are you trying to do yourself more damage, Niall O'Byrne?" she scolded, wondering if the healer had heard him. "Isn't it enough that your clansmen found you looking like a prickly hedgehog with all those arrows stuck in you? Lie still now, or you'll only make things worse!"

Her indignant tirade was rewarded by a wan smile, but it was fleeting.

"How long has Ronan been gone?" Niall asked, his concern plainly etched on his forehead.

"Since dark last night, and I imagine now it's almost dawn." Triona sighed with exasperation. "I wanted to go with them, too, but Ronan wouldn't allow it. Do you know what that fine brother of yours said to me?"

"Whatever it was, Triona, please don't hold it against him. You know how much he loves you."

She grew silent and looked away, only meeting Niall's eyes again when he squeezed her hand.

"I'm truly sorry all this came along to spoil things for you."

"Begorra, Niall, what nonsense! As if you personally invited those MacMurroughs to visit Glenmalure—"

"Aye, but this should have been your wedding day."

"Well, mayhap Ronan might think to bring a priest back with him and surprise us," she tossed out, the idea secretly thrilling her. But she sobered when Niall groaned. "You're in a bad way, aren't you?"

He didn't have to answer, his handsome face gone white from the pain.

"Rest easy, Niall. I'll fetch the healer."

To her astonishment, he held fast to her hand when she tried to rise. "God, no, Triona, spare me that torment. He'll just make me drink some foul-tasting brew."

"Unpleasant, mayhap, but a brew that should make you feel better or at least help you to sleep."

She sighed when Niall shook his head stubbornly, but the boyish grin he somehow mustered truly amazed her.

"A brimming cup of ale would do the job nicely, don't you think?"

Now she knew that he was going to recover, besides that she didn't have the heart to refuse him. "Well, it would certainly taste better than the healer's remedy. I'll fetch one for you only if you promise not to try to rise from that bed again until the healer says you may. Are we understood?"

"Aye, Triona, I promise."

She smiled, clasping his hand. "Then a cup of ale it is."

Chapter 31

TRIONA WAS STILL sitting by Niall's bedside hours later, Aud stitching a shirt near the flickering oil lamp while Maire was working quietly at her embroidery, when Flann O'Faelin appeared at the door. Niall was sleeping peacefully, so the huge Irishman kept his voice low.

"I thought all of you might want to know, the O'Byrne's back."

Her heart lurching, Triona rose from the chair. "Ronan's here?"

"Aye, miss, and from the looks of it, there's wounded among his men. I hope you can spare the healer—"

"Maire and I can see to the O'Byrne's brother," Aud broke in, her brown eyes alight as she turned to Triona. "Go on with you, sweeting! You've been waiting all these hours. . . ."

Triona needed no urging, careening past Flann in her haste to get outside. She squinted in the brilliant midday sun. The stronghold yard was alive with sounds: horses whinnying, dogs barking excitedly—aye, she heard Conn barking, too—people calling to each other, women and children rushing through the melee to find husbands and fathers. But she didn't see Ronan anywhere.

At once Triona began to fear that he might be among those wounded, Flann not having the heart to tell her. She plunged with a racing heart into the throng, her anxiety increasing by the moment. Then it occurred to her that Ronan might have gone first to their dwelling-house to look for her, which sent her running in that direction. But the instant she opened the door, she knew he wasn't there, the place disconcertingly quiet.

Once more she began to think the worst—until she realized that Ronan must have gone to see Niall, the two of them just missing each other in the crowd. Ninny! Of course he would go first to see his brother.

Triona cut back across the yard, almost to Niall's house when she suddenly spied Ronan talking with several of his men outside one of the stronghold's grain houses. He seemed to be giving them orders. Strange. He seemed unconcerned for her or his brother.

Stung, Triona turned her back the moment she realized Ronan had seen her.

"Triona, wait!"

She ignored him and kept walking, though she didn't get far. He caught up with her almost at once, grabbing her by the waist and spinning her to face him.

"Woman, have you gone deaf?"

Triona jutted her chin, her eyes flaring. "Are you so busy already that you can't take a moment first to find me and let me know you're safe?"

Recognizing her distress he swept her into his arms. "Do I look sound, Triona? Healthy? Whole?"

She had to fight hard not to smile at his low teasing, thinking that Ronan had never looked more handsome to her despite his smelling strongly of sweat and horses. But that wasn't so unpleasant either, she decided, a shiver racing through her.

"Aye, you look well enough, but Flann said there were men wounded. I didn't know—"

"I'm fine, Triona, and fortunately no one suffered any grave injury. Our attack was a surprise after all." Releasing her, Ronan sobered, looking almost as grim as when he had been speaking with his men by the grain house. "Flann told me the moment we arrived that Niall was doing better, so I saw first to another matter."

"And that was what?"

Ronan looked out across the yard, his tone grown harsh. "I had a prisoner to attend to."

"A prisoner?"

"More a hostage. But come, we can speak of this later."

He took her hand and steered her toward Niall's house, his expression easing. "Tell me about my brother. When did he wake?"

"Early this morning," Triona murmured, startled by Ronan's swift change of mood. Clearly, he had dismissed his prisoner altogether from his mind and now Triona did, too, eager for him to see how well Niall was doing. "I was with him when he awoke, Ronan, just as you wanted."

This news made him pull her close, hugging her as they came to Niall's door. "I hope you're not angry with me for asking you to stay."

"You didn't exactly ask me," she reminded him, slipping free of his embrace to enter the dwelling-house ahead of him. Then she just as quickly spun, throwing her arms about his neck as he crossed the threshold. "But mayhap I might forgive you for being such a tyrant if you'd say you were sorry—"

His lips capturing hers was just the apology she craved, his strong arms circling her to crush her against him. He kissed her so passionately, his mouth warm and urgent, that she almost forgot where they were and why they'd come. Niall's wry voice carrying to them from his room was an instant reminder.

"Do I get a greeting before the two of you disappear for the rest of the day?"

Her cheeks beginning to burn, Triona could see from the heat in Ronan's eyes that the idea appealed to him as well. She took his hand and led him into Niall's room, which was bright now with sunshine, the cloth covering at the window drawn back to emit the light.

Remarkably Niall was sitting up, several pillows propped behind him while Aud stood at his side, plumping another. And Maire was smiling happily, looking from Ronan and Triona back to Niall. Yet for all Niall's welcoming grin, he looked pale and physically weak, his voice holding a slight quaver.

"Good to see you again, brother."

Ronan left Triona to take the chair beside Maire's. When he had ridden from the stronghold, he hadn't known if Niall would survive the night. He swallowed against the tightness in his throat.

"Aye, it's good to see—" Ronan stopped, suddenly smelling the distinct odor of ale emanating from his younger brother. Casting a glance at Aud, who shrugged as if acquitting herself of any blame, and Maire, whose smile now appeared a bit uncertain, Ronan looked back to Niall.

"Has the healer adopted some new method of cure for arrow wounds?" he demanded with mock sternness, trying hard not to smile. "A little something extra added to the poultice?"

"Not at all, brother," came Niall's somber response. "But I see no harm in washing down those nasty herb brews with a good draft of ale . . . when the healer's back is turned, of course."

"Of course." Ronan saw the glance Niall shot at Triona, who'd come up behind him and laid her hands upon his shoulders. "And, of course, you've enlisted someone to keep your cup well filled, have you not? You're certainly in no shape to walk to the kitchen yourself—probably even less, now."

"Aye, I've a kind helper," Niall said at the same moment Ronan caught Triona by the wrist, pulling her around into his lap.

"A brazen redhead, mayhap?"

"All right, all right, it was me!" Triona cried, squirming in Ronan's arms. But she wriggled even more when he began to nuzzle her neck, which brought a low chuckle from Niall as Maire and Aud glanced at each other with very pleased expressions.

"Any chance you might have brought a priest back with you, brother?"

"Aye, I'd say that would be a wise thing from the looks of it," Aud interjected with a soft laugh.

"And it's a beautiful day for a wedding," Maire added, a note of excitement in her voice.

"Aye, so it is, but I've no priest," Ronan said regretfully, feeling Triona grow very still against him. Sensing her disappointment, he gently swept some bright copper curls off her shoulder. "But now that I've seen for myself that my brother is well on the mend, I plan to send some men within the hour to Glendalough. Early afternoon tomorrow sounds like a fine time for a wedding, wouldn't you say?"

"Oh aye!" Maire exclaimed before Triona could reply, her outburst seconded as Aud gave a distracted gasp.

"Why, the cook will have to be told at once if there's to be a proper marriage feast!" Aud took an instant to lay her hand upon Niall's forehead, clucked her tongue with satisfaction and then hurried across the room. "If I hear of you moving around too much, young man, you'll have to contend with me!" she warned as she disappeared out the door.

Triona looked from Niall to Maire to Ronan, all of them bursting into laughter. But their mirth was short-lived when Niall groaned, Triona slipping from Ronan's lap to stand beside the bed. "Niall?"

"I'll fetch the healer," Ronan said, rising from his chair.

"Aye, hurry, Ronan!" came Maire's cry.

"No, no, it was the laughing, is all," Niall tried to calm them, gesturing weakly for Ronan to resume his seat. "I must have bruised my ribs when I fell off my horse. And the healer's got enough to keep him busy from the sound of it. I wasn' sleeping so hard that I missed hearing Flann O'Faelin say there were men wounded."

"Aye, but none seriously," said Ronan.

"So tell me what happened—"

"He's brought a prisoner to Glenmalure is what's happened," Triona cut in, moving to the empty chair on the other side of the bed. "No priest, mind you, just a hostage. Or so was told."

Triona had been jesting, but she wished she hadn't said word about the prisoner when she glanced at Ronan. His face had taken on a harsh cast unlike anything she'd ever seen from him, even those times when she'd made him furious. Nor had she seen his eyes so cold.

"Is this true, brother?" Niall asked. "A hostage?"

"Aye, a MacMurrough."

Triona shivered at the hatred in Ronan's voice. But Niall continued before she could say a word.

"So you rode on Gorey and captured one of the bastards who attacked me?"

Ronan shook his head. "They would have been waiting for

us, spoiling for a battle, so we went deeper into Wexford instead."

"Then who did you bring back?" Triona's curiosity overcame her.

"Kin of Donal MacMurrough."

Triona was astounded, Donal the most powerful chieftain of the MacMurrough clan. "You attacked his stronghold in Ferns?"

"Aye, I decided the offense against my brother was worthy of such a strike. And it proved an easy matter, the place no more well guarded than a church. Donal MacMurrough should have thought more of protecting his own rather than riding off to join his precious Norman king."

Ronan rose to his feet, the matter clearly so detestable to him that he didn't seem to want to discuss it further. But Niall persisted.

"What ransom did you tell them you wanted for this hostage?"

"Enough grain and cattle to last us for several winters"—Ronan's hard expression eased as he glanced meaningfully at Triona—"and mayhap then I can forgo raiding so often to spend time in Glenmalure with my new wife."

Warmed by the look in his eyes, Triona nonetheless couldn't help bristling. "You make it sound as if I'm going to be waiting for you at home while you're traipsing about the countryside, Ronan O'Byrne. Don't forget that I'll be raiding with you."

"Begorra, here we go," came Niall's low murmur as he laid his head back upon the pillow.

"What do you mean, here we go?" Triona demanded, her gaze flying from Niall to Ronan. Maire kept her silence. "I am going to be riding with you, aren't I? After our marriage?"

When Ronan didn't readily answer, Triona spun back to Niall. "So your brother likes me just the way I am, does he? Mayhap you might want to ask him again, Niall O'Byrne! It seems you might have read him wrong!"

As furious tears blistered her eyes, Triona raced from the room before Ronan could stop her, slamming the outer door with all her strength. Immediately she felt a sharp twinge of guilt, wondering if the noise had hurt Niall's aching head or startled Maire, but in the next instant she was running across the yard as Ronan came out after her.

"Triona!"

She ignored him and kept running, dodging clansmen and their families who still lingered about the yard. She even went so far as to spout hoarsely, "If the O'Byrne asks any of you to fetch a priest for him, don't bother!" as she headed for their dwelling-house.

But to her dismay when she got inside, there was no bolt to lock Ronan out. Instead she braced her back against the door as Ronan butted his shoulder against the stout wood.

"Damnit, woman, do you truly think you're strong enough to keep me out?"

Triona shrieked as he leaned into the door, shoving it open so forcefully that she went tumbling to the floor. Scrambling away from him on hands and knees, she gulped air when she felt herself being lifted by her belt, Ronan catching her in his arms.

"You . . . you spawn! Let go of me!" she cried, fighting harder than she'd ever fought him. But her wild struggling only got her thrown across his shoulders much as he'd done the first day she came to Glenmalure, her arms and legs tightly pinned.

Yet that didn't keep her from shrieking that he release her right up until Ronan dumped her upon his bed. Her cheeks wet with frustrated tears, she barely had a moment to catch her breath before he was on top of her, his weight pressing her down into the mattress before she could make any motion to rise.

"Damn you, O'Byrne, I said let me—"

His mouth silenced her, his kiss so incredibly possessive that it didn't take long for her to cease struggling altogether. Yet when he lifted his head so she could draw breath, she blurted, "I won't be a Lady Emer! Do you hear me? I won't—"

He silenced her again, kissing her more soundly than the last time, his powerful body making it impossible for her to move. She was dizzy when he raised his head to stare into her eyes, a taunting smile on his lips.

"What makes you think I could ever content myself with a

docile Lady Emer after I've tasted the likes of you?"

Although she flushed furiously, Triona still wasn't ready to give in to him. "Why didn't you answer me, then? Why didn't you say I'd be riding with you?"

"Because of where we're lying, Triona."

Confused, she looked around her. "What does this bed have to do with raiding?"

"Only that we're going to make children here, you and I." He brushed his warm lips against her mouth, his eyes burning into hers like quicksilver. "A whole brood if I have anything to say about it."

"Aye, I want children, too," she murmured, made breathless by the way he was looking at her. "But I still don't see—"

"They're going to need their mother with them, don't you think?"

Actually, Triona had never thought that far ahead, given she'd never imagined she would find a man she could marry. She had to admit that Ronan's argument made sense, but even so . . .

"You hesitate, Triona."

"Only because I never considered how things might be after a babe or two," she admitted, her face on fire, "or three."

"Ah, now, I can see it well. You'll be teaching the girls how to ride like wild hoydens, how to hunt and swim—"

"And the boys how to shoot a bow as well as their father."

"Aye, woman, all that and much more. Do you think I would ever take those things from you?" He kissed her so gently that Triona went limp beneath him, delicious tremors radiating all the way to her toes. But when Ronan looked again into her eyes, his expression was somber. "There would be no raiding, is all. And I wouldn't be worrying at every turn for your safety—"

"But we've no babes yet," she broke in softly, "and until that happens, I want to be with you, Ronan. Someday you might be glad that I'm there to watch your back. If you could just grant me that much . . ."

He sighed, still reluctant, but then a roguish smile came to his lips. "No babes yet, you say? I guess I'll have to see what I can do to hasten matters along."

As his hips pressed suggestively into hers, Triona somehow steeled herself against the yearning ache kindled like flame between her thighs. "No, Ronan, not until you say that I can ride with you. . . ."

His husky chuckle thrilled her, his second taunting thrust nearly undoing her.

"Aye, woman, you can ride with me. Right now."

She sharply sucked in her breath as his mouth came closer and closer to hers, but he stopped as if to tease her when their lips were only a hair's breadth apart. "You're . . . you're not talking about raiding anymore, Ronan."

"I'm not?"

She never got a chance to answer.

Chapter 32

"RONAN..."

Triona tossed her head, caught in the grip of a whirling nightmare.

"Ronan, behind you!"

Her cry waking her, Triona lay trembling as she stared at the raftered ceiling. She must have roused Ronan, too. In the next moment she felt his arms tightening around her, pulling her close.

"Sshh, Triona, it was a dream. Only a dream."

"But you were fighting for your life, Ronan," she breathed shakily, burying her face against his neck. "And—and there was someone else behind you but I couldn't help you! I couldn't—"

"Easy, Triona, I'm here with you and there's no one behind me. Go back to sleep. I'll not have my bride's beauty marred by dark smudges under her eyes. . . ."

Triona tried to oblige him, but even the wonderful warmth of Ronan's body could not lull her back to sleep. Yet her closeness must have lulled him. Soon she realized that he was once more slumbering soundly, his deep steady breathing fanning her cheek.

Tenderly she kissed him, willing the troubling fragments of her dream to go away. But still that terrible helpless feeling lingered until finally, she sighed and quietly rose from the bed.

It was easy enough to find her clothes in the soft spill of moonlight pouring from the two windows, the garments lying in a heap on the floor. Remembering as she dressed how impatiently Ronan had stripped her, she couldn't help smiling and at once she felt better. But she decided to go and sit by the hearth anyway until she was certain she could fall back asleep. Carefully she closed the door behind her so as not to disturb Ronan.

The outer room was dark, lit only by the orange glow of the hearth. Lying close to where it was warm, Triona found Conn, her wolfhound raising his head as she drew near.

"Sshh, I'm going to join you for a while," she murmured as Conn's long, bony tail thunked a welcome on the floor. Settling into the nearest chair, she leaned over to stroke his ears until Conn's eyes began to close sleepily. Then she sat back once more, drawing up her legs as she stared into the crumbling red embers.

Unbidden, that same impotent feeling returned but she did her best to thrust it away, telling herself firmly, "You've always claimed you've no fear of dreams, Triona O'Toole, and now's not the time to start being frightened." She wasn't Aud, after all, who was as superstitious about such things as anyone Triona had ever known.

Instead she thought of Ronan and the wondrous day they had shared, her memories making her smile again.

He'd left her side only twice, the first time to send an escort to Glendalough after the priest and the second, much later in the evening, to check briefly on Niall and the other men who'd been wounded. The rest of the time they had been together, just the two of them, exhausting themselves with the sensual demands Ronan had made on her and those she'd in turn, made upon him.

It was a bit wicked, really, this night being the eve of their wedding, but they'd never before had so much time alone. They had enjoyed a bath earlier in the afternoon, much of the soapy water ending up on the floor, while supper—thoughtfully brought to them by Aud—had been savored sitting cross-legged on the bed, each taking turns feeding the other mouth-watering morsels of baked salmon dipped in honey and fresh oat bread.

Talk had been little, kisses and husky murmurings in endless supply, the lightheartedness of the evening broken only when Ronan renewed his vow to avenge her father now that King

John would most likely be sailing soon for England. Baron Maurice de Roche wouldn't have his liege lord's royal robes to hide behind much longer. Ronan was as determined as ever to seize him by surprise and stretch his murderous neck. But even that somber moment had been brief, Ronan's fierce lovemaking carrying them to the point where they'd collapsed in each other's arms, sleep like a sweet bliss finally overcoming them.

Yet for all that, Triona hardly felt tired now as she was swept by sudden excitement. Surely there couldn't be but a few hours left until sunrise, her wedding day having come at last.

"You were right about Ronan all along, my brave Conn," she whispered, reaching down to pat her dog's back. "He is a good man. An honorable man. It just took me a while longer to see it—Conn?"

Startled that the wolfhound had gotten up from the floor so abruptly, Triona watched as he trotted to the front door and stopped to cock his head. She listened, too, until she heard the anxious mewing coming from outside. Triona rose at once, realizing Aud must have forgotten to let Maeve back into the dwelling-house.

"Some Warrior-Queen," Triona murmured, hurrying to the door.

Aye, she should have named Maeve after Lady Emer for all she liked the out-of-doors, the feline much preferring a soft downy pillow to sleep upon than chasing mice all night long. But the moment Triona swung open the door, Maeve darted into the yard, the skittish creature clearly taken by surprise.

"Stay, Conn," Triona bade the wolfhound as she dashed outside, following her cat's sleek white shape past a long line of dwelling-houses. "Maeve, come back! Maeve!"

Triona had called out softly, but the night was so still she felt as if she had shouted at the top of her lungs. She saw immediately that her presence had attracted the attention of the guards standing watch over the stronghold.

"I'm trying to catch my cat," she said to the first one who approached her, the clansman looking at her as if she might be half mad. Shrugging, she rushed past him, searching the moonlit yard for Maeve. But after long moments had passed and she still hadn't spied her, Triona gave up. It was ridiculous to—

Triona suddenly stopped, listening.

Jesu, Mary and Joseph, was that a woman weeping?

A sick feeling rose in her stomach as she wondered if one of the wounded men might have taken a grave turn for the worse, his wife now pouring out her grief. Yet surely Ronan would have told her if that was so.

Triona listened again, the piteous sobbing a heartrending thing to hear. Whoever was crying sounded overcome by despair, inconsolable. And it was coming from somewhere nearby.

Looking around her, Triona saw to her surprise that she was almost to the grain house where she'd seen Ronan earlier that day. She noted, too, that a trio of clansmen were standing guard by the double doors, confirming her suspicion that the prisoner was being kept there. Yet surely the weeping couldn't be coming from the grain house. That would mean Ronan's hostage wasn't a man as she had assumed, but a—

"I found your cat, miss."

Triona would have jumped out of her shoes if she'd been wearing a pair, the young clansman had startled her so.

"Th-thank you," she murmured, hugging Maeve against her hammering heart as she turned and hurried away. Almost at that same moment, the sobbing abruptly ceased. Triona glanced over her shoulder to find that one of the clansmen standing guard had disappeared inside the grain house.

As if her bare feet were stuck to the ground, she stood in the shadows watching . . . watching and waiting for the man to come back out again. She felt she couldn't breathe, wondering what he might be doing to Ronan's wretched prisoner. But finally he ducked outside, grousing, "That should keep the damned wench quiet."

"You didn't tie the gag too tightly, did you?" asked one of the others.

"Tight enough to silence her wailing. If it's hurting her, who cares? The O'Byrne said to do whatever was necessary to keep her under control. I'd wager he'd have done the same thing if he were here."

Stunned, Triona didn't wait to hear more. She kept well to the shadows as she raced back to the dwelling-house. She didn't stop until she was inside, Maeve clearly not having enjoyed the jostling and jarring at all as she wriggled out of Triona's arms with an indignant yowl.

But Triona barely heard her. She paid little heed either as Conn playfully chased the spitting cat across the room. Her one burning thought was that she must wake Ronan.

Surely he would mind if his clansmen were mistreating his valuable prisoner, wouldn't he? A woman hostage, too, not that that was so unusual, just that Triona hadn't expected it. And just because the poor thing was a MacMurrough shouldn't give them leave to be so cruel.

Inside their room, Triona stopped cold at the foot of the bed and stared at Ronan as he slept peacefully.

Could he have given such a ruthless order to his men? To do whatever was necessary? Suddenly remembering the harshness in his voice and the sheer hatred in his face whenever he'd spoken of his hostage, Triona feared it was so. Ronan had always been merciful to women and children during their raids, but maybe he despised the MacMurroughs even more than the Normans and that was making him cruel. The MacMurroughs, after all, were responsible for bringing the accursed invaders to Eire. And he probably was being driven, too, by what had happened to Niall. So what good, then, would waking Ronan do?

Feeling strangely sick at heart, Triona undressed and slipped back into bed, Ronan in his slumber reaching out to hug her close. Yet the two of them might as well have been miles apart.

All she could think of was the woman's pitiful weeping, the sound echoing in her ears even as she closed her eyes to somehow try to sleep.

"Wake up, Triona! Are you planning to dream away the day?"

Triona dazedly opened her eyes, then promptly shut them at the bright sunshine streaming across the bed.

"Aye, sweeting, it's morning and a fine beautiful day for your wedding, too."

Triona's eyes flared wide open, her mind instantly clear. She glanced beside her to find that she was alone in the huge bed.

"Aye, the O'Byrne's been up for hours. I've never seen a man so interested in wedding preparations, but he's determined to make the day as special for you as he can."

At that moment, Triona wasn't thinking so much about Ronan. Stunned and not a little angry with herself that she could have slept so hard after what she'd seen last night, she sat bolt upright and looked around her. "Aud, have you seen my clothes?" But her maid apparently hadn't heard her, rattling on and on as she set about tidying the room.

"You won't believe what the O'Byrne's been doing, Triona. He's had the feasting-hall bedecked with herbs and flowers, aye, primroses and bluebells and the sweetest smelling honeysuckle. He's had the finest casks of wine tapped, the stronghold swept from top to bottom and everything put in order, and he's even been twice to the kitchen to see how your marriage feast is progressing. You can well imagine how nervous he's making the poor cook—"

"Aud!"

Startled, her maid spun to face her.

"Have you seen my clothes?" Triona repeated impatiently. "I left them right here by the bed."

"Why, I sent them to be washed, sweeting." Aud suddenly looked dismayed. "Surely you're not thinking to wear a shirt and trousers on your wedding day, are you? And here I've just laid out this lovely silk gown for you—look, the green one that so matches your eyes—"

"I'll be wearing a gown when I marry, Aud, don't fret," Triona said distractedly, sweeping the linen sheet around her as she rose from the bed and headed for the door.

"Where are you going, then? There's nice hot bathwater coming soon from the kitchen and . . ."

Triona didn't hear the rest of Aud's words as she rushed into her former room and made straight for the clothes chest.

As she flung aside the sheet and hurriedly tugged a clean shirt over her head, Maeve watching her from the bed with drowsy eyes, Triona imagined Conn must have tagged along with Ronan. But it wasn't Ronan she was going to seek out this morning, at least not right away. First there was something else she had to do.

"Sweeting, what of your bath?" came Aud's reproachful voice from the doorway.

Triona spun and fastened her trousers. "I shouldn't be gone long, Aud. Have them keep the water warm for me on the hearth."

"Keep the water warm for you?" Aud propped her fists at her thin waist. "You're up to some mischief, Triona O'Toole. I can tell, you know. Did you and the O'Byrne have a quarrel last night?"

"No quarrels. Everything's fine." Triona shrugged into her leather jerkin. "Have you seen my belt, Aud—no, never mind, I won't need it."

She didn't bother with shoes either, but darted past Aud as the older woman threw up her hands.

"It's your wedding day, sweeting! What else could be so important?"

Nothing was more important, Triona thought as she hastened outside. Yet she couldn't ignore that someone was suffering so wretchedly only doors away from her. It wasn't right.

Triona was so intent upon her purpose that she gave little notice to the bustle of preparations as she made her way to the grain house. Seeing three guards standing sentinel outside the doors, she wondered if they were the same ones from last night but then imagined those clansmen must have been relieved to get some sleep. These new guards looked very surprised to see her, glancing in puzzlement at each other as she approached.

"I'd like to go inside, please. To see the prisoner."

"Sorry, miss," came the response she'd fully expected from the stout bushy-bearded clansman who appeared to be in charge. "We've orders to allow no one—"

"Am I not soon to be the O'Byrne's wife?"

"Aye, miss."

"Then I demand to be given entrance. Or mayhap I should scream for the O'Byrne so he can tell you. And I will scream, I promise, loud enough to make everything in this place come to a stop. Ronan won't be happy that you've upset me on the morn of our wedding."

Obviously growing nervous, the clansmen still appeared reluctant. But Triona wasn't daunted, lifting her chin.

"Very well, then. You can't say you weren't warned—"

"All right, miss, don't be calling for the O'Byrne! You may go inside, but only for a moment."

Grateful that they had succumbed to her bluff, Triona waited impatiently as the doors were opened, the burly clansman who'd granted her permission following her into the building. Other than the sunlight streaming behind them, the place was dark as a freshly dug grave, the walls lined with huge sacks of grain.

"Where . . . ?"

The clansman gestured to a side door, opening it for her. Triona was relieved to see as she stepped closer that light emanated from the tiny room, however dim, a sputtering oil lamp set in the middle of the floor. At least the poor woman hadn't been left completely in the dark—

A frightened whimper drew Triona's gaze to the corner and she froze, staring in shock.

Chapter 33

"BEGORRA, SHE'S ONLY a girl!"

"Hardly a girl," the clansman said with a snort. "She may be a slight little thing, but she's seen at least sixteen winters if I'm any judge. You can't tell when she's all huddled up as she is now, but when she's standing—"

"As if she could with her feet trussed like an animal's!"

"Orders from the O'Byrne himself, miss. She's to remain bound hand and foot except for the times when she's given leave to eat and see to her personal needs."

"And how often is that?"

"Once in the morning and then again at night."

Sickened that Ronan's hatred could make him treat a defenseless young woman so wretchedly, Triona exploded. "Jesu, Mary and Joseph! What's the poor thing to do if she can't wait until nightfall? Sit in her own filth?"

When the clansman shrugged callously, Triona had heard and seen enough. Silently cursing that she hadn't worn her belt with the dagger she could have used right now, she looked instead at the clansman's belt. Before he'd guessed her thoughts, she'd wrenched out his hunting knife, brandishing it at him.

"I'd wager you've heard of my skill with the bow?"

His Adam's apple lurching, the man nodded as he took a few steps backward. "Aye, miss, I was in the hall that very day—ridden on raids with you, too."

"Then I'm asking you not to try to stop me for I can wield a knife as well. If I'm to be the mistress here at Glenmalure, I've a right to say when I feel something is unjust. And

I say that this hostage deserves better, no matter she's a MacMurrough. Are we understood?"

The man bobbed his head but Triona was already moving to the corner where she sank down on her haunches, so close now that she could tell in spite of the meager light that the young woman was of unsurpassed loveliness. Yet even silky blond hair and large green eyes hadn't spared her from Ronan's wrath.

Triona saw, too, that the young woman had begun to cry albeit silently, for she could do aught else with that disgusting gag in her mouth.

"Aye, I don't blame you a bit for weeping after what you've been through," Triona murmured as reassuringly as she could. "Don't be frightened by the knife. I'm going to cut away your gag, is all."

She did so quickly and with a deft hand, tossing the sodden cloth to the floor. Then she made short work of the cords tied far too tightly around chafed ankles and wrists, flinging them away in disgust. She looked up to find the young woman staring at her, fresh tears filling her eyes.

"Th-thank you . . ."

"Triona. Triona O'Toole."

The young woman nodded, a trembling smile on her lips as she gestured to herself, saying brokenly, "Caitlin MacMurrough." But she just as quickly sobered, tears tumbling down her pale cheeks as she rubbed her reddened wrists. "My father is Donal—"

"Aye, so I guessed, but that's certainly no sin of your own making." Triona rose, saying over her shoulder, "Could you come and help me lift her to her feet?"

When she got no answer, Triona turned around to find that the clansman had fled. Imagining the alarm he must be raising, she felt nervousness bubble inside her, but she did her best to tamp it down. "Well, Caitlin MacMurrough, it seems we're on our own. Your ankles look like they must be hurting you. Can you stand?"

"Aye, I think so."

"Then take my hands."

As Triona pulled the younger woman up in front of her, she saw at once that Caitlin stood no taller than herself which made her grin.

"You must come from a family of short women."

"You, too."

Glad to hear that Caitlin's tone had brightened if only a little, Triona gave a shrug. "I never knew my true mother, but aye, I suppose she was small like me. Lots of copper hair, too." She took Caitlin's arm. "How about a bit of Wicklow sunshine?"

Triona wasn't surprised when Caitlin held back, fear shining in her eyes.

"You . . . you can truly do this? What if Black O'Byrne—"

"I'm marrying the man this very day," Triona broke in, hoping she sounded confident. "Once I explain things, Ronan will understand it's only right that you should be treated better during your stay among us. A wife's feelings must stand for something."

With that, Triona led Caitlin from the tiny room, hoping too, that the young woman wouldn't sense that her nervousness was mounting. It didn't help either that there was a silent crowd of clansmen standing outside. Caitlin cringed at her side.

"Your father's a proud chieftain, aye, Caitlin Mac-Murrough?" she gently chided as they drew closer to the door.

"He—he is."

"Then hold your head high as if you were walking among your own people . . . and don't forget I'm right beside you."

Triona wished she had someone to bolster her courage as they stepped outside, the clansmen's stern faces truly a daunting sight. But it was the hostility in their eyes that struck her most acutely, as if all the resentment the O'Byrnes had ever felt for the MacMurroughs and their traitorous past deeds was directed toward this one poor girl. Triona could hardly blame Caitlin when she hesitated again.

"Don't worry, Caitlin, I'm going to take you to my house. We've an extra room where you'll be more comfortable—"

"Triona!"

She stopped as Ronan strode toward her through the crowd, his face thunderous. Bracing herself, she held onto Caitlin's arm that much more firmly, certain that if she didn't the young woman would bolt like a terrified rabbit right back into the grain house.

"Ronan, if you'd let me—"

"By God, woman, have you lost your senses?"

He'd gestured to his clansmen before Triona had a chance to speak, Caitlin yanked from her grasp and surrounded by guards. Immediately the young woman burst into tears.

"Now look what you've done!" Triona shouted indignantly, only to have Ronan seize her by the shoulders and shake her. Shake her! In front of his clansmen, some wives, even wide-eyed children.

"Damnit, Triona, you've no leave to countermand my orders! None!"

"Even if your orders are unjust and cruel? She's barely more than a girl, Ronan!"

He shook her again, not as roughly this time although his voice hadn't grown any less ominous. "There's no such thing as cruel when it comes to dealing with a MacMurrough. The wench's treatment here is no less than she deserves—"

"She deserves to be trussed like a wild animal? Her bindings so tight that in another day's time, her wrists and ankles will be bloody and raw?"

"Aye, if it prevents the chit from causing any trouble." Ronan jerked his head toward the grain house, his clansmen at once hustling their weeping prisoner through the door.

"No!" Furious, Triona wrenched free of Ronan's grasp and spun to race after the clansmen. But Ronan caught her again, pulling her around to face him.

"Come away from here now. Do not shame yourself, woman."

"Shame myself?" Incredulous, Triona felt tears searing her eyes. "You're the one who should feel shame, not me! I thought you might understand. That you might care for my feelings. Damn you, Ronan, I'm to be your wife! Have I no say in what I think is right or wrong?"

"Aye."

"Then allow Caitlin some better treatment. Surely you can

see the wisdom in releasing her to her father unscarred from this ordeal. She could have my old room until the ransom comes—the door can be locked after all and guards posted at the windows—"

"No MacMurrough will ever sleep under my roof!" Ronan cut in so harshly that Triona flinched. "I'd burn the place to the ground first, just as they helped the Normans torch our homes in Kildare. Just as they did to all that once belonged to the O'Tooles, Triona, a fact you'd do well to remember." He took her by the arm, pulling her along beside him. "The hostage will remain at the grain house. A fitting place since her ransom is going to help fill it."

"Then I have no say, do I?" Triona demanded, angry tears slipping unchecked down her flushed cheeks.

"Not in this matter."

"Aye, well, then you have no bride!"

Her vehement outburst breaking through his fury, Ronan stopped to face her, incredulous. "You would let this mar our wedding?"

"What wedding? There won't be one as long as Caitlin MacMurrough is being treated like an animal."

His ire rising again, Ronan tightened his grip on her arm. "Everything will soon be in readiness, Triona. I've been up since before dawn to ensure that it would be so. And the priest is here—"

"Then he can damned well go back to Glendalough! I'll even help him to his horse! Do you think that I could enjoy this day knowing a poor defenseless girl was suffering so miserably right in our midst?"

"Others are suffering, too, Triona. Don't forget that her clansmen nearly killed my brother."

"Caitlin had no hand in the crime. Her only offense is that she was born a MacMurrough, and for that she's already been wrested from her home and people. Are we such barbarians that we can't show her some compassion?"

Ronan heaved a sigh of utter exasperation, the tears drying upon Triona's face moving him more than her words. "Very well, you can visit her if you've a mind to. But she's to remain bound and at the grain house!"

Ronan had truly thought this concession would appease her until she shook her head.

"She can't stay tied, Ronan. Her skin's already chafed and it might be days before her father has news that she's been captured. Then there's the time it will take for the ransom to be gathered and brought to Glenmalure. . . ."

Triona's beautiful eyes pleading with him, Ronan almost relented. But he had only to think of how close Niall had come to death the other night . . . how it could have been Triona struck by one of those arrows, to know that he could not stomach coddling any accursed MacMurrough.

"You heard my offer, woman. I can do no more."

She looked momentarily stunned. Then she lifted her chin a good two inches.

"Very well, Ronan. Send the priest home."

He could only stare at her, the realization that she would abandon their wedding because of a MacMurrough almost more than he could bear. Before he could say anything he might regret, he turned and stalked away.

Chapter 34

"AYE, I'VE NEVER seen the like in all my days. Two people who love each other allowing a fuss like this to come between them? It's plain foolishness, is what it is!" came Aud's reproach from across the room.

Triona didn't need to look from the window to know that her maid was frowning at her. Aud had been grousing and scowling for the past five days, and she wasn't the only one.

A pall had descended over the stronghold, Ronan's black mood affecting his clansmen, their families and the servants alike. A freakish run of summer storms hadn't helped matters. Triona had never seen so much rain, even now the windows being pelted by a wicked downpour that had begun an hour ago. Well, two windows. The one she had shattered over a month ago was still boarded up, the rain making a nerve-wracking clatter upon the thin planks of wood.

"How much longer are you going to play this stubborn game of yours, sweeting? A week? Two?"

Triona gave an exasperated sigh. The last time she'd heard that question, Aud had called her spiteful. Had it really been only ten days past that she and Ronan had gone hunting together, ending up in that horrible deer trap? It seemed so long ago. She glanced over her shoulder to find Aud wielding her needle with a vengeance upon the pair of dark trousers spread over her lap.

"This 'fuss' as you call it, Aud, could have been settled the very morn of what should have been my wedding day."

"Aye, if the O'Byrne had given in to your demands about the MacMurrough girl. But he didn't because he can't, and

271

instead of showing him some understanding, you carried your bluff to the end out of pure stubbornness. Now he's miserable, you're miserable, and that poor priest is sitting in Glendalough wondering what in blazes happened!"

"Aud!"

"Shocked you, have I? Good! I've a few more curses up my sleeve, and I'd be happy to use them if it will force some sense into your head."

Triona spun back to the window, but Aud kept on, giving vent to emotions long stewing.

"You've allowed five days to go by, Triona O'Toole. Five precious days that you should have spent as the O'Byrne's wife instead of avoiding him at every turn."

"He's been avoiding me, too," Triona countered, staring unseeing at the rainwater trickling down the glass.

"Aye, and how you've both managed such a feat while sleeping under the same roof is beyond me!"

What sleep? Triona thought unhappily. She'd spent more time tossing and twisting than slumbering, her mind replaying over and over the ugly confrontation that had led her to this mess. Yet she wouldn't have done a thing differently. How could she? All she had to do was remember Caitlin's wretched sobbing to know that she'd been right to follow her conscience. Now if Ronan would only listen to his. . . .

"And as for sleeping under the same roof," Aud's stern voice broke into her pained musing. "Yours is a vain hope that the O'Byrne's going to change his mind and let his hostage stay in this room, Triona. You'd do better trying to find a way for the two of you to be sleeping in the same bed again!"

"Don't you think I want that?" Triona exclaimed, whirling around. "You make it sound as if I don't miss having Ronan's arms around me. Miss his teasing—his kisses, everything! Well I do, more than I can say!"

Aud sighed, softening her tone. "Then what's holding you back, sweeting? You told me yourself that Caitlin even urged you to mend things with the O'Byrne when you went to visit her this morning—"

"Aye, she did," Triona murmured, looking away. "Because she's tenderhearted and as kind as Maire and doesn't want her

unhappiness to be the cause of mine." Triona met Aud's eyes.
"Can you imagine that? Even after the cruel treatment Caitlin's
received here, she's concerned for me—for Ronan. For *our*
happiness. But if I told him that, do you think it would make
a difference?" Triona shook her head resignedly. "He'd still
despise her. He'd still treat her no better than an animal."

"That may be so, sweeting, but you can't blame him for
not being able to see her as more than just a MacMurrough.
After so many years of bitterness—and when you think of what
happened to Niall—"

"Aye, Ronan will never be able to see beyond that," Triona
said to herself, thinking aloud. "Unless someone could convince him that no grudge should be held . . . at least against
Caitlin. Someone who might prove a bit more tolerant . . .
a bit more understanding. . . ." Suddenly she swore under her
breath, her mind racing.

"Triona O'Toole, I know that look. What mischief are you
scheming now?"

"No mischief, Aud." Triona felt like kicking herself as she
hurried to throw her cloak around her shoulders. "I'll need you
to accompany me, so be quick and find your cloak."

"Accompany you? Oh no. Not until you tell me exactly what
you're up to—"

"Do you want Ronan and me to be together or not?" Triona
broke in impatiently. She knew she'd convinced Aud when her
maid dumped what she was sewing on the chair and walked
stiffly to the door, her cloak drying near the hearth. "I knew
you wouldn't fail me, Aud. I'll meet you in a moment. I have
to grab something first."

As Aud muttered under her breath and left the room, Triona
went at once to the clothes chest. She flung back the lid with
such force that she startled Maeve into jumping under the bed,
but Triona didn't have time now to comfort her cat. She dug
deep and pulled out a new gown she'd never worn, a deep blue
silk that would look lovely on Caitlin. And they were closer in
height and size than Triona was to Maire, so that would offer
no problem.

"Ninny! You should have thought of this solution days ago,"
Triona muttered as she stuffed the rolled up gown inside

her cloak. The only other item she would need, a comb for Caitlin's hair, was already over at the grain house. She'd helped her bathe just that morning, not an easy thing to accomplish with the guards insisting that Caitlin's ankles remain bound. But they'd managed and so they would now, with Aud's help.

Triona hastened from the room, pleased to see that her maid was wearing her cloak and waiting by the front door. Conn was there, too, but one gesture from Triona and he headed back to his sleeping place by the hearth, his tail drooping between his legs. But Triona knew that he wouldn't have liked all the rain anyway.

"We'll need our hoods," she said to Aud, throwing her hood over her hair. "And you mustn't say a word when we get to the grain house."

"The grain house! Triona . . ."

"We're going to visit Caitlin, is all. Aye, and remember to keep your head down when we get there as if you don't want your face to get wet." Triona didn't give Aud a chance to reply but left the house, the downpour so heavy and the clouds so thick and gray that it appeared almost dusk.

Aye, maybe all this rain had been sent for a good reason after all, though she doubted Ronan and his men would think so. They'd been hard at work for several days now shoring up the massive earthen embankments surrounding the stronghold that were threatening to become great mountains of mud—which right now was a good thing, too. She didn't want to be running into Ronan for the next few hours if she was lucky.

And if she were truly lucky, Triona thought nervously as the grain house came into view, the guards wouldn't question Aud's presence. They'd become used to Triona's visits; Ronan at least hadn't rescinded the offer he'd made her. But she'd always come alone before.

"Remember, Aud, let me answer if they say anything to you," she cautioned as they approached the doors.

The guards looked perfectly miserable; the three clansmen were drenched despite their heavy cloaks. Triona hoped the rain would work to their favor and prove a distraction. But she groaned to herself when the same burly clansman whose name she'd since learned was Fiach O'Byrne raised his hand for them to stop. He warily eyed Aud's hooded figure.

"My maid," Triona explained before he could ask questions. "Caitlin's gown has a tear and I brought Aud to mend it." When the man still looked doubtful, Triona said indignantly, "My skill lies with the bow, not the needle! How else will the damned gown be fixed if my maid doesn't do it?"

"Very well, go ahead," Fiach muttered, clasping his hand over the wooden hilt of his hunting knife as they passed by him into the building. "But the wench will remain tied during the sewing. You already talked me once into stretching the O'Byrne's orders so she could bathe, but I'll not free her hands again."

"I wasn't thinking to ask," Triona said honestly, for she didn't have to. She had her dagger with her, safely hidden in the deep pocket of her cloak where she'd been keeping the weapon for that time she might need it.

There had been occasions enough already when she had been tempted to cut Caitlin's bonds, the raw redness around her wrists and ankles growing worse by the day, but she'd resisted for fear she might lose her privilege to visit. But today she would take that risk. Grateful when Fiach showed no inclination to follow them, Triona waited for Aud to catch up with her.

"So I'm to mend, am I?" Aud hissed when the door was closed with a heavy thud, leaving them in darkness. "With no needles? No thread?"

"Sshh, Aud, he might hear you," Triona silenced her as she pushed open the door to Caitlin's cell.

"Triona, is that you?"

Her eyes adjusting to the dim lamplight, Triona pulled Aud along with her. "Aye, Caitlin, and Aud's with me. She's going to help us."

"Help?"

Nodding, Triona left Aud's side to drop to her knees next to the pallet where Caitlin was struggling to sit up. Before the young woman even realized what was happening, her bonds were cut, Triona smiling as she deposited the dagger back into her pocket.

"There. That should make sitting and standing a bit easier. Walking, too."

"Walking?" came Aud's low exclamation as Caitlin stared at Triona in astonishment.

"Aye, and we've no time to chat about it, either." Triona rose and helped Caitlin to her feet, then she pulled out the silk garment she'd been clutching under her arm. "Here's a nice clean gown, Caitlin. After you put it on we'll run the comb through your hair. I want you to look pretty for—"

"Triona O'Toole, have you forgotten what happened the last time you tried to take her from the grain house?" Aud said, her expression growing more skeptical by the moment.

Gesturing for Caitlin to hurry, Triona went back to her maid. "Aud, another outburst and you're sure to bring the guards down upon us," she whispered, pleading in her voice. "I think I've come upon a way to fix this miserable mess so everyone can be happy, but it won't work unless you help us. Now I'll need your cloak."

Aud hesitated, her worried eyes searching Triona's face, then she sighed heavily and wrested the sodden garment from her narrow shoulders.

"You know I'd do anything to help you, sweeting. I made a vow of it from the time you were a babe, and there's no sense in stopping now."

Triona gave her maid a quick hug, then glanced behind her to find that Caitlin was almost dressed. She waved Aud to the pallet. "You'll have to lie down, Aud, so I can cover you with the blanket. While we're gone, just remember to keep your face to the wall like you're sleeping—aye, and your wrists and ankles close together so the guards have no reason to doubt that you're tied—"

"I know, sweeting," Aud cut her off gently, curling onto her side as Triona spread the blanket over her. "Just make sure that you cover my hair. I've no pretty blond tresses like Caitlin's to fool them."

"I never heard any complaints from Taig O'Nolan that your dark hair was any less lovely," Triona murmured, smiling when she heard Aud's low chuckle. But she sobered when Caitlin touched her arm.

"I'm ready."

Triona straightened, knowing at once that she'd been right about the blue gown. Caitlin MacMurrough was a vision, her long golden hair combed to a glistening sheen. She was struck by the queer feeling that she might be looking into her own eyes, so closely did Caitlin's resemble hers, but she shrugged it off, handing her Aud's cloak.

"I know you urged me this morning to think of myself instead of worrying so much for you, but I'm determined to have you out of this wretched cell, Caitlin. I've thought of a way, too—that is, if you're willing to trust me—"

"I trust you."

Warmed by those simple words, Triona gave her a reassuring smile. "Then do exactly as I say. Keep the hood low over your face and keep your head down. And say nothing to the guards." Triona quickly swept up the rumpled gown Caitlin had discarded and stuffed it under Aud's blanket. "We'll be back as soon as we can, Aud."

"Aye, be careful, girls."

Triona and Caitlin slipped from the tiny room, both of them stopping at the outer door.

"Remember, Caitlin. Keep your head down and say nothing."

The young woman nodded and Triona thrust open the door, clearly startling the guards who spun to face them.

"That didn't take long," Fiach noted, rain dripping down his long nose and into his beard.

"The tear wasn't as bad as I'd thought," Triona said with a shrug, hurrying with Caitlin out into the downpour. "We'll be back in a short while with more blankets. It's so chilly in that cell, the poor girl might catch her death."

Fiach gave an unsympathetic grunt but held his tongue until they'd moved away—but not so far that Triona couldn't hear him grumbling to the others, "You'd think from all the fuss there was a queen in there and not some stinking MacMurrough."

Triona felt Caitlin stiffen beside her; she knew the young woman had heard him, too.

"I'm sorry," she began, feeling she must apologize for Fiach. But Caitlin shook her head, meeting Triona's eyes as they made their way across the muddy yard.

"To hate my clan is all those men have ever known, Triona. You can't expect otherwise."

Her throat tightening, Triona wondered suddenly if she had made a terrible mistake to bring Caitlin with her but they were already at their destination. Hoping her plan wouldn't meet the same outcome of five days ago, she held open the door and pushed Caitlin gently inside.

Chapter 35

"WHO LIVES HERE, Triona? Is this your house?"

She didn't have to reply as Niall's voice called to them from the other room.

"If you've come to make me another one of your nasty herb brews, man, then turn right around and go back whence you came! It's bad enough I have to lie here like a log while this damned leg of mine mends without having to down any more of that foul-tasting stuff."

"The O'Byrne's brother?" Caitlin asked incredulously, her wide eyes telling Triona that the young woman had realized it was Niall at once from everything she'd been told about the attack.

"Aye, Caitlin, but don't be frightened. Niall's not at all like Ronan—well, he is but he isn't. I mean their looks are similar, they're both terribly handsome, but—"

"What's all that whispering out there? Is that the healer or no?"

"No, Niall, it's Triona," she called, giving Caitlin's arm a reassuring squeeze.

"Well, come on with you, then. I've been wondering when you were going to pay me another visit given all the trouble between you and Ronan."

"You see?" Triona hissed, hoping she appeared more confident than she felt at that moment. "He's in a fine humor, so come on." Grasping Caitlin's hand, she began to steer her toward the door.

"Is that Aud with you? Now this is a pleasant surprise. Mayhap I can hope you brought me a sip of ale, too—"

"It's not Aud." Triona smiled nervously in spite of her best efforts to remain calm. She stepped into the room, drawing a reluctant Caitlin with her. "I've someone I want you to meet, Niall . . . Caitlin MacMurrough. I hope you—"

"Good God, Triona, have you lost your mind?"

Why was everyone demanding that of her? she thought, feeling affronted despite her stomach performing an anxious flip-flop at Niall's outburst. But he didn't look entirely furious; no, he looked more stunned, which gave her a boost of courage.

"Not at all, Niall O'Byrne, I've my wits about me. But is shouting how you welcome your guests? I remember you once chided Ronan for his lack of hospitality, but I never thought I'd be doing it to you. The least you could allow us is the chance to remove our hoods. They're dripping wet, you know."

Triona didn't wait for his assent but lowered her sodden hood as Niall gaped at her, Caitlin following her lead. In the next instant Niall wasn't staring at Triona anymore, but at the beautiful young woman who was standing at her shoulder.

"Would it pain you too much if we sat down?"

Silence reigned in the room, Triona's light query receiving no answer.

"Niall?"

He started, to her amazement a flush racing across his handsome features. "I'm sorry, Triona, did you say something?"

She had to fight hard not to smile, suddenly feeling very much heartened. "Just that we'd like to sit a while and visit . . . if that's all right with you."

"Of—of course. I mean, I suppose there's no harm in it, though Ronan might . . ." Niall shot a glance at Triona, but his eyes almost at once skipped back to Caitlin. "Ronan has no idea that you're here, does he?"

"I doubt we'd have made it this long if he did," Triona said wryly, taking the straight-backed chair at the foot of the bed. The closest one she left for Caitlin who, so far, hadn't uttered a word though her cheeks were as flushed as Niall's.

"Begorra, it's warm as Hades in here," Triona continued, hoping to spur some conversation. "Why don't you take off your cloak, Caitlin?"

"Aye, that damned healer ordered the hearth be kept roaring at all hours for fear the rains might bring on some fever," Niall said in a rush of explanation.

Caitlin gently pushed the cloak from her shoulders. "I hope you don't catch a fever. That would be terrible after everything you've suffered."

He stared at her, clearly as stunned by the fetching sight Caitlin made in her snug fitting blue gown as by the lilting sound of her voice. But he couldn't have looked more shocked when she added sincerely, "I'm sorry for what my clan did to you, Niall O'Byrne. Truly sorry."

Triona's breath jammed as she watched Niall's face, the momentary tightening of his jaw reminding her ominously of Ronan. Wondering if she'd been too quick to think that her plan was going well, she was relieved when Niall finally murmured, "It was no fault of yours, Caitlin MacMurrough. I accept your apology."

Silence fell again for the longest moment, but this time it seemed strained . . . almost as if Niall felt inhibited talking further with Caitlin in front of Triona. Realizing suddenly that *she* had become the third wheel on a cart needing only two, Triona rose hastily from her chair.

"Aye, well, I should see about that cup of ale you've been wanting, Niall."

"You're leaving, Triona?" Caitlin asked, half rising herself as if Triona expected her to come, too.

"No, no, sit," she insisted, not missing the flicker of pleasure across Caitlin's face. "I'll be back soon. Stay and talk with Niall."

"Aye, tell me how you managed to elude the guards who've been watching you night and day," Niall said as Triona made her way from the room and closed the door behind her. She leaned upon it for a moment, astounded in the next to actually hear Niall chuckling, Caitlin joining him.

Triona had herself seen this lighter side of Caitlin, the young woman growing less intimidated over the past days at Triona's assurances that all would be well. But to hear Caitlin laugh as she must at home in Ferns was a welcome sound, and for that, Triona had Niall to thank. Now if Niall might be able to convince Ronan that their innocent hostage was hardly deserving of the scorn being heaped upon her . . .

"Ale," Triona reminded herself when Niall's laughter burst through the door, grown teasing this time. She threw her hood over her hair and set off through the rain toward the kitchen, feeling more hopeful than she had in days.

"Those stout timber posts should hold no matter how heavy the rains, Lord. But we'll check on them again in the morning just to make certain," Flann O'Faelin informed Ronan.

Ronan nodded, though his mind was hardly on timber posts any longer. He parted ways with his drenched, mud-splattered clansmen at the stronghold's inner gates and strode full face into the stinging rain.

"You're not coming with us to the hall, Lord?"

Ronan gave no answer; the last thing he wanted was to spend another late afternoon and evening downing ale. He was wet and cold and muddy and most of all, sick to death of avoiding the woman he loved. He wanted a hot bath and he wanted Triona, not necessarily in that order.

And if the only way to have her back with him was to yield to her requests, then aye, he would do it.

Four restless interminable nights had convinced him that no MacMurrough wench was worth the strife between him and Triona. In a few weeks' time the damned girl would be gone, maybe even sooner. He could suffer her presence in his home for Triona's sake, no matter that the thought of catering to a MacMurrough still disgusted him.

"You men have a new post," he commanded as he approached the grain house, his three clansmen casting startled looks at each other. "I'm moving the hostage to my dwelling-house. From now on, you will stand guard at the windows outside her room."

The men stepped aside as he got to the door, Ronan already imagining the delighted look on Triona's face when she saw that he had relented. Anticipating as well the feel of her arms around him and the soft grateful kisses he could almost taste, he couldn't enter the grain house fast enough, shoving open the door to the cell.

"Get up, girl."

He saw her start beneath the blanket, but she made no move to rise which angered him.

"Didn't you hear me, wench?" He went to the pallet and bent down to wrest away the blanket. "I said get—"

"Forgive me, Lord!"

Astounded, Ronan straightened as Aud threw back the covering and clambered to her feet, her small plain face gone white. But she appeared no more stricken than his three guards as Ronan shot them a glance and then turned back to Aud.

"I-I'm sure this looks worse to you than it is, Lord—"

"Where's Triona taken the hostage?" he demanded. "To our dwelling-house?"

"I don't think so," Aud said in an anxious rush. "She didn't really say. All she told me was that she'd thought of a way to set everything to rights . . . a way to bring the both of you back together and—and I could do aught but help her—taking the MacMurrough girl's place—"

"Your lady left here no more than an hour past," broke in Fiach O'Byrne, the brawny clansman's face red with chagrin. "She said she was coming back in a short while"—his questioning gaze skipped to Aud—"with blankets for the hostage."

"Aye, Lord, Triona told me herself that she'd be back for me as soon as she could," Aud seconded.

Ronan didn't stay to hear more, the guards following close behind him as he stormed outside into the rain.

"Gather more men and search every corner of this place!" he ordered, setting out himself. But he didn't know where to search first, much of what Aud had said making little sense.

A way to set things right? A way to bring them together? Yet Triona had planned to come back? Surely if she had left the grain house with the MacMurrough wench posing as Aud, Triona knew she would have to return in the same way to get Aud out again without the guards suspecting . . .

"Unless Aud was deceived as well," Ronan muttered, his gut knotting as his gaze flew to the stronghold gates. All of them had been left open much of the day so his men could come and go while repairing the outer embankments.

By God, had Triona taken it in her head to aid the wench in an escape?

His heart pounding fiercely, Ronan ran toward the stable, his first instinct to check and see if Laeg was gone. But he'd gotten no farther than Niall's dwelling-house when he spied a hooded figure stepping out of the front door, wooden cup in hand.

He thought at first it might be the healer until the figure glanced up and saw him, uttering a most femininelike gasp. Before he could call her name, Triona had spun back into the house, slamming the door behind her.

"By God, woman, if I find . . ." Ronan didn't finish, bursting inside to a scene that he'd hardly expected. Triona was standing just beyond the door, her rain-streaked cloak still swirling, her expression the very picture of indignation as she pressed her hand over her heart.

"Jesu, Mary and Joseph, Ronan, do you have to come upon a person so suddenly? You can't blame me for being startled and running back inside—"

"You didn't duck inside because I startled you, Triona."

"Of course I did! And it's a good thing this cup was empty or I would have spilled ale all over myself. I was just going to the kitchen to fetch Niall another—"

"Where is she, Triona?"

His harsh tone appeared to rattle her, but she stared at him as blankly as a fish.

"Who? Aud? Why, I left her doing some mending when I came over to visit Niall—"

"Enough tales, woman! I just found Aud posing as the hostage I'd expected to escort to our dwelling-house. Now where is she?"

Triona couldn't have been more stunned, wondering if she'd heard him correctly. "Escort to our . . . You were going to let Caitlin come and stay with us?"

"Aye, but it seems you got to the grain house before me—"

Triona didn't let him finish, flinging her arms around his neck to hug him tight. "Oh, Ronan, I knew you would come around to seeing it my way! I knew you couldn't be so heartless!"

He embraced her, too, crushing her slim body against him. But he just as swiftly pushed her away to arm's length so he could look into her face.

"Triona, the hostage. You didn't help her escape, did you?"

"Caitlin's in here with me, brother."

Now it was Ronan's turn to look stunned, doubly when Niall's door was opened by the MacMurrough wench herself. She stared back at him, her eyes wide and apprehensive, her fingers twisting in her blue gown.

"What in blazes . . . ?"

"I brought her to meet Niall because I didn't know what else to do," came Triona's hasty explanation. "I thought if he could see that it wasn't right to hold a grudge against Caitlin— even after what he's suffered, mayhap he could influence you to think so, too. But I'd planned to have her back at her cell before you and Niall talked, so I ran inside the house to tell Caitlin to hide until you were gone. It never occurred to me that you might have already been to the grain house—"

"And you would have assisted in this ruse?" Ronan demanded of Niall, who was smiling reassuringly at Caitlin. Noting the heightened color of the young woman's cheeks and the furtive smile she threw back at Niall, Ronan didn't need to see more.

"That will be enough influencing for one day," he muttered, lunging for Caitlin and catching her by the arm. As she gasped, Niall exploded.

"Good God, Ronan, you don't have to be so rough!"

"And you'd do well to remember where your allegiance lies," he countered harshly, pulling Caitlin to the front door. "We'll talk of this later, Niall O'Byrne."

"Wait, Ronan, it's pouring out there!" Triona objected, running into Niall's room and snatching up Caitlin's cloak. But Ronan didn't wait for her, dragging his hostage into the rain. Triona could do no more than cast an anxious glance at Niall before she dashed outside.

"Where are you taking her?" she demanded, doing her best to fling the cloak around Caitlin's hunched shoulders as Ronan wrenched the sobbing girl along with him.

"Our dwelling-house, woman. Do you think your little plot has changed my mind? Now I've all the more reason to keep an eye on the wench, thanks to you!"

Knowing that he meant Niall, Triona swallowed nervously. She fell back a bit, starting when Aud caught up with her, a soaked blanket pulled over her maid's head like a cloak.

"I'm so sorry, sweeting! There wasn't anything I could do."

"It's all righ, Aud. Ronan's taking Caitlin to my room. It was his plan before he even came to the grain house."

"But where did the O'Byrne find you, sweeting?"

"At Niall's house," Triona said distractedly, cold rain lashing at her face. "But we can't talk about that now, Aud. Promise me you'll look after Caitlin. She'll need a hot bath, dry clothes—"

"Aye, I'll see to it."

"And send a bath at once to our room. And wine, Aud! Lots of wine. Ronan's in a terrible temper. . . ." Glancing ahead of her, Triona winced as Ronan practically hauled Caitlin over the threshold. "I've got to go to him, Aud. I'll see that the key is left for you in Caitlin's door."

Aud's reply was lost as Triona splashed across the yard, anger sweeping her that Ronan could be so cruel. Yet for once she prudently held her tongue when she got inside, Ronan's face truly ominous to behold as he slammed the door behind Caitlin and ground the key in the lock. Then he turned his wrath upon her, jerking his head toward their room.

"Inside. Now."

Chapter 36

TRIONA SILENTLY OBEYED him, bristling at his harsh command yet determined to keep her own temper in check. She'd gotten what she wanted after all, and most importantly, she and Ronan were back together. Now if only she could diffuse his fury—

She jumped as the door slammed shut, spinning around to face him. She doubted she'd seen him angrier, at least where she was concerned. Hoping to somehow lighten the tension, she gave him a small smile.

"Close the door any harder, Ronan, and you'd have brought the roof down upon us."

When he didn't readily reply, instead wresting his sodden cloak from his shoulders and hurling it with a wet smack to the floor, Triona knew her attempt had failed. Especially when he moved toward her, his storm gray eyes burning into hers.

"You think this is a jesting matter, Triona?"

"If . . . if you mean Niall," she began, edging backward.

"Aye, I mean Niall," Ronan broke in tightly, advancing upon her. "You're playing the matchmaker again, woman, but this time with fire and water, two things that can never mate. Each can only consume or smother the other—"

"And you're making much more of this than there is!" she blurted, half stumbling when she suddenly backed into a chair. Ronan caught her by the shoulders before she could fall but she didn't try to wrench away from him despite that his grip was punishing. Instead she lifted her chin and faced him squarely. "I hoped Niall might see things differently than you, is all."

"It seems he has," Ronan said. "Swayed by flowing blond hair and a face and form any man might lust over, no matter that the cursed wench is a MacMurrough."

"Oh, so you have noticed how pretty Caitlin is," Triona spouted indignantly, realizing, too, that she didn't like it one bit. To her surprise, a flicker of amusement crossed Ronan's face but he quickly sobered as if trying hard to hang on to his anger.

"Aye, with eyes as lovely and green as yours. And skin almost as fair."

Triona's mouth fell open; vexation overwhelmed her. Now she did try to twist away from him, nearly managing it when she stomped on his foot. But if she'd hurt him, he gave no sign, grabbing her around the waist in such a way that her back came up hard against his chest.

"A wee bit jealous, Triona O'Toole?" came his hot whisper against her ear.

"Not at all," she lied, still struggling against him despite the delicious chills racing through her. "You can look where you will, you spawn! We're not married yet, after all."

He twirled her around so suddenly to face him that she felt lightheaded, his powerful arms closing so tightly around her that she could scarcely breathe.

"Do you truly think that I could look further than eyes that shine with the spirit of ten women and copper curls with enough gold fire to rival the sun? Soft skin the color of finest cream and a body so perfectly fashioned as to haunt a thousand dreams?"

"Only a thousand?" she could not help teasing him though her voice was no more than a whisper.

"Aye, greedy as she is brazen," he countered huskily, his lips so close to hers that she ached to taste them. "Very well, woman. A lifetime of dreams."

He lifted her and kissed her so passionately that Triona was certain if her feet had been touching the ground, her knees would have buckled beneath her. It was so wonderful to feel his mouth on hers again! So wonderful to feel the strength of his arms, his honed body pressed so intimately against her breasts, her belly, her hips, a blazing heat rising between them despite the cool dampness of their clothes. Her head was truly spinning when he finally released her, but even so Triona couldn't resist teasing him further.

"So I'm to be marrying a poet, am I?"

"Aye, I've been known to have a way with words—at least I did before Conor . . ."

Seeing the sudden pain in his eyes, Triona reached up and gently touched the side of his face. "All's forgiven, remember? And forgotten. If I'm to haunt your dreams, Ronan O'Byrne, there can't be any more room for Conor. Let's leave him rest, or at least smile when we think of him. Agreed?"

Ronan nodded, burying his face in her hair as he enveloped her in a crushing embrace. His voice was hoarse when he finally spoke long moments later, his gentle teasing only endearing him that much more to Triona's heart.

"So it seems I'm to be marrying a sage."

"A sage is it now? I thought I was your angel?"

"Aye, you're that, and a good bit of a troublemaker, too." He drew back to look at her, his expression growing sober. "But I'll keep you all the same if you promise not to meddle again in matters best left for me to manage."

"What? And let you have all the fun?"

That comment brought a frown to Ronan's face, but it fled when Triona rose on tiptoes and kissed him. She even teased his lips with a darting swipe of her tongue just to make him smile, but that only made him groan, and pull her close, funneling his fingers through her hair.

"By God, woman, it's been too long since I've held you like this. Too long—"

The sudden knock at the door made Ronan groan again, but this time out of frustration. Reluctantly releasing Triona, he bade her as he moved across the room, "Stay right where you are."

"I have no intention of going anywhere," came her low-spoken reply, her seductive smile making it all the more difficult for Ronan to take his eyes from her. But he did, opening the door to find Fiach O'Byrne.

"We heard you found the girl, Lord. I wanted you to know that guards have been posted outside her windows as you ordered. Do you want a man stationed at her door?"

"No, the lock will be enough," Ronan answered, not wanting any of his clansmen standing guard in the outer room just in case he and Triona might decide to enjoy the hearth fire together.

As Fiach nodded and turned away, Ronan began to shut the door only to hear another sharp rap. Exhaling with impatience, he discovered Aud standing outside, the poor woman drenched and breathless, her face drawn with worry.

"The water . . . is here for your bath, Lord."

"I ordered no bath," Ronan began, only to hear Triona come up behind him.

"No, but I did. And some wine."

"Wine?" he queried, raising a black brow.

"To soothe you," she said simply, glancing past him to give Aud a reassuring smile. When Ronan turned back to the older woman, he could see that she had visibly relaxed, the sparkle returned to her large brown eyes.

"Aye well, since it seems to me you won't be needing as much soothing, I'll just send one of those casks back to the kitchen," Aud said as she gestured for the servants lined up behind her to start carrying in the water for the tub.

Ronan glanced wryly at Triona as they both stepped out of the way. "*Two* casks of wine? I would have been senseless, not soothed."

Triona shrugged as she looked up at him, though she curled her hand into his large warm one. "I wasn't sure my kisses would prove enough for the task, so I came up with a secondary plan."

She was thrilled when Ronan drew her close against him, his impatient expression matching her own eagerness that the servants quickly finish filling the tub and then leave them in peace. But Ronan's husky whisper thrilled her all the more, his words meant only for her ears.

"Your kisses would have found you tossed upon my bed if we'd had no interruptions, woman. I need no wine to feel drunk from the taste of you."

Her breath caught at the scorching look in his eyes. Triona was scarcely aware that Aud and the rest of the servants had left the room. But Ronan had noticed because he made a move to close the door only to suddenly stiffen. A frown marred his features as he stared at the six brimming buckets waiting near the hearth, then to Aud who was looking at him wide-eyed and worried again.

"Is that water not for our bath as well?"

Triona quickly came to Aud's rescue. "The rest is for Caitlin, Ronan, at my orders—"

"Your orders?" he cut in, a muscle flashing at his jaw. "I'd rather it be thrown outside into the mud than—"

"Please, Ronan," Triona said softly, squeezing his hand. "Let Aud see to Caitlin's needs. Please."

He didn't answer for what seemed to Triona the longest time, but finally she felt some of the tension ease from his body.

"Very well, bathe the accursed chit. And Aud . . ."

"Aye, Lord?"

"See to yourself as well. I don't relish answering to Taig O'Nolan if you catch a chill."

Aud smiled, a blush warming her cheeks. "I'll change into some dry clothes straightaway, Lord."

"It's Ronan. Call me Ronan."

"Thank you, Lord. I mean, Ronan."

"As for the rest of you," Ronan addressed the servants who stood waiting for Aud's direction. "Tell the cook that I'll be expecting a fine supper to be served tonight in the hall. We've known little merriment these past days but that sorry state"— he glanced meaningfully at Triona—"I'm pleased to say has changed." He closed the door on a ring of astonished faces, leaving him and Triona finally, blessedly, alone.

"Thank you, Ronan," she murmured, seeing that his face still bore a hint of hardness. "It was a very kind thing you've done for Caitlin—"

"I've done nothing for the girl," he broke in, though Triona knew his harsh tone was not directed at her. "All I've done is for you, Triona. Never forget that. I wouldn't care if that MacMurrough wench sat in her room shivering the night away. But I care about you and for that reason alone, I will yield to your wishes." He swore fluently under his breath as he stepped away from the door. "Though I grant you, it's not going to be easy for me. Just the thought that she's under my roof . . ."

Triona heard the sheer loathing in his voice and shivered, grateful that she had his love and not his hate. Quickly she shed her wet cloak, but she didn't hasten overmuch as she began to slip her jerkin from her shoulders.

"Then what can I do to distract you, Ronan? Since you've given me so much, surely there must be something I can give you."

"Aye, there's something," he murmured, walking toward her. Within the blink of an eye he had hauled his drenched tunic over his head and tossed it aside, his hands moving to his trousers. "Are you going to undress, Triona O'Toole, or is it your plan merely to stare at me?"

Triona gave a saucy smile as her gaze roamed appreciatively over his bare chest. "But there's so much for me to admire . . . Ronan!" She shrieked as he lunged for her and caught her around the waist.

"Don't you think I'd like to admire you as well?"

Ronan had slid her sodden shirt over her head before Triona could shriek again, her breasts bared to his admiring gaze. But he didn't stand there looking at her for long, opting instead for sweeping her into his arms and tossing her onto the bed.

"What of our hot bath?" she blurted, made breathless as he straddled her hips, his eyes blazing into hers like molten silver. "You must be chilled from being so long in the rain—"

"With a wild one like you beneath me?" he cut in huskily, bending down to tease a roused nipple with his tongue. As Triona arched beneath him, he laughed, a deliciously wicked sound that excited her as much as his suckling. After he'd played with her breasts for a heart-stopping moment longer, he lifted his dark head to stare into her eyes.

"You'll keep me warm, Triona. I've no doubt of it. Now since you're giving things away, I'd like another one of those kisses. . . ."

He didn't have to say more, Triona wrapping her arms around his neck and blissfully obliging him.

Chapter 37

THE FAINT RAP came at the door an all too short two hours later, Triona snuggling closer to Ronan as a female servant's voice called out, "I was sent by the cook, Lord. All is in readiness at the hall."

"We will attend shortly," he called back, turning his head to brush a kiss on Triona's brow. But she raised her chin so he caught the tip of her nose instead, which made him chuckle. "I fear, beautiful lady, that it's time to rise."

"I'm staying right here." Triona threw a slim leg over his thigh as if she could pin him down. To entice him further, she rubbed her toes up and down his hard calf, nestling against him even closer. "Supper will just have to go on without us."

"Not this night," he murmured, though his deep voice held regret. "My people need to see that all is well between us, Triona. These past five days have been hard on everyone, not just ourselves."

She sighed, knowing he was making perfect sense but not wanting this wondrous time together to end.

"We have only to stay an hour or so, Triona," he whispered into her ear as if reading her mind. "Everyone will understand if we slip away." He slid his hand down the curve of her back and playfully squeezed her bottom. "They'll understand that we have other things to do."

She smiled, but she was still reluctant to leave him. At least until he tweaked her bottom—and not so gently!—making her gasp and spring from the bed.

"Ronan, I'll have a bruise!"

"Then I'll be sure to massage it for you," he said wickedly, rising. Yet he didn't get far, staring at her in so lusty a manner that she was certain he was reconsidering stepping even one foot from their room. But finally he turned away and went to his clothes chest, the decision clearly costing him for the many times he glanced at her as he pulled out fresh garments.

Triona, meanwhile, swept up her damp cloak and wrapped it snugly around herself, then headed for the door.

"Triona?"

She half turned, expecting his query. "My clothes are in the other room."

"And they'll be moved into this room come morning," he said, frowning. But Triona had expected that, too, so she threw him a teasing smile.

"Aye, then you can watch me both dress and undress." As his frown eased just as she had hoped, Triona was struck by a sudden idea that filled her with nervous excitement. "You don't have to wait for me, Ronan. I'll meet you at the feasting-hall."

"You'll do no such thing," he began. "I want us to walk in together."

"Please, Ronan. I've a surprise for you, but if you insist on waiting, you'll spoil it."

She lingered only long enough for him to nod reluctantly, then she hurried from the room, her heart racing. Her idea was so silly, really, but she wanted to please him. And she'd thought of the perfect way, spurred on by the memory of how he'd looked at her that first night she'd entered his hall. . . .

Conn's tail thunking heavily upon the floor drew Triona's attention to the hearth; she took a moment to go over and give her wolfhound a pat.

"Poor dog, I don't blame you for hiding back here out of the fray," she murmured, stroking his ears. "But all's well now, I promise. So get up with you and go see Ronan. Mayhap he'll let you accompany him to the hall for a bit of supper. Go on. Find Ronan."

As Conn heaved himself to his feet and obliged her, Triona went to her former room, feeling guilty that she'd been paying so little heed to her pets of late. Her poor Ferdiad least of all.

Deciding that she would ask Ronan if they might take her beautiful falcon on a hunt tomorrow, Triona turned the key in the lock, the room lit softly with oil lamps as she entered. She was pleased to see Caitlin nestled in bed, Maeve curled into a sleek white ball on the young woman's lap and purring contentedly.

"I see you've found a friend," Triona said as she closed the door behind her, Caitlin throwing her a welcoming smile that was truly dazzling.

"Three friends, Triona. You, Aud, Maeve . . ." The young woman paused, a becoming pink blush suffusing her cheeks. "Well, four friends."

Realizing that Caitlin meant Niall, Triona nodded but said nothing more. She had only to remember Ronan's fearful wrath to know that would be akin to playing with fire. And for that reason she decided to tell her no more about Maire either, and the other way around. She imagined if the two young women ever met, they'd like each other well enough to give Ronan another fit.

Instead, Triona checked to see that the window coverings were well drawn against the clansmen standing guard outside and then went to her clothes chest, thinking guiltily that she'd been a ninny to feel jealous about Caitlin. How could a man not look twice at such rare beauty? With her delicate features and golden hair, Caitlin MacMurrough appeared more an angel than any woman Triona had ever seen.

"I came to change for supper," she said, lifting carefully from the chest the emerald green gown she was supposed to have worn at her wedding.

"What? No shirt and trousers this night?"

Triona blushed at Caitlin's gentle ribbing, suddenly feeling a bit ridiculous. Here she'd always sworn up and down how much she hated gowns, and now she was actually eager to wear one. But before she could say a word, Caitlin had climbed from the bed and hastened to her side.

"I think it's wonderful you and the O'Byrne have reconciled, Triona. Aud told me. And you'll look so lovely for him in that gown. Let me help you."

As Caitlin drew a finely textured camise from the chest, Triona was touched that the young woman could be so giving after the rough treatment she'd received at Ronan's hands.

"Here, put this on while I hold your gown."

Triona did as she was bade, letting the cloak drop to the floor as she settled the delicate camise over her head. Next came the silk gown, Caitlin uttering so many compliments that Triona grew embarrassed and asked her to stop as she drew on some soft leather slippers.

"Why should I stop?" Caitlin objected, showing a hint of the spirit that Triona had always suspected she possessed. "You should know how pretty you look, Triona. The O'Byrne might not mind you wearing trousers, but you'll surely turn his head tonight. Now if you had some ornaments . . ."

"I've these." Triona carefully lifted a small silk-wrapped bundle from the chest. As she drew forth the jeweled arm-ring and the lustrous strand of pink pearls Taig O'Nolan had brought her from Carlow, Caitlin gasped.

"Oh, they're beautiful. Put them on! Put them on!"

Caitlin's excitement matched Triona's, wearing such baubles truly a new thing to her. And she found she liked the effect very much, though she hoped Ronan wouldn't mind that she'd donned gifts given to her by another man, albeit a friend.

"Now let me brush out your hair for you, Triona, and you'll be ready," said Caitlin, but Triona firmly shook her head.

"You're not here to wait upon me." She went herself to the low table by the bed and got her brush.

"I don't see it as that at all," Caitlin countered, looking hurt. "You've done so much for me, Triona. If there's at least some small way I can repay you . . ."

Triona relented at once, anything to bring the light back to Caitlin's eyes. "Very well, but my hair's a fine mess. Always has been."

"I think it's lovely," Caitlin said as Triona handed her the brush and then sank onto the edge of the bed, preparing herself for the sharp tugging that would be involved. But to her relief, Caitlin's touch was deft and gentle.

"I used to brush my grandmother's hair before she died. It was wild with curls just like yours, though it had long since gone gray. But my father told me her hair had once been as fiery red as can be."

"Is his hair red, too?" Triona asked absently, the soft swish of the brush lulling her.

"Aye, but with lots of gold in it, like yours. Funny, isn't it?"

Triona nodded, realizing, too, that Ronan would be wondering what was keeping her if she didn't appear soon at the feasting-hall. With a long contented sigh she rose, smiling at Caitlin.

"Any more of that and I'll surely fall asleep."

"I was finished anyway. Do you have a mirror?"

Triona laughed. "I hardly need to look at myself after all the fine compliments you've given me, Caitlin MacMurrough!" She hurried to the clothes chest and swept up her cloak, looking down when a dull thud sounded near her foot.

"You dropped something, Triona. Here, I'll get it."

Caitlin had retrieved her dagger before Triona could bend down herself, but the young woman didn't readily hand it to her. Instead Caitlin stared at the weapon as if stunned, her face gone strangely pale.

"Where . . . where did you get this?"

"It was my father's," Triona murmured, surprised as well by Caitlin's odd behavior. Especially when the young woman glanced up at her, staring at Triona, at her face, at her hair as if she couldn't believe her eyes.

"Caitlin . . ."

"I thought I saw a resemblance from the very first," said the young woman almost to herself, her expression incredulous. "But it never occurred to me—I never thought . . ."

"Thought what?" Triona demanded, a strange chill coursing through her. But Caitlin was gazing down again at the dagger, turning it over and over in her palm.

"My father has one exactly like this—he always wears it in his belt. Only it's much bigger to fit his hand but he told me that a matching one"—Caitlin held out the glittering weapon—"a smaller one, was fashioned especially for his younger sister, Eva, when she so admired his."

"Eva?" Triona asked, feeling the blood creep from her face.

"Aye, he presented it to her on the eve of her wedding to Richard de Roche of Naas."

A wedding between Irish and Norman, Triona found herself thinking, Caitlin's words suddenly bringing to mind the story Ronan had told her on her first night at Glenmalure about his cook Seamus toiling at such an occasion. And Seamus had called her Lady Eva just before he died, gaping at her in terror as if she were a ghostly phantom come back to haunt the living. . . .

"This has nothing to do with me!" she lashed out, willing away her heart-stopping niggling of intuition. "The dagger belonged to my father, it's as simple as that." She snatched the weapon from Caitlin and stuffed it back inside her cloak. "There could have been more than two that looked like this—"

"Did your father give it to you?"

"No, I found it hidden—" Triona didn't say anything more, clamping her mouth shut as she fled across the room. But Caitlin flew after her, catching her by the arm to stop her.

"You said you never knew your true mother, Triona. You said that she must have had lots of copper hair. But what if I told you that your mother looked much like me—or so I've been told. I never knew my father's sister because she was killed by a wild boar four years before I was born. But she was blond—"

"I told you this has nothing to do with me!" Triona cut in, desperation seizing her as she yanked her arm free and bolted for the door.

"This has everything to do with you, Triona, don't you see?" Caitlin cried, running after her. "Eva had an infant daughter who was thought to have died in the forest as well—carried off by wolves. At least that's what Maurice de Roche later told my father. He was the one who found my aunt's body and brought her back to Kildare."

Triona had halted her flight and spun, her eyes riveted to Caitlin's. "Maurice de Roche?"

"Aye. Richard's younger brother. A foul evil man, too. My father never found proof, but he's always suspected that

Maurice murdered Richard for his rich barony, then sought to make Eva his wife. But she ran away with her daughter, Juliana—my father is certain that she feared for her young babe. Maurice de Roche could never have made the barony his own with an heiress in the way."

"No more," Triona said almost in a whisper, sickened. But Caitlin pressed her all the same.

"How did your father say he found you?"

"In the forest," Triona murmured numbly. "He was hunting and found me crying, my parents dead beside me. Killed by wolves. He brought me home to Imaal and adopted me into the clan as his daughter."

"It was Eva he found dead beside you, Triona. He must have found the dagger, too, then hid it just as you said."

"Aye, in that small coffer," she admitted without thinking, tears blurring her eyes as she glanced beyond Caitlin to the furnishings still stacked against the wall. "Behind a false bottom."

"Mayhap your father had planned to keep the dagger there until he could rid himself of it, but forgot—"

"Enough, Caitlin! I will hear no more!"

"But you must listen! This makes us cousins, you and I, and your name isn't Triona. You're Juliana Margaret de Roche, heiress to one of the richest baronies in Eire if you only lay claim to it. And you must, for your true parents' sake! You owe that to them—"

"I owe them nothing!" Triona broke in, tears tumbling down her face. "My father was Fineen, chieftain of the Imaal O'Tooles, my mother the Lady Alice. I would die before I ever called myself a de Roche!"

She fled to the door and this time, Caitlin made no move to stop her. The last thing Triona saw before she dashed from the room was Caitlin's stricken face, then she slammed the door shut, her fingers shaking so badly she could barely turn the key in the lock. But somehow she managed, swiping the tears from her face as she rushed past the hearth. She noticed at once that Conn was gone, imagining the wolfhound had tagged along with Ronan.

Ronan.

Dear God, what was she going to do now? If he ever found out that she was everything he hated—

"Triona?"

She started, her gaze flying to Aud as her maid entered the dwelling-house carrying a covered platter.

"I just saw the O'Byrne—I mean Ronan, in the hall. He's beginning to pace a bit, sweeting, so I suggest you hurry—"

"Tell me what you know about this dagger," Triona demanded, racing up to her and yanking the weapon from her pocket. Her spirits sank even lower when Aud blanched, but her maid quickly recovered herself, shrugging as she walked past her.

"You found it with your father's things. Inside a brass-fitted chest, as I recall."

"Aye, and you know well enough why he put it there," Triona accused, following her. "You were shocked when I first showed you the dagger, Aud, and I thought it strange. But you said it was only because you were tired, snapping at me as you've never done before."

"A body can become weary now and again, but if you're holding a grudge against me for being short with you that day, then I'm sorry."

"Aye, but you acted just as strangely when I told you about Seamus, Aud. Remember? When I said the poor man seemed to know me, calling me Lady Eva?"

"I thought it was queer, is all," Aud said stiffly, though her determined step had faltered a little. That was enough to bring fresh tears to Triona's eyes, her voice gone hoarse.

"Aud, you can't hide the truth from me any longer. You can't! I know about my true parents."

The older woman stopped, her face gone deathly pale. But she nonetheless made a brave attempt to change the subject. "Ronan is waiting for you, sweeting. Shouldn't you go to him? And . . . and Caitlin's supper is growing cold—"

"Please, Aud," Triona broke in, smudging away tears with the back of her hand. "My father told me that my parents were killed by wolves, but that's not the truth, is it?"

For a long moment Aud simply stared at her, but finally she shook her head. "No, it wasn't the truth."

"And my real mother's name was Eva."

Aud nodded, tears clouding her eyes. "Saints helps us, sweeting, how could you have discovered—"

"Caitlin told me."

"Caitlin?" Aud looked stunned, but she seemed confused as well. "No, that couldn't be—"

"She recognized my dagger, Aud, just a few moments ago. Her father, Donal, has one just like it, matching exactly the weapon that once belonged to my mother. Eva MacMurrough."

"MacMurrough?" Aud blurted. "But I've always thought your mother was Norman. And I'd never have known that if I hadn't come into the house of a sudden and overheard the O'Toole telling the pitiful tale to Lady Alice shortly after he brought you home. He made me swear on a crucifix right there and then that I'd never say a word to anyone, and I did so gladly. You were my sweeting from the first moment I laid eyes upon you, no matter your Norman blood."

"Half Norman, Aud. And half MacMurrough. I don't know what could be worse." Triona thought again of Ronan, despair filling her. But she couldn't allow herself to succumb to it. The last thing she needed was for him to sense that something was wrong. "I must go, Aud. Ronan is waiting."

"But your true father, Triona. The O'Toole never mentioned any names and if he ever found out the identity of the Norman baron who wanted to see you dead, he said nothing of it to me."

"So the spawn did try to hunt me down," Triona murmured, Caitlin's words coming back to her.

"Oh aye, and he might have found you, too, if the O'Toole hadn't come along when he did, saving you from a pack of wolves as well. The O'Toole heard you crying, and it's a good thing you were so young that you don't remember what happened to your brave mother. She died protecting you from a wild boar, sweeting. The O'Toole found that dagger sticking from the beast's throat."

Triona stared at the bloodred rubies studding the hilt, for the first time pitying the mother she had never known.

"It was when the O'Toole was about to bury the poor soul that the Normans came upon him," Aud rushed on. "He hid behind a tree and heard everything—the baron saying how he'd planned upon murdering you if the wolves hadn't found you first."

"But how would he ever have thought that wolves—"

"The O'Toole had thrown your bloodied swaddling blanket to the wild creatures to flush them from the trees. The baron's men found what shreds were left. Then they took up your mother's body and rode away, but not before the O'Toole heard the baron say he'd murdered your true father to make Eva his bride."

"Richard de Roche," Triona said under her breath although Aud had heard her well enough, her maid's eyes growing very wide. "Baron of Naas—at least until his younger brother saw fit to slay his own blood for the land and title."

"His brother?"

"Maurice de Roche."

Aud gasped, her eyes nearly popping from her head. "So the O'Toole *was* warning you in that dream, sweeting! Warning you to stay well away from that monster! Saints preserve us, you're in terrible danger just as I thought."

"Aye, of losing the man I love." Her throat was so tight that she thought she might choke. Triona pocketed the dagger and then whirled the cloak around her shoulders, walking on wooden legs to the door only to have it suddenly open in front of her.

"By God, woman, what surprise could keep you this long from my side?"

Chapter 38

"RONAN!" HEARING AUD echo her, Triona practically pushed him back outside, fearful that her distraught maid might say something they'd all regret. But she was quickly able to cover her action, spouting with feigned lightness as she looped her arm through his, "Black O'Byrne, you've no patience at all!"

"Not when it comes to you," he countered with a roguish smile, clearly finding no fault with her odd behavior. "Now where's my surprise?"

"You'll see at supper," she tossed back although she was finding it very difficult to talk. But she couldn't allow him to think that something was wrong. She couldn't! She began to tug him playfully in the direction of the feasting-hall only to have him sweep her into his arms.

"If I didn't know better, I'd say you're wearing a maiden's soft slippers," he said, kissing the sensitive shell of her ear. "And if that's the case, we can't have you ruining them in the mud. The rains might have stopped, but the yard looks as wet as a bog."

With a start, Triona realized that it was no longer raining; she felt so distracted that she hadn't even noticed. Somehow she managed again to keep her voice light, though she felt inside as if her heart were breaking.

"Ronan, just pretend you didn't see any slippers or you'll spoil my surprise. Now are we just going to stand here or . . ."

She fell silent as a clansman suddenly came around the corner of the dwelling-house, the night so dark that she didn't realize it was Fiach O'Byrne until he was almost upon them.

The man looked so grim that Triona went tense, swept by another terrible niggling of intuition.

Jesu, Mary and Joseph, if Fiach had been standing guard just outside Caitlin's windows, then he must have overheard everything! He knew!

"By God, Fiach, you've been guarding that wench all day," Ronan said with easy good humor before the clansman could speak, setting off with Triona toward the hall. "I'll send replacements at once so you and the other two guards can join us for supper. The cook has outdone himself tonight. I've already tasted a bit of roast mutton."

"But, Lord—"

"Later, man! My bride-to-be has a special surprise for me that cannot wait."

Triona's heart was pounding so fiercely at that close call she was certain Ronan could hear it. But he seemed oblivious to her distress, and thankfully so. Wiping her hand over her cheeks as swiftly as possible to rid herself of any last traces of tears, she masked her purpose by saying, "I think I just felt a bit of rain."

"Then we'll have to hurry, won't we?" He pressed another warm kiss against her ear. "Don't think I've forgotten our plan, Triona. A bite of supper and it's back to our room."

Triona didn't reply, the husky promise in his voice only filling her with dread.

Realizing now that she would have to tell him before someone else did what she still found so hard to believe herself, she prayed when the moment came she would find the right words. But would Ronan be willing to listen to anything further after he heard that she was both MacMurrough and Norman? The heiress to vast lands that had been stolen from the O'Byrnes?

"Smile, Triona, so my people can see that all is well."

Somehow she did, blinking at the brilliant torchlight as Ronan carried her into the feasting-hall. He didn't set her down straightaway but conveyed her to the head table amid rousing shouts of approval.

To her surprise Niall was there, reclining in a makeshift litter drawn to the table, his wide grin telling her that he must already know Caitlin was faring better. Maire was there, too, the most curious smile on her lips, her gray eyes alight and her cheeks flushed bright pink with color. Triona wondered fleetingly what they both might say if they knew she and Caitlin were cousins, then she thrust the thought away as Ronan gently put her down.

"Is my surprise underneath your cloak?" he whispered in her ear, his teasing expression leading her to believe that he had guessed she wore a gown. When she nodded, her smile pasted upon her face, he chuckled and drew the garment from her shoulders.

Triona almost burst into tears at the look he gave her, his eyes so full of love that she couldn't bear to think of the contempt that would soon replace it. "You're pleased?" she asked brokenly, the emotion between them so palpable that she reasoned he wouldn't think anything was amiss if she looked about to cry.

"In all ways, Triona," he murmured, bending his head to kiss her soundly in front of everyone. Cheers were rocking the hall when he finally lifted his mouth from hers to whisper against her ear, "What became of all those little presents I gave you when you were a child? The ribbons, the gold trinkets—"

"I—I threw them in a bog," Triona stammered, his question taking her entirely by surprise. "After Conor—"

"Aye, and you had every right," Ronan murmured, pulling away to stare into her eyes. But Triona saw no pain in his eyes, only love, and again, she came very close to tears. Then she felt his large strong hands capture hers and bring them up to his chest, a small silk-wrapped package pressed into her palm.

"What . . . ?"

"A gift, Triona." He gave her a wry smile. "I only hope this one doesn't end up in a bog. It belonged to my mother."

She was stunned, staring dumbly at the bundle until Ronan began to chuckle and unwrapped it for her himself. A low gasp rippled through the hall as he held up the most beautiful necklace Triona had ever seen, delicate gold beads alternating with sparkling gems of every hue: emeralds, blue sapphires, topazes, red garnet and amethysts.

"These pearls from Taig O'Nolan are very lovely, Triona," Ronan said huskily as he lifted the pink strand over her head and replaced it with his glittering surprise. "But I want only my gifts to adorn you."

Triona had to blink away tears as he replaced her jeweled arm-ring, too, with a heavy bracelet of purest gold.

"Aye, and you'll need a coffer for all of your beautiful things," Maire said behind Ronan, her voice oddly catching.

Triona understood why when Ronan stepped aside, Maire rising from her chair with only the aid of her crutch while Ita stood close by, the plump serving woman's eyes shining as brightly as her young mistress's. Maire gestured to the jewel chest a servant placed upon the table, the same elegant coffer Triona had seen at Maire's house that first day she'd gone to visit.

"It's for you, Triona. I've a gift for Aud, too, for helping me. . . ."

"Then you know?" Triona blurted, meeting Ronan's gaze.

"Aye. Maire had a special surprise for me tonight as well." He took her hands and brought them to his lips, his breath warm as he looked into her eyes. "You're a kind, compassionate woman, Triona O'Toole. Thank you for helping my sister."

As he gently kissed her fingers, Triona had never felt more wretched, the evening that should have been so perfect become a nightmare.

She had never seen the O'Byrne clan so merry, the feasting-hall alive with good cheer, while she was miserable. Yet she continued to smile and tease and banter, to sample the smoked salmon, venison sausage and roast goose Ronan set upon her plate though she tasted nothing, to drink the scarlet wine he poured into her silver cup though it made her want to choke.

It soon became clear when the meal was nearly done that Ronan was enjoying himself far too much yet to leave, Triona noticing the looks his people were casting him as if astonished to see him smiling and laughing as easily as Niall. Yet they appeared wholly pleased, too, and for that reason Triona guessed Fiach O'Byrne had chosen to remain at the back of the hall with the two guards who'd entered with him.

She had seen them at once, her heart lurching in her breast as she wondered if Fiach would make his terrible announcement to the entire clan. But he merely ate his supper, apparently loath to disrupt the night's merriment. But she didn't doubt for a moment from the somber way he was staring at her that if he found Ronan alone, he would tell him.

She had one more scare when a clansman came to their table, a cloaked guard as drenched and muddy as Ronan had been earlier that day. Just to hear the man mention the name Maurice de Roche was enough to make her blanch, her fingers trembling as she gripped her wine cup. But she relaxed the tiniest bit when she heard that the guard had just come from Kildare with news that the baron would be returning to his castle as soon as King John sailed home from Dublin.

"Did you hear that?" Ronan roared to his people after he'd bade the man to go warm himself by the fire. "The Norman king is receiving homage from his vassals at Dublin castle. Mayhap the loyal Donal MacMurrough is there as well, licking that dog's stinking feet!"

Triona winced as the hall erupted in jeers; she dropped her gaze when she saw that Fiach was watching her. She said nothing, even when Ronan leaned over and whispered, "We'll have our vengeance soon, Triona. Even if I have to flush the good baron from his castle by setting fire to his fields just as you suggested. That I vow. And if it pleases you, you may send de Roche to hell with one of your arrows. It would be fitting."

She had no time to dwell upon his offer, for in the next moment his voice had sunk to a whisper. "Sing for me, Triona."

She was stunned, though it made sense that he would make such a request. Yet she shook her head, her emotions too frayed to bear it.

"Aye, woman, you must. You know how much it would please me."

She swallowed hard, his slate gray eyes burning so intently into hers that she could not refuse him. As Ronan gestured for the gaunt harper to come forward, Triona rose and went around the table to join the man, her cheeks afire at the knowledge that Ronan's gaze was upon her.

She could not sing of love. Not when hers was being so horribly threatened. Instead she sang of Cuchulain and his heroic deeds, and of his noble death on the battlefield, his back to a rock and his face bravely to the foe.

When she was done, the last shimmering strains of the harp fading into the air, there was a great silence in the hall. All faces were turned toward her as if spellbound until at last, the harper's voice shattered the stillness.

"If ever fairer singing has been heard in Eire, let me cast down my harp and play no more!"

Immediately the hall erupted in cheers, Ronan's people using their silver cups, their cutting knives, their shoes to bang upon the tables. It was such a wild din that Triona didn't hear Ronan walk up behind her. She jumped when she felt his strong hands encircle her waist.

"Aye, woman, you've pleased me well," he said against her ear, embracing her as the deafening tumult raged around them. "Come. It's time we take our leave."

If he'd pronounced a death sentence upon her, the effect would have been the same. Stricken, Triona somehow made her legs carry her from the hall after he'd settled her cloak around her shoulders, Ronan leading her by the hand. And this time he noticed her distress. As soon as they stepped outside, he faced her, concern etched upon his handsome face.

"Triona, are you feeling well? You're so pale."

"The . . . the hall was overwarm." She shrugged, mustering a smile to reassure him. "Or mayhap the wine was too rich."

"Or too plentiful. You emptied your cup four times."

If she had, Triona possessed no recollection of it. She had been so preoccupied with what lay ahead, she was surprised she hadn't drunk more.

"Here, I will carry you."

She didn't protest. When he lifted her, she wound her arms around his neck and buried her face against his shoulder, his clean male scent doing little to soothe her. She didn't look up again until they were almost to their dwelling-house, when Triona glanced back toward the hall. She saw a dark male shape standing outside the doors and guessed at once it was

Fiach, her stomach twisting into knots as Ronan carried her into the house.

At least the main room was empty, Aud nowhere to be seen. Ronan set her down gently just inside their room and then left her for a moment, Triona watching him as he went to Caitlin's door and pulled the key from the lock. He was frowning when he returned, his jawline set angrily in the orange glow of the hearth.

"I long for the day when that accursed wench is finally gone from Glenmalure."

Triona felt suddenly as if she couldn't breathe. She stepped out of his way as he tossed the heavy key onto a bench against the wall. But she gasped when he suddenly pulled her into his arms, kicking the door shut behind her. His breath was warm and scented with wine as he looked down into her face, though they couldn't see each other at all in the dark. Yet she knew when he spoke that his lips were very, very near.

"Forgive me, Triona. It wasn't my intent to spoil our evening."

She remained mute, tears welling in her eyes when he reached up to stroke her cheek.

"Woman, when I said I loved you before, it was nothing to what I hold in my heart this night. You are everything to me. Life. Hope. Happiness . . ."

As his mouth tenderly covered hers, Triona could hold back her tears no longer. She let them come, the low sob breaking from her throat causing Ronan to draw back in surprise.

"What's this?"

"I . . . I have something to tell you," she began, only to fall silent as memories of the past days suddenly flashed through her mind. The hatred written on Ronan's face whenever he spoke of Caitlin. His cruelty toward the young woman . . . the way he'd dragged her through the mud and rain just that afternoon. The rancor in his voice only moments ago.

"Triona?"

She started, grateful for the darkness so he couldn't look into her eyes. She doubted she could have hidden her misery from him as she swiftly decided to do now. She couldn't tell him. Not yet. Not yet! In the morning she would, but first let them share one more night where he knew her only as his Triona O'Toole.

"You're everything to me, too, Ronan O'Byrne," she whispered brokenly, a low chuckle sounding in her ear as he bent his head close.

"So many tears for those few words?" he teased, his warm fingers cradling her chin. Again his lips found hers, his kiss so achingly tender that Triona went limp against him. She felt him lift her, then she was laid gently upon his bed, Ronan leaving her for a fleeting moment to shed his clothes before returning to her side.

"You looked so lovely in your gown that I hate to take it from you," he whispered, slipping the silk past her thighs and over her hips. "But what's underneath is lovelier still." He slid both her gown and camise up over her breasts. "I need no lamplight to see it."

Ronan drew his arm beneath her shoulders and lifted her, a gentle tug freeing her of the garments to leave her lying naked beside him. Naked, that is, except for the gold bracelet and the jeweled necklace which he drew slowly back and forth across her nipples.

"Can I tell you what I see?" he asked huskily when Triona moaned deep in her throat. The smooth gold beads and precious stones were cold against her heated flesh, the sensation nearly overwhelming her. Somehow she murmured a breathless "Aye," but already his fingers were sliding along the inside of her thigh, his voice low and seductive.

"Begorra, I see a woman so beautifully formed"—his hand slid higher—"with silken legs honed and lithe from years of wild rides through the forest." He chuckled wickedly, his warm palm gliding along her hip to her waist. "Soft curves that could defy Eire's finest poets to do them justice—wide here and narrow there, aye, just as they should be, and this tempting hollow in the middle . . . so deserving of a kiss."

Triona gasped as his lips found her navel, his hot breath tickling her belly and making her arch beneath him. But she began to tremble when he tunneled his fingers into the thick wet curls at the juncture of her thighs and tugged gently.

"Ah now, this is one of the sweetest places of all—"

"Ronan!"

She cried out at the same instant his fingers slid deeply into
er, his tongue no longer toying with her navel but swirling
round and around a swollen nipple that he'd taken into his
nouth. She couldn't say how long the exquisite torture lasted
or she had grown quite dizzy, either from the pleasure, the
vine she'd drunk or both. All she knew was one moment she
vas lying on her back and the next she had been rolled over
n top of him, his hard body stretched out beneath her.

"Straddle me, Triona. I want to feel your thighs gripping
ve as when you ride."

She obliged his raw-spoken demand, her hair spilling over
er shoulders to cover her breasts as she sat upright upon
m. Trembling uncontrollably now, she wasn't surprised at
e turgid bulge pressing between her legs, his body straining
enter the hot wetness her woman's flesh had become.

And she wanted him inside her, deep, deep inside her,
ars springing to her eyes as fresh misery assailed her. But
mehow she swallowed them back, lifting her hips as Ronan
oaned raggedly in the darkness and guided his swollen flesh
to the very heart of her.

With a broken cry she sank down upon him, enveloping him
her tight heat while he drove upward to fill her body. There
as such power in his movements as he began to thrust inside
r, such power in his hands as he caressed and gripped her
ttom. She held onto his thick wrists as she rode him, her
easts bobbing, her breath panting, until her wild craving to
closer to him made her sink forward upon his chest.

"Hold me, Ronan!" she pleaded, but she hadn't needed to
y a word, his arms going around her to clasp her fiercely
en as his body began to tremble and stiffen beneath her.

She was quaking, too, her body being consumed by the
e blazing outward from where their flesh was joined. One
ment she still had some semblance of conscious thought
d the next she was engulfed entirely, the heat, the ecstasy
erwhelming her, overwhelming him.

It was wonderful and yet terrible, for somewhere in the
dst of her mind-shattering pleasure the pain began again,
ona finally collapsing upon Ronan's chest in mute despair.

She said nothing, could say nothing, beginning to wonder if she would ever say anything at all. To see his love become hate would surely kill her.

That thought remained long hours later, Ronan sleeping sated and peacefully beside her despite the violent thunderstorm raging outside.

But Triona had only dozed fitfully and now lay wide-awake, watching the jagged lightning cut across the sky and wondering what she was going to do. A particularly blinding flash was followed by such a rumbling of thunder that she didn't hear the loud pounding upon their door until the sky grew still.

"Lord, it's Flann O'Faelin! Lord!"

Chapter 39

HER HEART RACING in her throat, Triona gave no answer. She hoped desperately even as Flann kept pummeling at the door that he might give up and go away. But already Ronan was roused, his arms going from around her as he vaulted from the bed.

He seemed alert at once, and though he said nothing to her, Triona could sense that he felt something was wrong. Wondering if Flann knew the truth of her birth and was about to expose her, she could only watch frozen, her hands clutching the sheet, as Ronan flung open the door.

"Lord, an entire quarter of the outer embankment is close to washing away! And still more of the ramparts are threatened, those damned posts no match for this storm. We need to sink more of them—"

"Aye, call out every man if you have to," Ronan commanded, Triona feeling relief so great she could taste it. But it was horribly short-lived when he added, "I'll meet you there."

As Flann disappeared, Ronan began searching for his clothes. Triona, gone numb from the thought that he might soon run into his clansman Fiach, somehow managed to throw aside the covers so she could rise and help him. But Ronan came over to her at once, pushing her back down upon the mattress and pulling the blanket up under her chin.

"Stay here, Triona, and keep warm. I'll return as soon as I can." He brushed a kiss upon her cheek and then he was gone from her, dressing swiftly. With a last glance toward the bed he left the room, the sound of the front door slamming an instant

313

later followed by another deafening thunderclap.

Triona lay there for long moments, stricken, until finally she tossed back the covers. She had never felt like a coward before in her life, but she knew she wouldn't be able to bear Ronan looking at her in any other way than with the love he had last night in the hall.

She rose, stepping over the gown lying in a silken heap upon the floor. Instead she found the shirt and trousers that were still damp from yesterday's rain. But it made no difference. Soon she would be soaked through to the skin, no matter the cloak she settled around her shoulders as she hurried to the bench by the door.

She grabbed up the key and went at once to Caitlin's room, the thunder crashing so loudly as she unlocked the door that it seemed to shake the house.

"Caitlin!" Triona hissed, keeping her voice down as low as she could so any guards outside wouldn't hear her. She saw her cousin sit bolt upright in bed, Caitlin's sleeping gown a stark white in the darkness.

"Get up! We're leaving."

"What? Leaving?"

Triona spared no time to explain, hurrying to the chest to pull out another pair of trousers. Spying Maeve curled upon the pillow as a bright flash of lightning lit up the room, Triona felt a terrible stab of regret but she couldn't turn back now.

"Here, put these on underneath your gown," she directed, Caitlin already having climbed from bed. Her cousin obeyed as if sensing her urgency, tucking the long linen garment into the trousers and next throwing on the spare cloak Triona had found her. Meanwhile Triona strapped on her leather belt and sheathed the dagger she had drawn from her cloak pocket.

"Come on! My bowcase is in the other room."

As Caitlin followed close on her heels, shutting the door quietly behind them, Triona felt another stab at the empty space near the hearth where Conn enjoyed sleeping. She imagined her dog was lying under a table in the feasting-hall with his belly swollen from eating too much. At any other time she might have smiled at the thought but now she thrust Conn, too, from her mind as sh

ouldered her bowcase and moved with Caitlin to the
ont door.

"How well do you ride?" She dragged her hood over her hair
Caitlin did the same, her cousin stuffing her telltale blond
esses inside her cloak.

"Well enough."

"Do you need a sidesaddle?"

Caitlin shook her head and Triona didn't wait any longer.
e thrust open the door, the yard nearly pitch-dark, pounding
n coming down in sheets. Fortunately, there were clansmen
shing about the yard to mask their flight, some running
t the stronghold gates on foot while others passed by on
rseback.

"Keep your head down! Say nothing!"

Triona knew Caitlin was right behind her from the sound
her splashing as they raced through ankle-deep water to
e stable. As they ducked inside the meagerly lit interior,
iona saw at once that Ronan's midnight steed was gone, her
artache so fierce at that moment she almost reconsidered.
t she had only to glance at Caitlin to remember Ronan's
uelty. She immediately bridled the nearest horse and led the
imal from its stall.

Too late did she realize it was Niall's mount, but there was
time to bridle another horse. As Caitlin hoisted herself
to the powerful gelding's back and wheeled him around
th evident skill, Triona ran to Laeg's stall.

At least she would have her own horse with her, she thought
she bridled him and mounted, though that did little to ease
r pain. She tensed as a trio of clansmen suddenly entered
e stable; she gestured nervously for Caitlin to keep her
ad ducked and ride out. Triona followed, wincing as she
erheard one of the men say, "Begorra, wasn't that Niall
Byrne's horse?"

She didn't hear an answer for the earsplitting thunderclap
at boomed overhead, the sound startling Laeg into a gallop.
hich was just as well for Caitlin was already riding well
ead of her toward the first set of gates. To Triona's relief,
e saw that they were unguarded, every clansman no doubt
listed to help shore up the ramparts.

Triona didn't dare take a breath until she and Caitlin h
cleared the last gates, the commotion of posts being hammer
into the ground and men shouting above the storm quick
receding as they rode into the night. Only when the strongho
was well behind them did Caitlin finally pull up her mou
Triona reining in beside her.

"We'll be in Ferns by daybreak if we ride hard," Trio
cried, raising her voice against the howling wind, lightni
streaking like bony fingers across the sky.

She realized at once that Caitlin was overcome with reli
her cousin wiping more than rain from her eyes. Triona's ey
were stinging, too, but she willed the tears away as she kick
Laeg back into a hard gallop.

Crying wouldn't change anything; she'd shed enough us
less tears already. It was time to think ahead to vengeanc
Nothing else was left to her now.

A bright rosy dawn had risen over the glen by the tir
Ronan rode back into the stronghold, the sunlight glisteni
upon myriad puddles a mocking sight after the despera
efforts of the past hours. But the outermost embankment h
been saved, barely.

If Flann O'Faelin hadn't gone to check the massive earth
ramparts at the height of the storm, no amount of lab
would have prevented them from crumbling altogether. .
least now Ronan still had the fortified defenses he needed
case Donal MacMurrough was planning to attack rather th
pay ransom for his daughter, a foolhardy plan to be sure b
a possibility.

Muttering a blistering oath at the thought, Ronan left h
horse to a servant waiting outside the stable doors and stro
across the yard, his shoes squishing in the mud.

Most of his exhausted men were headed to the feasting-ha
for a warm meal and cup or two of ale, then back to the
homes for much needed rest. But all Ronan wanted to do w
see Triona. To climb back into bed with her and hold her tigl
That was all the warming he needed.

As he drew near his dwelling-house, he saw that the do
was standing ajar, but he thought nothing of it. The wind ha

been so fierce last night that many a door and shutter must have been banging upon their hinges.

"Lord!" called a male voice from behind him.

Ronan turned, his eyes narrowing as Fiach O'Byrne hastened to catch up with him.

By God, what could be so damned important that his clansman had been dogging him since Ronan had left his house in the wee hours of the morning? Three times he'd had to wave Fiach away, the man having a gift for approaching him when he least had the time to talk. And now here he was again, just when Ronan could almost feel the warmth of Triona's body in his arms.

"Lord, I've something I must tell you," Fiach said, his eyes shifting around them to see if anyone else was near. "I've been trying since last night but—"

"So what is it, man?" Ronan impatiently set out again, Fiach forced to keep pace with him.

"It's about your lady."

"Triona?"

"Aye, Lord. I fear to tell you she's not—"

"Saints help us, Ronan! She's gone!" Aud was yelling as she suddenly came running out of his dwelling-house, waving her arms and half stumbling in her haste to reach him.

Ronan stopped cold.

"Triona's gone! My sweeting's gone!"

Ronan caught the frantic woman just before she stumbled again, Aud clutching onto his arms.

"What are you saying, Aud? I left Triona in bed."

"She's not there, she's not there! I came to talk to her—I've been awake all night just thinking about what's happened and . . . and I came to urge her to tell you everything—"

"Tell me what, woman?" Ronan demanded, his eyes cutting from Fiach's grim face back to Aud, who suddenly burst into hysterical tears.

"She's half MacMurrough, Ronan! Aye, and half Norman. But she didn't even know herself until last night and now she's gone! Oh God, my sweeting's gone!"

Aud collapsed, Ronan barely catching the weeping woman as her knees sank into the mud. Stunned, he picked her up and

carried her inside, depositing her into a chair by the hearth.
Then he went to his room, his heart thundering in his chest
when he saw that the bed was empty. He saw, too, that the
key was gone from the bench just as Fiach called to him from
the opposite room.

"Lord, the MacMurrough wench!"

Ronan spun, his clansman's expression telling him that
Caitlin was gone as well. Yet he went to the room anyway,
taking in the empty bed, the chest lid flung open, the clothes
scattered upon the floor and Maeve mewling plaintively, the
cat left by itself for who knows how many hours.

It was only then that Ronan recalled another clansman coming up to him not long after Ronan had reached the crumbling
embankment to say that he'd seen Niall's horse being ridden
from the stable. But Ronan hadn't given it a thought. Who
cared how his men got to the ramparts as long as they were
there swiftly to help? Yet that must have been Triona and
Caitlin—Ronan certain that if he went now to the stable he'd
find Laeg missing, too.

"By God, Fiach, was this what you've been trying to tell
me?" Ronan exploded, Aud's weeping growing louder. "That
Triona is—"

"Of MacMurrough blood. Aye, Lord, and Norman blood.
My men and I heard everything last night through the prisoner's windows. Your lady was getting dressed for supper,
the MacMurrough wench helping her, when she must have
dropped her dagger."

"Aye, that cursed thing!" Aud cried, tears coursing down
her face as she twisted in the chair to look at Ronan. "I wish
I'd done away with it right after Triona found it, but I didn't
see the danger. I didn't see . . ."

As Aud fell into another fit of weeping, Ronan felt he was
suddenly living a nightmare as he turned back to Fiach. "Tell
me everything you heard. Quickly, man!"

Fiach did, Ronan listening in grim astonishment as the
incredible story unfolded, Aud tearfully embellishing it.

Triona and Caitlin, cousins? Her mother, Eva Mac-
Murrough, her father, Richard de Roche of Naas? And
horribly enough, Triona's uncle the very man who'd helped

end Fineen O'Toole to his grave?

"No wonder Seamus thought he'd seen a ghost," Ronan
said almost to himself, recalling the dead cook's stricken face.
Seamus must have served at that very wedding—must have
heard as well how Eva MacMurrough died, gored to death by
a wild boar. Then, when he saw Triona in his kitchen, no doubt
looking much like her mother and with what he believed to be
blood upon her gown . . .

"The MacMurrough wench finished by saying that your
lady should lay claim to her inheritance, Lord," Fiach added,
breaking into Ronan's thoughts. "Mayhap that's why she fled
with the hostage—"

"Are you mad?" Aud shrieked as she vaulted from the chair
to face them, swiping the tears from her cheeks. "If you believe
that of my sweeting, Ronan O'Byrne, then I hope you never
hold her in your arms again! She feared losing you—aye, she
told me so herself just before you came to fetch her for supper
and no wonder, after she saw how you mistreated Caitlin. If
she left for any reason, it was because she thought you might
hate her once you knew the truth!"

Ronan suddenly felt sickened, thinking back last night to
how pale Triona had been when they left the hall though she
had smiled and teased the entire evening as if nothing were
wrong.

And her bout of tears when they'd finally been alone.

She must have been about to tell him the truth after he'd
said he loved her, but something had stopped her. By God, he
hadn't made it any easier for her by venting one last time how
he couldn't wait until Caitlin was gone from Glenmalure!

Cursing the blind hatred that had made Triona flee from him,
Ronan strode from the room, but not before grabbing Aud by
the hand and commanding that Fiach follow him.

"Where are we going?" Aud demanded though she didn't
resist, her shorter legs working hard to keep up with him.

"To the hall. My men must hear of Triona's true parentage
and that no matter her blood, I intend to take her as my
bride."

"Ah, Ronan, I knew you wouldn't abandon her!" Aud cried,
her eyes growing wet with fresh tears.

"But what if they object, Lord?" Fiach threw in, Ronan glancing at the man over his shoulder.

"Then the O'Byrnes must seek a new chieftain. I won't live my life without her."

"Aye, you must find her, Ronan, as quickly as you can!" Aud broke in, her fingers digging into his arm. "She's in danger, I feel it! If she's taken refuge with Caitlin in Ferns, aye, all will be well. But if my poor sweeting's decided upon some other course . . ."

Aud didn't have to say the name Maurice de Roche for Ronan to understand. His gut in knots, he began to run toward the hall, Aud and Fiach close behind him.

Chapter 40

TRIONA SQUINTED IN the early afternoon sun as she approached Dublin's towering walls. She hoped the same ploy that had gotten her into Kilkenny weeks ago would work now. As soon as she'd come upon the main road she had dismounted, walking Laeg the rest of the way among the rush of pedestrians and heavily loaded carts going to and from the city.

It was just as well for Laeg's sake. He needed a rest after the long hours of riding, but at least they hadn't had to come all the way from Ferns. The sun had barely begun peeking over the horizon when she'd left Caitlin just north of Gorey to ride to her father's stronghold by herself.

That hadn't been pleasant, Caitlin insisting at once that she accompany her when Triona admitted she was riding north to Dublin. She had been forced to yell, telling Caitlin there wasn't a damned thing she could do to help her as Triona wheeled Laeg around. Even now the memory of the hurt in her cousin's eyes made her wince, but she'd been thinking of Caitlin's safety after all. If anything happened to her, she didn't want to be worrying about Caitlin, too.

"Nothing's going to happen to you," Triona chided herself, smoothing her cloak a bit to better conceal the bowcase clutched under her arm.

Not when justice was on her side. All she had to do was find Maurice de Roche and see that the bastard confessed his crimes to King John, the deadly point of an arrow the perfect incentive for him to do so. Hopefully he would receive the punishment he so richly deserved, while she . . .

Triona sighed. She had no idea what she was going to do then. The future without Ronan looked so bleak that she didn't want to think about it, and, with her fast approaching the city gates, right now she didn't have time to.

After she made sure that her hood was pulled securely over her hair, Triona veered Laeg closer to a creaking wooden cart full of ripe-smelling goat cheese and asked the wiry driver in a gruff voice, "Bound for the market?"

The man cast her a sideways glance then looked back to the road. "Aye. What's it to you, lad?"

Keeping her voice low, Triona shrugged. "I just wondered if it was near Dublin Castle, is all. I've never been to the city before. Don't know my way around."

The driver glanced at her again, this time looking her up and down before he focused once more in front of him. "The castle's not hard to find. You just look for all the stinking Normans." He gave a grunt. "Follow alongside me if you want . . . but you'd best grab that blanket from the cart and throw it over your horse. It might keep the guards from asking you where you got so fine a steed."

"T-thank you," Triona murmured, hastily doing what he said.

"And another thing—miss."

Triona gasped, meeting the man's sharp eyes.

"I'd suggest you say as little as you can if you don't want anyone else to guess there's a wench under that cloak."

She gulped, lowering her head as they came to the massive gates. Her relief was intense when no one stopped them, the cheese-seller giving her a quick wink when she dared to look up again.

As they wound their way along streets wider than Kilkenny's but just as crowded, Triona had no choice but to stick close to the cart, so many people bustling here and there it was an amazing thing to see. Most astounding were the number of Norman soldiers, but she shouldn't have been surprised considering it was rumored seven hundred ships had been needed to carry King John's army across the water to Eire.

"Dublin Castle, lad. Straight ahead."

Grateful that the cheese-seller was playing along with her ruse especially with so many Normans around, she gave him a small smile only to have him frown at her.

"None of that now," he muttered, nodding her along. "You'll give yourself away for sure."

With that, he clucked to his horse, the cart rumbling onto another street before Triona could even thank him. Left alone, strangers passing by her on every side, she gave in to a moment's hesitation. But all she had to do was remember Fineen, aye, and the cruel fate of her true parents as well, and she found the courage she needed.

Somehow she had to get inside the castle walls, for surely if King John was holding court, Maurice de Roche couldn't be far from his side. Her heart hammering at her sudden idea, she pulled the blanket from Laeg's back and mounted, carefully clutching her bowcase under her arm as she kicked her horse into a trot and rode toward the guarded gates. She knew she was drawing attention to herself, but better to be brazen and look convincing for the mission she would soon profess.

There were others waiting to gain entrance, mailed knights on horseback and still more people approaching on foot, but Triona slowed Laeg to a walk and pushed right through to the front.

"A message for Baron de Roche," she said gruffly to the nearest guard, a harried-looking man who swept her with a glance and then waved her on. Her breath stilled, she didn't tarry, but she'd no sooner urged Laeg through the arched gateway when a strangely familiar voice sounded behind her.

"For the baron, you say? I was just going to meet him myself, boy. I'll take the message for you."

It was the "boy" that struck her like a jolt. Triona dug her heels into Laeg's sides and spurred him across the huge yard toward the building she hoped wildly was the hall.

"God's blood, didn't you hear me?"

Aye, she'd heard him, Triona's heartbeat slamming so loudly in her ears that it nearly drowned out the sound of Laeg's hooves hitting the earth.

"Stop that rider! Stop him at once!"

She gasped as guards suddenly came running at her from all directions. She shot a glance behind her to find several mounted knights riding hard on her heels, one of them the man who was shouting. With no hope now of reaching the hall, she tugged up on the reins and veered Laeg sharply around, crying out in dismay as she lost her hold on her bowcase, the leather sheath tumbling to the ground.

She had wanted to make a dash for the gates but already she was too late. Within an instant, she was surrounded by Normans. Hands reached out to snatch the reins away from her while someone grabbed her cloak from behind and yanked her violently off Laeg's back. She hit the ground so hard that she could only lie there on her side, stunned. But not for long.

"Get up!" that same familiar voice commanded, Triona hauled to her feet so abruptly that her head spun. As her hood was pulled back, her hair tumbled free. A gasp went up from her captors, Triona jerked around to face the blue-eyed de Roche knight who she'd last seen in Kilkenny.

"You!" he grated, clearly incredulous. "You're the Irish bitch who cut me. Tricked me, too, you little whore! Jumping with your black-haired friend from that window—"

"Aye, too bad it was only your hand I slashed and not your damned throat!" Triona cried, reaching desperately inside her cloak. But the man grabbed her wrist before she could pull out her dagger, a tight smile creasing his face as he yanked the weapon from her belt. Yet he sobered when he held it up, another gasp sounding from the men gathered around her.

"God's nightgown, William, you've a king's treasure in your hand!" someone breathed behind her. "Diamonds, rubies . . ." But William ignored the man, holding the dagger only inches from Triona's face.

"Was this the message you intended for Baron de Roche?" he demanded, staring furiously into her eyes.

"She had this with her, too!" added another knight, the tall man pushing through the crowd with her bowcase.

"You've come to Dublin well armed, wench," William grated when Triona lifted her chin, remaining silent. "Since you're so clearly unwilling to talk to me, perhaps you might enjoy speaking to the baron instead. It's only fitting after all.

He's the one you came to murder."

The knight thrust her ahead of him so roughly that Triona stumbled and fell hard to her knees, but he caught her by the collar and hauled her once more to her feet. "Bring her horse!" he called out as he dragged Triona along with him. "You've a fine steed, wench. Fine weapons. I'd wager you've got a fine story to tell us as well."

Triona said nothing, stubbornly holding her tongue though her apprehension was close to overwhelming her. Yet she forced herself to keep her head. It was clear she was being taken to the hall, which was right where she had wanted to be in the first place. God willing if King John were inside, she would denounce Maurice de Roche to the very rafters.

"Hold her here," William commanded as they approached the huge doors, two guards coming forward to grab her by the arms. "She's caused enough commotion for one day without disturbing the king's audience."

"No, I demand to go with you!" Triona cried, only to be silenced by such a blow across her cheek that she saw brilliant lights flare in front of her eyes. Dazed, she slumped between the two guards, tasting blood. Tears threatened but she refused to give in to them, not even when William returned moments later to wrench her head up by the hair.

"Here she is, Baron. The same bitch who made me look such a fool in Kilkenny."

Triona opened her eyes, staring into the swarthy face of a man she knew at once recognized her. She wanted to scream, to shriek, to rail at him, but all she could manage was a hoarse whisper. "Murderer."

Maurice's cold dark eyes narrowed, then he struck her, his backhanded blow so violent that she was knocked nearly senseless to the ground.

"Fetch me your horse, William."

"My horse, Baron? But why—"

"Just do as I say!"

Through slitted eyes, Triona saw Maurice turn to face those Normans still standing near, her jeweled dagger clutched tightly in his hand.

"Go back to what you were doing, the rest of you. Nothing more than a jealous Irish chit who's showing her claws over my new mistress."

Triona heard male laughter like strange echoes in her ears, the crowd dispersing. Then the harsh voice of her uncle sounded once more as he looked down at her.

"Say a word and you die right here."

Her wits slowly coming back into focus, Triona nonetheless remained very still as if she were still stunned from the blow. Her condition seemed to satisfy Maurice for he sheathed the dagger in his sword belt and picked her up in his arms while William came forward with his horse.

"Here. Take her while I mount, then lift her up to me."

Willing herself to remain limp, Triona wanted desperately to make some move against them but she was still so dizzy she didn't know if she might collapse during the attempt. Better to wait for a few moments longer.

"I'll be back before sunset, William. Tell the rest of my knights. If anyone else asks for me, say to them just what you heard me tell the others."

"Very well, my lord."

Triona kept her eyes closed as Maurice kicked the steed into a gallop, his muttering not so low that she couldn't hear him.

"I don't know how you survived the wolves, wench, or how you found out about your parents, but I'll not have you laying claim to all that I've gained. This time I'll make sure you're silenced."

His words chilled her, but Triona told herself to keep calm. She knew they had already passed through the gates, the street noises growing loud and boisterous. She didn't want to wait until they were too far from the castle; she wasn't giving up so easily no matter his threats. She waited one more moment, then she grabbed wildly for the reins, jerking up on them with all her might.

"God's teeth, wench!"

They were both thrown to the ground as the horse reared, Triona landing on top of her uncle. But she no sooner rolled from him and tried to scramble away than Maurice caught her by the foot, the fall apparently having done the powerfully built man little harm. Shrieking, she kicked at him with her other leg as shocked passersby began to stop in the street. But still Maurice pulled her toward him, his hand fumbling at his sword belt.

"Fiend! Murderer!" she cried, using her elbow to smash him in the face. It was enough to throw him off balance, and Triona seized her chance. Within an instant, she'd grabbed her dagger and was on top of him, the razor-sharp blade pressed to Maurice's throat.

"Make a move and you're dead, de Roche!" she rasped, her breath coming so hard that she'd never felt such a pain in her lungs. But she gave it little heed, wondering how she was going to get her uncle on his feet so she could march him back to the castle and King John.

Nor did she pay much attention to the thundering of hooves, so intently was she glaring down at her uncle. She saw him look beyond her, his eyes widening, then an Irish sword appeared in front of her, aimed, too, right at de Roche's throat.

"Aye, woman, you've always been one to take care of yourself. I'm beginning to wonder if you need me at all."

Chapter 41

"RONAN . . . !"

Triona had no sooner breathed his name in disbelief than he pulled her to her feet and crushed her in his arms, holding her so fiercely that she could feel the pounding of his heart against her breast.

It was only when she heard Maurice's vehement curses that she looked down, astonished to see her uncle pinned to the ground by a half dozen armed Irishmen. Some she recognized at once as Ronan's clansmen—Flann O'Faelin and amazingly enough, Fiach O'Byrne—but as for the others she had no clue.

At least not until she glanced beyond Ronan to the coppery-haired chieftain seated atop a huge roan stallion, Caitlin at his side. Behind them, the road was packed with mounted Irishmen as far as she could see. Stunned, Triona looked back to Ronan.

"You rode here with Donal MacMurrough?"

Ronan nodded, pulling her closer. "My men and I came upon them this morning while riding south to find you. They were preparing to head to Wicklow with the ransom when your cousin arrived safely home, so they changed their course to Dublin." He pressed a fervent kiss to her brow. "The MacMurrough and I shared a common cause this day, woman. You."

"Then . . . then you must know everything," she began, only to have him touch a finger to her lips.

"You're my Triona O'Toole and always will be. The blood in your veins bears no weight on my love for you."

Triona felt foolish Lady Emer tears leap to her eyes but she couldn't help it, staring at Ronan like the besotted maiden she was while he gestured to his men.

"You should have seen how readily they chose to come with me. You've won their hearts as well. And Niall . . ." Ronan shook his head. "I practically had to tie him to his bed to keep him from joining us, while Maire was beside herself, pleading for me to hurry—" Ronan suddenly stopped, glancing past her to where Donal MacMurrough had dismounted. "We can talk of this later, Triona. There's someone who wants very much to meet you."

Triona left the warmth of Ronan's arms as the Mac-Murrough chieftain approached her, Donal standing as tall as Ronan. She could swear the man's eyes were wet, his voice slightly hoarse when he spoke.

"Aye, you look like Eva"—a small smile came to his lips—"except for your wild hair. For that you've my mother to blame, though as I recall, your father Richard's hair bore some red as well." He sobered then, glancing to where Maurice was scowling at his captors before looking back at Triona. "We've some business with King John, though you and Ronan can leave at once for Glenmalure if you've a mind to—"

"I haven't come all this way not to see that spawn pay for his crimes," Triona broke in, warmed when Ronan reached out to squeeze her hand. "Maurice de Roche not only murdered my true father and caused my mother's death, but he and his kind struck down the man who reared me as his own daughter."

"Lies, all of it!" Maurice shouted, only to have a sword pressed to his throat to silence him.

"King John will determine your guilt or innocence," Donal MacMurrough muttered, his eyes narrowed with fury. He turned to Triona. "I'd prefer if you and Caitlin ride near the back where it's safe."

"Near the back?" Triona blurted, bristling. "I'll ride at the front, Uncle, with the man I plan to marry when all this is done!"

"Aye, you're a stubborn one, just like your mother," Donal observed dryly though his gaze softened as he glanced at Caitlin. "I fear it's rubbed off on my daughter as well. She refused to stay home, insisting she ride to Dublin, too."

Triona shot a smile at Caitlin, a warm look passing between them that clearly meant no apologies were needed. But in the next moment, Ronan was leading her to his horse; he mounted and held out his hand to her. Yet first Triona went up to Maurice, who'd been hauled to his feet, his guards keeping him well subdued. As she rested her dagger point against his belly, he glared at her with impotent rage.

"I wish you had moved so I could stick my mother's knife in your throat," she said icily. "But no matter. If your King John is just, you'll soon be rotting in hell."

Maurice couldn't answer, a sword blade resting beneath his Adam's apple. Satisfied for the moment, Triona sheathed her weapon and returned to Ronan.

"Begorra, woman, if glances could kill we'd have just won our vengeance," he murmured, hoisting her up in front of him. He clasped her close as their huge entourage set out down the street, Maurice de Roche being driven on foot toward the castle gates followed by three hundred grim-faced Irishmen.

It must have been an astonishing sight because the guards fell back without any protest, recognizing Donal MacMurrough at their lead. Word of their approach reached the hall well before their arrival, King John and his courtiers awaiting them outside the massive stone building.

Triona was amazed by the Norman king's small stature, most of his mailed knights towering above him. Surely he stood no more than half a head above herself, with dark hair worn long to the neck, his rather ordinary face sporting a moustache and trim beard. But if he appeared unassuming, he more than made up for it with his thunderous countenance. King John looked furious.

"You herd one of my most loyal barons before me like a sheep, Donal MacMurrough?"

"For good reason, my lord. There are serious crimes to be stated against him—"

"Aye, he's a murderer!" Triona shouted, sliding from Ronan's horse to stand beside her uncle. "He slew his own brother Richard de Roche of Naas to lay claim to his land and title."

"And who are you, young woman?" the king demanded.

"Triona O'Toole, daughter of Richard and his wife, Eva MacMurrough."

"And who is that?" the king added when Ronan dismounted ? well to stand at Triona's side.

"Black O'Byrne, the devil!" a portly knight interjected, ushing forward from the throng. "He and his foul band of bels robbed me blind last year . . . holding me at sword point my own tub! I'd never forget that face."

"So they've done to me!" another knight shouted. "While e were north these past weeks fighting at your side, my rd king. Harrying south Leinster they've been, the thieving astards, when there were few at home to defend against it!"

At that, a great rumbling went up from the crowd, several ormans pulling their swords. But King John waved for lence, his expression all the darker as he addressed Donal MacMurrough.

"One of the most powerful chieftains in Leinster riding de-by-side with rebels? The very man whom I've always usted and counted upon to keep the allegiance of his people rmly with the Crown?"

"My allegiance has not been swayed, my lord. But Ronan 'Byrne and I share a like cause—to protect the only child of y sister, Eva. And it was that man"—he pointed at Maurice— who hounded my poor sister to her death twenty years past nd who would have murdered her child had he found her! He ight have done so today, too, if Triona hadn't known how to ield a knife!"

"Lies!" Maurice countered heatedly, but King John waved m, too, into silence.

"Your elder brother, Richard, was long a friend to me ere I new you," he said grimly to the outraged baron. "I will hear full accounting of this matter from Donal MacMurrough."

As the chieftain obliged him, Triona felt Ronan squeeze er fingers reassuringly. Mayhap they could hope that justice ould be served this day.

But as if sensing that the tide was turning against him just y the king's ominous expression alone, Maurice barely waited r Donal MacMurrough to finish before roaring, "A judicial

trial of combat will prove my innocence!" He fixed his dark
burning eyes upon Triona, demanding, "Choose a champion
wench, for it is your right as my first accuser."

Everything was happening so fast that Triona had no sooner
looked to Donal for counsel when Ronan's voice rang out.

"I will fight him."

"No!" she cried, grabbing his arm. But Ronan shook his
head.

"I promised you vengeance, Triona—"

"So let it begin," King John suddenly announced, his eyes
shifting to the silk-clad officials at his side who nodded solemnly. "I see no better solution for this prickly matter of word
against word."

"No, there has to be another way!" Triona lashed out at
him even as Donal threw her a cautioning look. "You're only
allowing this because you hope that Ronan will fall, not your
loyal baron!"

"God will defend the right," King John said cryptically,
waving for the battle to begin. And he'd barely done so before
Maurice flew at Ronan, drawing his sword so violently from
its sheath that the metal sang.

Courtiers, knights and Irishmen alike scattered out of the
way, Donal wrenching Triona to his side. She watched in
horror as Ronan dodged the first blow, his sword still
lodged in his belt. But he managed to pull out the
weapon before the second blow came, the heavy Norman
sword hitting his much lighter Irish sword with an ominous ring.

"It's not a fair fight," Triona breathed, her eyes wide as
Ronan barely ducked in time to save his skull. "Ronan's
weapon is no match—"

"Have faith in the man you will wed, Triona O'Toole,"
Donal chastened her, his voice low. "The O'Byrne has at
least ten years on de Roche. The baron will tire—"

Triona's gasp cut him off, her stomach flipping as Ronan
continued to dodge and parry blow after vicious blow,
Maurice's enraged roars rending the air.

"You call this a fight, Black O'Byrne? You sidestep like a
frightened ferret looking for its hole!"

"If anyone should crawl into a hole, it's you, de Roche," came Ronan's taunting reply. "Like the evil serpent you are!"

Cursing at the insult, Maurice intensified his attack. Triona watched with mounting alarm as Ronan was driven back farther and farther until he came up hard against one of the castle's defensive walls.

Above him, Norman guards jeered and spat from their high walkway, Ronan ducking and twisting away just as Maurice struck the wall where his head had been an instant before. But the worst came when Ronan was forced to retreat through the doorway leading into a great round tower, Maurice disappearing after him.

"No, this must stop!" Triona shouted, but Donal held on to her tightly, whispering into her ear.

"Think, Triona! The O'Byrne knows what he's about! What better way to exhaust a foe laden with chain mail than to wage an upward battle around a staircase?"

She couldn't reply, her throat so tight as she waited to catch a glimpse of Ronan at the top of the tower that she could hardly breathe. She could hear the muffled ringing of swords, at least that being a hopeful sign that Ronan hadn't fallen. But she nearly choked when he finally appeared on the walkway, a bright red slash across his left arm.

And still Maurice attacked on the offensive, though he was showing signs of tiring just as Donal had said. His labored breathing and broken curses could be heard over the hushed yard, all necks craned as the battle raged atop the walkway.

It was then Triona spied two de Roche knights slipping into an opposite tower, the bastards obviously fearing for their lord's life. Yet she had no sooner grabbed Donal's arm to tell him when another man appeared at the top of the tower, Triona's eyes flaring when she recognized William. Crouching in the doorway, he looked down at King John as if for a signal. Then he rose swiftly, aiming a spear right at Ronan's back.

"Oh God, no!" Horrified, Triona wrenched herself free of Donal's grip. "Ronan, behind you! Look out behind you!"

Chapter 42

HE MUST HAVE heard her for in the next instant, Ronan lunged into a gap between the battlements as the spear hurtled past him to strike Maurice. The baron's high-pitched death scream sent chills plummeting down Triona's spine. Clutching wildly at the shaft protruding from his chest, Maurice pitched from the walkway to the ground below, his body landing with a sickening thud.

Silence reigned for the longest moment, everyone appearing as if in shock. But Triona had never known such relief as she raced to the tower to meet Ronan when he exited the doorway.

"Your arm . . ." she murmured, blanching at the blood oozing from the gash through his clothing.

"It would have been far worse, woman, if not for those fine lungs of yours." His breathing hard, sweat dripping from his face, Ronan still managed to give her a smile. "Your dream was wrong. You were able to help me after all—"

"Seize the O'Byrne rebel!"

As the king's furious command echoed around the yard, Triona looked unbelievingly at Ronan. But she had no chance to say a word as a dozen Norman guards suddenly descended upon them. Triona was shoved roughly out of the way as Ronan was overpowered despite his fierce struggling.

"What . . . what is this?" she cried, rushing to Donal who appeared just as stunned as she. Instead her answer came from King John, his decree directed to everyone though he glared at Triona.

"You've won your justice, young woman, and now I will have mine. I declare Ronan Black O'Byrne a traitor to the Crown and hereby condemn him to hang!"

"No!"

The roar had come from Donal MacMurrough. All eyes turned to the chieftain as he drew his sword, the loud buzz that had greeted the king's pronouncement swiftly become a shocked hush. Every MacMurrough and O'Byrne likewise drew his weapon, their grim faces now turned to the irate king.

"You raise your sword against me, Donal of Ferns?"

"Aye, my lord king, in this matter I do. Ronan O'Byrne and his clansmen came into the city under my protection, and so they will leave. Rebel or no, the man is the betrothed of my niece. She loves him and, therefore, I stand with him this day. If you proceed, you will fight all of us."

Triona had never seen so many gaping mouths, the king's courtiers and officials taking a few steps backward as if ready to lift their fine silk tunics and run like rabbits. Meanwhile, every Norman knight drew his sword, clearly eager for a fight. Several began to close ranks around the king to protect him. But King John waved them back, a dark brow lifting shrewdly at Donal MacMurrough.

"You've always served me loyally, Donal of Ferns. Always striven to help maintain order in this unruly land, especially among your people."

"I have, sire."

"And you give me your oath that your fealty will continue, no matter this"—he glanced with distaste at Ronan—"unpleasant dispute?"

"I do, sire."

"Very well. I renounce my sentence of death upon the rebel Black O'Byrne and grant him safe conduct from the city. But I vow," King John added swiftly, fixing a warning gaze upon Ronan as his captors reluctantly released him, "that if you're ever caught raiding against my vassals, you *will* hang." The king then turned his eyes to Triona, who raised her chin and stared back at him though she wanted nothing more than to run to Ronan.

"You're aware, young woman, that you now are the heiress to one of my richest fiefs?"

"Aye."

"Then you can understand if I say you will lose all rights to the land if you marry this man. I'll not have an Irish rebel as lord of Naas."

"Aye, I understand, so you might as well find some other de Roche to take it off my hands." That said, Triona couldn't hold herself back any longer. She ran to Ronan and flung her arms around his neck. "I'd trade all of Eire to become the bride of Black O'Byrne," she announced for everyone to hear, smiling into Ronan's eyes as he embraced her. "My only regret is that I can't give back to him the lands which are rightfully his."

"Enough!" King John shouted, outraged by Triona's defiance. "Take these rebels from Dublin at once, Donal MacMurrough, or I promise I'll hang them all!"

The chieftain hastened over to them, saying in a low firm voice, "I suggest you mount your horses." But when Ronan began to veer Triona toward his stallion, she balked, pursing her lips to give a sharp whistle. Immediately she heard an answering whinny, courtiers scurrying out of the way as Laeg came galloping to her side.

"Aye, Laeg, we'll soon be gone from this foul place," she murmured, her heart doing a flip-flop when Ronan's strong hands went around her waist to give her a boost onto her horse's back. "Your arm must not be hurting you too badly if you can lift me with such ease," she teased him as he mounted, the heat in his eyes assuring her that he was hardly maimed. Growing flushed, she sobered as she looked out across the yard.

"What is it, Triona?"

"My bowcase." Spying the leather sheath clutched in a tall knight's hand, she spouted, "He has it, there! And I'll not be leaving without it."

"Give her the damned thing!" King John commanded, the man nearly stumbling over his long legs in his rush to obey.

"My thanks, sire," she said sincerely as she shouldered her bowcase, the familiar weight a comfort. Yet she couldn't resist adding, "I hope swift winds carry you soon and safely across the water . . . and far, far away from Eire."

"Triona . . ." Ronan murmured with a warning frown as Donal MacMurrough bowed his head to his king, then led their huge party back through the gates. But once outside the castle grounds Ronan smiled, the warm teasing look Triona so loved back in his eyes. "Did anyone ever tell you that for an angel, you've got a bit of the devil in you, too?"

She snorted. "Devil? I gave the man a good Irish blessing, is all." Triona laughed as Ronan shook his head, Caitlin soon falling back from her father's side to join them as they rode through the bustling city. But they still had a good way to go when Ronan suddenly pulled up on the reins and called for a halt.

"Don't tell me Triona forgot something back at the castle," Donal said with tight-lipped exasperation.

"Not at all," Ronan reassured him, dismounting. He gestured to the stone church they'd just passed. "It's time your niece and I were wed."

"Here? In Dublin?" Triona blurted, her emerald eyes grown wide.

"Why not? I'm sure the priest knows the right words just the same as those in Glendalough."

"But Aud isn't here, Ronan," she began.

"Aud will understand," he said firmly, reaching up for her. "Now come."

Still Triona hesitated, the stubborn set of her chin leading Ronan to wonder what she was going to demand of him next. He had a good inkling when she glanced first at Caitlin, then at Donal, and finally back to him again, soft pleading in her eyes.

"I know it might be hard for you, Ronan, but I'm asking you here and now to make peace with the clan MacMurrough. Not just a truce for a day but lasting—"

"Done."

She gaped at him, clearly astonished. "Truly?"

Ronan nodded, the deep gratitude he felt toward the MacMurrough chieftain far outweighing any of the hatred that had gone before. Without his aid, he might never have gotten into the city to find Triona, and that to him was worth any price.

"On behalf of the O'Byrnes of Glenmalure, I offer peace." Ronan somberly met Donal's eyes. "I hope that the MacMurroughs will accept—"

"I accept," the chieftain stated, his expression just as solemn though there was a hint of humor in his eyes. "Now if you'll kindly make this willful niece of mine an honest woman, I'd be a happy man. And quickly, Ronan, before King John changes his mind."

Their wedding was probably the briefest on record in that lofty church, considering the long weeks it had taken Ronan to get Triona to say her vows. A priest's blessing, a fervent kiss, then they were mounting their horses again. No more than a few moments later they had left the city, MacMurroughs and O'Byrnes riding south together in the waning afternoon sun until the time finally came for the two clans to go their separate ways.

It was an awkward parting but heartfelt, hope that all would continue to be well between them on everyone's mind. Especially Caitlin's, whose eyes were brimming with tears as she brought her steed close to Triona's to give her a hug.

"Will we see each other?" the young woman asked brokenly, Triona giving her a reassuring wink.

"Aye, I'm sure of it."

Then, with an embarrassed laugh, Caitlin began to dismount until Triona stopped her.

"But this is Niall's horse."

"Exactly, cousin." Triona glanced at Ronan and her uncle, pleased at least to see that the two men weren't frowning. She leaned forward and whispered in Caitlin's ear. "Niall can't fail to come to visit if he wants to get his horse back, now can he?"

Caitlin's brilliant smile was a fine thing to see, Triona wondering to herself how long it might be before her pretty blond cousin would be joining them in Glenmalure. Not too long if she had anything to say about it. And, of course, there was Maire who so wanted a husband. . . .

"Playing the matchmaker again?"

She started, meeting Ronan's eyes as the MacMurroughs rode away. "You object?"

"Would it matter if I did?"

She could hear that he was teasing, but he looked serious all the same. "Of course it would, husband. I wouldn't want to do anything to displease you. Don't forget I just promised to love and obey, though . . ."

"Though what, Triona O'Toole?"

"Triona O'Byrne, you mean."

He chuckled, his slate gray eyes taking on a most lusty cast. "Aye, so it is now."

"Well," she continued, growing quite flustered and a bit embarrassed, too, that her O'Byrne clansmen were all glancing sideways at each other behind them. "I don't expect to have any trouble at all with the first one, but the second—"

"I'll settle for love, woman. That's enough for me." Ronan reached out suddenly and grabbed her to him, kissing her so soundly that Triona nearly lost her balance and fell from her horse. But at his next words, she wondered if he'd done so on purpose just to give him unfair advantage.

"How about a race back to Glenmalure? And let's say whoever wins can console the loser—"

"Ha! You'll not be consoling me!" she cried, kicking Laeg into a gallop. "You know I'll beat you, Ronan O'Byrne!"

"I dare you to try, woman!" he called after her, their laughter ringing out as they rode headlong into the wild Wicklow hills.